Roland Vernon lives and writes in Somerset, where he also runs his own marquee company. He is married with three sons. His previous books include a biography of the philosopher Jiddu Krishnamurti and two other acclaimed novels, the award-winning *A Dark Enchantment* and *The Maestro's Voice*.

THE GOOD WIFE'S CASTLE

Roland Vernon

BLACK SWAN

TRANSWORLD PUBLISHERS
61–63 Uxbridge Road, London W5 5SA
A Random House Group Company
www.transworldbooks.co.uk

THE GOOD WIFE'S CASTLE
A BLACK SWAN BOOK: 9780552775533

First publication in Great Britain
Black Swan edition published 2012

Addresses for Random House Group Ltd companies outside the UK
can be found at: www.randomhouse.co.uk
The Random House Group Ltd Reg. No. 954009

The Random House Group Limited supports the Forest Stewardship
Council (FSC®), the leading international forest-certification
organization. Our books carrying the FSC label are printed on
FSC®-certified paper. FSC is the only forest-certification scheme endorsed
by the leading environmental organizations, including Greenpeace.
Our paper procurement policy can be found
at www.randomhouse.co.uk/environment.

Typeset in 11/13pt Giovanni Book by
Kestrel Data, Exeter, Devon.
Printed and bound by
CPI Group (UK) Ltd, Croydon, CR0 4YY.

2 4 6 8 10 9 7 5 3 1

MIX
Paper from
responsible sources
FSC® C016897

Dedicated to the English teachers who inspired my love of writing – Angus Graham-Campbell, Francis Moran, Michael Meredith, and the late magnificent Christopher Dixon

THE GOOD WIFE'S CASTLE

Prologue

I could tell by the look in his eyes, that afternoon in the milking room, that my father knew that I knew he deserved to die. But he didn't have long to think about it, because he'd already stepped off the chair. That was the very moment I came into the room. I was thirteen years old, and two days before I had seen him with that village girl, the one who helped with the cows, a *kaffir* child not much older than me. He didn't talk to me for those two days, couldn't even look me in the eye for shame, and then, one hot afternoon, he decided to string himself up in the milking room. But just after he kicked away the chair he saw me in the doorway and tried desperately to pull up on the rope, or ease the grip of the noose, or anything, but not die. He hadn't managed the thing at all well. Not enough drop. It took him a long time to quieten down, and all the while he stared madly at me, dancing in the air, trying to tell me something. Perhaps he was begging for help, it was impossible to say exactly. Then his eyes lost their wildness and I think his mind departed, though his legs continued to kick and flutter with an energy he'd never shown in life. I happened to have some paper and a pencil to hand, because I had come straight from school, so I picked up the chair, sat down and did a couple of drawings of him. I still have the drawings somewhere. At the top of the page I put, in very neat writing, 'Father's last dance.'

As he danced his way to hell at the end of that rope, with me nearby on the chair, I remember thinking to myself: am I supposed to step up and help? It was not my job to put things right. That's what fathers were supposed to do. But he had chosen to let the family drop into ruin and just watched from the sidelines as my mother fell apart. That was his choice, now I had to make mine. As it happened, I was too absorbed with my drawing and hadn't resolved the dilemma by the time he stopped shaking. By then, of course, it was too late. But I did not have long to wait before the messenger came to me, and then I knew for sure that I had done the right thing.

It was a few days after they buried my father that I received the visitation that would change my life. In my mind's eye he had golden hair, blue, peaceful eyes and a sword sheathed at his belt. He was silent and stern, but infinitely kind – a kindliness that I had forgotten existed. He held aloft his robed arm as if to point out the way and, strange to say, I knew immediately what I had to do, though it wasn't as if he spoke any words of instruction. In my own way and in my own time, diligently and apart from the world, it was my task to redress the balance, to even up the family account, as it were. And that marked the start of my long journey.

Be not unequally yoked together with unbelievers, we are commanded, but *come out from among them, and be ye separate*. It is a wisdom as old as the hills, of course, but generally neglected. We are citizens of heaven and not of this earth, except that we are temporarily imprisoned here. A holy life is a life that separates a man from the world and from an interest in worldly things. The angel pointed out that path to me and it has guided me through the rough and smooth of the years. It has brought me to my present circumstances, to this place, in order to start my work afresh.

This morning I left the cottage early and went over to the other place to have breakfast with her. After I had finished, I put my knife and fork together and thanked her very much for it. It is important to give credit where credit is due. I told her it had been an especially good breakfast, which was true. She nodded and with a sweet and seemly smile took my plate to the sink and began to wash up. That was it for today because I had quite a lot to do back at the cottage, so I left her and locked up behind me, as usual. I could tell that she was disappointed to see me leave so soon. She hungers for company, of course, it's only natural. But her time is well apportioned and the routine will see her through until I go back at teatime. Then, so long as our more serious business goes smoothly, we will have a pleasant and relaxing evening together.

There is dignity between us nowadays, good manners, too, both of which please me. I am proud of her. Not that we're home and dry, not by a long chalk, but she doesn't complain openly or express herself through acts of defiance any more. I can tell that she sometimes hides her feelings – it is written in her face – but it is good that she can hold her emotions in check. I applaud self-discipline, and I let her know of my approval. She responds to encouragement of this sort, just like a child or a pet. One day we will weed out the ill thought entirely, in the same way that we have already successfully weeded out the ill words. There are challenges ahead but she is stronger in herself now and can see right from wrong. The worm has turned, as they say, and I have good reason to think that we can achieve a state of stainless wedlock in due course.

Chapter 1

It was suddenly there again, only this time it was happening in his bedroom. The immense benediction. It would always arrive unexpectedly, but never before had it actually roused him from sleep. So early to be woken, and yet he felt electric and his eyes were wide open. It had the grandeur of a symphony but there was neither movement nor sound. What are you? Granville silently asked, as he had asked so many times before, and there were tears in his eyes. The question was absurd, he knew, but it was a way of acknowledging the presence, a salute of welcome.

It bestowed equal splendour on everything in the room, regardless of size or status: the two people in bed, the cat, the scattered clothes and rubbish, the dust, the air and sheets, alike. All of it became extraordinarily vivid, as if sharpened to the eye by the glass of a superior lens. Everything that was previously lowly had become significant, even noble. The worn-down protrusion of her lidless lipstick now glistened pink and voluptuous like a miniature totem. A green plastic bottle top gathering fluff by the skirting board now proclaimed perfect circularity and indestructibility, against all the odds, a heroic boast. The wide variety of shapes all around, their depth and colour, became essays in figurative perfection.

It came on a second time, a sudden, silent surge of voltage, and a renewed wave of wonder passed through Granville. He quietly gasped with relief and joy at the encounter, like a diver who has pulled away from the cusp of calamity and emerges into God's clean air. He could see so clearly in that moment that everything had to change. His life must change, once and for all. Everything, other than this, was pointless.

Then, out of the blue, the telephone began to ring downstairs and magic fled the room like a startled deer when it spies the hunter. It vanished into nothingness, trust betrayed.

The second ring. He wondered who could be calling so early. Still night time, really. It was an old-fashioned Bakelite phone, a silly vintage folly, with a heavy, unapologetic ring that might wake the girls. He knew he'd never get to it in time before the answer service cut in, but it stopped prematurely, which was good, if a little strange. An uncomfortable question mark hung in the silence.

The intense energy that had greeted him when he awoke was gone and its afterglow fast receding. Everyday objects that had just now been elevated became banal once again, and beside their tawdriness drifted in a sadness. A pair of her knickers lay in a roll on the floor. They'd been peeled off with lazy resignation late at night and dropped there; and another pair quite near from another night. His old Florentine stud box, which wouldn't close for the mountain of cufflinks he hadn't needed for years. Random copper coins, irrelevant receipts and business cards, an unused crumpled tissue, the contents of emptied pockets that sat for weeks on top of his chest of drawers. Also there, propped, in its silver frame, because the velvet stand had broken off, the signed sepia photograph of Rocco Campobello, finest of all the golden age operatic tenors, a personal gift from the great man himself to Granville's grandfather in 1924. He looked over the familiar melange of detritus and treasures, and thought that it was a fitting metaphor for the muddle of his own past and present life.

He climbed out naked from under the covers, and quietly, so as not to disturb her. He would have given anything to share the departing miracle with her, as he had once liked to share everything, but it was out of the question in these wintry times. If he was honest, she had probably never truly understood him, even in the old days when their love had billowed unfettered like a laundered sheet in the wind. She had nodded and smiled and held his hand as he'd droned on, as he'd feebly searched for words to describe the indescribable; but nowadays she didn't even pretend to listen, didn't try to understand, and would look the other way when he began, preferring to notch a point against him by keeping silent counsel. Or, when the benediction came with great intensity and left him dazed for an hour or so afterwards, she would tell him that he should go and see the doctor. Better to nip it in the bud, she would say. But he knew very well that this was no ailment; quite the opposite; and he had been experiencing it, though not as powerfully, since he wasn't much more than a boy. He had therefore decided a while ago that it would be better for both of them if he did not mention it any more, and that was how things had remained.

He removed himself lightly from the bed. Movement seemed easy because the spell had left him feeling unburdened, as if he had shed the greater mass of his body and acquired the lightfootedness of a sprite. He walked thus weightlessly the few steps over to the window, passing in the shadows the ill-defined presence of an ancestral portrait on the wall close by, and he parted the curtains a finger's breadth.

The other houses of the estate were over to the left, five of them, dark blocks in the gloom. They, and his own home, comprised the tail end of a medium-priced, brick housing development built at speed for quick profit in the mid-1980s, not a particularly pretty site, but just now these buildings pleased him, safe cubes of warmth and homeliness that they were. Dawn was still at least an hour away and it was a cold clear night. Beyond the houses' garden fences, invisible in this light, was the little stretch of grassy scrubland where his girls would take their bikes and forget to bring them back. He would forget too, so that they were left rusting on their sides in the rain, sometimes for weeks on end, in the company of armless dolls staring skyward, or any number of dispensable kitsch and pink toys. Irksome neighbours, with nothing better to complain about, would toss them crossly back over the garden fence from time to time.

On the far side of that piece of grassland lay the woods, which he could just about make out. The woods. Their tops etched giant black cauliflower shapes against the slightly paler sky behind, and there were stars discernible between their branches, flickering in and out of view as the treetops swayed in the breeze. High above them the barest slit of a moon gouged a clean wound in the night's skin, and even further, on a distant sweep of hillside, a single light shone square and yellow from a farmhouse window. He wasn't the only one up so early.

It was on nights like these, as a child, that he would look from the windows of his parents' country home and imagine himself not in a pleasant corner of Surrey, but on the banks of the Rhine, no less, in a *schloss*, looking out from a lichen-crusted mullion beneath battle-scarred ramparts. Once, in a madly romantic moment, he stole out into the woods that surrounded his old home and found a dark oak to sit beneath, where the cries of the owls and the rustles of creatures in damp bracken fed his fantasies. That gentle English woodland became for him an impenetrable Gothic forest, thick with legend and romance, laden with chivalric doom, dangerous but alluring, the home of nature's secret whisperings; and, deep within, at the core of his adolescent longings, some immaculate maiden perchance awaited him, with huge melancholy eyes, and tumbling raven hair. There was something of that spirit even here, even now, within his small cavity-walled, insulated, tan brick housing estate house, with the rise of the meadow to the right, and the dark hump of Rodyard's Ridge imprinted against a paling sky in the east. In a funny way this place, too, was his *schloss*. The wonder and mystery of those juvenile longings were still alive within him.

As it happened, Granville had not chosen this house; it had come with the job, but he liked it all the same. For years before coming here he had hankered after this kind of democratic unpretentiousness, and now that he had been part of it for a while he was glad that it was every bit as pleasant and manageable as he had hoped. Edwina hated it, of course. It wasn't at all the sort of home she'd envisaged for herself in the days when she'd played her princess games as a child. Edwina would never confuse this house, number 3, Tennyson Terrace, with a Black Forest castle; nor had she spent very many days in their years of living here without undertaking some piece of research to see how they could escape it. It wasn't as if they couldn't afford something better, she had said again and again over the years until the words lost all meaning. 'Take a look at that view,' she would add with exasperation, standing at this same bedroom window, 'just take a look out there, for God's sake.' And he would look and he would have to agree. 'Out there' had the crisp predictability of an architect's model, a low budget residential development, complete down to the cutest details: clean hatchbacks on curving driveways, law-abiding citizens dressed sensibly, walking well-behaved dogs on leads, with a smattering of children rejoicing in front gardens. The orderliness of the general scene was only spoilt, as it happened, by the untended lawns and overgrown borders that surrounded his own home. Granville was never much interested in gardening.

Yes, he could understand exactly why Edwina didn't like it here but he couldn't share her anger. It was fine, he would say, it was solid Middle England, a good community and a lovely area to bring up children; but he knew in his heart that it couldn't go on for ever. He could recognize a terminal illness when he saw one. He'd had to sit by a lot of dying people in hospital beds over the years and it was a matter of when the end would come, what might be done to postpone it, and how much good, if anything, could be salvaged from the wreckage.

The light was changing, and he turned away from the window. The gilded frame of the huge eighteenth-century portrait, now gaining slight definition, looked grotesque in this low-ceilinged bedroom. There wasn't a room in the house that was right for the picture, and Granville was too embarrassed to have it on show downstairs, particularly as the title plate showed that the man portrayed bore exactly the same name as his own. The young aristocrat was depicted in front of a princely Leicestershire home, one of the former family estates. Determined to shed the burden of so valuable and ostentatious a picture, Granville had once promised it to a gallery that housed several of this painter's works, but Edwina wouldn't hear of it. For the children's sake, she said.

Still conscious of not wanting to disturb her, he crept quietly over to where his dressing gown was slung on top of a chair. He looked at her sleeping form as he pulled the gown around his shoulders. She was bigger than of old, not just a little plumper but a different shape altogether. And her hair, despite all the care and attention, had thinned. This was the raw woman, stripped of artifice and crafty cosmetic effect. It was rather touching. For all her proud defences, her elegance and deportment, she would still bleed if pricked. Lying there, curled and rumpled, there was something of a lost child about her, and the sight squeezed his heart.

Her breathing was shallow and rasped at the edges, which informed him that she was probably far away, dislocated from the disappointments of her life; transfigured, perhaps, back to the pretty provocative girl she once was. Such feisty irreverence had not only been permissible in an attractive young woman but positively alluring. When he had first met her she was felling men like skittles, and the wreckage she left in her wake had given him reason to pause for thought before committing himself to her completely.

Now that she lay sleeping on her side, he observed the prettily embroidered strap of her nightie and the fine pleated linen which hid the heavy droop of her breast. He was pleased that she still kept her standards, that she bought exclusive brands and treated herself to the best bathroom products. She always thought that he was her enemy in such matters, because he was by nature frugal, but the truth was that it was a delight to him that she

19

should spend money on herself. He liked that she had not given up, that her general disenchantment with life had not expunged all trace of the old zest.

As he moved towards the door, his foot clipped something – he couldn't see what it was; an old clothes hanger, one of the girls' toys, perhaps – but it caused the cat on the bed to stir and raise its head, assessing the scene. It concluded that some better option lay beyond the bedroom, stood up, stretched and jumped off the bed. It was turbulence enough to evoke a grunt from Edwina, as though the sunny paths along which her dream was rambling had met with a sudden, unwelcome barricade. Granville froze, hoping she could retrieve the thread. He did not want to start the day off on the wrong foot. There was so little tolerance between them right now, so little understanding or will to forgive. The smallest slip might cast a shadow over the whole day, perhaps longer.

'What's happening? What are you doing?' she said.

'It's OK,' he whispered. 'You can go back to sleep.'

'What's the time?' She raised her head from the pillow, squinting.

'I don't know. Early. Go back to sleep.'

'God,' she said with something like disgust, 'why so much noise?'

He didn't say any more, but removed himself from the room and closed the door quietly behind him.

He remembered that Sunday was only two days away and thought he had better get to work on his piece. It was quite a big Sunday and there would doubtless be a fuller house than usual. He would work on it until it got a bit lighter outside then take the dog for a walk; but not for long, because Edwina was leaving early for the station and he had to be back in time to drive the girls to school.

He flicked on the landing light and caught sight of

his reflection in the mirror on the far wall. His dressing gown had fallen open and he observed his nakedness. The early morning always flattered his virility, he thought with some amusement. He hadn't noticed the phenomenon for years, but there it was. He pulled in his stomach and turned his jaw to one side, instinctively trying to eke out the best from the raw material on show. He had never got used to the premature white hair, though supposed he should be thankful there was still no sign of it thinning. Perhaps achieving grey-haired status in early midlife lent a degree of gravitas to a man's looks. It would certainly dilute the impact of the next thirty years' ageing. Get the transformation over with early, and the turn of the seasons later on would be less noticeable. He glanced over the rest of his body and thought it wasn't so bad for a man well past forty, one who barely had time to walk the dog, let alone get to the gym. Perhaps his large, dark eyes had grown a little more hooded over the years. They were less dreamy, probably less romantic, but this gave him a sternness which was not entirely unwelcome. For most of his life he had worked quite hard not to look too good, for all the obvious reasons. There had been a few near misses with women, sometimes clumps of them in the same community. Anyone with half-decent looks in his position would have had the same problem, he imagined. He had learnt to spot the signs early on: ladies a little too eager to lend help with jumble sales or the weekly flower rota, sacrificing time which would be better spent at home with their families. He had had to watch himself, every word he said to them, every dart of his eyes. In the early days – at university, soon after his big experience and when he was still full of it – women had flocked to him. They found his blind passion irresistible, they said. If ever there had been a

21

test of his convictions it had been then. Today's dangers were pale by comparison. The shy but meaningful smiles of the cake-baking, jam-jarring ladies of central Dorset were pretty easy to defuse.

He went downstairs to the study and turned on the desk light. His glasses were sitting there from the evening before, with that orange lanyard still attached to them. Edwina had given it to him so that he could hang the glasses around his neck when he was in the pulpit, and had chosen a bright colour, she said, so that he wouldn't lose them so often. It had been a birthday present, and he only used it to please her, the latest in a succession of superfluous gifts. There'd been the new pair of slippers (his old ones were fine), the juicer (given on the eve of her own short-lived health drive), and, of course, regular additions to his redundant cufflink collection.

He put the string around his neck, the glasses on, and cast an eye over the notes he'd yesterday begun to make for the ten-thirty. They were jotted as usual on folded scraps that he'd retrieved from the bin to save paper. He'd already scribbled down a few biblical references to prompt himself, the bare bones of an idea, with a question mark next to the title of a funny anecdote he might throw in. Or perhaps they'd heard that one before, hence the question mark. He let out a heavy breath. The standard formula. Arrest them with the unusual, develop the hook with a story, a peppering of wit here and there to spice it up, get a good instructional theme going, and then go and spoil it all with the obligatory scriptural references.

There were a few books piled on the desk, old ones that he'd had since before he was married. He had pulled them out yesterday in the hope of tapping some of his former enthusiasm and noticed that the shelves had become discoloured where the books had been sitting all these years; little profiles of faded paint and ingrained dust, the marks of more than a decade of neglect. Spinoza, Marcus Aurelius, St Augustine. How relevant it had all seemed to him once upon a time, this wealth of words, a glittering canon of thought and theory, huge, intricate and multi-layered. Too big, too grandiose, unwieldy; and maybe empty at the end of the day, he pondered. The whore of Babylon. He got up and stood in front of the shelf to look for something new. Squashed between a couple of paperbacks was the bleached spine of a theological book he himself had written a long time ago. He hadn't looked at it since before the children were born, for fear of laughing at everything he'd once thought so important. The congregation wouldn't be interested in that. Or maybe he was underestimating them. He half pulled it out, but then pushed it back in.

The phone started to ring again. Its suddenness was amplified by the peace of the early hour, and it took a moment for him to absorb the shock. He glanced at his wall clock. Twenty to six. It rang for nearly ten seconds before he moved over to pick it up, but once again it stopped before he had the chance to answer. He dialled 1471 to see who it might be. It was a mobile number that he did not recognize. He contemplated returning the call straight away, but thought twice and placed the phone right next to him in case it went again.

The interruption had helped clear the cobwebs from his thinking, and he pushed all the old books away from his workspace, accidentally knocking a couple of items off the edge of his desk. They clattered onto the floor and he looked down to see what they were. An old boys' directory from his former public school, and a sphinx paperweight that one of his parishioners had bought for him on a holiday in Egypt – something he had never had the heart to throw out because the cheery lady who gave it had got cancer and died just a year later. The old boys' directory he now took the opportunity to put in the bin beside him, where it lay perched precariously on a top-heavy stack for recycling.

He stared at a fresh sheet of paper and held his pen poised. This Sunday's sermon called for something new. Ring out the changes. It would be good for them and it would be good for him too. He glanced around the room for inspiration. On top of a bookcase stood a black and white stylized photograph of Edwina, taken at the time of their engagement, making her look like a 1950s starlet, fetching and sexy. He looked away from it, deciding after all that he couldn't concentrate, and his sermon had better wait until he'd freshened up. Walking the dog would bring some ideas to mind. In the meantime he turned to other bits and pieces that needed to be tidied up, starting with the agenda for the Spring Prayer and Study Circle. There was a meeting tomorrow evening, but it would be a breeze. The handful of members – a mildly intellectual parish hard core of five or six – would devour any old theological claptrap he tossed them, like ducks who hone in on a child with a bagful of stale bread at the water's edge.

It was half-past six and almost properly light outside when he took his tracksuit from its peg in the understairs cupboard. He kept it there specifically for times like this, so that he could pull it on and go out early without having to get dressed properly. The bull terrier, Luther, knew the form and tap-danced expectantly on the tiled kitchen floor, sneezing with excitement. A glance through the window told Granville that the earlier crispness of the clear night sky had vanished, and that the morning had dawned grey and dull. He grabbed a stick, pulled on a waxed coat and went outside. A light drizzle had commenced and he heard the faint patter of it on shrubs and grass as he closed the door behind him.

He considered walking eastwards to the edge of the village, where there was an old airstrip, unused since the war, its tarmac now largely reclaimed by grass. The farmer who owned it was applying for planning permission to develop it into a business park, but the vociferous not-in-my-backyard element of the village had stalled his application, and until the stalemate was broken it made a great place to exercise the dog. However, Granville decided on a whim to take the path west from his garden gate instead, the one that led down to the woods at the other side of the village. Luther had already anticipated the route and was trotting joyously along the pavement in the right direction. It was too early for traffic. Only residents from the housing estate used this lane, and then only rarely, because the way to the main road lay on the other side of the development.

The narrow road and the entire housing estate were constructed on what had once been the Old Rectory's capacious garden, adjacent to the church. Tarmac sliced straight across the sweeping lawns of former times and led to open countryside south of the village. Before the new homes had usurped half the Old Rectory's original plot, Granville's predecessors, the incumbents of St Peter's, Cheselbury Abbas, would have enjoyed uninterrupted views towards the interlocking hills and combes that framed the southern edge of the Blackmore Vale.

Edwina had never understood Granville's love of walking, especially when the weather was anything less than perfect, and she did not attempt to hide her annoyance about it. Granville did not rise to her jibes, and doubted she could even hear herself any more, but equally would not compromise the daily time he allowed himself in the open countryside. It fuelled his faith and irrigated his dreams. He only had to walk a few hundred yards before losing himself in a timeless reverie, and it mattered little to him what the weather was doing. On the hardest winter days he would feel a kind of kinship with the rugged hunters of old, the sort who left hearth and home at dawn, with dog and gun, and returned late, weighed down with game, to dry themselves by the fire and taste the stew their womenfolk had kept warm on the inglenook range. Conversely, in glorious summer sunshine he would sense the spirit of the fresh-faced lads who toiled till the golden light faded across the fields, their work accompanied by the buzz of hedgerow bees and spiced with the scent of wheat husk in the summer evening air. Today, dreary, damp and mild, the climate conformed to no particular cliché of pastoral idyll, but there was a freshness about, the turf and moss were soft underfoot, and this alone was enough to make him rejoice in the earth, giving thanks for its fertility and abundance.

Adrift in private musings of this sort, he hadn't realized until fairly late that he was not alone.

Chapter 2

A man was approaching from the other direction. He had one fist buried in the waist pocket of his old brown bomber jacket, and the other clasped the hind legs of a rabbit that bobbed limply at his side. Granville saw that the man was older, with untidy grey hair, but he walked with a brisk, determined pace that suggested unusually robust fitness for someone of his age. It was not until he was more than a few yards away that Granville recognized his face, though he hardly knew him at all and couldn't recall his name. All he could remember was that the man was a relative newcomer to the area, a foreigner, who kept himself to himself in a cottage right at the edge of the village.

Granville stopped and smiled. 'Another man who likes to get out early?' he said.

The man did not immediately answer, but raised his chin and looked Granville over. His mouth hung open slightly and there was quiet concentration in his eyes. 'Best time of day, in my opinion,' he eventually said. His accent was pronounced.

'Been hunting?' Granville pointed his stick at the dead rabbit. Its head was disfigured.

'I picked it up off the road.'

'I should chuck it in the hedgerow. The foxes will have it.'

'It's not badly damaged, apart from the head. The meat's OK.'

'You mean . . . ?'

'I've eaten a lot worse, I can tell you. No point in wastage.'

Granville smiled and sought refuge in a pleasantry. 'Not a very nice morning, is it?'

'I don't mind the weather. For me every morning is like a gift from the Almighty. A reason to rejoice.'

'Quite right,' replied Granville. 'We take so much for granted.' The man did not comment. 'You don't have a dog?' Granville asked.

'No.'

'Very sensible. They're an absolute menace. Luther!' he called to the bull terrier, who had trotted on without waiting. At the call, the dog looked mournfully ahead for a moment, and then decided to return to its master. 'You're from South Africa?'

'You can tell.'

'I'm no expert.' Granville held out his hand. 'I don't think we've met properly. Granville St Clair. I live just over there.'

'Sin what?'

'St Clair. Spelt like Saint Clair but pronounced Sinclair. An English idiosyncrasy. Funny old language.'

'OK.'

'And you?'

'Me what?'

'I was wondering what you were called.'

The man did not answer straight away, but again seemed to be assessing Granville. 'You are the padre, right?'

'That's right.'

'Glad to meet you, Father,' he said. 'My name is Piet Steyn.' He shook hands formally. It was a cast-iron grip.

'Please, call me Granville.'

'I prefer "Father." I'm a little old-fashioned, I suppose.' His head was tilted back, his mouth still slightly ajar.

'Are you going this way?' asked Granville. 'It's pretty down by the stream behind the church. There's the remains of an old mill. The path goes round over there – ' he waved a finger vaguely – 'behind the Old Rectory, past the abbey ruins and comes out back on this road about half a mile down that way. I'll show you if you like.'

'Actually, I was . . .' began the man hesitantly.

'Don't let me keep you.'

'No, it's all right,' he changed tack. 'I'll come with you for a while. I'll leave the rabbit here and pick it up on the way back.'

Granville called again for his dog, who turned with something like reluctance to follow his master's latest caprice. Meanwhile, Steyn took out a penknife, spliced open a ligament in one of the rabbit's hind legs, and fed the other leg through the aperture to form a secure loop from which he could hang the animal on a branch. 'So that your foxes won't steal my supper,' he said.

They left the lane and headed down the little path beside the churchyard wall.

'I expect you haven't enjoyed our lads giving yours a thrashing these past few days,' said Granville.

'A what?'

'The final test.'

'I'm sorry, I don't understand.'

'Cricket. England versus South Africa. The test match. Have you got Sky?'

'Ah. I see. No, I don't own a television.'

'You can get it on the radio. Long wave. Ball by ball.'

'Actually, I'm not interested in cricket.'

'Silly of me to make the assumption.'

'I'm probably an exception amongst my countrymen.'

They walked for a few paces in single file where wildly overgrown brambles had narrowed the passage. Granville failed to notice an oak tree's root across his path, one that had writhed out of the ground over many years, and he tripped on it, nearly falling.

'All right, Father?' asked Steyn.

'Just about. Watch out along here, there are hidden stones and all sorts lurking in the ground just waiting for the opportunity to bring you down. The Old Rectory's kitchen garden wall used to run along here, but it fell to pieces long ago. No-one ever cleared the stones from the path.'

'An Old Rectory? Is that it?' Piet Steyn pointed to the fine Georgian building across the lawn to their right. He whistled. 'So the pastors of old used to live in places like that?'

'They had a fine time of it. A very rich man lives there now with his young family. Half his time here and half in the City,' said Granville.

'I think you could say your job has been economically devalued by modern society, Father.' The heavily accented words came slowly and cut through the quietness of the morning air like old gravestones through a ground mist.

'Perhaps not just economically. I sometimes wonder if most of the people who live in these parts would care or even notice if they lost their rector altogether.'

Steyn stopped and leant back, eyeing Granville carefully once more. 'You sound like a man disappointed with his lot.'

Granville shook his head. 'Don't mean to. Just turning

into a grumpy, glass-half-empty old misery guts. Must be the time of life.'

'Have you thought about a change of direction?'

'No, no, no, nothing like *that*,' he answered quickly. 'But I'm all for the Church of England having a bit of a shake-up. Got to do something to boost the dwindling congregations, after all.'

'There's more to a community's pastor than just leading church services.'

'Tell me about it,' muttered Granville. 'But what about you?'

Steyn tilted back his head again. 'What do you mean?' There was an old guardedness about him. He was not going to be free with his responses.

'What do you do for a living?'

'This and that.'

'Oh yes?'

'Let's say I'm semi-retired.'

'More time for hobbies, then?'

'In a manner of speaking.'

'Like what?'

'I'm sorry?'

'How do you like to spend your time? If you don't mind me asking.'

'I like to potter about in my workshop. And I write a bit.'

'What sort of writing?'

Steyn looked away and it seemed as though he was not going to reply, but then he looked up again. 'Mostly about my faith in the Lord.'

'Really?' replied Granville, and smiled as if he had been presented with a small, beautifully wrapped gift. 'Perhaps you'd like to pop into our church some time?'

Steyn shook his head. 'Nah, Father. I'm pitched in

a different camp, so to speak. I belong to the Dutch Reformed Church.'

'Oh, come on. We're beyond all that nowadays, aren't we? I don't care much for the differences between the faiths, let alone the niceties that divide Christian brethren.'

'In times gone by priests were put to death for less.' If there was humour intended in the remark it did not show in Steyn's expression, but Granville chose to interpret it that way.

'*That's* what they're doing down by the duck pond! I wondered what they'd put that stake there for.' Steyn now allowed himself a smile as well. 'OK, then,' said Granville. 'Let's just say we're children of the same Father and we all follow the example of the man Jesus.'

'You have a point.'

'I'll have you on the church council before you can say "I am not worthy." Only kidding.' But Steyn did not hear this last comment because his attention had suddenly been distracted. He was looking over Granville's shoulder.

'I think your City friend is up early this morning, as well,' he said.

Granville turned and looked behind him. It was still not quite fully light, and he could see, across half an acre of perfect lawn, that the lights were on in the Old Rectory's drawing room. He knew the house well, because Bertie Gosling, the current owner, and his wife were stalwarts of the parish and the church, and had hosted a number of village events there. 'I suppose we shouldn't be looking,' Granville said with a grin when they both saw that Mr Gosling was walking about the room completely naked. He had opened up a tall stepladder in the middle of the room, and was climbing to the very top of it. 'What's he

32

up to?' muttered Granville, as he saw Gosling fiddling with something above his head. 'Changing a bulb, or something?' The ceiling was high, and he seemed to be teetering at full stretch. Granville had seen enough, and turned away, but Steyn's gaze was fixed on the scene inside the house with the concentration of a patient hunter.

'I don't like the look of this,' he said quietly. 'Well I never!'

'What?' Granville swung around, but his eyesight over longer distances was not as sharp as it had been. 'What is it?' Then Granville did see something: Bertie Gosling dropped suddenly from the ladder some four or five feet, and came to a stop at the end of a rope with a little bounce. The naked figure began to rotate with its face upturned, rudderless, like a paper boat floating on a park pond.

Chapter 3

Neither man exchanged a word but Steyn was the first to vault the fence. He was already running across the lawn towards the house while Granville – less agile – climbed over to follow him. Their footprints left a trail of untidy smudges in the veneer of the dewy grass. The bull terrier, excited at the thought of some new game, hopped and cantered enthusiastically at their heels. Granville stopped at the large sash window of the drawing room and banged a flat palm against the pane. The man on the other side of the glass was swaying in a circular motion, and his face was misshapen by the sideways strain of the rope. A sudden kick from one of his feet sent the stepladder clattering to the ground.

Steyn rattled the handle of the French window that led from the lawn into the house. It was locked. 'Where is the main door?' he called.

'This way!' shouted Granville, and they both ran around the side of the building. Granville fumbled with the latch of an antique garden gate that was stuck, but Steyn pushed past him and kicked at it, so that the hinges snapped cleanly off the old iron post. They hurried on past the pillared main entrance of the house, which was not often used, round to the boot room door at the side where the cars were parked, and this they found unlocked. Granville led the way along a stone-tiled passage, on, into an elegant hall, leaving dirty boot prints on the rug behind him. 'Over there,' he pointed, hurrying to an architrave doorway across the hall, but Steyn overtook him and flung the door open.

'I'll deal with it,' said Steyn, moving without hesitation towards the hanging man. The bare feet dangled in front of his chest. 'You go and see who's in the house. If there are children—'

'Of course,' said Granville, and turned back into the hall. Moments later he heard the sound of a heavy thud from the drawing room, and went to see what had happened. He saw Steyn kneeling in a pool of urine on the parquet floor, and leaning over Bertie Gosling's body. His fingers were held against a raw lesion on the naked man's neck, feeling for a pulse. He pressed his ear to the bare chest.

'Is he alive?' asked Granville. 'We should call an ambulance.'

'It would be a waste of time.'

'He's dead, you mean?'

'There's still a heartbeat. Technically his body's still alive, but he won't recover consciousness. His neck's completely broken and everything's closing down fast. In a minute or so his heart will stop as well. That's the way it happens.' Steyn looked up at the ladder. 'Your friend has done his mathematics. He knew how to kill himself quickly.'

'If there's a heartbeat there's still hope. Bertie!' He leant down over the inert body. 'Try to resuscitate him. Where's the phone?' Granville looked around and spotted a telephone in the corner of the room, but before he had taken a step towards it they both heard a voice from the hallway.

35

'Hello?' It sounded like a young girl. The two men looked at each other. The voice called again. 'Is there somebody in there?' She was closer. 'Bertie? Where are you?' Granville leapt across the room and managed to get to the door before it opened.

She took a step back into the hall and caught her breath when she saw him. Then she raised her forearms, hunching her shoulders forward in an attempt to hide her breasts. She was barefoot, quite slender and pale, and was wearing nothing but the briefest white knickers. She was recoiling from Granville, who held up his hand to stay her retreat and calm her. He had never seen this girl before.

'You'd better not go in there,' he said.

'Who are you? Where's Bertie?' Her accent was local and she was young, more than a child but less than a woman. Her cheeks were pink, quite pudgy, and her nakedness struck Granville like a distant memory – something familiar, in a sense, but affirmatively irrelevant and precluded from his present circle of reference.

'I'm called Granville. I'm the rector. It's all right.' He walked towards her, but she stepped back at the same pace, maintaining the distance between them.

'What's happened to Bertie? Why are you here?' She tried to scuttle away but he caught up with her easily.

'Take your hands off of me!' she yelled, and he raised them instantly from her bare shoulders.

'I'm sorry,' he said.

'Keep off.'

'All right.' She had a brace on her teeth. Of all the schoolgirl clichés, he thought. 'Something bad has happened, I'm afraid,' he said.

'Are you going to tell me, or what?'

Granville hesitated. 'He's killed himself, hasn't he?' Granville nodded. 'Oh God.'

36

'Father!' Steyn called quietly from the drawing room. Granville went back in and saw that Steyn was on his feet, stretching his back and shoulders with a sigh, as if easing an old stiffness. 'He's gone. The heart has stopped now.'

'I'd better call the police,' said Granville softly. 'Would you look after the girl in the hall? She shouldn't see this.'

'Who is she?'

'I haven't a clue.'

'Not one of his children?'

'No. He's got two sons, and they're younger.'

'Are the children here? And the wife?'

'I don't know. Ask the girl. Maybe she's an au pair or something.' Steyn went out to talk to the girl and Granville crossed over to the telephone again; but as he picked it up, something occurred to him. He took his BlackBerry from his pocket and flicked quickly at the buttons, eventually finding what he was looking for. He stared at the screen for quite a few seconds before letting his hand drop to his side. He was still there, head hanging, when Steyn came back into the room.

'Did you call the police?' he asked.

'No.'

'I think you should come and have a look at this. There's a note.'

'Bertie tried to call me.'

'What?'

Granville let out a long breath. 'This morning, early. My home phone rang twice but I didn't get to it in time. I've just checked the address book on my mobile. It was Bertie Gosling. I didn't recognize the number at the time.'

'That's not your fault.'

'He needed help.'

37

'You don't know that for sure.'

'Why else would he have called?'

'Perhaps to get you to help the girl.'

Granville turned to look at Steyn. He was standing in the doorway and holding a piece of paper. 'Read this. It seems the family are away for a few days. This girl . . . it's not good.'

Out in the hall, Granville took the paper and quickly read what was written. It did not take long to digest the situation. He looked up at the girl, who now stared at him with alarm.

'Where are you from?' asked Granville.

'Bournemouth.'

'How long have you been seeing him?'

'I don't know. A few months. I didn't want to hurt no-one. We were going to finish it.'

The flesh on her thighs had come up in blotches from standing still in the cold air, and goose pimples spread up her arms. 'Does anyone else know about your relationship?' asked Granville. 'Does anyone know you're here?'

'No. Nobody. I haven't told anyone. I wouldn't do that.'

Piet moved up to Granville and cut in, quietly. 'Don't you think we should let the young lady put her clothes on?'

'Yes. Of course,' said Granville, blinking and looking away from the girl. 'Why don't you go upstairs and get dressed? We can have a chat in a minute.' She hesitated for a moment, then turned and walked towards the broad oak staircase. When she reached the landing she made her way to one of the bedroom doors and closed it behind her. Granville turned to Steyn. 'This is unbelievable,' he said. 'The note. He sounds desperate.'

'Very sad,' said Steyn.

38

'His wife and children are at their cottage in Cornwall for a few days' holiday, then. Did you read what he wrote about her?'

'I did.'

Granville looked at the note again and began to read out: '"I don't love Janet, I haven't loved her for years. In fact, I don't think I ever did truly love her. I have been living a lie and I can't bear the thought of spending another day like that, let alone the rest of my life." Poor Janet. How is she going to cope with this?'

'The wife?'

'They seemed perfectly happy on the outside. Had everything. And she's a delightful, beautiful woman. A good wife and mother. The perfect household, or so you'd have thought. The secrets and pain that people conceal.'

'Indeed.'

'You're absolutely sure there's no hope? Shouldn't we at least call an ambulance?'

'You can call one by all means, but he's stone dead. The second and third vertebrae have snapped cleanly, which would have ruptured the spinal cord instantly. After stepping off the ladder he would have been conscious just for those few milliseconds of falling.'

'Have you got a medical background?'

'Me? No.' Steyn almost laughed. 'I've just picked a few things up along the way.'

They stood facing one another for a moment, until Granville said, 'I don't like to leave the girl. I think I'll go and see how she's getting on.'

'Maybe I should call the emergency services now.'

Granville hesitated. 'Just leave it a couple of minutes, would you? I'll be down in a moment.' Without waiting for Steyn to reply, he bounded up the stairs, two at a time, and went up to the door through which the girl had earlier gone. He raised a hand, paused, then knocked gently before turning the door handle.

She was already dressed and leaning over a bay-window seat, searching for something in her handbag. Granville glanced around the room. It was huge, smart and expensively furnished with voluminous chintz curtains and an antique four-poster bed – everything his own wife, Edwina, would have liked. The sheets on the bed were wildly disarrayed and a pillow lay on the floor.

The teenage girl in skin-tight jeans and ankle boots by the window seat seemed misplaced in so palatial a room. She glanced up as he came forward, and looked older now that she was dressed, more able to cope, though her hands were shaking. He could picture her in a shopping mall or smoking on a bench with a group of under-aged mothers at an urban playground. But her face was ashen and there was a hunted look in her eyes as she turned to face him.

'What you going to do?' she asked.

He tried to smile, to ease her worry. 'Just have a chat. Who are you?'

'Nobody.'

'What's your name?'

'Rhian.'

'Pretty name.' Granville walked over to her. 'Why don't you sit down, Rhian?' She did as she was told, and looked up at him the way a patient looks to her doctor as she waits for laboratory results. Her eyes were large and clear, their whites without stain or blemish. Granville sat down too, on the edge of the bed, leant forward over his thighs and placed his hands together. He forced a smile. 'How did you get here?'

'Bertie picked me up.'

'All the way from Bournemouth?'

'No. He got a taxi to bring me to Sturminster. That's where he met me and took me out. We went for an Indian.'

'Yesterday evening, you mean?'

She nodded. 'It got, like, late and he said he'd bring me back to stay the night and take me back home in the morning. And then it . . .'

'It's all right. I understand.'

'He was so unhappy, last night, like, and I felt so sorry for him. I had to stay.'

'You can't blame yourself,' Granville added, though he wondered if he really meant it. 'Tell me, how did a young girl like you get involved with a man so much older, like Bertie Gosling?'

Her face looked as if it would crumple. 'Don't you go judging me.'

'I'm not. I just want to know how you met.'

'He always asked for a latte.'

'He what?'

'At the airport. In the departure lounge. I work in the cafe.'

'Bournemouth airport?'

She nodded. 'He used to go on lots of business trips. Early flights. I got to know him after a bit. Am I going to get into trouble?'

'It's not going to be easy. He's a family man.'

'I know. I didn't want to hurt nobody. I've never done anything like this in my life. I don't know what I'm going to do. It's going to break my mum's heart. And my dad . . .' This latest thought brought tears to her eyes as quickly as if a valve had been switched, and she buried her face in her hands. 'Isn't there something you can do to help me?'

'I wish I could.'

She sniffed heavily to clear her nose. 'Are you Bertie's friend?'

'Sort of. I'm the rector here.'

'Is that some sort of vicar?'

'That kind of thing.'

'Then you must be able to help me.' She looked up at him, pleadingly. 'My grandad was a vicar.'

'Really?' He wasn't sure if he believed her. 'Whereabouts?'

'Bournemouth.'

'Do you want me to phone your mum and dad?'

'No!'

'OK. I can wait here with you while the police do all their stuff, if you like.'

'Are they going to take me away?'

'I shouldn't think so. They'll just have a few questions. They might call a counsellor. No-one's going to give you a hard time. Bertie left a note which shows he was a very unhappy and disturbed man.'

She began weeping again, and edged forward, taking Granville's hands. He could feel the wet warmth of her tears on his fingers. The nails were stubby, unmanicured. They were kid's fingers. 'I can't face it,' she croaked.

'My dear,' said Granville, squeezing her hands and rocking them comfortingly, 'I'll do anything I can to help, but I can't undo what's happened. I can vouch for you, talk you through your problems, visit your mum and dad, even, but I can't bring Bertie back to life.'

She listened in silence, her sobs gradually subsiding into little convulsions.

Downstairs, Piet Steyn was sitting on the edge of the sofa and staring down at the naked body on the floor.

His lips were pursed and he was nodding slowly, acknowledging a valid point in some internal debate. He then sighed and got down onto his knees next to the corpse, cupping Gosling's cheeks in both hands and turning the head from left to right and back again. It moved freely. 'You poor sinner,' he said, and looked up at the remaining portion of the rope dangling from the ceiling. It was fixed with a heavy steel screw to an old beam. Steyn had cut it with his multi-tool to get the body down. The noose end was still attached to Gosling's neck, and its heavy twisted knot looked as if it might have dislocated his jaw in the drop. 'No dance for you, then.' Steyn smiled almost nostalgically. The dead man's eyes were half closed, the expression on his face one of discomfort rather than pain. 'Come on, then, old fella,' Steyn said, and took hold of the two lifeless hands. He placed them together between his own palms, held them over Gosling's abdomen, and began to mutter a prayer in Afrikaans.

He was still bent and reciting quietly when Granville came back into the room, saw what was going on and lowered his head. As soon as the prayer was finished and the Amen uttered, Granville opened his eyes and said, 'We need to talk about the girl.'

They walked along to the kitchen, which was neat and tidy, cupboards closed and sink wiped down, with no sign of recent use other than a warm teapot to one side. A brown drip beneath its spout had started to dry on the polished granite surface, while on the other side of the room there was a single drained mug. Granville crossed his arms and explained his proposal in a subdued voice. He let his words sink in and watched Steyn closely, waiting for his response.

'I don't like the idea,' Steyn said.

'You're worried about trouble with the police?'

'No-one wants trouble with the police.'

'Believe me, the police are more likely to wrap this case up and be on their way if we do as I suggest. The real story could make things drag on for some time.'

'God's law has been broken in this house.'

Granville contained himself and replied simply, 'Who's to say?'

'Would your conscience rest easy? As a man of the cloth?'

'If I take into account the bigger picture, yes. The tragedy of a family man killing himself is bad enough. But think of the fallout if the whole story comes into the open, and think of all the people whose lives will be shattered by it. His wife, Janet, for one. Then this girl, of course, and her family, not to mention the two boys, Bertie's sons. Bad enough to lose their father, but to grow up thinking there was something like a disease at the heart of their family, that their mother might have driven their father to suicide, that he was an adulterer, and that he went around picking up waitresses thirty years his junior. God knows, she might even be a minor. Now think of the alternative. We send the girl home, destroy the note and treat it as a straight-forward suicide. We'll get the police over and everything else we tell them can be the truth: we happened to be walking, looked in through the window, and so on.'

'Truth is sometimes bitter, but that's no reason to corrupt it.'

'But hiding this truth is not going to hurt anyone or cause harm. Just the opposite. And if we tell the whole truth we'll be handing out a punishment of life-destroying magnitude. Can't we instead offer forgiveness? Wasn't that what Christ was all about?'

44

Piet looked straight at Granville. There was a ruggedness in his gaze that told of hardship in times past, of weary entrenchment. 'What do you say?' asked Granville, now less urgently. 'I can't do this unless you are with me. And we have to decide straight away.'

Piet said nothing, but looked down to the flagstones.

'I can see you are an upright man,' continued Granville, 'and I admire that. I'm sure I'll get to know you better but we don't have the luxury of time right now. Moral issues are not always straight-forward. And the law doesn't always have the monopoly on right and wrong.'

'That is the purpose of the law,' murmured Steyn: 'to decide right from wrong.'

'Sometimes we have to break free, have to be courageous. Life isn't black and white.'

'It is where I come from.'

'That's another issue. Look, you won't be alone in this. If everything goes wrong you can put the blame on me. I'm on your side.'

Steyn once again examined him, and after a few seconds of expressionless hesitation seemed to relent. Whether he decided of his own accord, or was persuaded or felt in some way compelled, a door within had been opened, as if for the first time in decades, it seemed to Granville, though the view of what lay beyond it was still far from clear.

'You might have a point,' he said quietly.

'I just want to do the good thing,' Granville endorsed his position. 'Surely every good act, fed by love, is a religious act.'

Steyn nodded to himself. 'All right,' he conceded. 'Let's move.'

Granville already had a plan. He would take Rhian down a sheltered path that followed the high yew hedge, at the bottom of which was a gate that led straight to the north end of the churchyard. He would let her into the church vestry and keep her there until he had a chance to organize transport. Then he would come back to the Old Rectory and join Steyn with the police, as quickly as he could.

'We can tidy up all trace of her. She won't even have been here,' he said.

'You can leave that side of things to me,' replied Piet. 'I've got an eye for detail.'

*

There was not a hint of a breeze in the air and a relentless light drizzle had settled in for the day. The clouds over central Dorset were low and heavy, and it was still rather dull when Granville hurriedly ushered the girl he thought was called Rhian out through the back entrance of her dead lover's home. He was unaware that across the yard Leo Flowers had put a finger between the curtains of his bedroom in the caretaker's annexe and was squinting in the direction of the moving figures.

Leo had worked at the Old Rectory for forty years before retiring six years previously. At that time, Bertie Gosling had barely arrived in the village but generously offered Leo life tenure in the little cottage annexe beyond the garage barn, on the understanding that the old man would keep an eye on the place and feed the dogs when the family were away. Leo was aware that Mr Gosling was at home at the moment, and so he was officially off duty, but was in the old habit of scanning the yard from top to bottom every morning when he opened his curtains, to make sure everything was as it should be. He struggled to see clearly at the best of times, having lost an eye and disfigured himself in a tractor accident in the 1950s. The injury had made it difficult for him to find a job and impossible to find a wife, which was one of the reasons a charitable former rector of the village took him into full-time employment all those years ago. Nowadays his good eye had clouded with age and overuse, and on dark mornings like this he couldn't see clearly at all, which is why he was squinting like a fairground halfwit to try and see who was scurrying around the back of the house so early in the day. It definitely looked like a man and a woman, that much he could be sure about. But it was over so quickly, and as he turned away to go and put the kettle on he wondered if he could even be certain of that.

A little later he saw the flashing police cars come and he went out and heard the awful news. Then he watched as the undertakers struggled to carry out the heavy zipped bag. He found them the key to the front door, which made things easier because it was a wider access and meant that they could reverse their van right up, though they parked it a bit too close to the stone pillars for Leo's comfort. Much later in the day poor Mrs Gosling and the little boys arrived back from Cornwall, and Leo watched that, too, but didn't want to go out and disturb them. They walked into the house with their heads bowed.

Yes, it had been a long day for Leo, and by the end of it the strange little early morning scene he had witnessed in the yard seemed to have been swallowed up in his memory, much as lovers' initials on a tree trunk are distorted and eventually absorbed by the advance of new organic matter. And yet, something about it would not be smoothed away altogether, then or in the weeks that followed. Time and again it would prick through the blanket of his comfortably uneventful daily routine, and jar him. He wanted nothing more than a quiet time, a cup of tea every two hours, a little bit of telly, a daily glance at

47

some very old dirty magazines, and the occasional stroll down to the stream, weather permitting. But this little business chafed annoyingly at his peace and quiet. Had that been a female out there, so early in the morning? Leo wondered from time to time if he should say something to someone about it, just to put the thing to rest in his own mind, but more often than not the whole business would slip from his memory again, sometimes for days on end.

Chapter 4

Edwina St Clair awoke that morning to a faint but welcome scent of the erotic, something which hadn't happened to her in a long while. She had no memory of a specific dream, nor were there the remains of carnal shapes in her waking mind's eye, but she felt luxuriant, and, half asleep, spread wide her limbs beneath the quilt with a sigh. The alarm clock had not yet gone off, and it was still quite dark in the room. Without raising her head from the pillow, she reached across to find some flesh in the vague direction where she imagined her husband's midriff to be, but her fingers encountered nothing but empty sheets. Another stretch of the hand, and a moment's floundering, informed her of the fruitlessness of the venture, and the zest of the moment withered away.

Definition was restored and thoughts about the day ahead sank on to on her shoulders like a coat of drenched felt. Not that it was going to be as depressing as most days. By normal reckoning she was in for something of a treat: off to London by the early train, the hairdresser, some shopping. But dreariness had some years ago institutionalized itself in her life, joining forces with irritation and resentment, and these, like three sibling witches, had become her constant companions, weaving a dismal counterpoint in and around her daily activities. It made little difference how much she tried to vary her normal routine, because everything – play, work and family living – was acted out beneath dull skies. Sleep was an escape, but moments after waking every morning the careless freedom of the night would evaporate as the programme of her day, her life, took shape: a grid of time management and planning, a plague of administrative boxes to be ticked, with no promise of reward, no guarantee of better times to come. It felt even worse this morning because she had woken to such a delicious urge. Her first words of the day were therefore a muttered curse.

She climbed out of bed and padded, yawning, across the landing to wake the girls. 'Hurry up now. Your father's taken it into his head to go off before any of us have got up, so you're going to have to be extra quick. I've got a train to catch.' Groans from the bunk beds were her response.

Edwina got herself ready more hurriedly than she would have liked and went down to the kitchen to prepare the girls' breakfast. Granville still was not back and there was no sign of the dog. Could he have forgotten that he was taking the girls to school this morning? It was worse than absent-minded, worse than thoughtless. He was growing ever more erratic and deluded and it seemed she was expected to do nothing more than sit back like an obedient wife and watch quietly from the sidelines as he fell apart, as their world crumbled. If he would just agree to go and see someone about his problem, if the underlying cause could be investigated and rooted out, she might be able to drum up a modicum of sympathy – support, even – but as it was, Granville seemed content just to swim round and round in a private pond of supernatural hocus-pocus, to which neither she nor the girls, nor anyone else, for that matter, could ever hope to share access. Not that she wanted access, if truth be told. She'd had enough of it over the years and didn't care any longer to watch Granville's eyes mist over as he tried to 'explain the inexplicable'. The crass terminology, the pseudo-mystical jargon and semantic escapism of it all had really begun to grate.

Edwina had never had anything against religion per se, nor the priesthood as a job, but her own present role as country rector's wife and glorified local social worker was not one she had either sought or anticipated at the start of their lives together. She could see now, of course, that she had been wrong to imagine Granville might have wanted to do a little better in his career, but after such a dazzling student record, she couldn't be blamed for thinking it. Anyone would have. Even after his so-called awakening, when he grew his beard, lost his looks and began to wear clothes that he'd forgotten in the bottom of his drawers for more than a decade, he still seemed to have more than enough good cards in his hand to take him all the way to the top. He came through his vocational crisis pretty much intact, and, by the time she married him, turned himself into a tidy and studious young clergyman, with an outstanding gift for writing and an enviable job in his sights. She could be forgiven, therefore, for having pictured a future of ground-breaking theological publications and bishops' palaces.

Her gradual discovery that the nuts and bolts of a vicar's life ranked, on the scale of glamour, probably lower than that of teacher but above male nurse, was sobering but not devastating. Worse – heart-sickeningly worse – was the way in which, over the next twenty years (potentially the two most explosive decades of his life, when his old university friends were conquering the world) Granville allowed himself to drift on the periphery of nowhere, surrounded by nobodies, neck deep in a sea of irrelevancies. Whenever she thought about it her exasperation turned to indignation, and from that quickly to tearful anger.

But she tried hard not to burden her daughters with her malaise, and did her best to keep up her spirits whenever they were at home; so that when they came downstairs in their school uniforms, carefree and smiling, she tried to adopt a more positive outlook. She chirped happily with them over breakfast about plans for the week ahead and kept up a pretty good show of being happy Mum right up until the moment when she looked up and saw, through the drizzle outside, her husband walking back up the driveway on his way towards the house. By the time he came into the room she had completely succumbed to misery again and turned away so as not to have to face him.

She spoke through the noise of the running tap as she rinsed the cereal bowls at the sink. 'You know I'm catching the seven-forty, don't you?' He did not answer, but then he often ignored her if he detected a provocative tone. Still, she did face him but turned the tap off and shook the drips off her hands. 'Can you take over here? I've got to go and get ready. We're running late, hurry up, girls.' Her voice was flat, unyielding. When, eventually, she did turn around, it was because of something Amelia, her younger girl, said, which took her by surprise.

'Daddy, what's the matter? What's the matter, Daddy?'

*

An hour earlier, after leaving the Old Rectory, Granville had crossed the garden with Rhian and let her into the church vestry by the outside door. Once inside, she visibly shrank at the unfamiliarity of her surroundings, its antique scent and masculine austerity, and did not move from the doorway until he encouraged her to sit down. He put the kettle on for some tea and dialled a succession of numbers for taxi companies, deliberately avoiding the very local ones. When at last he found one that was open for business, he arranged for a car to come to the village school car park and pick the girl up in twenty minutes. There was a paved path across the church meadow, he explained to Rhian, that came out by the post office, right next to the village hall. It was a short walk from there to the school. No-one would take any notice of her getting into a taxi in the middle of the village.

While she was waiting for him to sort out the taxi, she spotted a man's hairbrush and a little square mirror propped up on a mullioned sill at the side of the vestry. She crossed over to it and began to brush her hair, staring at herself, trance like, with large, unblinking eyes, while her head was tilted slightly to one side. When she had finished, and as Granville was pouring boiling water into two mugs, she leant forward close to the mirror and began to apply mascara to her eyelashes. Granville caught sight of her in the reflection and watched for a moment too long until she noticed him looking, and then he quickly looked away.

As they drank their tea Granville found he had to do most of the talking. There were only a few minutes to kill but Granville found them heavy going. He could see that she was desperately nervous and disoriented, and did his best to comfort her, assuring her it would turn out fine and she'd be able to put the whole painful business behind her in time. He would do everything he could to

53

protect the secret. She stared doubtfully into space, clung to her mug with both hands, and said nothing. When it was at last time to go he helped her with her coat. 'We're in this together now,' he said, warmly, and squeezed her shoulders. 'You're not to worry, OK?' She nodded. 'If you start showing you're worried then someone will pick up on it. Try to act as normal as possible, and if you feel wobbly just get in touch with me. I can help.' She nodded again and smiled up at him.

In a moment she was gone, and after waiting a few more minutes in the vestry, watching her disappear at the end of the flagstoned path, Granville locked up and went back to the scene of the incident at the Old Rectory. The police were just arriving.

Half an hour later, he made his excuses and told the officer in charge that he lived a few hundred yards away. He'd be happy to answer any more questions just as soon as he'd got his daughters off to school. Arriving at the garden gate of his house, he could see from the light in the kitchen that the family were all up. He saw their heads moving around, and his elder girl, Serena, did a little hop which made her pretty long brown hair bounce. He could tell by its shiny texture, even from this distance, that she'd already brushed it.

He went indoors and held the door open for the dog. Edwina must have heard him come in but she did not call a greeting nor look round from the sink. It was only after he had been in the kitchen for at least a minute that she said anything to him: a deliberately barbed reference to the train she had to catch, as she flicked the drips pointedly from her fingers and dried them on a tea towel. He did not respond, but looked at his girls and felt an overwhelming urge to hug them. He crouched down to their chairs and scooped them, one into each arm.

He pulled them in tight and held them there, which Amelia must have found sufficiently unusual behaviour for her to ask, 'Daddy, what's the matter? What's the matter, Daddy?' At this, Edwina did turn to look at him, and he could see from her expression that she realized immediately that something was up. She also understood, from his return look, that she shouldn't say anything out loud, but when the girls were facing away from her she mouthed, soundlessly, 'What is it?'

Granville closed his eyes at her and nodded, indicating everything was all right but she should just wait a minute. He then released the girls, telling them to go and brush their teeth and collect their school bags from their room because it was nearly time to leave.

When they had gone he gave Edwina an outline of what had happened.

'Did he leave a note or anything?'

'No.'

'Naked? How awful!'

'The South African guy, Piet, was great. Seemed to know exactly what to do with the body.'

'Oh God. I wonder if they've got hold of Janet. Do we have any idea why he did it?'

'No. He seemed to have everything life could offer.'

'Poor woman. And those two boys. How will they ever get over it?' said Edwina.

'I'll go back there when she gets home. Better if someone's there for her, not just the police.'

'I suppose her family will come down. Hasn't she got sisters? Or maybe she'll go to them. It's half-term for private schools, isn't it?'

'That's why they're in Cornwall, I guess.'

'So you just saw him through the window? How long before do you think he did it?'

'The police think about an hour.' That was it. He had lied to her thrice. He hadn't particularly planned to, but it had just happened. It was unfamiliar territory, there was no way back, and it made him feel faintly nauseous.

'Maybe I shouldn't go to London.'

'Of course you must. I can handle everything. You'd better get going.' She did not dispute it but turned to go. Just then, Granville recalled something and asked her what train she'd be coming back on. 'I've got the old ladies here tonight,' he said, 'you know, the Bereavement Fellowship.'

'Couldn't they meet somewhere else this once? In the circumstances.'

'It's all right. You don't need to be here. I'll do it on my own. I can get some ready-made stuff from Sainsbury's. They're not fussy about what they eat. I'll cut short the Youth Group and get back here in time to pop it in the oven. I'll have to excuse myself before the end because Beth Longman and her fiancé are coming round for a marriage prep session straight after.'

'Isn't today the hospital rounds?'

'That's earlier.'

'Will you have time to get from the hospital to the Youth Group and still leave early?'

'I'll manage.'

'I don't know why you bother with those delinquents anyway. It's not as if they've got anything to do with the church. The Youth Group should be run by the local council or something.'

'They're good lads. It's quite fun, actually.'

'But you've got so many other . . .' She stopped herself when she saw his eyes close, held up her hands in wordless surrender and turned to go upstairs. Just at that moment, a muffled ringtone sounded from Granville's trouser pocket. 'Your phone,' Edwina said, before calling up to the landing for the girls to get a move on.

Left alone for a moment in the kitchen, Granville took the phone from his back pocket and pressed a button to retrieve the text message. It was short, clean and inconsequential; yet he found himself staring at it for far longer than it took to read, as if it were some puzzle or obscure monogram needing to be deciphered.

'*Thankyou xxxx*,' it said, simply. It was from Rhian. He had given her his mobile number; in case of emergency, he had told her. Less than an hour ago. It had seemed the appropriate and compassionate thing to do.

Chapter 5

Piet Steyn's garden was substantial for such a small cottage. It stretched to nearly an acre all told, though half of this – the half further away from the house – was overrun by brambles and apparently impenetrable, which is exactly how he wanted it to remain. The rest comprised a weedless lawn framed on three sides by symmetrical borders with ruler-straight edges. The beds themselves were immaculate, if understated at this time of the year, because the winter cut-back had yet to be superseded by the burst of new spring growth. But evidence of warmer weather was on its way: pale buds swelling, perennials springing up in straight lines through well-turned compost, and fourteen old-fashioned roses (seven on each side) sprouting green and burgundy shoots beneath the scars of past pruning. In the three years that Piet had been living here, he had transformed the plot from what had been a neglected stretch of wasteland into a sanctuary, which, if not exactly pretty or adventurous, was a model of order and planning. A casual passer-by would probably judge it to be the work of a conscientious, disciplined and well-informed horticulturalist, so long as the incongruous wilderness at the end of the plot was not taken into account.

But it would be difficult to reach such a judgement

because there was hardly anywhere for a passer-by to stop and get a decent view. The garden was enclosed by a high wall on one side and an old box bush hedge on another. A deep border of hawthorn, beech and ivy separated the remaining flank from the little road that ran alongside the property, and the dense scrub at the top stretched as far as the eye could see, all the way, in fact, to the edge of the old wartime airstrip that was up for development. Curious observers might have been able to crane their necks around the box hedge at the point where it was breached by a small garden gate, and just about get a glimpse of what lay behind, but to do so might have seemed nosey or invasive and therefore few attempted it, not that there were many pedestrians this far out of the village, anyway.

Piet Steyn liked to keep a rigid routine but had been delayed this morning and came out of his cottage rather later than usual. He was carrying four plastic bags that he had earlier brought back from the shop. He walked across the lawn with them, down to the end of the garden, and then, after looking around, disappeared into the cover of brambles at the far end. He was following a hidden path, one that he had deliberately carved out in a zigzag pattern so that it would not be obvious to potential onlookers. After turning three hairpin bends within the undergrowth he was completely obscured from the main garden, and the path then took him a further forty feet deeper in towards what looked like a raised hump in the ground. This, too, was surrounded by untended trees and covered in nettles and brambles. A few secret snowdrops had sprung to life here, because of the time of year, but they were lonely outposts of prettiness and seemed almost apologetic for raising their heads in such a wasteland.

Piet climbed onto the top of the little hump and began to walk the length of it, checking some mesh grates that were sunk into its top. Each he swept with his hand, clearing leaves and twigs away. He noticed that here and there the concrete beneath his feet had cracked and ivy was eating away the mortar between the bricks. The exterior skin of the place was immensely thick because of the purpose for which it had been built, and he did not want to clear away too much of the overgrowing foliage, for obvious reasons, but it was definitely time for some basic maintenance work, especially now that the weather was improving.

Returning to the left end of the concrete hump, he bent down with a large key and unlocked something on the ground between his feet. He then heaved with both hands and a thick steel lid groaned open on its hinges. Retrieving the carrier bags he had earlier put down on the ground, he hooked them one by one to an apparatus in the cavity beneath the lid. He reached down, found a rope which he pulled taut, and with the other hand released a lever hidden from view. This transferred the weight of the hooked bags to the rope that he was holding, and he lowered them, gradually feeding rope over a lubricated pulley, down into the hole, until the bags gently reached the bottom. He coiled the rest of the rope on a hook under the lid and sat down with his legs hanging over the edge of the hole. Finding a foothold, he climbed inside, flicked a light switch just beneath the rim and finally pulled the steel above his head until it crunched to a close. A final tug from the underside nudged the lid firmly into its rusted groove, and he secured it with an anticlockwise turn of a locking wheel.

Normally he would clip the seat attachment to the block and pulley system but today he had to use the old ladder rungs to get down to the bottom of the shaft because the shopping bags were still clipped on to the descent rope. It was the same every time he had to take down something heavy and it was tiring on the legs. When he had originally done the place up, he'd had to use the ladder for every single descent; but then the physical strain had seemed like nothing compared to the logistical challenge of getting everything he needed down there: months of preparation, taking all the kit apart, piece by piece, and reassembling, or building it from scratch, down below; installing air circulation pumps, heating and air conditioning, repairing antique ventilation shafts and drains, updating the plumbing, putting in a boiler, rewiring the circuitry, linking it to the cottage three-phase supply (in the old days they would have used generators), and more. Then there was the matter of setting up a foolproof alarm system, and, the most important part of all: styling the place in the appropriate manner. He had gone to a lot of trouble to get it just right, and had had to work hard and sporadically, mostly at night, so as not to attract attention or make the place look like a building site. When it was all finished, he had waited a further three months to let the dust settle on the whole job, before embarking on the project proper.

Stepping off the last rung at the bottom of the shaft, he unclipped the carrier bags from the rope, took out his bunch of keys and walked across a dark vestibule towards a steel door on the far side. He unbolted the door, top and bottom, before turning a large antique key in the lock. It was a heavy door, with reluctant old hinges that no amount of lubrication seemed to ease up, and once it was unlocked he needed both hands to pull it open.

He took the shopping bags through to the next chamber, locking the first door behind him. A disused latrine was on his left, and a tiny room – some sort of guard post – on the right. Both were unlit, full of cobwebs and had a coating of rubble on the floor. He hadn't thought it necessary to restore this area but just kept a passage swept through to the next door, straight ahead. This one was the same as the first, made with thick sheet metal, riveted together in sections. He unlocked and unbolted it before proceeding through to a second room, little more than a wide corridor, but less derelict than the previous one. He had re-mortared the brickwork here, repaired the cracks and painted the walls, so that it looked like an ordinary domestic cellar, lit by two dim bulkhead lamps along the centre of its brick vaulting. The door at the far end of this chamber was secured with a pair of modern mortice and cylinder locks as well as bolts at the top and bottom. He opened them all and went through, closing it firmly behind and locking it before turning round to survey the scene within.

'Rose!' he called, his accent rolling heavily over the first consonant. 'I'm here.' There was silence. 'Where are you, my dear?'

The room he had entered was large and drenched with golden light, as if lit by the early morning sun, but the sources of the light were cleverly concealed behind screens and curtain pelmets. There was one large window, which seemed to open onto an idyllic country landscape; but it was an illusion because the scenery was in fact a huge, brightly lit photographic poster, and the area behind the glass was nothing more than a shallow recess, backed by bricks. There could be no real windows this far underground.

It was a perfect specimen of a large family kitchen, tidy, prettily upholstered and well equipped, but reminiscent of a stage set. Part of this was due to the lighting and the symmetry of the layout, but there was something else unusual in the detail. Every appliance, each article of furniture, the ornaments, pictures and fixtures, the tablecloth, linoleum flooring and lampshades, everything, down to the Bakelite cupboard handles, the rose print upholstery and the enamelled bread bin, conformed to a period of home design and kitchen technology that had disappeared decades before and was familiar to the modern eye only through period dramas and photographs. And yet this was no film set or museum interior, but an orderly, working kitchen. At any moment a gaggle of red-cheeked Enid Blyton-esque children might suddenly spill into such a room, with grey flannel shorts, caps and satchels, ready for their glasses of milk and breakfast porridge.

'Rose!' Piet called again, now a little more forcefully, and a door at the other side of the kitchen opened. A woman stood there and rested her hand on the door frame.

'Good morning, husband.' Her face was made up heavily like an old-school actress, its light umber foundation evenly applied and finished with a powder compound. She wore eyeliner thick like Cleopatra, and her scarlet lips were drawn wide into a smile that neither drooped nor flickered.

'Good morning, my dear,' replied Steyn. 'You look lovely today.'

'Thank you.' Her expression held still and her wide eyes barely blinked. Her heels were quite high, and the full circle of her white skirt showed the ruffled edges of a net petticoat at its hem. The waist was narrow, the blouse short-sleeved and red with white polka dots.

Piet held up the bags. 'I've got you everything you asked for.'

'Thank you.'

He lowered them onto the kitchen table and she went straight to unpack the first. He studied her reactions carefully as she regarded the groceries item by item, but her expression did not change.

'I've also brought you today's newspaper and the bill for the food.' He squinted at the slip of paper, then put on a pair of spectacles and looked at it again. 'This lot, together with those small bits on Tuesday, come to . . .' he made a silent calculation, 'forty-seven pounds and twenty-three pence. Do you mind if I have a look at your accounts?'

She walked smoothly over to a bureau, opened it and took out a large ledger with leathered corners. She passed it to Piet, who flicked through its pages to find what he was looking for and then traced his finger down a column filled with neat handwritten figures.

'That makes ninety-two pounds and twenty pence exactly for the week. Is that what you were expecting?'

'That seems about right.'

'I don't think there's any point in increasing the household management allowance next quarter. You seem to be getting the hang of a decent budget. I like the way you avoid wastage and still manage to cook good meals.'

'Thank you.'

'You've drafted out our requirements for next week?'

'Why don't we see how we get on? I may need some soap and a new tin of polish but there's quite a lot of food left over that will last.'

'Spoken like a good and responsible housewife. Look – ' he took a parcel out of one of the bags. It was wrapped in white tissue and crossed with pink ribbon. 'I've got something for you.'

At the sight of it she drew breath sharply and withdrew the fingers of one hand to her chest. Her nails were finely shaped and red.

'A little something to show my appreciation.'

She took it, pulled open the ribbon's bow with a single tug and the tissue paper seemed to fall away of its own accord. Holding out her arms, she allowed a folded white nightie to tumble open. It was embroidered all over with little pink blossoms. 'It's beautiful,' she said, holding it up by the shoulder straps and staring at it.

'I'm glad you like it. The flowers are roses. As soon as I saw it I thought of you.'

At this, she seemed to suffer an involuntary convulsion and with another sharp intake of breath let the garment drop. Embarrassed, she turned away from him, searching for something.

'Please don't cry, my dear,' said Piet.

'It's all right,' she said, finding a freshly pressed handkerchief in a drawer, and stooped to pick the nightdress up off the floor.

'You are happy? They're tears of happiness, I hope?'

'Of course.' She turned her back to him again as she put the handkerchief to her eyes, carefully trying not to disturb her make-up.

Piet looked away discreetly and continued to unpack the shopping bags. When they were done, the woman was at his side and he stood back to look her up and down. He shook his head with awe. 'You are turning into a beautiful woman, Rose, truly. Your hair has grown long and – ' he ran his fingers through it – 'seems almost to shine. A picture of health, eh?'

She acknowledged the compliment with a tilt of the head. 'You were later today than usual,' she said. 'I was beginning to worry.'

'Yes,' he sighed. 'I've had a bit of trouble from the locals again.'

'What was it this time?'

'An unpleasant message sprayed onto the garden path. If these people think they can frighten me away with such playground antics they have another think coming.'

'Who do you think did it?'

'The same ones, to be sure. I shall have to deal with them. The son is meddlesome but harmless. It's the father who is the real menace. I had to purchase a chemical agent to clean the lettering off the paving stones. Over twelve pounds, that bottle cost!'

'How can you be sure it's the same people?'

'It's as if they leave a scent behind. They have the ignorance of pigs. I can smell it, trust me.'

'Of course I trust you,' she said.

'I know you do,' he said, and nodded benignly, resting his hand on the bare skin of her arm above the elbow. 'The trouble is they are getting a little bit braver every time. I suppose they are encouraged by my long absences from the cottage. They must be wondering where I go.' He shook his head. 'I can't have them sniffing around the property behind my back. Not when there's so much at stake. I'll have to put a stop to it.'

The woman's smile faltered. 'Perhaps you should go and meet them. Talk to them and make friends. As soon as they get to know you they'll stop doing bad things. I'm sure they only do it because they think—' She cut herself short and looked down.

'They think what?'

'They might think that you're a bit unusual. People are frightened by what they don't understand.'

Piet put his hands on his hips, closed his eyes wearily and shook his head. After a pause, he said, 'So I should throw a little party for them, is that what you say? Drinks and food and paper hats, perhaps? And maybe you'd like to come to the cottage and help serve? Be the hostess, receive them at the front door?'

She looked away quickly. 'Of course I can't do that.'

Piet examined her face closely. 'Or perhaps you see some kind of opportunity for you in all this.'

'What do you mean?'

'Perhaps you hope these people might do some harm to me and that will help your cause.'

Her eyes widened. 'How could you say such a thing? If anything happened to you, I'd be finished.'

'Is that the only reason you do not wish to see me come to harm? In order to save your own skin? Hardly reassuring.'

'No! But—'

'But what?'

'But if something did happen to you . . .' There was an edge to her voice. 'After all, no-one knows what's around the corner. What if you get done in by these people—'

'That is an unpleasant and undignified turn of phrase.'

'I'm sorry. What if something unexpected did happen and you were hurt or killed? What would happen to me?'

'The Lord would make provision for you in His own wonderful way. Or not, if He sees fit. We cannot hope to predict what He intends.'

'So I would sit here and rot? Die of thirst and starvation?'

'That's enough, now,' said Piet quietly.

The woman turned away, blinking, and went to open the fridge. She squatted elegantly, knees locked together to one side, and took out some bacon wrapped in grease-proof paper. She held the little packet with the first three fingers of her right hand, while the other two hovered in the air.

'No, I shan't be inviting those halfwit idiots in for a friendly chat,' Piet went on. 'Unless it's to give them a stiff caning. Back home a man would have his tongue cut out for less. I've seen worse happen, believe me.' The woman said nothing but put a pan with two slices of bacon onto the gas flame of the cooker. Piet passed her a gingham apron that was hanging on a hook and she tied it around her waist. She then cracked an egg into the pan, and it instantly began to crackle and pop in the hot oil.

'I always feel better for seeing you, my dear,' Steyn said, sitting down and resting his elbows on a freshly ironed tablecloth. It was edged with white lace and printed with spring daffodils. A place had been laid for him at the table with a plastic knife and fork. He yawned. 'And you don't have to worry about a thing. Our secret will be safe for ever.'

She brought his bacon, eggs and toast over to the table, holding the warmed plate with a folded tea towel, and put it down in front of him. He held up his knife and fork, leaning over to sniff appreciatively at the food, but was distracted by a pain in his neck and twisted his head from left to right to ease it.

'Stiff again?' the woman asked.

'Always stiff.'

'Would you like me to massage it?'

'Perhaps later.'

'The breakfast will do you good.'

'Thank you,' he said, and she turned to fetch her own plate of toast and jam from the side. 'This looks delicious,' Piet said, unfolding a napkin on his lap. The woman went to the other side of the table and sat down.

Steyn frowned affectionately. 'We must introduce you to meat again. You lack protein in your diet. Remind me, how long it is since you ate meat?'

'Not since I was much more than a girl.'

'I asked how long.'

Her eyes moved rapidly from side to side and she answered quickly, 'About twenty-six years.'

'Not good for you. The Lord means us to eat animals. You don't have to search far in the Bible to see that. We'll start you on meat soon.'

The woman thought better of making a response and stifled the impulse with a smile. Piet noticed. 'Did I say something amusing?'

She looked up sharply. 'No, husband.'

'Well then?'

'It's just that I don't think I can start eating meat again after so many years.'

'We shall see about that.'

'The taste of it would probably make me sick.'

'Not if there's no alternative. You'd quite soon be grateful for anything. You've never been really hungry, have you?'

'No.'

'Well, I have, and I know.' His face had hardened but he looked across at her and the grim expression melted away. 'One thing at a time, eh?' He stretched over the table to pat her hand, and she smiled back but said nothing. They sat in silence for a few minutes, eating.

'So,' Steyn said at last, not looking up from his plate, 'tell me about your morning so far. You did your penance?'

'Yes.'

'How much did you accomplish?'

'I got up as soon as the lights came on, as usual, and spent an hour in prayer before going to my desk.'

'Where have you got to in your manuscript?'

'The Book of Jeremiah, chapter thirty. I've completed nearly three thousand pages.'

'You keep the writing neat, as befits the Holy Word?'

'Of course.'

'Jeremiah thirty, you say. Let me see.' He picked up a copy of the Bible that always sat on the kitchen table. He was still turning pages when the woman spoke in a soft monotone.

'For thus says the Lord: Your hurt is incurable, and your wound is grievous. There is none to uphold your cause, no medicine for your wound, no healing for you. All your lovers have forgotten you.' She paused and her eyes met his for an instant before she looked away again. Piet put on his reading glasses, looked at the text, pursed his lips and nodded at her approvingly. 'Very good,' he said, 'I'm impressed.' He closed the Bible gently and placed it back on the table.

He took off his glasses and put his knife and fork together. 'I have had an interesting experience,' he said, 'and I think I will share it in part with you.'

The woman looked up quickly, her flawless demeanour mildly stung by this novelty. 'Oh yes?'

'I won't bore you with the details, but I have met the local padre, a man called Mr St Clair. Did you come across him in your former life?'

'I don't think so.'

'He's been here about six years. A spineless sort, thinks he's a bit of a wag. He's asked me to join his congregation, be part of his church community.'

'What did you say?'

'These sorts of people are hypocrites but you don't want to go offending them.'

'So you won't go to the church?'

'We'll see. This pastor seems very keen. He wants to know about my faith and how I choose to live. It sounds like he's dipped his toe in all sorts of pools – different philosophies and beliefs – Hindus, voodoos, you name it – and he thinks his broad-mindedness is some kind of recommendation!'

'Ungodly fool.'

'Amen, well said. On the other hand, a man of his standing in the community might help this business with the locals. If I had someone like him as an ally, he could act like a kind of bridge. A pressure valve, you might say.'

'Did you talk to him about it?'

'No. It's just an idea. What do you think?'

She hesitated. She could see that he was monitoring her response. 'It's impossible for me to say,' she replied.

'It would mean entering into a kind of friendship,' Piet explained, 'which is something I usually avoid. There might be risks, but there might also be benefits. Do you have an opinion?'

She shook her head vigorously. 'You are a good judge of character, husband. And I'm sure the Lord will help you to decide.'

This seemed to satisfy Piet and he nodded. 'You're right. Now – ' he stood up from the table. 'We are not going to do our usual work together this morning. I have some writing to do and then must get on with a few essential repairs to the building.'

'Repairs? Is there a problem with something?' Again, there was a flicker in her eyes.

'Of course not.' He put a hand on her shoulder. 'I just want it to be perfect for you here. Rule number one to all who come after me – ' he held up an index finger: 'A good wife deserves to take pride in her home. If you aspire to be her lord, you must provide her with a castle. She must never have need to reflect upon the alternative of a better life. She must be honoured, her fragile nature protected, as befits the weaker vessel, as St Peter says. This place will be your fortress, my dear, your sanctuary, and you its princess.'

She looked at him and held steady her smile, even as he stooped to give her a light kiss on the cheek to say goodbye. He would be back in time for supper, he said.

Later, after he had gone altogether, her tears began to fall, as they always did, even before he was through the first of the locked doors, and she pinched her nose to stem them. One by one she heard the familiar sound of the doors clang shut, heard the apparently innocuous click of the levers turning in the locks followed by the coarse slide of the cast-iron bolts. The tears would always stream down her cheeks for a good while before she got to her feet, took off her shoes and shuffled off to the bedroom to change. Then she would go to the bathroom mirror and begin removing the make-up. She took her time because time she had plenty, and with every wipe of every cotton-wool pad her ashen complexion would begin to re-emerge. From beneath the manufactured comeliness her true situation would stare back at her, beseeching and powerless; the grey, drawn and hunted face of a prisoner.

Chapter 6

Granville had everything ready in the church by midday, so that he could nip back home and have a bite to eat in good time before the funeral party was due to arrive. Edwina was still upstairs getting changed when he got in, so he went out into his back garden to take a last look at the site where the statue was going to be positioned.

He had been planning it for months – drawing, measuring, choosing the right materials – and the workmen were coming to install the base section this afternoon. He was glad of the distraction, if truth be known. The funeral today and the tea reception afterwards were going to be an ordeal because he still wasn't convinced, in his heart, that he had done the right thing on the morning of the suicide. The widow's dark-rimmed eyes and the fatherless boys' empty faces weighed heavily on his conscience; and none of it was made any easier by the regularity of the one-line messages that kept pinging up on his phone from the girl, Rhian. One had chimed its arrival when he was actually sitting with Janet Gosling, his arm comfortingly squeezed around her shoulders. It had made him feel almost sick inside, and now he hoped more than anything that the passage of time would wipe all doubts about what he had done from his memory, in the way that oil slicks dilute and eventually vanish into the enormity of the ocean.

He stood on the lawn with his hands in his overcoat pockets looking down at the quadrangle he had sprayed on the ground with orange paint. It was a brash colour against the unassuming green of the grass. The spirit scent of paint still hung in the air, a biting, masculine smell, and he felt guilty for having so much enjoyed doing the spraying. He should just as well have marked out the space for the workmen with bamboo sticks.

This was going to be the most expensive purchase he had made in years and he knew that a lot of people would consider it a folly. Edwina, for one. When he first showed her the drawing she scoffed out loud. Later, after he had convinced her that he was serious and tried to explain the reasons behind the design, she turned sarcastic, and added that such recklessness in a fully paid up penny-pincher was a sign of a midlife crisis. But he suspected her objections had nothing to do with money or aesthetics; it was more that she could not stand the idea of putting down roots in this house when she was secretly counting the days before they could leave. His wanting to install something so permanent in the garden here depressed her beyond belief, and she was deaf to his assurances that they could take the sculpture with them if ever they moved.

There never seemed to be a spell, nowadays, when there wasn't a problem with Edwina. If Granville was not openly quarrelling with her, he was most likely navigating a path between hazards to avoid a quarrel. After all these years, they had landed themselves in a strange, cold territory, and he tried to picture the stages of descent, or perhaps it was more like stepping-stones, that had brought them here. He wanted to believe that she was as blameless as himself, and it broke his heart to think of her, too, feeling desolate and lonely, in a place of unkindness and misunderstanding. Was it too late to claw back some warmth? Did she even enjoy his company any more? There were twenty or more people in Edwina's life, he was sure, that she would prefer to spend time with than himself. Plenty of stepping-stones crossed to get to that shore.

Their adventure together had begun when she first came down to visit him in the Sussex cottage, straight after university, before he had even seriously thought about becoming a priest. He and two college friends had rented the place for cash to find spiritual purity close to nature and without modern amenities. It was little more than a hovel, and icy in winter, with no electricity or running water, which meant that they were probably breaking some Environment Agency regulation just by occupying it. The entire fabric of the cottage was crumbling around them but they loved it. With the arrival of spring and summer, they rolled up their sleeves, picked up spade and scythe, and threw themselves into open-air toil, brushing inquisitive bees from their sweating brows and sneezing through clouds of sun-baked pollen. They grew vegetables for most of the year, bought a cow and chickens, but otherwise used money as little as possible. When not labouring until their nails cracked, they would spend their time silently in prayer or reading religious texts by candlelight.

For a year they led a life of diligent calm in a primitive utopia, with periods of enforced silence and fasting, free of what they considered to be the impoverishing influence of technology, and Granville began to write a book about the project. Local people were amused but kind to them, and offered lifts in cars, which were usually declined. The starry-eyed friends preferred to walk, even when going to see their families, which in Granville's case meant an eighty-mile round trip. There were occasional visitors to the cottage and they were usually reluctant to leave, because the quiet, spartan paradise was strangely enchanting. One of them was Edwina. She came as a friend of Bindy, the sister of one of Granville's companions, for a long weekend in late summer. Edwina immediately took to Granville, enthralled by his enthusiasm and innocence, and by the second night they were in bed together. He remembered the novelty of waking up with her warm beside him and the nutty scent of her skin in the sheets. He remembered the single bed they shared, with a window and a pair of worn old floral curtains right beside it. They would lean through the window, kneeling together on the bed, and look out across the sun-drenched fields, thinking they were like shepherds in a Samuel Palmer idyll.

The sweet life that the three young men shaped for themselves at the cottage came to an end as autumn began to turn and they realized they could not endure another winter there. They justified their decision to leave by saying they should no longer run away from the world but engage in a life of service within it; and so they went their separate ways, Granville to theological college, Robert to teaching, and Billy to a fiery death on the M4, a few miles short of Swindon. Granville found a publisher for his book but its appearance caused less than the smallest ripple of interest and soon went out of print.

Standing now in his housing estate garden, Granville glanced up at the sky and wondered if the drizzle would clear. The grass underfoot was wet, and his pale fingers felt damp and chilly in his coat pockets. The workmen would make a real mess of the ground in weather like this, which would mean wellies for the girls and mud on the hall carpet for a fortnight or more. Edwina would moan like anything about that. He could already hear the words forming in her mouth, and the clean metallic edge in her voice when she was irritated. The clouds were breaking slightly in the west. In between some trees in the same direction he caught a glimpse of the ruined abbey's walls, but a change in the breeze altered the configuration of branches and the interesting view was obscured again. There were times when life seemed so flat compared to the old days, he thought; dull and hopeless.

He heard the sound of clinking china behind him and turned to see that Edwina was in the kitchen, and so he went back inside to join her for lunch.

She was hurriedly laying the table for the two of them, and glanced up at him as he came in. He noticed her eyes dart towards his clerical shirt and dog collar, but she didn't say anything. He knew, of course, that she didn't like dog collars at all and particularly loathed his choice of wearing one with a blue shirt, something which she described as desperately plebeian. She was in a tight-fitting black dress, knee length, and looked sophisticated, elegant and voluptuous. Her shining dark hair was scraped back high, tied with a black silk rose, beneath which it tumbled in a thick ponytail. Her high black shoes had earlier been parked in a corner of the room, waiting until the kitchen chores were done, and she went over now to retrieve them. Brushing the dust off her stockinged foot she slipped on the first shoe, and it must have hurt her a little because she sucked in her breath and let out a high-pitched sound that he found slightly arousing. Enough to make him recall the statistics of their infrequent sex life, which he preferred not to dwell on.

They sat down opposite each other at the kitchen table and helped themselves to the salad she had made. There were some slices of cold beef and a jar of pickle on the side, next to Granville's plate, but Edwina touched neither.

They ate for a while in silence until Edwina asked, 'How do you think she'll hold up?'

'Janet? I think she'll be OK. Quite a few of her family are coming.'

'Two sisters, isn't it?'

'And a mother.'

'Essex girls, the lot of them. Made good, of course, but you can spot it a mile away.'

Granville smiled into his plate.

'Sorry,' Edwina added. 'I probably shouldn't say that in the circumstances.'

Granville ate some more. 'Piet's been good to her, which has made my job easier. She's on more of an even keel.'

'Who?'

'Piet. The South African guy.'

'Oh, your new buddy.'

Granville smiled again. 'The day after she got home he went around to her house with a bunch of flowers to pass on his condolences.'

Edwina stopped mid-chew. 'Serious?'

'Can you believe it? He'd never met her. Dressed up smartly, flowers in hand, did a little bow.'

'Did she tell you that?'

'He's a very proper chap in his way. He says he's going to start coming to the church.'

'What did she think?'

'She was touched, actually. And he's good with the

boys. Takes them fishing, does a bit of carpentry, odd jobs, that sort of stuff. Janet's up to her eyeballs with the funeral and all the admin, and it's half-term, so it's been good to get them off her hands. Poor things.'

Edwina raised her eyebrows. 'Nice for Janet to have a good strong man about the place.'

'Oh, come on!'

'Cometh the hour, and all that.'

'He's a bit old for her.'

'How old?'

'Hard to say. About sixty.'

'That's nothing.'

'Don't. Please.'

'Playing with fire.'

'I would think she's mature enough to be on her guard,' said Granville and checked his watch.

'Bereaved women are notoriously vulnerable,' concluded Edwina, and stabbed a last asparagus spear on her plate.

Granville was grinning through his mouthful and began to shake his head.

'What's so funny?'

'Just the thought of it. He's pretty rough and ready. Hardly her type. And I wouldn't think she's the rebound sort.'

'There'll be loads of men after her money.'

'And not just her money.'

'You fancy her too, then? Along with everyone else.'

'Don't be absurd.'

'She'll have to play her cards carefully.'

'She'll be OK. Men are put off women with small kids, and there aren't many single men around anyway.'

'There's your new buddy, for a start. Anyway, it's not the single men I'm talking about.'

79

Granville put down his knife and fork. 'So you think all the marriages in Dorset are going to start clattering down like houses of cards because Janet Gosling's putting herself on the market? Don't you think this conversation's a bit premature?'

'Maybe.'

'When the time's right I'll have a chat with her. Point out the dangers.'

'You knight in shining armour, you.'

'No. Just the rector.'

'Just warn her off that weirdo. You should hear what people say about him.'

Granville took a tired-looking napkin from a silver ring and wiped his mouth. 'It's all rubbish. Parochial xenophobia of the worst kind. Just because the man chooses to be a bit of a loner. He's actually a very decent bloke. He's agreed to do the tombola at the fete. And other stuff at the church. He's even going to repair the gutters.'

'Oh, pardon me for tarnishing his halo.'

'Consider yourself forgiven,' replied Granville and they both got up to clear. He took his plate over to the sink and checked his watch again. 'I'd better get going in a minute.' He glanced down at her black-stockinged calves and the tight black dress as he moved around behind her. This had been the warmest few minutes they had spent together for quite a few days, and he almost put out his palm to touch her on the bottom, but thought better of it.

Granville quickly rinsed the plates as Edwina faced the mirror to apply some last-minute touches to her eye make-up. 'Are you going to ask him over, then?' she said out of the blue.

'Who?'

'Your new friend.'

'Still talking about him?'

She moved on to the lipstick. 'Just wondering.'

'I don't think you need to worry. I'm pretty sure he doesn't think much of me.'

'Why do you say that?'

'I can tell. He's very stern in his beliefs. Very old-fashioned. A sort of Calvinist.'

'Fire and brimstone?'

'And the rest. I think he thinks I'm a lightweight.'

'But he's going to join your flock?'

'Who am I to stop him?'

Edwina took her eyes off her full scarlet lips, and gave him a wry smile in the mirror. 'Don't give me that,' she said. 'You've made him a project, haven't you? You want to save him.'

'Not at all.'

'Oh yeah.'

'Got to go.'

'I'll be along in a minute.'

Granville had his coat and was about to walk out of the door when the phone rang and Edwina answered it. When she heard who it was she closed her eyes. 'Yes,' she sighed and flapped her hand at Granville, 'he is here. Hold on, would you?' She handed him the receiver, despite his silent protests and watch-tapping, and he had to take it. It was the stonemason, saying he would be there by three o'clock. Granville briefly told him where he could park his truck, plug in the cement mixer and about how to find the painted square on the back lawn. After he put the phone down, Edwina muttered, 'Do we have to have something so big out there?'

'Don't start again.'

'It'll be like that thing in *2001: A Space Odyssey*. We'll

have bearded hippies creeping up at dawn to touch it with their fingertips.'

Granville checked his pockets to make sure he hadn't forgotten anything. Keys, wallet, phone, glasses. 'Like that old traveller bloke who camped out by the standing stone in the church paddock, you mean?'

'Another weirdo friend of yours.'

'He was very interesting, actually. He'd travelled all over—'

'Here we go. Remember what happened in the end? He shacked up with that scraggy woman in her caravan on the top of the hill and started dealing weed. Until the police got wind of it and then he was off.'

'Those sort of people don't live life by the same rules. It's not as simple as right and wrong. If you'd taken the time to—'

'Bertie Gosling was the one who went to the council to complain about vagrants on the hill, as I remember. Good on him. They towed her caravan away and that was that.'

'And I nearly fell out with Bertie over it. She wasn't hurting anyone and she wasn't even there when they took her stuff away. Shocking, what they did.'

'Did she ever show up to complain?' asked Edwina.

'Not as far as I know.'

'That's hippies for you.'

'You're prejudiced.'

'You'd better go.'

'Hmm?'

'You said you were late.'

Granville looked at her absent-mindedly for a moment.

'You're not having one of your turns, are you?' she asked.

'What?' Granville blinked back to attention. 'No. Of course not.'

'Have you rung the doctor yet?'

'I don't need to see the doctor.'

'If you don't make the appointment, I will.'

'Waste of time.'

Granville went over to the sink, poured himself an inch of water into a glass that was upside down on the draining board, and swallowed it, before hurrying from the house.

Chapter 7

He observed himself in the long vestry mirror as he robed for the service and wondered, not for the first time, if he was a fraud. He tied the rope cincture around the waist of his polyester-cotton alb and draped a black stole around his neck. Some of his clergy friends said that the robing procedure inspired a sense of piety, but for Granville the anachronism of church vestments had grated ever since he was ordained.

Wordlessly he rehearsed the order of points he would make in his homily about Bertie. It was fairly straightforward. The congregation would be hungry for any scraps of comfort to ease the atmosphere, which meant they would be on his side and easy to please. He could hear beyond the vestry door that people were already taking their places in the pews, and the organist had begun extemporizing soothingly in the run-up to the family's arrival with the hearse.

He had seen a lot of Janet Gosling in the past few days and had been drawn into the predictably intense drama of affection that this sort of situation usually engendered. Bereavement wove its own special kind of magic to fast-track relationships, elevating a light acquaintanceship to a binding friendship in a matter of minutes. Some mourners would develop an urgent dependency on him, and his hand had been squeezed countless times over the years by widows, swearing through tear-filled eyes their lifelong devotion to him and the Church for the comfort he brought. But the vows of friendship would evaporate pretty quickly in the weeks and months that followed. The lives of widows, orphans and grieving parents eventually reconstituted themselves in a new mould and his former indispensability would become just a quaint memory; but that was fine by him; the alternative would be too tiring by half.

He had felt a particular need to look after Janet this past week, knowing what he knew about Bertie. It had been difficult to look her in the eye at times. Again and again, during their talks, she had been gripped by a spasm of remembrance coupled with incomprehension. She had clenched her fist around her handkerchief and shaken her head in disbelief that Bertie would do such a thing. It was so out of character, she said; this happened to other people but couldn't be happening to her. She would chop the air with frustration, questioning repeatedly why he hadn't left a note, or anything, for God's sake, any clue to help her understand why he'd done it. At one point Granville felt his defences crumbling and thought that she might cope better if she knew the truth, but silent inner counter-arguments quickly filled up the breach, and his resolve did not waver again.

Without warning, the vestry door opened and Brigadier Finch, the churchwarden, came in. The Brigadier would never knock, on principle, it seemed. He liked to think that his management of the church premises and his role as senior congregation representative placed him on an equal, if not superior, rank to that of the ordained incumbent. The time had come, the Brigadier explained, for Granville to make his way to the west end door for the arrival of the hearse.

A number of people were approaching along the path, locals and strangers alike. They walked up to the church slowly, almost apologetically, and hung their heads as they greeted Granville. Then Piet Steyn appeared on the road beyond the church wall, not shuffling along like the others, but striding purposefully, as was his way, like a man setting out on a hike. He was dressed in a cotton plaid jacket with wide lapels over a dark rollneck sweater. They greeted each other quietly and Granville said that it was good of him to come.

'I wouldn't miss it for the world,' he replied.

'You've been good to Janet. It's much appreciated.'

'That's OK. She needs the help. She is a fine woman but she's too fond of the bottle, I'm sorry to say. One family tragedy is enough for those poor boys.' Granville was more taken aback by the baldness of the statement than its kind intent, but he did not have long to contemplate either because the cortège had appeared and was slowing to a halt in front of the church gate. A veiled Janet Gosling with her two smartly dressed sons and a distinguished looking elderly gentleman climbed out of the first car. She approached the church on the arm of the older man, clutching a handkerchief, but broke away when she saw Granville and gave him a tight hug. Her handkerchief fell to the ground and Piet, hovering nearby, picked it up for her. He turned and winked at the two boys who were standing behind, waiting for their mother to disengage herself, but neither responded.

The thick walls on either side of the small sanctuary at the east end of the church were perforated by the slenderest and most ancient of lancet windows, through one of which sunlight streamed as Granville approached the altar there to commence the service. This was the oldest part of the church, the last remnant of the small thirteenth-century thatched structure that had first been consecrated on this spot, though there was evidence of pagan shrines having stood here for centuries before that. Light from stained-glass windows above cast a fiesta of coloured smudges over the pews and across the pale plastered walls of the nave. On days like this Granville felt bolstered by the thought of the generations who had worshipped in this building in times gone by; the streams of Victorians, Edwardians, Georgians, Jacobeans, farmers and gentlemen alike, who never missed a Sunday, who sat bolt upright and hierarchical in their ordered rows, hats clutched on laps, earnestly contemplating every word of what they heard from the pulpit, because it seemed so vital to their lives, in this world and the next.

'We have come here today to remember before God our brother Bertie, to give thanks for his life, and to commend him to God, our merciful Redeemer and Judge.'

He turned to face the congregation, aware that they looked to him to guide them through the rough waters of grief. His training had equipped him for the task and he took care to keep his voice strong, his manner warm and imperturbable.

'Almighty God, you judge us with infinite mercy and justice and love everything you have made. In your mercy turn the darkness of death into the dawn of new life, and the sorrow of parting into the joy of heaven.' Onwards he progressed through the prescribed paragraphs, led the hymns in his solid baritone and nodded reassuringly to the timid young brothers when it was their turn to come up and do the readings. Then, sitting back to listen, he observed the comfort everyone present seemed to derive from the familiar contours of the Anglican procedure, the old crutches they trusted. The very structure of the ritual seemed to stem their tears. It was ironic, he thought, that he, the master of ceremonies here today, was perhaps the only person present to feel unaffected by it.

It was about halfway through the service, just as he was gearing himself to ascend the pulpit and deliver his sermon, that he heard the distinctive clang of the great west door's latch being raised to let in a latecomer. He glanced down the aisle and saw the girl enter. She stood for a moment at the far end, looking down the length of the nave directly at him; then she sidestepped into an empty pew at the back, and sat down. One or two others looked around at the noise but did not particularly register anything; apart from Steyn, who was sitting near the front. He saw who had entered and stole a quick glance up at the rector.

Granville went on with the homily and they hung on his every word. He wove into the narrative of Bertie's life the odd thread of measured flattery and sentiment, seasoning it here and there with humour, in keeping with his informal, modern way of doing things; and yet, for all his upbeat style, the mood collapsed, as it always did, at the point when the undertakers stepped in to shoulder the coffin for the outward procession. The west door was opened fully and sunlight streamed onto the medieval font at the end of the aisle as they made their solemn way out towards the waiting hearse. Granville was going to follow the funeral party in his own car to the crematorium in order to take a short committal ceremony, before returning for tea at the Old Rectory. As he passed Rhian in the last pew he did not look directly at her but could sense her eyes following him all the way to the door.

Most of the visitors from further afield thanked Granville with regretful smiles as they shook his hand. The locals were more forthcoming, some bordering on the hearty, including one or two who did not usually come to church. One of the last to emerge was old Leo Flowers, who lived in the caretaker's annexe at the Old Rectory. His voice was high and fluty, and he wore a black patch over his redundant eye socket. The surviving eye regarded Granville defiantly as he shook hands. 'I would have liked more music,' he piped, 'not just hymns and organ playing. Mr Gosling liked his music. Some instruments or something, perhaps.'

'I'm sorry, Leo. I'll remember for next time,' Granville replied, but if he'd hoped to raise a smile on Leo's bulbous, scarred face, he was disappointed. The old man turned without another word and hobbled, bow-legged, away down the path. However, after a few steps something made him stop and turn back to look at Granville and the couple of people who still lingered outside the large arched doorway. He squinted his eye at them, trying to give shape to whatever it was that had made him pause to think, but it had slipped out of reach, and he turned on his stick and walked off in the direction of the Old Rectory.

Rhian was one of those standing outside. She was on her own a few yards off, waiting until Granville had finished shaking hands. He knew she was there and that she would not leave until she'd had the chance to speak to him. He therefore told Edwina to go on to the car and wait for him there because he had to go back to the church to get some things that he would need at the crematorium. She did as he said but not before pausing

89

for a moment to put a hand on his arm. 'You were wonderful, by the way,' she said. 'Perfect sermon. One of your best.' He thanked her and she walked towards the car, pulling down her sunglasses from her forehead. She looked unutterably glamorous, Granville thought.

He now turned his attention to Rhian, knowing that it would have to be brief and inconspicuous. People were getting into their cars behind him, and he turned his back to them, to shield the girl from view.

'What do you think you're doing coming here?' he asked.

'I wanted to see you.'

'Can't you see how reckless this is? You might be noticed.'

'I had to see you.'

'What about Bertie? This is his funeral, you know.'

'I know.' She looked as if she would burst into tears at any second.

He was lost for words momentarily and looked sideways. He wanted to take her by the shoulders and shake some sense into her but could not risk a scene. She wasn't dressed like any of the other mourners. Her skirt was short, too short, over black woollen tights, and she wore a tight, strappy vest top. He faced her again and spoke in a quiet, urgent voice. 'You stick out like a sore thumb.'

'I'm sorry.'

'Look, I'm going to say this once, and once only. What we did the other day in order to protect you—'

'What *you* did.'

'Several people's happiness is at stake here, not to mention my job, my reputation, my whole life. One sniff of this and the papers will be full of it. And it won't help your cause one bit.'

'I know that.'

'Then why did you come back? Why take the risk?'

She just looked at him.

He sighed. 'I've got to go. Don't do anything like this ever again, d'you hear me?' He resisted the temptation to raise an index finger in case someone behind was watching. 'I don't want to see you again.' He turned to go.

'That's not what you said before.'

He half turned back. 'What do you mean?'

'You said if ever I needed to talk to you I could.'

'I meant in an emergency. If you want to get through this you've got to put the whole business behind you. And the sooner the better.' He began to walk away. He could see Edwina looking at him from the driving seat of their car. He smiled and waved at her.

'I have to see you,' called Rhian. It was too loud, much too loud, and he almost crouched at the sound of it. He turned back to her.

'Keep your voice down!' he said in a stage whisper.

'But I have to see you. You're the only one I can talk to. Otherwise I don't know what I'll do. I can't take this any more.' She was right on the verge of crying.

He looked straight at her. 'OK. OK. Call me tomorrow. After ten o'clock. We'll make a time to meet. Just this once. Now please go, and don't make a spectacle of yourself.' Rhian's desolate expression now lifted and a smile arose like the dawn sun. She gave a furtive little wave of the hand from waist height, but he turned quickly away and went around to the passenger seat of his car.

They'd been driving for a minute or so before Edwina made her first comment. 'Got everything you need, then?' she asked.

'Yes,' he replied, 'I think so. Why?'

'Because you said you were going back to the vestry to

get some bits, but from what I saw you never got there. You were held up talking to that peculiar looking girl.'

'Occupational hazard.'

'Who was she?'

'I don't know any better than you. I suppose she must have known Bertie. Why else would she come to his funeral?'

'Well, what did she want?'

'To know who was welcome for tea.' He surprised himself with the speed of his invention.

'She seemed pretty agitated. It looked important.'

'Well maybe it was, for her. How should I know?'

He said no more on the matter, but had to work hard to make up ordinary conversation all the way to the crematorium.

Chapter 8

Rufus Futcher squatted over the hole in the side of the bank with the knob of his stick raised and ready. It was shaking from the tension, and his arm was getting tired, but he could not relax it because he knew that any minute something was going to happen. His terrier, Skip, had torn down the hole like a mad thing as soon as Rufus had released him from the leash. That was a good ten minutes ago. Skip was a hunter to the last hair on his head, determined, hungry and vicious. Early this morning, when Rufus had crept downstairs in his socks, Skip had guessed what was going on and had started to jump and yelp, so much that he'd earned himself a clip on the muzzle to shut him up; but that hadn't stifled the dog's joy nor stopped the stub of his tail wiggling madly. It had still been dark when Rufus had parked his van down by the field gate, but now, as he crouched beside the hole, on the higher ground just beyond the village, the sky was paling, ushering in a grey, damp dawn. In the distance, the ruined abbey's silhouette began to gain definition, black above a thin ground mist.

Rufus had raised his stick as soon as he heard a noise from inside the hole. He wasn't sure yet if it was Skip who'd made the sound but he was an experienced trapper and knew that something was about to break. At moments like this he felt a savage bond with his dog. His family had always joked that he was part dog himself. As a toddler he had made barking noises as he stumbled around the house, 'Ruff, ruff,' which was enough to earn him the nickname Rufus – a dog's name, they all said – and it had stuck with him ever since. His real name was David, but hardly anyone knew that.

Suddenly it happened. There was no warning other than a silent anticipatory trickle of soil falling back into the hole. Then the terrier's back legs came into view. It was reversing out, its muzzle clenched around a badger's neck, dragging it into the open air. The badger was fighting back, teeth bared and the claws of one paw embedded in the dog's shoulder. Skip was straining and growling for all he was worth, tossing his head from side to side, bleeding and twisting too fast for Rufus to decide where or when to strike. The stick hovered in the air. Skip's hind legs tore at the soil, straining to pull the heavy brock inch by inch away from the hole. Rufus thought it might be better to separate them, but when he tried to get a hand in he was nipped quite deeply by the terrier. 'Bastard,' he said in disbelief, and struck angrily with the knob of the club. It cracked against the badger's skull, but the creature still held fast to Skip's flesh. One of its eyes was now dull and half-closed, deadened by the blow, while the other glared madly, wide enough to burst from its socket. Rufus thumped his stick again, but missed the badger altogether and his fist landed in a bed of nettles. 'Fuck it,' he said, and lifted the knob for a third blow. This one struck home hard and direct, and the badger recoiled, abandoning the fight in a desperate last scramble for the safety of its sett. But it was dazed, broken and disoriented, and did not make the entrance of the hole before Rufus intercepted it with a *coup de grâce* on the crown. He took care not to hit too hard this time, because his father didn't want the animal too messed up. 'Good shot,' he muttered to himself as the badger shuddered in the wet grass, and bent down to inspect the corpse. The twitches of its hind legs slowed and eventually stopped. 'You're a fat old bastard, ain't you? What you done to my dog? Tosser.' Skip sniffed and nipped triumphantly around the dead animal until Rufus kicked him out of the way.

He was at the vet by opening time to have Skip's wounds stitched before going on home. His mother was in the kitchen as he came in with the bandaged terrier in his arms. She was already dressed and ready to leave for work at the Cheddar factory. 'That'll cost you some,' she said. 'Them vets don't come cheap. Don't you be thinking I'll be paying for it out my wages. You brought that on yourself.' Rufus did not answer but put the dog in its bed and went to get himself a bowl of cereal.

His mother worked for a thriving cheese company and made sure to wash thoroughly every morning, pinning her hair up in a white net before leaving for the factory. High levels of hygiene were expected at work and she did her best, because she loved her job, but it was a challenge, for her husband and only son were employed at a pig farm. The acrid scent of pigs – a blend of human body odour and stale urine – was impossible to shift completely, from either skin or clothes, no matter how much they were washed. It permeated the very fabric of the Futcher household, the walls and furniture, and they took it with them wherever they went. It even followed them to Portugal every summer for their beach apartment holiday, and returned relatively intact, despite a fortnight of sea, sun and tanning oil.

'Dad'll pay for the dog,' grunted Rufus as he ate his sugared wheat puffs. His mother was reaching for her coat.

'What d'you want a dead badger for, anyway?'

'You know.'

'I don't understand why you hate that man so much. Just 'cause he's foreign. What business is it of yours what he does and doesn't do?'

At that moment an older man appeared at the bottom of the stairs. It was Rufus's father, Colin, and he was buttoning up his flies. He glanced at his wife but quickly looked away. He had been asleep when she'd got up an hour earlier. 'You still 'ere?'

'No, I've gone. As you can see.'

'Get a bloody move on, then.'

'Mum's asking why don't we leave the weirdo be.'

'Is she now?' muttered Colin Futcher inconsequentially and lowered himself into a chair at the table. 'Put the kettle on, would you?' he said in the direction of his wife.

'Put it on yourself,' she answered, checking herself in the mirror. 'I'm already late. What's wrong with the bloke, anyway?'

'Thief.'

'What's he stole?'

'Them plastic drums out the back of Jennings' farm, for a start.'

'Is that all? Phil Jennings only chucks them fertilizer cans out there 'cause he can't be fagged to take 'em down the tip.'

'And he nicked some wire,' added Rufus. ''E was seen coiling it up an' taking it on home.'

'Where'd 'e take that from?'

Rufus shrugged. 'Said 'e just found it.'

'Did you ask him why he took it?'

Colin sniggered. 'He says he don't like to see perfectly good stuff thrown out for no good reason.'

'What's wrong with that?' asked his wife.

Colin slumped back in his chair. It seemed too frail to support his bulk and a buttock hung off the edge. 'It's not his to take, though, is it?' he said.

'What's made you so holier-than-thou all of a sudden?' Mary Futcher was tying a scarf around her hairnet. 'Times I've met 'im 'e's behaved like a gentleman. Which is more than I can say for some of your friends.' The men did not respond. 'An' 'e went out and helped when Eggers' Land Rover got stuck down the ditch that time. Weren't no-one else who would go out to help on a Saturday night. Helped 'im get it out, he did, and then went back on Sunday morning to check for damage. Whiles you two were still sleeping it off in bed. Fred Eggers said 'e ain't never known anyone know so much about old Land Rovers.'

'What about what 'e did to me down at the abbey that time?' said Rufus, and a look of fierce wonder came into his eyes.

'You got what you deserved,' said his mother. 'You shouldn't'na been spying.'

'Nothing wrong with 'aving a look,' replied Rufus. 'Fuckin' weirdo. Hangin' about round them graves at night and hidin' an' like. Then he starts catapulting me.'

Colin Futcher began to chuckle. 'Where'd 'e get you then, Ruf, go on, tell us, give us a laugh.'

'You know already,' said Rufus sulkily and returned to his cereal.

'Go on,' insisted his father. 'Got you ping on the end of your dick, did 'e?'

'And the rest,' muttered Rufus.

'That's the one good thing 'e done, then,' laughed Colin.

'It weren't you got a stone catapulted in your balls. Fucking weirdo. Then 'e pops his head up from behind some old gravestone an' gives me this cold blood stare. Scary, 'e is. Fuckin' weird. Starin' at me like this and not sayin' nothin'. Sooner 'e's gone the better.'

'Load of nonsense. I'm off,' said Mary.

Colin pretended not to hear his wife, but went on as if talking to Rufus. 'Here's something neither of you's heard yet, though.' Rufus looked up and his wife paused at the door. 'He got a parcel in the post the other day. Wrongly delivered. Ended up down at Pete Garvey's, who opened it *by mistake* before he realized it weren't for him.' Colin sniggered again.

'What was in it, then?' asked Mary, impatiently, 'I haven't got all day, you know.'

'Packed full of ladies' clothes.'

'What?'

'Old ones. Second-hand an' that. Stuff you'd find at the jumble sale. Dresses, nighties, panties, suspenders an' all.' He started laughing. 'Old Garvey just taped the whole lot up again and took it down the post office in the back of his pickup.'

'Surprised he didn't try on them knickers 'imself,' chuckled Rufus.

'You're having me on,' said Mary.

'The bloke's a weirdo, that's all there is to it,' muttered Colin and reached for the cereal. 'Snooping around other people's property seeing what he can pick up for nothing. If I see 'im round 'ere, I'm goin' straight for the twelve bore.'

Mary Futcher tutted and left the men to their breakfast. She closed the front door gently behind her, as she did every morning, breathing a sigh of relief to be free of the stench of pigs at last, though she knew a trace of it remained with her. She could tell by the looks on people's faces when they came too close.

*

At nine o'clock the same evening Rufus picked up his dad from the village pub, as they had agreed. Colin hadn't quite finished his pint and brought it along with him in the van.

'So. Checked it all out?' Colin asked as they set off.

'Dead as a doornail down there. Not a soul about.'

'Good,' said Colin, and raised a buttock to fart. 'As we thought.'

'Aw. That fuckin' stinks.' Rufus rolled down his window.

They parked off the road, some way from Steyn's house, on a piece of crumbling tarmac at the edge of the old wartime airfield. Rufus opened the back doors of the van and took out a heavy sack. Colin carried a smaller cloth bag and a claw hammer. They made their way quietly to the cottage's entrance gate, knees bent like caricature pantomime villains, and crept down the stone path towards the front door. All lights in the house were off, and they tested the water by throwing a succession of stones at various different windowpanes. When they were convinced that the house was unoccupied, they approached the door and Rufus tipped the badger out onto the doorstep. It fell like a clod to the floor and

Colin stooped down to have a look at it, still holding the remains of his pint in one hand. 'You'll have to break its legs,' he whispered to his son.

'Why?'

'How else are you going to do it?'

'OK.' Rufus bent down to the dead animal and grabbed one of its legs. 'It ain't 'alf stiff. Pass me the hammer.'

'Don't be daft. Just get hold of it like you're pulling off a chicken leg.' Rufus did as he was told and the leg cracked free. 'There you go. Now do the other ones.'

When he was finished, he lifted the rigid animal up to the door and held it there while Colin put down his pint glass and took four six-inch nails from his bag. Three of them he held in his mouth, while, squinting and swinging the hammer expertly, he drove the fourth through the badger's throat, securing it to the timber of the door. Then he held up one of the forelegs, limp in its socket, and hammered a nail through the soft tissue of the paw. The pressure of the piercing made its claws distend. He did the same for the other foreleg, so that they were both splayed horizontally. Rufus was now free to let the animal go, while his father plunged the final nail through the paws of both hind legs. They stood back to inspect their work, before Rufus raised a finger, remembering something, and drew an old penknife from his jacket pocket. The blade was rusted up and he cursed and tugged at it with his thumbnail. Once open, he plunged the knife to its hilt into the badger's abdomen and left it there.

'That'll be a warm welcome for the bastard when he comes home,' said Colin Futcher. 'Where the fuck does 'e go, anyway?' He bent down to retrieve his pint glass. There was only a mouthful left. 'Hang on a minute,' said Colin, draining the pint; then, grinning, he forced the tall glass over the badger's snout, wedging its head firmly inside. Drips of ale fell onto the oily fur of its haunches, and the two men turned to go. They walked in silence back to their van at the edge of the old airfield and moments later its diesel engine fired up. A cloud of fumes billowed, lights came on and the vehicle juddered off into the night.

Chapter 9

The only times Granville had been to the doctor's surgery in the past few years were to take one of his daughters, and only then if Edwina was busy doing something else. A secret fear of physical decline, blended with a suspicion of doctors' reliability and the fact of his own apparently indestructible good health, had ensured that Granville remained a relative stranger to the neat little health clinic in Cheselbury Abbas. On arrival, he could not even remember the last time he had needed to go, and the layout of the place seemed unfamiliar. He looked to left and right, wondering which way to go, until the receptionist caught his eye. She explained in antiseptic tones that the entrance lobby and waiting room had been modernized a couple of years previously, and asked him to take a seat until called.

He looked around the room. There were posters doling out advice with a mixture of humour and menace. Smiling cartoon hearts pumped iron beside ominous close-up photographs of lit cigarettes. Plastic toys littered the floor, magazines were piled up on a low table, the room's windows were sealed, and a warm, stale smell hung in the air. There was a small assembly of people hunched on padded chairs around the edge of the room – young mothers and pensioners, mostly – while children spilled over onto the floor, trying to find something of interest in the half-broken toys, and yelling at will between fits of coughing. Granville expected to recognize one or two faces here, having served the community for six years, but there was no-one he knew. He smiled, nonetheless, when a few bored patients looked up at him, then took a seat and picked up the nearest magazine. Its cover felt well thumbed and slightly oily, and he put it down again. As it happened, he did not have long to wait before an illuminated board showed his name and instructed him to proceed to room number three. The others looked resentful as he got up, presumably because he had been called before them despite having just arrived. He smiled apologetically and they looked away.

He knocked on the door of the doctor's room and went in. The light in here was immediately more bald and penetrating. It pronounced that this was no murky waiting room but a place of straight talk and clear methods, where time meant money. The doctor was one he had never met before, a broad-shouldered, down-to-earth man slightly younger than himself, wearing a dark tie, a perfectly ironed shirt and monogrammed gold cufflinks. He sprang to his feet athletically, and held out his hand with a smile. A happy family of five – including the doctor, in a T-shirt – beamed from a silver frame on his desk.

'So. What can I do for you?' the doctor said, returning to his chair. Granville described in brief what had been happening, the history of his episodes going back to his university days, the increased frequency in recent months and the new development of early morning activity. The doctor kept his eyes earnestly locked on his patient for a few minutes, nodded silently from time to time, keeping his counsel, and then began to glance through Granville's records on the computer screen. He asked if he was taking any medication, had changed his diet, routine or work pattern – anything that might explain the recent intensification of his seizures.

'They're not seizures,' Granville corrected him.

'How would you describe them?'

Granville considered the question. 'Moments of extreme perspicacity. And joy.'

The doctor nodded again and typed a sentence into his notes. 'You say you sometimes find yourself speaking involuntarily?'

'It's not exactly speech. Just voiced sounds. More like a reflex, a gasp, but a bit more pronounced.'

The doctor typed again. 'Any bad headaches, passing out, dizziness?'

'Nothing like that.'

'Any feeling of pressure in your head, any particular aches?'

'No.'

'Otherwise perfectly fit?'

'Absolutely.'

A string of further routine questions were asked, all of which received predictably brief and non-alarmist answers, which were duly typed into the records. Granville was impressed with the cavalier flair of the doctor's fingers as they tap-danced across the keyboard, and presumed that spelling and punctuation were being sacrificed for haste. It was always thus with GPs, he thought, remembering the surgeries he went to as a child, and kind old avuncular doctors scribbling out prescriptions as if speed with the pen were a sign of competence.

The doctor finished with his notes and swung around

to a second computer, whose screen faced away from the patient's chair.

'So,' he began again, as he tapped and looked into the screen. 'I think we'd better organize an MRI scan for you. Have you got private health insurance?'

'A what?'

'An MRI. Routine precaution in cases like this.' He spoke as if he dealt with a dozen of them a day. For a moment Granville could not find the words to respond, and the doctor added, 'A magnetic resonance image.'

'I know what MRI means. What do you think this is, then?'

'It's not what I think it is,' replied the doctor and his schooled assurance almost turned his expression into a smile, 'it's what we ought to rule out. Did you say you did have insurance, by the way?'

'Yes,' said Granville. 'My wife took out a family policy, but I'm happy to go on the National Health. I don't mind waiting like normal people.'

'We should probably get you seen pretty quickly if we can.'

'What is it you want to rule out?'

'There are several possibilities. Some perhaps far-fetched, but you don't want to hang around if there is something there.' Granville waited for further explanation but the doctor had opened a manual.

'Possibilities like what?'

'Penduncular hallucinosis. Or hypnagogia. Particularly, daytime parahypnagogia, DPH, as it's called.' He drew down the corners of his mouth and wagged his head from side to side, toying indecisively with the options. 'It would explain why it seems to happen in the no-man's-land between sleep and wakefulness. On the other hand . . .'

'A kind of daydream, you mean?'

'Have you been overworked, stressed, unusually tired recently?'

'Aren't we all?'

'That can contribute to DPH. Or it could be caused by compression on the brain, a tumour or lesions. I personally doubt it because you've been experiencing something similar for so long and there's no history of surgery or intervention in that area. On the other hand, it sounds as though the condition is getting worse, so—'

'I wouldn't exactly describe it as getting worse.'

'The episodes are becoming more frequent, then. An MRI will show if there are any abnormalities in specific areas.'

'And if there's nothing? If it's not any of those conditions?'

'Then,' replied the doctor, slowing again and glancing at the screen that faced away, 'we'd be looking at a psychiatric condition. Do you mind me asking if there's any history of mental illness in the family?'

Granville shook his head and looked down. Part of him felt like laughing. His father was a basket case, of course, but he didn't suppose that was what the doctor had meant.

'No, we're all completely sane,' he said.

The doctor picked up on the humour. 'You should meet my family,' he said. 'Complete nutters, the lot of them.' Granville doubted it. The doctor sparkled with well-brought-up wholesomeness.

'What kind of psychiatric condition do you mean?'

The doctor's chin dimpled and he attempted a chummy smile. 'Trouble with these things,' he said, 'is that the terminology can sound so alarming. Certain words are so loaded in common parlance.'

106

'What sort of terms?'

'Psychosis. Schizophrenia, perhaps, or a form of it. I'm no expert.' The sudden and shattering weight of his words did not seem to change the relaxed slant of his expression. He might as well have just shared another little quip about his family. 'If the MRI scan doesn't show anything, I would suggest we refer you to a psychiatrist.'

'Schizophrenia?'

'It doesn't have to be as bad as it sounds. There's a whole range of possible psychotic disorders that can be bunched under the umbrella heading of schizophrenia. You're not showing the symptoms of an extreme case, by any standards. But the situation is getting worse, you say, so we should get you seen to as soon as possible.'

'What symptoms does your computer say I do have in common with schizophrenia, then?'

The doctor blinked at the implication that he might not have been able to diagnose the symptoms without help, but took it in his stride. 'Well, there's the hallucinations, of course, then the delusions, the disorganized speech episodes. And the fact that you first had this when you were twenty-one. There is a pattern to these things.'

'That's what it says?'

The doctor now assumed a kind of false modesty. 'You can look it all up yourself when you get home. Probably end up knowing more about it than me.'

Granville shook his head. 'I've lived with this for years, I know myself, I'm a perfectly level, straightforward, family man, and I know, I just know you're barking up the wrong tree. I hesitate to explain how I know this is a spiritual thing rather than anything clinical or even psychological, because I know it's in your job description to look down on anything that can't be empirically proved.'

'A religious experience, you mean?' asked the doctor, adopting utter sincerity, and unperturbed by Granville's flash of emotion.

'Exactly. A religious experience.'

The doctor replied as though he were ready and waiting for this. 'Would you explain the involuntary speech episodes as speaking in tongues?'

'No.'

'Well, the religious dimension could be a sign of temporal lobe epilepsy, TPH. It's another possibility we should investigate, and related to a form of schizophrenia. Gives people the feeling that they're going through some sort of spiritual awakening. Talking to God, angels, and the like.' And the like? Granville wondered if the doctor knew what his patient's job was. 'Another symptom is having vivid flashbacks, images from the past suddenly appearing out of nowhere. Has your memory been playing on you very much recently?'

'Well,' Granville sounded reluctant to yield his ground; his hesitancy answered the question more accurately than his words. 'Doesn't memory play on everybody of a certain age?'

'Maybe.' The doctor glanced up at the clock and smacked his big hands together. 'So. Shall I go ahead and book the MRI? You could go to Bournemouth. Or Yeovil would be nearer.' He was back at the first computer again, and typing as he talked.

'No. Don't bother. It'd be a waste of time.'

The doctor was momentarily nonplussed by this and gave Granville a serious look. 'I have to advise you that—'

'Please assume your opinion has been heard and digested. Thank you for what I'm sure must seem to you very sensible advice.'

'As a precaution, you—'

'Thank you.' He repeated himself in a gentler tone. 'Thank you, but I know that sort of treatment would be a red herring. And a waste of money.'

The doctor smiled, leant back in his chair and brought his pen to his lips. 'Which begs the question,' he said, 'why you bothered to come here in the first place.'

Granville rose to his feet and shook his head. 'I really don't know. I'm sorry to have used up your time.'

Chapter 10

Very early that morning there was a bad smell in the air around Steyn's garden that would have caught the attention of passers-by, had there been any, and made them walk quickly on. It spread far afield, carried by the breeze, and a faint scent of it, some way off, was enough to make a superstitious local builder screw up his face. 'The smell of the damned,' he muttered to his young apprentice as they drank their early morning tea.

'Why?' asked the boy.

'Can't you smell it?' came the reply. 'Burning flesh and hair. Hell itself.'

Steyn could smell it more pungently than any because he was standing right next to the fire. He held a long stick which he was using as a poker. At one point the pyre beneath the badger's carcass caved in, and the carbonized torso rolled onto the lawn at his feet. It lay there, smoking and singeing the grass, its paw stumps rigidly saluting the sky, until Steyn impaled its gut on a stick and flung it back onto the fire, where it began to blacken and fizz once again.

As soon as the fire was safe, he washed his hands and walked down to the end of the garden. As usual, he looked around before taking the hairpin path through the brambles and disappearing from sight.

*   *   *

'What was it this time?' she asked.

'They crucified a badger on my door.'

Shock showed in her repeated blinking but she quickly recovered a porcelain-calm demeanour. 'I'm sorry to hear that.'

'It's not your problem. It's between me and these people. Thankfully they cannot touch the beautiful home we've built here together.'

'Do you think someone suspects something?' she asked, and he looked up at her sharply.

'No I do not think anyone suspects anything.' She met his eye and looked away. 'So,' he sighed, took off his jacket and slumped onto a kitchen chair. 'Have you put your recent wickedness behind you?'

'Yes, husband.'

He nodded. 'I am glad to hear it.' He held out a hand to her. 'Indulge an old man. Let me hear you say it. Here we go: would you still like me to consider getting you a television set?'

She took a step forward and held his hand lightly with the tips of her fingers. The nails were perfectly shaped and coloured. 'No, I would not.'

He bowed his head approvingly. 'And may I ask why not?'

'Because television is a modern-day river of filth that streams unimpeded into the homes of the godless. It is created by the profane and greedy and it is promoted through blasphemy, obscenity and violence.'

'Correct in every sense. And as master of our home, I must fulfil the role of God's prophet, as priest and protector of my family. How can I say that I am protecting my family against evil influence if I allow the sewer of television to run freely through our home?' The woman

111

did not answer. 'Rose?' he barked and her eyes snapped to life.

'You are quite right, husband.'

'I know, I know,' he said and stood up from the table. He yawned and picked up his empty plate.

'I'll do that,' she said, taking the plate from his hands.

Piet got up from the table and stretched his neck, side to side, before leaving the kitchen by one of the two doors on the far side of the room and closing it behind him. He was now in a small sitting room, more dimly lit, with a sofa, two armchairs, a *faux* tiled fireplace, an old desk and a standard lamp. The atmosphere here was more cosy and cocooned, like that of a low-ceilinged farmhouse with shutters closed against a howling wintry gale outside.

He looked around the chamber, as he often did, silently approving the intimacy and serenity that he had fashioned. Room by room the bunker had turned out exactly as he'd intended. It was comfortable but not luxurious, nothing unnecessary or ostentatious; a degree of decorative prettiness had been allowed here and there, but kept to a low key.

It had taken years of trial and error to fix upon the right template for his home. This one – his most successful to date – had been inspired by an exhibition piece at the Imperial War Museum which he read about in a newspaper and went specially to London to visit. When he got to the museum he found a full-scale replica house from the London Blitz reconstructed in the main hall, and he walked around it, upstairs and down, in a state of wonder. He decided there and then that he was close to what he had long been seeking, though he wanted his new home to be a happier place than this. Honest, straightforward frugality should underpin the way of life, of course, but it would be achieved in pursuance of a righteous path, through choice rather than because of forced austerity and government ration books. He straight away set about constructing it, consciously recreating a time of wholesomeness and domestic rectitude, a time when personal cravings were the result of need, not a desire for surplus, when gratitude took precedence over greed; a time when husbands were pillars of leadership, lords of their homes, and women were the glory of their menfolk.

He was sitting at his desk and he noticed that his trousers were hanging too loosely from his thin, sinewy thighs. All this hard work must have made him lose weight. Or maybe it was something else. His appetite had shrunk and he sometimes wondered if there might be some undetected, slow disease eating away at him from the inside. There were plenty of little aches and pains in his abdomen, if he chose to notice them. But he supposed everyone of a certain age had the same and therefore refused to let himself dwell on the matter further. He pulled a cord to click on a brass library lamp on the desk, and, putting on a pair of glasses, began work on his large old Bible, the one he had taken everywhere since adolescence. It had travelled the high veld with him, traversed a desert wilderness and scaled arid mountains; it had seen the seasons advance and retreat, had been studied by night by the hissing light of a hurricane lamp, with insects flitting across its pages, and by day in the oven glare of a subtropical sun; it had been wrapped in blankets and hung from saddlebags, been rocked by oceans and jogged by transcontinental railways, and always under the watchful eye of its student who, over the years, had annotated its pages densely, in a tiny, meticulous hand, underlining much of its text in different coloured inks. Another leather-bound book lay open beside the Bible on the desk – his personal notebook – and he jotted slowly in this as well from time to time.

It was an hour before there was a knock on the door. Steyn did not immediately respond but finished what he was doing and then called out that the woman could enter. 'Is it time already?' he asked, and took off his glasses. 'Everything goes faster when you reach my age,' he added with a smile and beckoned her forward to take a seat. She walked towards him with a straight back and sat down on the edge of a chair facing him, knees together at a slant, heels tucked under. Her fingers were cradled on her lap and she turned her eyes downward.

'So,' said Steyn, unlocking a side drawer of the desk and removing a tall notepad. He quickly reviewed some pages of earlier handwritten notes before turning to a fresh sheet. Then he leant over to a large 1960s reel-to-reel tape recorder that sat on a table next to his desk. Replacing his spectacles on the end of his nose, he examined the tape feed and counter dial, put on a pair of headphones that were plugged into the machine and switched a knob to rewind the reel a few feet. Next, he pressed a button and the reels turned the other way, now more slowly. A second or two later he clicked the machine off, depressed the red 'record' button, removed the headphones and readjusted the angle of a plastic-cased microphone that sat on the edge of the table. Then he rested his notepad on his crossed knees and held his pen at the ready.

'I think we have dealt with number six in as much detail as necessary, so we'll move on to number seven.' He glanced up over his glasses at her. 'Is there something wrong?'

'Of course not.'

'You look nervous.'

'No.'

'You still recall the purpose of this exercise?'

'Yes.'

His face softened. 'I hope you are taking this in the right spirit, my dear.' The guttural quality of his accent lent a slow deliberateness to the words. 'I do not do this to persecute you. The intention is merely to draw out, lay bare and expunge the disease.'

She nodded, tensely.

'By this route, and by this route alone, we will cleanse you of your sinful past and build for a flawless future.' Still she said nothing, but kept her eyes down as he began. 'So. Number seven. What was his name?'

'May I ask you something first?'

Steyn looked up at her over the rim of his glasses. 'You want to ask something before we begin?'

She hesitated. 'Yes.'

'Well then?'

She drew her shoulders in and seemed reluctant to speak.

'Rose, don't be afraid. Speak up.'

'Why don't you want to touch me?'

Piet stared at her for a while before answering, 'Who says I don't want to?'

'You've never tried to.'

'Do you want me to touch you?'

Her eyes darted around the room. 'Won't it be part of being a . . .'

'Go on. If you have a sensible question, ask it.'

'Wouldn't it be part of me becoming a good wife?'

'Yes. In time. It's not something I want to hurry. And we must purify you first, of course.' She nodded and

115

looked down at her clasped hands. 'Well, then,' he added quietly.

'I've been here three years.'

'I know that.'

'It's just—'

'Yes?'

'Am I ever going to see another human being again?'

'What has that got to do with anything?'

'You are the only person in my life. The only person in my life.'

'We've talked about this many times before.'

'If you're going to be the only person in my life for ever, I need to be close to you. If I'm not close to you then I'll never be close to anyone ever again. Can you imagine what that means to a young – a youngish woman?'

'So, you are asking for sexual relations?'

She looked away and her frame seemed to shrink. 'I just need to know what to expect, what to work towards.'

'You need what I say you need. But I understand what you are trying to say, in your clumsy way. Everything we do here takes us further along the path, doesn't it? From the start we've been working our way towards our goal. I thought you had understood that.' She nodded and said nothing. 'Don't disappoint me, now.' She shook her head. 'Right,' he sighed, and pushed his spectacles up onto the bridge of his nose, returning his attention to the notepad. 'So. Number seven, is that right?' He glanced at the previous page. 'Yes, number seven. What was his name?'

'Flossy.'

Steyn looked almost wounded. 'What sort of a name is that?'

'A nickname, I suppose. I never got to know him very well. He was the wandering sort.'

'There seem to have been quite a few of those. How old were you?'

'Twenty-one.'

'How did you meet?' He was noting down the answers.

'It was short. Hardly anything.'

'You think that makes it any better? How did you meet?'

'I think—'

'Please – just the facts.'

'We met at a friend's house. A neighbour of mine who Flossy knew from years before and was visiting. It was a party. We got chatting.'

'How long was it before sexual relations began?'

'The same night.'

Steyn closed his eyes and sighed again.

'But it only happened once,' she added quickly. 'He was gone and I never saw him again.'

'How far did relations extend?'

'We'd had a drink. And a smoke.'

'Drugs again?'

'Cannabis.'

'And?'

'He was obviously after one thing only and I let it happen.'

'You freely admit it. That you were so weak.'

'I was a free spirit.'

'The freedom of Satan.'

'I suppose.'

'What did he do to you?'

'It was quick.' She lowered her chin. 'Just . . . normal penetration.'

'Ejaculation?'

'I can't remember exactly.'

'Is that a yes or a no?'

'Yes, I imagine.'

'Did you enjoy it?'

'It doesn't stand out in my memory.'

'Because there were so many.'

'Because it was insignificant.'

Steyn noted something on the pad. 'Anything else about this *Flossy*?'

'No.'

'Let's move straight on to number eight, then. Name?'

She paused before speaking. 'Ephraim.'

Steyn looked up. 'Ephraim? A Jewish gentleman?'

'I don't know. '

'Where did he come from?'

'I'm not sure. He was English, I think.'

Steyn did not say anything for a moment, but stared at his pad. 'Please don't start playing games with me, Rose.'

'I'm not.'

'Explain what you mean, then.'

'He wasn't white.'

'You mean this person was black skinned?'

'Not exactly. But he wasn't completely white, either.'

'A half-caste?'

'*I don't know*,' she burst out and her head trembled madly, spoiling the perfect set of her hair.

'Calm down.'

'I'm sorry.' She gripped her forehead between thumb and forefinger and squeezed at her temples. 'I'm sorry.'

'You were saying.'

'I really don't know where his parents came from. He spoke like an English person.'

'Right.'

Aside from the continuous hum of the air circulation fan, the close atmosphere of the underground chamber was punctuated only by the dry tick of a clock on the mantelpiece. It was a fairly low grade antique clock, a typical mid-twentieth-century hearthside accessory, its plain face framed by a Gothic-arched oak case.

Steyn exhaled heavily and paused before raising his pen to the pad again. 'Was this a passing fancy, again?'

'No,' she replied quietly.

'Ah. What, then?'

'It went on for quite a while.' A frown puckered the even paintwork on her brow.

'How did you meet?'

'In the street.'

'*What?*'

'He started talking to me by a shop window. Laughing, fun. A nice man. I agreed to go and have a coffee with him. Then he asked me back to his flat.'

'You didn't guess what he was after?'

'He was sweet.'

'What happened?'

'We talked about being free and uninhibited. Then he started undoing my blouse.'

'You just let him?'

'I'm trying to be truthful.'

'What next?'

'Suddenly I wanted him.'

'Wanted him how?'

She did not reply, and after a lengthy silence he encouraged her on. 'How many times, then, with this . . . Ephraim?'

'Often.'

'I said, how many times?'

'I saw him for quite a few months. And we did it a lot.'

'How many times?'

She hesitated, calculating. 'I don't know. A hundred. Two hundred. I really can't say.'

'A hundred here or there doesn't matter?'

She did not answer.

'What was so special about this fellow?'

'Nothing.'

'Rose. I asked you what was so special about him.'

Her eyes travelled over the carpet as she tried to think of something to say. Again, he had to prompt her.

'Was it the size of his penis that you found so alluring?'

She shook her head, blushing deeply, and looked towards her feet.

'What then?'

She spoke with her eyes still lowered. 'He seemed to want me all the time. Sometimes several times a day.' When Piet made no response, she looked up at him. 'Would you like me to go on?' She could see his jaw tense, but he said nothing, and she continued. 'He was a powerful man but it was more than just strength. Being made love to by him felt like . . .' She glanced around the room, searching for the right words. 'Felt like you had that thing, that essence of every desirable woman in the world, all rolled into one. When he decided he wanted me . . .' Again she watched Steyn carefully; he did not meet her eyes but was pressing his fingers to his ribcage, massaging himself there in a slow circular motion. 'When he wanted me,' she went on, 'there was nothing on earth that could stop him.' She fell silent.

'And?' Steyn eventually asked.

'That's all. That's how he would do it to me,' she answered quickly.

'Do what?' When she did not reply, he said, 'Primitive, you mean, like an animal?'

'No,' she said, shaking her head fast.

'Like what, then?'

120

'Like a master.'

'You mean he made you feel like his slave?'

'No. If anything, like his subject. His grateful subject.'

Their eyes met. Steyn's face suddenly flinched and he jolted forwards fractionally.

'What is it?' she asked.

'Nothing.' He closed his notepad and took off his glasses. 'That's enough for today.' He stretched over and switched off the tape recorder.

'That was short.'

'Yes.'

She frowned. 'Are you all right?'

'Yes.'

'I've only tried to be honest.'

Steyn opened the drawer of his desk. 'You can go now.'

She got up straight away and walked towards the door. 'Would you like me to make you some tea?'

He was facing away from her, tidying away the notebooks and the old Bible. 'No, thank you.' She hesitated before leaving, but only for an instant, and then walked noiselessly from the room, closing the door gently behind her.

As soon as he heard it click shut, Piet lowered his forehead onto his fist and squeezed the loose skin at the bridge of his nose. His eyes were shut tight, and he remained locked like this for some while before raising his head and locking up the desk.

Chapter 11

When Granville told Edwina at lunch that he had to go out and would be away all afternoon, she did not ask where he was going. She had hardly spoken a word to him all morning, and he hadn't had time to start trying to work out what was the matter; he simply had too much work to get through before leaving. In any case, he knew that talking about a problem would only drag it out and make matters worse. If there had been a particular issue to thrash out it might have been easier, but they hadn't quarrelled or even exchanged harsh words. There was just an ill climate between them, and any petty disagreement seemed to be pretext enough for hours if not days of resentment. It felt as if the old cushion of trust and affection – which in the past protected them from the bruises of daily living – had worn thin, and now every little bump of the stone-cold floor beneath felt harsh, undeserved. They were both too tired and sick at heart for a scene, and so they kept their misery to a low key, drawn out and dreary, like a persistent drizzle that sets in for the day with no prospect of a breeze or storm to help blow it past.

She had gone to bed early the previous night, peeved that he should want to watch television on their only free evening together of the week. He pleaded that it was a documentary about wartime defences and that it was apparently going to feature the airfield at the edge of their own village, but Edwina was unimpressed and went upstairs in silence without saying goodnight. Granville knew that the sourness would still be there when they got up in the morning, and he remembered it with a sinking feeling as he woke up. He was facing away from her, as he had been all night, with a large gap in between.

Whether their sex life had deteriorated because of the constant little fights or whether it had happened the other way around, was something Granville reflected upon quite a lot. Things had reached a low point about ten years previously, around the time she had Amelia, when they hardly came near each other; and then, a short time after the baby's birth, and still in the midst of this dark period, she seemed to go through a crisis of rejuvenation, restyled her hair, trimmed back her pubes and went on a diet of powder sachets. Granville did wonder suspiciously why she was suddenly going to such lengths to make herself more attractive, but then noticed that most of the other mothers in the school car park were doing likewise. He decided it must be something to do with the time of life and therefore didn't particularly warrant increased vigilance on his part. It was disappointing that her rediscovery of beauty and sexiness was never really tuned towards trying to please him, and so perhaps a grain of doubt about her motives remained. Maybe this had led him to distance himself from her, for safety's sake, and that was perhaps why she, in turn, had grown ever more jaded.

As he lay there, before getting out of bed, and with the shadow of yet another heavy atmosphere looming between them, a heinous thought presented itself and he could not ignore it: how long could either of them permit this charade to go on? But when he thought of the girls asleep next door, and saw, on his chest of drawers, a photograph of them all, smiling and healthy, at a pub garden table in the sunshine, he blocked the thought out. The ghost of it still hung there, though, biding its time.

Later in the day, as they cleared up lunch together, Granville thought he would try to ease the situation. 'The girls and I have come to a decision,' he said. Edwina neither replied nor looked up from stacking the dishwasher. 'We've decided that you do quite enough housework. From now on, after supper, you can just down tools and walk away from the kitchen – watch telly or whatever – we'll do all the clearing up between us.' Edwina smiled, but Granville knew it was not a good smile. Otherwise she made no response.

As he was about to leave the house, she mentioned in a deadpan way that his parents had called, inviting them to go to Glyndebourne with them later in the summer; and she added that there was no possible way she would endure the purgatory of an evening like that.

'How can I possibly tell them that?' he asked in his most reasonable tone. 'They'll be so hurt.'

'Tell them whatever you like. But after the last time I don't see why I should make the effort. Your father couldn't be more rude to me if he tried. I've had years of it, and I've had enough. Let's face it: they can't stand me.'

'That's just not true.'

'And I don't care for them, if I'm honest.'

Granville shook his head silently.

'Why should I make the effort?' said Edwina. 'You don't exactly go out of your way to visit my parents.'

'They live most of the year in Scotland or the Cayman Islands. And I don't get much time off.'

'You could come on the August grouse fortnight. Daddy's invited you every year.'

This needled Granville. 'You're the one who goes on at me about how time together when I'm not working is so precious. And now you suggest I spend my hard-earned fortnight away with a load of—' He cut himself short.

She sighed. 'Same old story,' she muttered. 'I come up with an idea and I get my head bitten off.'

'You know that grouse-shooting parties are not really my scene,' he added, but she did not answer. 'I'm late,' he said. 'I'd better go.' Again, Edwina smiled her private smile and the atmosphere for the next twenty-four hours was sealed.

Before he went through the door she found time for another comment, this time in a pleasant sing-song tone. 'Don't worry about your bloody dog. I'll walk it, for the third day on the trot.'

'What?'

'Nothing,' she sang again.

'Thank you. About the dog.'

'And when you get back you can go off with the girls and plot other ways of how to deal with poor old batty, tetchy Mummy.'

'That's not how it is. I'm trying to find ways to make your life easier.'

Now she looked at him with furious eyes. 'Then why don't you pass on some of your stupid parish jobs to other people? Fuck clearing up the kitchen after supper! What we need is the odd hour alone together so that we can try and sort out the bloody mess that we call a marriage.'

Granville looked at her. There was nothing he could say that would not take hours, if not days to iron out; and he had to go.

*　　*　　*

He left her the car and drove off in their old Volkswagen camper van. It started up with a great throaty rumble and he reversed it slowly off from the tarmac driveway. His family had had one of these vans when he was a boy, and the unmistakable sound of its rear-mounted engine reminded him of the camping holidays he'd been on with his parents. There had been plenty of them, each as lively and offbeat as the one before.

Granville's father was a hereditary baronet with no love of social conventions but a penchant for Indian jackets. He had been rich enough never to have to work for money and had dedicated his life instead to a succession of immense unpublished writing projects. Epic poems in the style of Byron, unfinished novels, maverick translations of the Greek classics. Their presence had hung over Granville's childhood like phantoms of gargantuan Parma hams, richly scented, rare and uncut. His father would spend whole days on family camping trips scribbling away, stripped to the waist, wearing a straw hat and sitting in the shade of a big tree, piles of reference books littered around and a Labrador at his feet. As a young man, Mountstewart St Clair – known to all as Mounty – had been swept along by a tide of beatnik revolt blended with intellectual liberalism. When he eventually inherited his own father's titles and land, he transferred quite well from bohemian London to country squiredom, but never shook off his unconventional ways. Granville's mother was equally nonconformist, but not as extrovert as her husband, nor as public spirited. When she became lady of the big house, she was happier gardening or collecting berries in wicker baskets than joining her husband in his succession of extravagant local schemes.

Edwina was right in a way. Neither of Granville's

parents had particularly tried to get to know their daughter-in-law, and had written her off early as a class-conscious social climber who had a tendency to treat their beloved son like a doormat. Granville had watched them going through the motions with Edwina, engaging her in chat and exchanging pleasantries, but he could detect their absence of conviction. When Mounty spoke to Edwina on his occasional visits it was pretty clear that he wanted to have done with it quickly so that he could get on with the more important business of talking to his boy.

It took Granville an hour and a half to get into the centre of Bournemouth, find a place to park and walk to the coffee shop that Rhian had specified. He was wearing jeans, brown suede shoes, a thigh-length corduroy jacket with its collar turned up, and his face was partially hidden by a pair of heavy-framed retro sunglasses. Proper disguise, he thought, and certainly not your average vicar.

She was already sitting at a table when he came through the door. She stood up, smiling broadly, and took a step towards him, but he waved at her to sit down. Her face fell when she realized from his serious expression that her effervescence was ill-judged. He ordered a latte for himself, a white chocolate cookie for her, pushed his sunglasses up onto his forehead and walked across to the table where she waited. Her hair was loose, artificially straightened, and he could smell the fresh apple scent of its shampoo from across the table. She greeted him warmly but he sat down without pleasantries and asked her to explain what the problem was.

As she spoke she played with a strand of her hair. Her head was tilted slightly and she did not look straight at him but let her eyes wander over the tabletop and around the cafe. She talked much about herself, how she couldn't sleep at night, how she felt tense with her friends and with her parents because it was uncomfortable to be hiding such a big secret. He listened in silence. Her tone was lively, peppered with smiles and giggles. There was no immediate evidence of the trauma that seemed to have engulfed her when she stood at the doors of Granville's church, a week or so before. 'I just feel,' she concluded thoughtfully, laying a palm flat down on the tabletop – her nails were freshly painted – 'I just feel that this whole thing is going to affect the way I make relationships in the future, because I'm pretending to be someone when I know that inside there's, like, this other person trying to get heard?' Her statement rose at the end, as if posing a question that expected a response. Granville did not respond. She went on, 'and if I don't, like, find some way of dealing with it, I think it's going to seriously mess up the way I relate to everyone in my life from now on? And—' He raised a hand to interrupt her and she stopped midstream.

'You've said enough.'

'What?'

'I think I've been pretty patient already.'

'What do you mean?'

'I mean the load of self-pitying, indulgent bilge you've been spewing, expecting me to feel sorry for you.' She opened her mouth to speak but nothing came out. 'Meanwhile that poor woman – his widow – is going through a hell on earth, and so are those boys. Suddenly told they'll never see their father again. Their lives have had their insides ripped out, and all you can think about is some little snag in your relationships.'

She gave him an injured look. 'How can you talk like that?' she asked. 'Being a vicar an' all.'

He sighed, shook his head and took a piece of paper from his back trouser pocket. 'You've got some explaining to do,' he said, unfolded the paper and smacked it flat onto the table between them. It contained her own details, name, address and phone number, written down in pencil by her in a hurry in the church vestry before he'd sent her off in the taxi on the morning of the suicide.

She looked at it, then up at him. 'Yeah? So what?'

'The only thing that's genuine here is the mobile number. I've done some checking. The address doesn't exist.' He jabbed his finger at the name on the paper. 'Neither does this person.' Her eyes darted around the cafe, and for a moment it seemed as if she was going to get up and run, but something seemed to overwhelm her. Her face crumpled, huge tears arose in her eyes and she pressed her palms against her ears. Granville tried to engage her line of sight but just at that moment she let her hand fall heavily, which jolted the table and overturned his latte glass. It rolled off, spilling its contents everywhere, and smashed on the floor. As Granville sprang out of his chair to clear up the mess, she turned her face to the ceiling and began to moan. He called to her from where he squatted on the ground, sodden tissues in hand, trying to distract her, and everyone in the cafe stopped talking to see what all the noise was about. Unable to quieten her, Granville went over and helped her to her feet, by which time she had started to wail with every breath. He dropped a crumpled banknote on the table and hustled her out into the street. Passers-by stopped and stared, so he grabbed her arm and hurried her off towards a side street, all the while reassuring her. 'It's all right, don't worry. I'm here, I'll help you.'

Eventually they found a quiet spot in a cul-de-sac and sat down on the entrance step of a redundant ironmonger's shop. An estate agent's FOR SALE banner stood above them, and one of the old shop's windows was curtained on the inside with towels. Her breathing was punctuated with little sobs which slowed as the fit began to subside.

She began stumblingly to confess the truth. Her real name was Hetty, she said. She had run away from her mother, 'who was a useless old cow who drank too much and spent most of the day watching television in bed'. Her father had been locked up for killing a child while drink-driving. She wished he'd stay there for the rest of his filthy life, she said, and her eyes blazed.

Granville let her burst of anger subside before asking, 'What about Bertie Gosling?'

'Everything I said about him was true. We met at the airport cafe, where I used to work. He helped me to get away from home.'

'Helped how?'

'He gave me money.'

'Why would he do that? Were you blackmailing him?'

'No, nothing like that. I think he loved me. He felt sorry for me and wanted to help.'

'How long did this carry on?'

'A long time. It would have been a year next week.'

'All that time? And he paid for you to live somewhere else?'

'A bedsit. Nothing special, but it's nice. I can't pay the rent any more and I've got to move out at the end of the month.' She looked up at him. 'I don't know what I'm going to do. I can't go home again. My old man will be coming out soon.'

'Why do you hate your father so much?'

'Don't ask me that,' she replied, and looked down again.

Granville waited for a moment and asked, 'Didn't you see what you were doing to Bertie? Did you really think things could go on?'

'I did my best to make him happy,' she said. 'He got something from me he never got from her.'

'From his wife, you mean?'

'He said she was a cold cow. She never properly loved him. Never gave him what he needed, from here.' She spread her palm across her chest. Her painted nails dug into the fabric of her T-shirt.

'And you did?'

'He was happy with me. Looking after him was the best thing I ever did in my life.'

'Yes, well, let's not get carried away with that theory,' said Granville. 'Don't forget he's no longer with us.'

'He would be if he'd left her and come with me.'

Granville sighed and looked up between the buildings to the avenue of clear blue sky above. An ambulance, with siren shrieking, pelted along the road at the bottom of the street where they sat. 'That just wasn't going to happen, was it, Hetty? Be realistic.'

'It's not my fault what happened.'

'No,' he said. 'No, it wasn't your fault. Bertie made his own choice.'

She turned to look at him. 'What's going to happen to me now? I can't go back to my mum's.'

'Have you got an alternative?'

Her eyes began to fill with tears again. 'You've got to help me. You can't send me back there. Not to him, not to my dad.'

'I'm not sending you back, it's your home. What do you expect from me? To pay the bill for your bedsit?' She said nothing, but continued to look at him, her hands clutched so tightly together that her fingers whitened. 'I could take your case to social services or something, but you'd be better doing that yourself. It's dangerous for me to be associated with you. I should have known better than to have come to see you in the first place. If this goes on, word about what happened will leak out, one way or another. We can't meet again.'

She closed her eyes and uttered a single word, high pitched and feeble, like a prayer, as the tears rolled over her pudgy cheeks. 'Please.'

'There's nothing I can—'

'Please.'

Granville got to his feet and looked left and right down the desolate alley. His back and knees ached from the way he'd been sitting. He felt old, well past his prime, and stiff. 'The best thing I can do for you is find a person more local to come and see you in confidence. A clergyman. I think I could manage that.'

'I don't want anyone else,' she said, looking up at him pleadingly, 'I only want you.'

'Well, you can't have me, I'm afraid.' He backed away from her. 'I'm sorry about your situation, but you've already lied to me, even though I risked so much trying to protect you. I can't even be sure you're not lying now.'

'I'm not lying!'

'You can't be mad enough to think I'm going to replace Bertie Gosling in your life.'

'I didn't say that.'

'Better by far if I keep away,' he said, and she looked down again. 'Look, I'll see who I can find. I'll put someone in touch with you who can help. All right?'

Still she did not answer, but her head sank and rested against her raised knees.

*　　*　　*

Half an hour later he was caught in rush hour traffic on the way out of Bournemouth and had to wait a long time at a succession of traffic lights. By chance, Hetty was walking in the same direction. He spotted her in his side mirror, and twice she went past him along the pavement. He watched her from the driving seat of his camper van, stuck in the jam, but she did not notice him, nor did he try to attract her attention. Her head was bowed and her hair fell forward, concealing her face. Once she almost ran into someone coming the other way and the person had to sidestep quickly over the kerb to avoid her. She walked straight on past, closed to all.

Chapter 12

After my father hanged himself, I went to live at my uncle's farm close by. We were all part of the same family settlement, the land, the people, the livestock; cousins, I suppose, but without the bonds of affection that word might suggest. It was a community of people who had no choice but to get along together, work side by side, share the same food, face the same dangers, endure the same hardships. Our parents, grandparents and great-grandparents had done likewise. They were bound together by the unwritten laws of the clan. When push came to shove, we would stand shoulder to shoulder, I guess, but that was for reasons of survival rather than loyalty. I was reluctantly accepted into my uncle's home as one more kid of the tribe to feed, but was always made to feel like a bit of a parasite. They certainly made sure to get their money's worth out of me. I was worked to the bone in that place.

I must have been there for about three years when the day came for the great bull's slaughter, an incident that was to mark a turning point in my story.

We all came out to watch: children, a crowd of farm-hands, even houseboys, because it was quite an event. My uncle and his sons led the bull into the smaller kraal and closed the gate behind them. They were experienced cattle men, farmers who had seen it all, and if they still harboured a trace of fear for the safety of their skins in situations like this, they were too hardened and proud to show it. They moved around the *kraal* with a lazy swagger, laughing and smoking, aware of the watching crowd, and wanting to show that they could do this job almost with their eyes closed.

They brought the bull in with ropes tied to each of its horns, one to its tail and another to the ring of its nose. We all knew this animal, and I had been close to it many times before, eyeball to eyeball, even. It was quiet and easy to handle, though massively built, one of the race specially bred to pull the heavy carts of the Voortrekkers hundreds of miles across the rough veld. It looked like a monster but behaved like a sleepy old dog because it had never had to regard its keepers as enemies, and that was why they did not bother to tie its legs.

They got down to the job straight away like a piece of routine work, and placed the captive bolt device against the animal's forehead. They fired it off and the bull went down, sending up a cloud of dust into the air. A few people cheered. One of the men put his knife to its neck and let out a torrent of blood into the dry clay. The job seemed to have been done quickly and people began to walk away, thinking the afternoon's entertainment over, but a sudden shout made everyone turn around. The bull was back on its feet and tossing its head. The blood was still spouting from its neck and sprayed the men who scrambled to pick up the restraining ropes. I wondered how could there be so much blood, and guessed it must be because the creature was so huge. It was wheezing badly. Blood bubbles filled and popped at the cut because its windpipe had been pierced. The two big black eyes, which just a few minutes before had been placidly blinking away the swarms of flies, now looked wildly about for a means of escape.

The bull's will to survive, his love of God's good air and earth, had wiped clean the slate. The old alliance with mankind was null and void and the fighter inside unleashed. The holding ropes were tossed aside like cotton threads and the lads hanging onto them floundered about in the dirt. The bull scraped the ground with its fore-hooves and stampeded towards the fence. A row of onlookers who were leaning on the timbers cringed back in fear, though the bull stopped short and turned and looked for another route of escape. My uncle, a fearless Boer of the old school, now approached the animal with a shotgun at the ready – not the most appropriate weapon, but the only one he had to hand. The bull turned angrily to face him and my uncle fired. The full force of the cartridge hit it close range in the face. The spray of pellets tore the fur and flesh from its skull and took out an eye, but still it came on, refusing to let go its life.

Now we were all uncertain. Everything had failed and the bull was still alive, free to choose its place of attack. Spectators retreated from the fence, children were swept up into the arms of their mothers, and in that moment of primal fear we actually asked ourselves: will this animal have done with us all? But my uncle stood firm in the kraal. Someone had handed him a rifle and he took aim. The shot rang out and the bull's legs buckled like daffodil stalks. One last huge sigh, a few more hopeless kicks of the hooves and it was over. The surviving great black eye went still and a film of dust settled over it. None of the onlookers was hurt, and the bull was now just another dead animal to be flayed, hung and jointed; people could get back to work. To me, it was one of the most extraordinary scenes I had ever witnessed, and I was surprised that nobody else wanted to talk about it – ashamed of their fear, I thought: nobody, except for one person.

She was a distant relative, another cousin of sorts, part of the same extended family at the collective farm settlement that was overseen by my uncle. I had met her before, of course, but this was the first time she had properly spoken to me. She was a year or two older and worked as a kind of nurse at the farm because of a disease that had set in amongst the black workers. They were developing unpleasant little sores that sometimes turned into ulcers stretching down the whole leg. Occasionally there were maggots, which meant amputation or, quite often, death. No-one knew what caused the disease, why it only attacked the blacks or how to get rid of it, but my uncle had already lost four decent men, which did not please him greatly because he was left to deal with the widows and children (and how those people would breed!). Anyway, the girl – the nurse, my distant cousin – remained at the kraal fence that afternoon longer than the rest, as did I, and together we walked back to the farmhouse where she lived. She talked of the slaughtered bull's nobility, about its righteous anger and strength of will, and said that she could sense the holy spirit in it. I was moved by her natural faith and sensitivity.

We began to meet more often. It was good to find someone I could talk to, at last. I told her about my parents, about my mother, who had once been a beautiful and devoted wife but who now surely burned because she failed the challenges the Lord had placed before her. My mother had been born into an English farming family and came to the Cape after the war as the bride of the South African soldier she had nursed.

They arrived back at the family lands in the Transvaal shortly before I was born. After me came my brother, and then the tragedy that broke the family apart. I told her the whole story. I told her of my mother's fall and the misery afterwards, right up to the morning when the old man lynched himself in his shame. It was the first time I had wept about it. I felt comforted by the girl's pious kindness. That was how our time together began.

I grew to love her, and all my disappointment and anger about the past began to dissolve. Her words and her smile cleaned the wound. I came to see her as an angel, immaculate, too good, in fact, for the place where we were both living. We took refuge in each other, kept ourselves as much as possible away from them all, and began to plan our escape. We believed in a dream world waiting for us in some other place, just the two of us, united in purity and godliness.

One night we slipped away from the farm on a pair of ponies and travelled far. We lived on a wing and a prayer. I kept watch at night, so that she could rest a little, and by day we rode the ponies or walked until our blisters turned hard as tree bark. I knew that my uncle would not care to search far for me; but for her? She came from a distant branch of the family and had been orphaned as a child. They were hoping to breed from her – to introduce fresh blood into the immediate family – and might go to some lengths to have her returned to the fold, having invested so much in the commodity, as it were. But I was clever in the open and knew how to cover our tracks. We were exhausted and afraid almost all the time, but it seemed we were living a miracle, especially at dusk and dawn, when the light went dim and the vast sky turned red. It was a silent wilderness and we felt boundlessly free. We were like the oppressed peoples of the Old Testament, the chosen of God, fleeing through the desert from our enslavers, and in that wondrous and dangerous paradise we consecrated our union.

We survived through grace and love but knew that at some stage we would have to return to conventional living. That moment arrived when we stopped one day at a small, lonely farmstead, and asked for food. The family there treated us kindly, fed us and offered us work. To this day I admit that I never foresaw what might happen next. It did not occur to me that my girl's goodness and beauty might be qualities greedily observed by people other than myself, but it was soon obvious that the farmer – our host and employer – had begun to take an interest in her. He was a big strong man, with money, wit and experience, beside which I looked like an adolescent fool. He flattered and spoiled her until her resistance crumbled and she allowed herself to be taken. Perhaps she was worn down by our hardships, or maybe she had just grown up and changed. My suspicions were aroused quite early on (my instinct for such things has never let me down), though I never found the opportunity of catching the two of them together. But one afternoon she went missing and when she came back to our hut there was something not quite right. She was short in her answers and her hair was too well brushed for the hour of day, and I felt my blood run cold. I commanded her there and then to remove her underwear, which she did, too compliantly, almost with resignation. She dropped her pants to the ground between us, a small white pile, and the evidence was all too obvious. She could not look me in the face.

We left the place with our ponies in the night and when we were far enough away, I sat her down and had it out with her. How we wept. My heart felt as if it was being torn from my chest. I had chosen this woman to redeem the wrongs of all womankind in the wake of my mother's fall, and she had betrayed me. For two whole days we sat in despair, unable to find a path through the nightmare, but, sad to say, I could see that her misery was one of disappointment rather than remorse.

At last, I went to the Lord for advice. I spent the night in prayer, reading my Bible and cleaning my mind of anger. Seek and ye shall find, we are told, and, of course, it was there before me. The Book of Deuteronomy told clearly what had to be done. It is written in chapter twenty-two, and as soon as I was absolutely sure, I thought it best to do it straight away, before the sun arose. Her face was down in a blanket and she would not have known what was coming, but I was no expert in those days and it took me longer than it should to finish her off properly. Afterwards, I bled her thoroughly as well, just to make sure.

When everything was tidied up, I actually sighed with relief and a miracle occurred. The weight of her sin evaporated and disappeared, as if it had never happened, and I realized the Lord was giving me a sign. I realized that the whole purpose of His having placed this girl in my path – perhaps even the reason she had been born at all – was to educate me, to take me one step further along the road of discovery. Step by step I would be led there, lesson by lesson, until the end was achieved, an end which would benefit all who came after me, in accordance with God's wishes. The Lord's healing comfort that morning was instantaneous, but the lesson was clear: there could be no short cuts. Women are frail creatures who need time, nurture and patience. In future I would have to distance myself from my feelings, which are weak and fed by desire.

First my mother, now this young woman. A state of unblemished matrimony can never be taken for granted. A man must be tirelessly vigilant, leave no stone unturned. There can be no rest, no relaxing of the guard. As I laid down the shovel after filling her grave, out of breath but relieved to have done with it, I knew I had to move on. A new chapter. I actually wept with gratitude. I was overwhelmed with the certainty and righteousness of what lay ahead. I was just a young man and it all seemed very exciting.

Chapter 13

There was no bell, so Granville rapped his knuckles against the door. As he waited, he glanced down the length of the flower beds either side of the perfect lawn. Neither a blade of grass nor a young shoot out of place. He was about to raise his hand to knock a second time when Steyn's voice called out from the other side of the door, 'Who's there?' Granville's bull terrier, alert at his heels, stopped panting and pricked up its ears.

'It's Granville.'

'Who?'

'Granville St Clair.'

There was a pause and then the sound of two bolts sliding open. Steyn held the door ajar and took a look at Granville before unhitching the security chain and opening it wider. He did not smile or step aside but leant back casually, thumbs in pockets, and observed his visitor. Granville was by now used to Steyn's manners. They swung between over-emphatic courtesy and the abruptness of an executioner; there was no predicting which might happen.

'What can I do for you, Father?'

Granville raised his eyebrows. 'May I come in?'

Steyn hesitated, took a step aside and allowed him through the door. The terrier tried to push its way in as well, but Granville blocked its path with his foot and hauled it back by the collar. 'Bloody numbskull,' he said. 'So determined. But I suppose anyone would be if their family business was killing bulls. I'll leave him in the garden, if that's all right. Wouldn't want him to mess up your house.' The dog looked unimpressed by Granville's command for it to stay, and when the door was closed began to sniff around the garden path.

Granville went into the small dark hallway. In front of him was a steep old-fashioned staircase, flanked by walls, leading to an upper floor. 'I've never been in here before.' He looked around. 'Cosy,' he said, because he felt he ought to say something. Steyn did not respond. The cottage had a dark and neglected feel, smelt of damp and contained no decorations or pictures. The windows had curtains but they were faded, and looked as if they must have been left behind by the previous owner after a generation or more of use. In sharp contrast to the atmosphere of decay was the large quantity of potted plants, squeezed close together in neat rows on every windowsill and shelf: cyclamens, azaleas, but mostly geraniums, red, white, pink and variegated. The scent of them soured the air, and Granville remembered his grandfather describing the aftermath of mustard gas attacks in the trenches. It had smelt just like geraniums.

'How long have you had this place?' he asked. 'Must be over a year now.'

'Four years come August,' replied Steyn.

'How time flies. You've made great strides in the garden. Puts me to shame.'

'Would you like some tea or something?'

'Thank you,' replied Granville. 'Which way?'

Steyn led him towards the kitchen. 'I'm sorry if I seem

distracted, Father,' he said. 'My mind's somewhere else. I was in the middle of writing.'

'Sorry to disturb you,' said Granville. 'What were you writing?'

'A sort of memoir, you might call it.'

'I should like to read something you've written. Your theological thoughts, maybe.'

Piet smiled. 'We might not see eye to eye.'

'Oh, I don't know. I'm pretty open minded.'

'That's the problem. I'm not.'

Granville laughed and they went into the kitchen. It was tidy but dismal. The old units were discoloured, their paintwork having faded in accordance with the seasonal movement of sunlight through the windows. One of the knobs on the control panel of the cooker had been taped over because of an electrical fault, and legions of dead flies hung from sticky brown tapes pinned to the ceiling. Piet filled an electric kettle and went to find a teapot from a high cupboard. He looked it over, lifted its lid and sniffed inside, before giving it a quick dust with a tea towel.

Granville sat at the table. He had come with the intention of bringing Piet up to date with the recent developments regarding Hetty. Straight after returning from Bournemouth he had done some research on the internet and contacted a couple of local news agencies. This time her story did add up. There had indeed been an incident of drunk driving in the town a few years before, in which an eight-year-old girl had died, and the perpetrator of the tragedy, a thirty-seven-year-old former Grenadier Guards corporal called Liam Swanley, had been sentenced to eight years in prison. Despite the protests of the dead child's parents, it seemed the man was shortly to be released on parole after serving only

144

three and a half years of his sentence. He was listed as having a wife, Jillian, and one daughter called Henrietta.

But now that Granville was here he hesitated to bring the subject up. Although it had been pressing on him day and night since the trip to Bournemouth he decided on the spur of the moment not to say anything. Voicing his concerns would edge the issue closer to the status of a crisis. Outside, he heard Luther bark a couple of times, and as the kettle began to stir he tried to think of something else to say to Steyn.

'Why did you decide to come here, Piet? It's a long way from home.'

'Well, I hadn't much to stay in Africa for. You know, things are not that easy there for the white man any more.'

'But why particularly here?'

'A sort of family connection, you might say.'

'Family in Dorset?'

'A long time ago,' Steyn dismissed the idea with a wave of the hand. 'My mother was born in this part of the world, but she left during the war.'

'I had no idea. Where did her family live?'

'I'm not sure exactly. Somewhere around here. It doesn't really matter.'

'What was the surname? There might be relatives.'

'I don't even know that. She died when I was quite young. I always thought she might have been called Newland, which is my second name. I don't see any other reason why they would have given me such a peculiar name.'

'It's not a name I recognize. I imagine you've looked online?'

'No.'

'Or the local phone book?'

145

'You know, Father, no offence, but I'm not very good with computers and things.'

'That's fine.'

Just at that moment there was the sound of barking from the garden and the bull terrier flashed past the French windows. Granville jumped up to get a better view of what was going on. 'Bloody dog,' he said. 'He's seen something in the brambles down the bottom of your garden. I'd better go and fetch him.'

'You stay put,' said Piet. 'I'll go.'

'No, really. He's a stubborn old clot. You'll have the devil of a time trying to pull him out of that. And I'd hate him to damage anything.'

'Don't worry,' said Piet, 'I have a way with dogs.' He did not wait for a reply, but headed out of the French windows and jogged down to the end of the garden, disappearing into the cover of the bramble thicket.

Granville turned away from the window and cast an eye around the room. There were plants lined up on shelves here as well, but otherwise not many clues to the nature of the man who occupied the place. Granville wondered if Piet was a genuine ascetic who chose austerity for spiritual reasons. It was not impossible, on the evidence he had seen, but he knew it was just as likely Piet was a lonely, lost human being, lacking initiative or cash, and waiting for someone to show him the way out.

There was another door that led off the kitchen, right next to him, with a key sitting in its lock. He glanced out of the window. Steyn had not yet emerged from the brambles, and so Granville turned the handle of the door. It was unlocked and he opened it to have look inside.

It was dark in there because of wooden shutters over the windows. His hand felt for a switch on the wall and a light came on – a solitary pendant bulb, without a shade, in the middle of the ceiling. The wallpaper was textured and yellowing with age, and the floor was covered with transparent plastic sheeting, beneath which the room's contents appeared to be organized into piles, as yet unidentifiable. A narrow path led between the piles from the doorway, splitting into two branches halfway into the room, allowing access to the far corners.

Right beside the doorway was a neat stack of newspapers. Granville's attention was drawn to them straight away because something seemed not quite right. Despite the familiar title of the top copy, the front page carried only a single photograph, the columns were unusually narrow and the headlines too understated. He took a closer look and saw that it was dated Monday, 3 March 1952, but the quality of print and paper was as if new. He lifted the top copy and had a look at the one beneath. Tuesday, 4 March 1952. And the next and the next, in a daily sequence, brand new copies of vintage newspapers, great piles of them, months, perhaps a year's worth. He knew that such things were available as commemorative souvenirs, quirky birthday presents boxed up with a bottle of brandy and the like, but a job lot this size must have cost the earth. He placed the top copy back neatly.

He looked around the jumble of contents and began to discern other things beneath the plastic sheeting: stacks of empty, flat-packed grocery boxes, cartons of soap, toilet paper and cotton wool, columns of tinned food, many with their wrappers removed; and three racks of women's clothing, each item zipped into a suit carrier, dresses, blouses, twinsets, fur coats.

Suddenly there came the crash of an outside door closing on the other side of the house and Granville moved quickly to leave the room. But before reaching the door, he noticed, at the bottom of a wall on the right, a panel of electric switches with dials and lights, a kind of sophisticated fuse box. It was outsize, almost cumbersome, more like a spaceship console from a low-budget 1960s sci-fi drama than anything normally found in a house. Some switches were up, others down, some lights illuminated, others flashing, and quite a few dead, everything minutely labelled. There was no time to look closely, and he backed quickly out of the room, switching off the pendant light as he went. He was only just back at the kitchen table when Steyn entered, slightly out of breath.

'I've had to tie your dog to the gate,' he said. 'I'm sorry, but I've got traps in the rough down there. I wouldn't want him to hurt himself.'

'Traps?'

'For foxes.'

'Ah.'

'Sit down, Father,' said Piet, and went back to the kettle which had boiled and clicked itself off. 'I'm looking forward to this Easter Grill of yours,' he said, pouring water into the teapot. 'Is it something you do every year?'

'Yes. Yes, every year.'

'Why do you have such an event at Easter in particular?'

Granville collected his thoughts. 'It's just a bit of a village get-together. I spent some time in Greece once, where they take Easter very seriously. Every family roasts a lamb and has a big feast. I thought it seemed like a lot of fun.'

'So you celebrate Easter in Cheselbury Abbas by roasting the Paschal Lamb?'

'Just a sort of barbecue, really.'

'And people like it?'

'Seem to. Though the organizing committee do their best to make everything as difficult as possible. You wouldn't believe how many petty problems a tableful of do-gooders can dredge up, given half a chance. I honestly think they enjoy making life harder for themselves.'

Piet smiled. 'I know what you mean. I've seen some of them in action already. I admire your tact at those meetings.'

'It's good to have you in the congregation. And helping out in all the ways you do. We're really grateful.'

'I enjoy it.'

'Different from what you're used to?'

'A little. But I like your hymns.' He put two mugs of tea on the table and sat down with Granville. 'They're a bit more tuneful than ours.'

Granville looked across at him with a mischievous smile. 'Perhaps I can tempt you to join us properly.'

'Join you?'

'You know, become a formal member of the C of E. I could write to the bishop. You might even like to apply one day to be a licensed lay reader. You seem to have a calling.'

'I don't think so.'

'Give it some thought. We're a very broad bunch, every colour of the rainbow represented.'

Steyn smiled. 'Are you trying to convert me?'

'I wouldn't use that term. Just offering you a home from home. In out of the cold.'

'I appreciate the sentiment.'

'And how's the barbecue thing coming along?' Granville asked. 'Do you think you'll have it finished in time for the Easter Grill?'

'Easily.' Piet patted the air in front of him. 'It will be the best *brai* you've ever seen.'

'Best what?'

'That's what they call barbecues where I come from.'

'You must let us know your costs.'

'Think of it as a gift.'

'What about all the materials?'

'Just bits and pieces I've picked up along the way. Cost me nothing at all. Basically just an old oil drum cut in half. Simple.'

'You're very kind.' He looked up at Piet. 'And I'm glad you're scooping up the Goslings. Janet needs the distraction. How's she doing?'

'An impressive woman.'

'Yes,' said Granville and nodded thoughtfully. 'A little confused at the moment, perhaps. Understandably. And vulnerable.'

'A woman who sacrifices everything for her family,' went on Piet, ignoring Granville's comments, 'is a rare creature in this day and age, a blessing for her husband. That fool did not deserve her.'

'Well,' mused Granville, 'we can't undo what's done. Poor fellow.'

'Did you know,' Piet continued, 'Janet has never had sex with any man other than her husband? Little does she realize that her love and fidelity was wasted on a philandering sinner.'

Once again, Steyn's frankness gave Granville a jolt. 'She's talked to you about such things?'

'Several times. She knows I admire her purity of spirit. Is there anything wrong with that?'

Granville shrugged. 'Not especially, I suppose. It just seems rather . . . intimate.'

'We've become good friends. I've persuaded her to stop drinking.'

'Right.' Granville hesitated. 'You aren't going to say

anything to her, are you? About the morning of the suicide?'

Steyn pursed his lips and took a sip of tea. 'I've thought long and hard about that, too. But I think we should stick to our plan.'

'I had no idea you were in any doubt.'

'It's all right,' Steyn held up his hand reassuringly, 'your secret's safe.'

'I thought we were in this together.'

'Don't worry, Father.'

'You're sure?'

'Hundred per cent.'

'Glad to hear it.' Granville settled back in his chair.

Steyn asked, 'What are you so frightened of?'

'What do you mean?'

'If the truth were to come out.'

'My credibility would be at stake, for a start.'

'Your job, you mean?'

'It wouldn't look great.'

'Would that be such a disaster for you, though?' Steyn narrowed his eyes, sharpening them like pencil points as if to penetrate deeper. 'I get the feeling that you're not a hundred per cent happy in your work. Maybe it wouldn't be so bad if something happened to help you change direction.'

'I've never said that.'

'Not in so many words, perhaps, but reading between the lines.'

Granville gripped his tea mug. 'You're quite perceptive, aren't you?'

'Nah,' Steyn said quietly. 'I've just seen a lot in my time.'

'It's not that I don't want to be God's servant in the world. There's nothing I want more. My faith is stronger than ever. I can't express it strongly enough. It's my whole being, but it's just . . .'

'You don't want to be a pastor any more?'

Granville looked at him. 'There's something extraordinary happening to me. I'm having experiences.'

'What kind of experiences?'

'They're not even experiences. That word would imply that something happens, but nothing does happen. Everything stays the same, but I get . . . get just overwhelmed. I can't describe it. It's a benediction. It's happening more and more often. It's the Holy Spirit descending on me, that's all I know for sure. I've always known it.'

Steyn was listening closely. 'How long has this been happening?'

'It first happened when I was at university, but I didn't really know what it was. It changed my life. It was my calling, you might say. At first I thought it was all about nature, a beautiful landscape, the simple splendour of God, a chorus of angels through birdsong, that sort of thing. It would come once in a blue moon. But nowadays it happens anywhere, at any time. In the street, in the bank, in a bus queue. I even felt it a bit on my walk here.'

'Is there a problem with this?'

'No. At least, I don't think so. Edwina made me go and see the doctor and he came up with a handful of crackpot suggestions.'

'You don't think there's anything wrong with you?'

'Definitely not. It's just that when I feel the Holy Spirit so completely, so choicelessly and overwhelmingly, when I see the face of God, if you like, I realize what a paltry business I'm involved in. Organized religion! How can God be organized? My antics at the altar are a joke!

Nothing to do with the divine, no relation to it whatever. Worse. To get up there and profess God through words, fancy clothes and superstitious incantations feels like insulting the Almighty, spitting in the face of the truth I know to be at the heart of all creation.'

'Steady, now.'

'I've seen enough of the world to know that we don't have a monopoly on truth. What I've been experiencing is completely in tune with what you can read about in wisdom philosophy the world over. It's *parabrahman*, the attainment of the absolute godhead, supreme awareness, the *Tao*, *Wuji*, whatever. We choose to call it the Holy Spirit, and that's good enough for me. I'm sorry. I can't possibly hope that other people will understand.'

'It's good you're getting this off your chest,' said Steyn. 'So let me ask you this: do you no longer see any value in teaching the Holy Gospel of Jesus Christ?'

Granville smiled at him. 'You must think me a bit of a heretic.'

'No, no,' replied Steyn, reassuringly, 'this is not about me. Tell me what you think.'

Granville's eyes glazed and he bit at his lower lip before answering. 'Of course I can see how much good the biblical texts can do, how people's lives are improved, comforted, all of that. But at the end of the day it's all just words.'

'The Word of God, some would say.'

'Just words. And to me, words are at best only an approximation of the real thing. Perhaps less than that. Words are just a bunch of symbols that detach people from a real experience of the living world. The word "tree" is not a real tree, it's a symbol used by thought to represent a tree, and that's what most people live by. Most of us live our whole lives through symbols like that. Words are man's undoing. You might say that when man discovered language he lost touch with reality and fell from grace. Perhaps the Garden of Eden story is a metaphor for man detaching himself from God by inventing his system of words and language.'

'What about the Law? The Law of God is the Word, and we are commanded to live our lives by it.'

'Again, just words.' Granville chopped the air. 'And they're all relative. Look, times change, cultures change, language changes. How could we expect it all to have pristine relevance today? We do not belong to a politically oppressed, illiterate, Middle Eastern race of two thousand plus years ago, pure and simple.'

Steyn raised his eyebrows. 'Phew!'

'And so, when I stand up there and preach about holy Gospels, the Word of God, and this or that commandment, what I'm really doing is spreading a load of ignorance. I can't help thinking I'm making things worse for these poor people I'm supposed to be saving.'

'So, let's get this straight,' said Steyn. 'This so-called benediction of yours, this visitation of the Holy Spirit, this thing that is better than all words – is it leading you out of the priesthood? Is that what you're saying?'

'Shall I tell you what my daily work as a priest feels like?'

'Go on.'

'It feels like ploughing up and down the same field for ever, up and down, day after day, neatly, perfectly, using all the tried and tested techniques, but without planting any seed. It keeps me busy, gives me a sense of purpose, it's good practice, but it completely misses the point of the exercise.'

Steyn looked down at the table and nodded. 'I feel sorry for you,' he said.

Granville smiled. 'Thank you. I feel quite sorry for my-self.'

'Would you like some more tea?'

'No thanks.' He looked at his watch. 'It's good to have someone to talk to.'

Steyn got up to clear away the mugs. 'Any time.'

'I should be on my way. There's a Deanery Synod meeting at six. The Rural Dean will be there. We'll be discussing the inter-diocesan "Growing in Grace" conference, scheduled for June, and the elections for the Deanery's Standing and Pastoral Committees. Can't possibly be late for that. See what I mean?'

'Would you like a sandwich? I can make one quickly. A bit of sustenance to keep you afloat for the evening.'

'Very good of you, but no thanks. Edwina's putting something in the oven for when I get back. She wouldn't be at all amused if I'd already eaten.'

Chapter 14

Steyn arrived at Janet's house, as arranged, at eleven o'clock precisely. He was holding a large cardboard box in his arms. It was a beautiful sunny morning, unusually warm for the time of year, which was perfect for what they had in mind. Janet was beaming when she opened the door, and she wore a light floral dress with a ribbon in her hair. Nearly five weeks had passed since her husband's death and she said she wanted to get out a bit more.

'I've brought these for the boys,' said Piet as he entered the hall. He put the box on the ground and took out of it two cars made entirely out of wire. They were expertly crafted, with opening doors, suspension and interior seats. They came with a pair of steering devices on long rods, that hooked over the front axle and twisted it to the left and right. One car bore a miniature Mercedes Benz logo on its bonnet, the other a Volkswagen.

'My God,' said Janet, putting a hand to her mouth, 'they're just wonderful.'

'We all used to have these when we were boys,' said Piet, pushing one of the cars around the hall with its steering rod. 'My *klonkie* taught me how to make them.'

'Your what?'

'A kind of child houseboy who looks after a little white

kid all day, one to one. Something between an older brother and a servant. All the kids had a *klonkie* on the farm.'

'Were there a lot of children?'

'Plenty. Five or six families, all related in one way or another.'

'It must have been great fun for you all.'

'It had its ups and downs.'

'Thank you. The boys will be just thrilled. I hope it'll get them away from their computer games. They're out for the day, but they'll be coming back this evening.'

Steyn parked the cars together to one side. 'Are we ready?'

'I've packed a picnic in the car and organized the insurance. We can walk out right now.'

They took the south road out of Cheselbury Abbas, with Piet at the wheel of her large Toyota four-wheel-drive. 'The best off-road vehicle in the world,' Piet commented, 'and I've driven them all.' Janet replied that its qualities were wasted on her; it had been her husband's choice of car and she would soon be trading it in for something smaller and more economical.

'Bertie liked to drive off road, then?' asked Piet.

'Of course not,' she scoffed. 'He drove it up to London. Ridiculous waste of money.'

They were heading for Dorchester, and from there on the coastal road to Abbotsbury. Janet had mentioned to Piet the previous week that one of her favourite outings on a fine day was to the swannery at Abbotsbury, even though the cygnets would not be hatching for at least another month or two. Piet offered on the spot to take her there, and the date had been set. As they drove along, she made a point of thanking him for his kindness. Her little speech came across rather formally, as if she'd rehearsed it to convey the appropriate sentiment without giving the wrong impression. 'I don't know how I would have survived without you and Granville,' she concluded.

'He's been attentive, then, Father Granville?'

'Just wonderful. He does so much for so many people, it's quite extraordinary. You wouldn't believe what he's done for the community over the years, the stories are endless. Always there, always puts himself out. He's a very, very special guy.'

'I suppose it's all part of a day's work for someone in his position.'

'He does far more than he has to. All the ladies of the parish are desperately in love with him, of course. He is pretty dashing.'

Steyn smiled. 'The village Superman!'

'You could say that.'

'Do you think he's a good priest, though? In the strictest sense of the word?'

Janet's window was rolled down. She looked out of it at the passing landscape, eyes half closed, and the warm air rushed through her hair. 'I've never met a person who so completely embodies what I think a man of God is supposed to be like. He doesn't even have to say anything, he just brings the presence of something very special along with him, like a blessing. Yes, he's a good priest all right.'

'I'm glad he's been able to help you. You deserve all the support you can get.'

She turned back and looked at him, smiling. 'You're a good man, too,' she said, and narrowed her eyes in thought. 'You make me feel I should be a better Christian. And just being with you makes me feel as if I already am, in a strange way.'

'That's a beautiful thing to say. I think I'd better stop the car and make a proper speech to thank you, now.' They both laughed and she patted him lightly on the wrist.

Later, they walked along the paths at the sanctuary of Abbotsbury, where other species of wildfowl, besides nesting swans, had flown in to take refuge and feed on the barrowfuls of grain. The grass was speckled all over with feathers, as if a party of giants' children had just been let loose there to have a pillow fight. Down by the shore a wiggling mass of plump white shapes with craning, snake necks marked the area where the adult swans had assembled, half in, half out of the water. Visitors were allowed to meander around amongst them. Piet was about to comment on the unpleasant odour but noticed the rapture of Janet's expression and withheld the remark. Then, with no prior signal or falter, Janet stopped in her tracks and bowed her head. She raised a hand to her face, hunched her shoulders and began to cry without restraint. Piet went up and put an arm around her. He spoke quiet and comforting words but she did not respond. She just continued to weep, letting out deep, guttural cries, oblivious to the people who skirted nervously around her on the path. A few minutes later she dried her eyes, blew her nose and, without another word, resumed her stroll through the colony of swans.

Afterwards, they drove a couple of miles along a lane westwards, parked the car and spread out a blanket on the high ground above Abbotsbury. The grass had been cropped short by sheep and an ancient hilltop chapel behind protected them from the breeze. There was not a cloud in the sky, and beneath them stretched the long, narrow spit of shingle known as Chesil Beach. It curved distantly round to the right, giving a view of the waves crashing white against the pebbles, all the way to the defiant outcrop of Portland Bill. There they sat and had their little picnic of cocktail sausages and ham sandwiches followed by a fruit salad.

After they had finished eating, Piet lay back in the grass while Janet got the coffee. She poured it, hot and steaming, from an old tartan thermos that had once belonged to her mother and now had much sentimental value. They sat, sipping their hot drinks and Piet gazed at the view. It was Janet who broke the silence.

'Have you ever been married?' Piet did not immediately respond, but took another sip of his coffee and continued to look into the distance, as if he had not heard the question. 'I hope you don't mind my asking.'

Piet placed his cup between two tufts of grass beside him and brought his knees up beneath his forearms. 'Not at all,' he said quietly. 'No, I haven't been married.'

'Don't you ever get lonely?'

His grim set of face eased and he nodded. 'Sometimes, yes, I do.'

Janet tilted her head, amused and intrigued to find a chink in his armour. 'Have you deliberately avoided getting married?'

'It isn't as straightforward as that.'

'You're a bit of a dark horse, aren't you?'

'I don't mean to be. Maybe I'm just not the marrying kind.'

'I don't believe that,' she teased. 'A good wife would be the making of you. I'm surprised there haven't been women in your life.'

'Who says there haven't been women?'

'Aha. Now we're getting somewhere.'

Piet took a deep gulp of coffee, tutted, and lay back in the grass, smiling. 'You're being mischievous, Janet.'

'Just trying to find out a bit more about you.'

'Feel free,' he replied and closed his eyes. The sun was shining full on his face. 'I'm an open book.'

She thought for a moment and plucked a grass stem from the ground. 'I hope you don't think . . .' She stalled and frowned. Piet opened his eyes and turned towards her.

'Go on.'

'I'm probably going to make a fool of myself.'

Piet heaved himself up onto an elbow. 'What do you mean?'

'You're being so kind. To the boys and everything. The presents, the flowers, the visits to see how I am. I just hope—'

Piet sighed and shook his head. 'The last thing I want to do is cause you any upset. What's up?'

'I'm sorry. I just hope you don't think there's anything improper going on.'

'What do you mean?'

'Because it's so soon after – you know. I hope you, or anyone else for that matter, don't think—'

'*What?*'

'Some people might say it's a bit odd to be doing so much with a single man so soon after my husband's death.'

'Ah.'

'You don't think it might seem improper?'

'It's possible, I suppose. But anyone who thinks that would be wrong, of course.'

'And you . . . ?'

'Don't trouble yourself worrying about me. I just want to help.'

'I know you do. I shouldn't have said anything.'

'It's probably good to get it off your chest.'

'I don't know what I'd have done without you.'

'Just mention me in your prayers. That's all I ask. I don't need thanks.'

'But perhaps it might be better . . .' She was still frowning.

'Yes?'

'Perhaps we should have a bit of a pause before we do something like this again.'

'You're probably right.'

'I think it might be more . . . seemly.'

'I hadn't thought, but now you mention it.'

'Do you see what I mean?'

He nodded solemnly and drew down the corners of his mouth. 'Yes.'

'I'm not saying that I never want to—'

Piet put a stop to her awkward stumbling by raising his palm. 'It's OK. It's OK,' he said.

Tears had come to her eyes again. 'I think it's probably time to go now, don't you?'

Piet drained his cup and sprang into action. 'OK,' he said, slapping his palms together, and leant down to pick up the blanket. 'You stay put for a couple of minutes, and I'll pack up the car.'

When everything was ready, he held out an arm for her as she negotiated her way across the field's pronounced grass tufts back to where he had parked the vehicle. Her pink peep-toed sandals had quite high heels, but she didn't want to risk going barefoot because of all the sheep droppings. He held the door of the car open and waited for her to scoop up the hem of her dress from the sill before closing it gently. An added push snapped the door onto its catch plate and Janet put on a pair of large sunglasses.

She seemed suddenly overwhelmed by exhaustion

and they drove along in silence until Piet leant over to her and said, 'I believe all adversity has a positive side. This terrible time you're going through. You can't see it now, of course, but you will come through it a stronger, bigger person.'

'Who knows?' she replied sleepily. It was very warm now, and her window was wound all the way down.

'I hesitate to say it,' continued Piet, not seeing that beneath her sunglasses Janet's eyes were closed, 'but you might even find that a new chapter is beginning. The start of a better life.' He was looking at the road and she turned her face away drowsily. He stole a glance at her. 'I have had some terrible things happen in my time,' he said. 'I'll tell you about them one day. But each of them has left me a better man. Stronger in faith and stronger in purpose.' Janet did not respond but drifted into sleep. A large flock of seagulls on the bank beside the road took to the air as the car approached. They flapped lazily, dispersing in random directions.

All at once there was an explosion of bedlam within the car. Janet screamed and put her arms over her head. It was a bird. One of the seagulls had flown straight in through her window and struck her on the face. It seemed huge in the confined space and now flapped wildly at the glass of the rear window. Piet swerved the car quickly to the side of the road, mounted a bank and yelled for her to get out. He was already at her door by the time she stepped out and he quickly closed her window, then slammed the door behind her. She was crying hysterically. He put his hands on her shoulders and tried to see if she was all right, while the seagull, trapped in the car, continued to lash its wings and bump its head against the window. 'Let it out, let it out!' screamed Janet, but Piet was leaning down trying to calm her. She struggled free and masked her face with her hands. There was a heavy red scratch on her cheek.

'Are you hurt?' asked Piet, coming towards her again, but she turned away. Instead, he walked back to the car, where the seagull had stopped struggling, and perched itself on the back of a seat. It was defecating on the headrest like a dribbling tap. Piet looked in at the window and chose his moment to open the door. The seagull flapped but settled again, while Piet moved forward slowly, raising his arm. When he was within reach, he shot out his hand and grabbed the bird by the neck. He quickly pulled it from the car. It was flapping madly again but Piet secured its body under his arm. There was a snap as one of its wings, which was angled awkwardly, broke under the pressure. Its expressionless face did not register the pain but it tried to turn its head sideways to get a proper view of its assailant. Piet would have none of it, and, with his free hand, grabbed the bird's head and twisted it, compelling it to regard him face on, in the way of mammals, not birds. Its beak convulsed open, but Piet shook it angrily and brought its fierce, yellow-ringed eye close to his own. Janet watched aghast from some yards off, her hands cradled over her mouth and nose like a mask. She saw Piet slip his fist around the bird's throat and twist violently. The neck snapped, its head hung limp and its wings flapped for a few seconds more. Piet tossed the body into the field and it hit the ground with a thump. There were feathers everywhere. He turned back to Janet and she flinched from him as he approached, still crying into her hands.

'Sshh,' he said as he tried to ease her hand away from her cheek. 'Let's have a look at that. Oh, it's a nasty scratch. We'd better get some disinfectant on it. Why don't you sit down for a minute while I tidy up the car, and then I'll take you home.'

All the way back to Cheselbury Abbas she seemed trapped in a kind of private paralysis, unable to speak. When he pulled up outside her house, she managed to thank him quickly but then ran up the steps without looking back. He brought in the picnic basket and left it next to the sink in the kitchen, placing the car keys beside it. On his way out, he paused in the hall to look up the staircase, and scanned the landing to see if any of the doors were open. He waited for a few more minutes, first on the bottom stair, and then on a chair at the kitchen table, but when there was still no sign of her, nor any sound, he gave up and walked out of the house.

Chapter 15

Later the same evening, Steyn was seated in the small sitting room of the bunker and the tape recorder beside him was rolling. In the world above, beyond the concrete, the colour of the dusk sky was a glorious twilight blue. The stars were out, the hush tangible, the moon close on full. The air in the garden, though cool, carried a scent with the promise of summer nights ahead, and a brace of bats wove figures of eight at lightning speed in and around each other. Yet in the underground chamber the atmosphere was the same as it had been all week, all year. It would have been the same if it had been howling a storm above, or the ground buried three feet beneath snow. Down below, the temperature remained constant, and the silence, above the noise of the air circulation fan, was impenetrable. The only other sounds, when she was not speaking, were the warm hum of the tape machine, the slight whirr of its reels, and the rhythmic ticking of the mantelpiece clock – wheels within wheels, perfectly aligned and synchronized.

There were candles alight around the room. This was the third time Steyn had returned to talk to her about her involvement with the man called Ephraim. He wanted to know the smallest details, to probe every recollection, but as time passed his questions grew less frequent, while Rose's answers flowed more easily. She seemed less subdued than in previous interviews and her eyes were alive in a way they had not been for months.

She was dressed all in white, with white shoes and a broad white hairband just above her hairline. Her back-combed hair was large, perfectly set; and glossy white globes, the size of Christmas tree balls, dangled from her ears. She had been talking for half an hour, almost unprompted, and had just come to a stop. Steyn was sitting perfectly still in front of her and staring blankly at his pad.

'Are you falling asleep?' she asked, but he did not reply. She stood up from her chair, advanced towards him and knelt down in front of his knees to get a closer look at his face. 'Husband? Dear?' she asked softly.

'Yes.'

'You *are* awake!'

'Yes.'

She hesitated. 'Can I ask you a question?'

'If you have something to ask.'

'Why do you call me Rose?'

'You're getting bold.'

'Do you mind me asking?'

'You've never wanted to know before.'

'I have. I just haven't said so.'

'Don't you like the name?'

'I do. But I just wonder why.'

'All my ladies have been called Rose.'

'All your ladies?'

'Yes.'

'How many ladies?'

'I thought I was supposed to be asking that sort of question.'

'Were they wives, as well?'

'Only two of them. But neither lasted very long.'

'What happened to them?'

'You don't need to know.'

'You can trust me.'

'I'll tell you when you're ready.'

'Why Rose?'

'That is not your concern either,' he said. 'Are you trying to make some kind of point?'

'No.'

'You're supposed to be doing the answering, not the asking.'

'I'm ready to answer anything. I'm yours to do with as you please.'

He looked at her. Her eyes were shining. 'I think you might be enjoying this,' she said.

'What do you mean?'

'You know.' Now her face broke into a smile.

'What about you?' he asked. 'Do you enjoy telling me these things?'

She was beneath him, on the carpet, her face directly above his knees. 'Would you like me to enjoy it?' she asked.

'What if I were to say yes?'

'Then I would do as I was told,' she replied. 'I always do what you tell me.'

'I need to know everything. Tell me more.' His voice almost faltered.

'More what?' she asked. 'More about Ephraim?' He nodded. 'What particularly do you want to know?' She put a hand on each of his knees and inched forward between them.

Steyn looked away from her. 'Whatever you think I ought to know.'

She narrowed her eyes and almost whispered. 'Do you

think there might be things I haven't dared to tell you yet?'

'There's more,' he murmured. 'I know there's more.'

'Would you like to know how big he was?' she asked quietly. 'Don't you think you should know that? Shall I tell you?'

His answer was an eternity in coming. 'Yes.'

She slowly raised a hand. The dark red of her nails made her little fingers seem ghostly pale in the candle-light. 'You see this hand?' she said, and spread wide her fingers in front of him. He did not reply. 'Do you see this hand?' she asked again.

'Yes.'

She curled her fingers around slowly, forming a C-shape with her thumb and index finger. Her little finger hung delicately in the air behind. 'That's about as far as I could reach around him.' Steyn closed his eyes, and the notepad slipped to one side. Rose edged forward between his knees and remained there, her hand held out in front, the tips of her painted fingers not quite meeting. 'I got used to it.'

Steyn shuddered. He mouthed a word. 'Whore.'

'If that's what you like,' she whispered, and rested her elbows on his thighs. They looked at each other for a moment without moving.

'Off!' he said, abruptly pushing her away. 'That's enough.' She eased back from him and got up off the floor. Steyn went over to the tape recorder and switched it off. His hands were shaking. He remained there, facing away from her, without moving. It was only when he turned back that she saw there were tears on his cheeks.

She gasped, hands to mouth and eyes wide open.

He tried to shield his face from view. 'Are you

surprised?' he said but she did not answer. 'After all this time! After all the work we've done together!'

'But I thought . . .'

He groaned heavily and curled over to pull a creased up old handkerchief out of his tight jeans pocket. He looked suddenly old, thin and round-shouldered. He wiped his face impatiently with the handkerchief. 'Well, whatever you thought, you thought wrong. You thought wrong.' He stuffed the handkerchief roughly back into the trouser pocket with his thumb.

When he looked up again he noticed that Rose's attention was focused on the armchair where he had just been sitting. She instantly shifted her gaze back to him and there was fear in her eyes. He glanced at the armchair and saw that his large bunch of keys was resting there. They must have fallen out of his pocket while he was interrogating her. He looked back at Rose and she instinctively took a step away from him.

'What?' he asked. 'Do you want to make a dash for the keys?' She did not answer. 'Is that what's on your mind? Go on, then.' He held out his hand. 'Take them, if you want. What would you do next?' He grunted, walked up to the armchair, picked up the keys and tossed them at her feet. 'Is that all you've been thinking about these past months? Escape? Has it all been lies, everything you've been saying to me? Hmm?' She said nothing. 'Have a go. Be my guest. Let's see what happens.' She remained tense, unable to move, like a wound-up toy soldier with a snapped spring. 'Are you trying to make a fool of me?' he asked. She shook her head vigorously. 'You think I can't see what you're playing at?' She stared back at him. 'Haven't you learnt that I can see the secrets of people's hearts?' His eyes were set hard. 'Yah,' he said at last, coarsely, so that the word seemed to rake up the loose fluid in his throat. He all but spat at the ground in front of her. 'I suppose you thought all this whore talk would soften me up. Is that it? You thought you'd found a secret weapon.'

'No!'

'You think you can break me down with your filth and catch me off my guard.'

'Never.'

'Why, then?'

'You seemed to like it.'

'*Like it?*'

'And I thought it might bring us closer. I was wrong. I'm sorry, husband.'

'Don't call me that ever again!' he yelled and raised his fist at her. It quivered, taut, in the air between them, and she edged back towards the door. When she had got far enough to know she was safe from being struck, she turned and fled from the room.

Chapter 16

It was unusual to have a Parochial Church Council meeting in the morning, but as all the members were elderly housewives or retired men, Granville asked if they wouldn't mind on this one occasion. The councillors were not keen on change and two of them made their excuses with a whisper of outrage but the others agreed to the morning meeting, though their amenability was stretched by Granville's subsequent request that they begin it as early as nine-thirty. His reason – though he did not tell them this – was that he had to get away for an appointment. He had agreed to another meeting with Hetty.

Ever since discovering that her revised story had been true he had felt a compulsion to telephone her, to ease her mind and maybe also to apologize, which he thought she deserved. It was a curious blend of protectiveness and responsibility, with some other ingredient thrown in which he couldn't quite identify. But every time he went to pick up the telephone he found he could not go through with the call. Then, one evening, when he was giving pre-marriage instruction to a hopelessly young couple of the parish, he noticed the screen of his BlackBerry light up and saw her number glaring at him. There was no ringtone because he had earlier turned it off, but he felt his stomach lurch. After half a minute the message icon sprang up, and he accessed it when he reached the privacy of his car.

As soon as he started listening to the message, he leant back in his seat and closed his eyes. His fears had been misplaced. Everything had come right since their last meeting, she explained cheerfully, and she wanted to tell him face to face what had happened. He phoned her back straight away and she asked to meet him up at the Hardy Monument, outside Dorchester. 'But that's miles from Bournemouth,' he said. 'How on earth are you going to get there?' She replied that she had a car now and was going to drive there. 'I didn't know you could drive,' Granville was trying to say when she chirped that she had to go, and turned off the phone.

It was therefore in a rather distracted state of mind that Granville listened to the administrative items on the PCC's agenda that morning, the apologies for absence, the approval and signing off of the last meeting's minutes and the brief assessment of matters arising. Then came the usual sparsely worded summaries of parish events from the previous quarter, the reports about Mothering Sunday, the Lenten Prayer Group and the children's Shrove Tuesday pancake bonanza, for which Edwina St Clair was formally thanked by all present. A heated debate followed as to whether to buy a new wall-mounted heater for the church nave or attempt to replace the faulty element on the existing one.

'Why do we live in an age where everything has to be thrown away as soon as it stops working for the first time?' complained Gordon Saunders, a self-made industrialist who liked to act the part of a country gent now that he had retired.

'Simple answer to that,' said Andy Turstone, a

former electrician. 'By the time you've taken the old one down from right up there, taken it apart and put it back together again, it'll cost you more than a new one. And them old ones are about twenty years out of date anyway. They'll pack up soon enough and there's much better ones available that put out more heat for less power.' After a few more minutes' debate, one of the ladies complained that men could never decide anything without quarrelling and suggested that the last word go to the rector. This was not an unusual occurrence, and Granville, who had been listening from the sidelines, nodded tactfully before replying that he thought they'd better repair this one, but that if any others blew in the near future they should think about replacing the lot. The matter was thus settled to the satisfaction of some but not others, before they moved on to a proposal that torches be placed in strategic positions around the church in case of power cuts. It was a health and safety issue, the proposer declared firmly, and Granville felt his attention wandering. He checked his watch and glanced at the agenda on his printed sheet, trying to estimate if he would get away in time. There was still the one per cent rise in Church Commissioners' statutory fees to be discussed, along with a variety of other financial matters. Then there were the elections – for a new treasurer, a sub-committee, and an administrator for the Kershaw Bequest – which distributed a ten pound cheque once a year to a deserving member of the parish.

Finally, when all motions had been proposed, seconded and approved, the meeting was brought to a close and Granville jumped up from his chair. Apologizing for his rush, he hurried out of the church hall towards his car but was barely halfway there when he was stopped by a call from behind. It was Alan Burnside, an immensely built retired farmer, and he was waddling over to Granville as quickly as he could on his two bad hips. There was a matter on his mind that he wanted to speak plainly about, he said, out of breath. Granville glanced at his watch again. The trees around the church paddock, Alan said, 'them which border on my field, are up for preservation orders from the District Council.'

Granville said that it wasn't, strictly speaking, church business. 'You'd be better off complaining to the local authority.'

Alan would have none of it. 'A matter of boundaries is a matter for the owners of the land to decide, first and foremost. Boundaries is boundaries, as my father used to say.' Granville at last managed to quieten the old farmer and turned to leave, but had only gone a pace or two when something occurred to him. He turned back and called to Mr Burnside.

'Alan, your family's farmed here since forever, hasn't it?'

'Far as my grandfather's grandfather, I know for sure. Before that, you'll have to ask my sister. She knows more about the family history than me.' He held out an index finger. 'Father to son, we've all been born in the same house, me included, and my son, for six generations.' The words rolled off his tongue with an easy familiarity. 'But my grandson's gone and been born in Taunton hospital. Broke the chain, you might say.'

'Very impressive,' said Granville. 'Have you by any chance ever heard of a family called Newland who may have farmed around here?'

Alan's eyes fixed for a moment on the flagstones of the path in front of him. If he was a touch slower than he had been in his prime, he was still proud that he knew what he knew, and none could dispute it. 'No,' he said with finality. 'That's not a family I've heard of. There's none by that name who's farmed these parts in my lifetime.'

'Never mind,' said Granville, and pressed the unlock button on his car key fob.

'But . . .'

'Yes?'

'There's a *place* called Newland. A farm as was. Split up and sold on long ago, back in the sixties I should think it was.'

'Oh, really? Whereabouts?'

'Close by Petershot. Six-hundred-odd acres. Holsteins, mainly, and a bit of arable on the higher ground. Eggers bought most of it when the place split up.'

'Jim Eggers?'

Alan laughed. 'Lord, no. You're well wide of the mark there. It'd be Jim's grandfather's time. But it was the old man's younger brother, what was he called?' He gripped his chin before raising his eyes again, triumphant. 'Neville Eggers. That's who bought up Newland Farm. Neville Eggers.'

'You don't know who was selling it, do you? The people who lived at the farmhouse before?'

'I haven't got a clue,' Alan replied defiantly, as if his ignorance of this particular detail was only right and proper in the circumstances and it was almost an affront to suggest otherwise. 'You'll have to ask someone a bit more local to that area, I'm afraid. Or Jim Eggers. He's still got cousins over that way, though you never know with families, do you?' With this enigmatic comment on the gossamer fragility of blood ties, Alan Burnside took himself off to his car.

Granville was now significantly late and travelling along roads that could not be hurried. Anxious that

176

Hetty should not feel let down by him, he hammered out a text message to explain the delay. Looking up a fraction later, he had to swerve to avoid a ditch at the side of the road and tutted at his recklessness. Within seconds his message was returned: a row of crosses, a smiley face and an exclamation mark. He was held up further on behind a tractor that was clipping the hedge at the stately pace of a steamroller, and which he could only get past when the lane widened at a field gate.

The weather, which had been grey and dull when he left Cheselbury Abbas, had closed in and turned misty the further south-west he travelled. He imagined it must have something to do with the cooler air rolling in from the sea. When he was past Dorchester and away from the main road, his route took him up a narrow lane through a patch of bracken-clad moorland, and the gradient rose steeply. The cloud was low and swallowed up the rolling hills, which meant having to put on his headlights. He remembered that the Hardy Monument was up here at the end of this winding lane, but he could see no further than the tarmac three yards ahead and the windswept gorse banks either side. And then suddenly the verge gave way, sweeping in to the left, and he knew he had arrived. There was one other car parked there, just short of the rise of the ground, but the hill's summit, and the monstrous phallic announcement that was the monument itself, was shrouded by mist.

He could see her sitting in the driving seat, though she had not yet noticed him; her head was bent over her phone as she tapped frenetically at its pad. He knocked on the window and smiled. In a flash her phone was thrown aside. She got out of the car and flung her arms tightly around him. 'I'm so, so glad to see you,' she said.

'OK. OK,' he replied, allowing his chin to rest on her shoulder for a moment, as she swayed, enraptured, in his arms. He let go of her first. 'OK,' he said again, with a hint of finality. 'So. Look at you. You're like a different girl. What's happened?'

She smiled up at him and grasped his hand. 'Let's go up to the monument,' she said. 'I love this place.' She pulled him along by the hand up the gravelled path that led into an abyss of white fog. At one point a man and a woman wearing bicycle helmets and blue Lycra shorts appeared out of the mist walking the other way, and Granville felt acutely conscious of his hand in Hetty's grasp. He noted the cyclists' polite smiles as they passed, the woman glancing at his dog collar, and he wondered what kind of judgement they had made.

They could not see it until they were right up close, and by then they felt the breeze whipping in from the Dorset shoreline, three miles south-west. It towered over them, grey, masculine and monolithic, caught in design somewhere between a medieval tower and an early industrial chimney. One front of its octagonal base had been defaced with graffiti – exuberant bright pink mutant letters – and they walked around to the opposite side to shield themselves from the sight of it. 'Bertie sometimes brought me here for picnics,' said Hetty. 'Normally there are great views.'

'Not picnic weather today,' said Granville, and freed his hand from hers at last. Her fingers were white and knuckly, the nails chewed short like a schoolgirl's. She was wearing jeans and a thick woollen jumper, the baggy neck of which swallowed the lower half of her face. She opened her arms, spread wide her hands and laid them against the flat stonework of the monument; then she looked up towards the bolt-like protrusion of its pinnacle. The wind caught her hair and blew it around her face.

'You haven't told me what's happened to make you so happy,' said Granville.

'It's Bertie,' she replied and laid her cheek against the grey monument.

'Bertie?'

'Yes. He must have thought about it all before he did it.'

'Before the . . .'

'Before he hung himself.' The joy flickered out of her eyes for an instant but returned straight away. 'I got a phone call from a man. He asked me to go over to his office and said it would be good news. He turned out to be a solicitor. Bertie left everything in place. He'd put some money aside for me secretly, the man said. And now I don't need to move out of my flat and I can afford a car. Everything's changed. I've seen this job advertised in Bristol, at a beauty salon, and I'm going for an interview on Thursday.' She hopped up and down on the spot. 'I might move away from Bournemouth altogether.'

'That's wonderful,' said Granville, who was rapidly weighing up the pros and cons of the news. There were implications for Janet and her sons, of course, deprived of money that should have come to them; but on the other hand this would protect them once and for all from the devastation of learning the truth. He inwardly concluded that there was probably more than enough cash in the pot to keep everyone safe and happy. 'I'm delighted for you.'

'I'm delighted for myself,' she yelped, flinging her arms in the air and scrunching her nose like an infant. Her buoyancy was almost too extreme, Granville thought. For all the change of circumstances, this effervescent child did not square up with the desolate tragedienne he had left on the pavement of that run-down Bournemouth cul-de-sac a fortnight before. They walked over to a crescent-shaped stone bench close by that normally would have served visitors admiring the view, and sat on it side by side. The greyness around them was drifting past. It lifted in patches and thinned in others, variegating according to the strength of the breeze. He tried to talk to her about the practical issues of her new life, where she would live if she moved to Bristol, how much she would need to earn on top of the income she received from Bertie Gosling's Trust if she wanted to remain independent of her family. He wanted above all to convince himself that there was now a platform on which to lay to rest his anxieties about Hetty and the morning of Bertie's death; but he struggled to pin her down on specifics and rarely got sensible answers to his questions. She seemed more interested in his welfare than her own. At one point she raised a hand and rubbed her fingertips against his forehead to ease the frown ingrained there.

'Why do you worry so much?' she asked. 'You look as though you've forgotten how to relax.' She smiled at him with a sudden and immense warmth. It was as if her youth had been suspended and replaced by a latent sea of maternal tenderness.

'You're right,' he said, and looked out at the fog. 'I mustn't let everything get to me so much.' For a brief moment he felt deliciously abandoned.

'Are you in love with your wife?' she asked out of the blue.

He did not look at her but kept his eyes fixed on the imaginary vistas beyond the mist. 'What sort of a question is that?'

'Just a question.'

'Of course I am.'

'Because you're so used to saying you are, or because you're really in love with her?'

'Being married for years is different from having a crush on a boyfriend, you know.'

'OK, then,' she went on. 'Are you only properly happy when you're with her? Does she light up your life when she comes into the room?'

'Of course.'

'Liar.'

'Hetty, this isn't helpful. What are you hoping to achieve by trying to make out my marriage is in trouble?'

'I just want to know if you love each other.'

'Well, we do.'

'You don't look very sure.'

'Look, when you've been together for a long time there are lots of layers to your love. You don't necessarily kiss all day long or go around holding hands, but it doesn't mean that your love is any the less for it. In lots of ways it's much greater.'

'Does she understand you like no-one else does? When you look into each other's eyes is it like the rest of the world's out there, but you two are here, joined?'

'We stopped gazing into each other's eyes years ago.'

'That's what I thought.'

Granville winced and shook his head. 'I'm being ridiculous even listening to you. You couldn't possibly understand. Edwina and I have been through so much together.'

'But do you want her all the time? Does it hurt to be apart?'

Granville sighed, exasperated. 'No it doesn't. Happy now?'

'I just don't think you love her.'

'Well, you just don't know.' He was quite angry now and turned to face her. The mist was moving in the breeze. A patch of it thinned to allow a flash of brilliant sunshine through before the pale cloud consumed it again.

'She's very beautiful,' said Hetty. 'More beautiful than me.'

'You . . . what? . . . why on earth are you making a comparison?'

She giggled and shrugged her shoulders. 'I've started going to church. Because of you. You make me feel like I want to be a better person. I thought you'd be pleased with me.'

Granville sighed. 'Hetty, Hetty,' he said and shook his head. 'You don't have to do things to please me. I am not a player in your life.'

'Come on,' she said, and nudged him in the ribs. 'Don't spoil things. I'm so happy today.'

He smiled at her. 'And I'm glad about that. Really.'

Without warning, she turned and put her arms around his neck. He was facing her and she pulled him against her face and planted her lips on his. She held him there; for a moment they were locked together, and their tongues touched, before he pulled himself away. He looked at the ground. 'Hetty, you can't do that sort of thing.'

She was smiling broadly and swaying victoriously on the stone bench, hands clutched together between her knees. 'Why not? No-one can see us. It's fun.'

'It's not . . . Listen,' he said, and took hold of one of her hands. 'I don't want you to get hurt any more. I can see exactly what you're trying to do, but it's not going to happen.'

'I just love being with you. That's all right, isn't it? It's like you're a bright light in the dark.'

'You need a father, not an older lover.'

'You can be my father, then.' She leant towards him again, and before he could pull away had placed another quick kiss on his lips. 'Hello, Daddy.' He quickly drew breath to scold her on impulse, but stalled as he looked into her seemingly innocent, carefree eyes. He tutted instead. There was nothing malign or calculating in her expression and he could no more quash her joy than deliberately tread on a kitten.

'Come on,' he said, 'no more of that,' and he got up from the bench. 'It's time to go.'

Hetty walked beside him to the car park, smiling all the way but not saying anything, and seemed perfectly content with what he had to say when they parted. 'I don't want to be unkind, but these sorts of meetings can't go on.' She nodded obediently, still smiling. 'It's not going to help you and it certainly won't help me.' She nodded again. 'Are we clear, then? I don't want to hear from you unless there's an absolute emergency. And then you should try everyone else before you come to me. Understand?' A third happy nod. He knew she was taking no notice.

She said goodbye too quickly. There was no sense of a final parting, more a kind of expectation on her part that they would be meeting again soon; and then again, and probably regularly thereafter. She had convinced herself, and there was nothing he could do about it. His reproaches scattered away like invisible spores in the mist breeze.

*

It did not seem as if he had been back at his desk long before he heard the crash of the front door and chattering voices tumbling into the hall, which announced the girls' return from school. Seconds later his study door burst open. It was his elder daughter, Serena, recently turned thirteen; and simultaneous with that milestone she seemed suddenly, mysteriously, elevated to a new, higher platform of sagacity. It unnerved him, partly because he recognized himself in her, but also because he was suddenly running out of places to hide. Even now she looked at him and he felt transparent. Until so recently she would have bounded up at a moment like this, happily ignorant of his inner world, and flung her arms around his neck; but now she stood still in the door frame and smiled at him, enjoying and exploring the silent eye contact with an almost conspiratorial glint in her look. She seemed too mature to be in a school uniform.

'Hello, Daddy,' she said and planted a kiss on his cheek. It was the second time that afternoon he had been addressed with those words.

'Hello, darling,' he replied, and hugged her with one arm; but he felt less comfortable than usual. She sensed it and eased back away from him, her smile clouding.

'Has something bad happened?'

'No, darling,' he replied, 'nothing bad at all. You go and change and I'll be along in a moment.'

Chapter 17

Serena nowadays liked to draw attention to the difference in age and maturity between herself and her younger sister; yet it seemed so recent to Granville that his two girls had been an indivisible twosome. They had been content to share bedtime stories, choices of films and rainy afternoon board games; they had exchanged dolls, clothes and trinkets, and frequently huddled themselves away in an alliance that was not always quaintly harmless. But a line of sorts had been drawn between them a few months ago, a boundary crossed, and whereas Amelia remained unchanged, Serena now aspired to pair herself with her mother rather than sister whenever possible. The divide was never clearer than when Granville and Edwina were preparing their home for the arrival of guests.

Serena took great care with her clothes and make-up this evening, even though she knew that she would only be around for the first part of the dinner, handing around canapés and filling glasses. Amelia, by contrast, got into her nightie and dressing gown early and came downstairs with her hair still damp and smelling of soap. She shared a sense of occasion, but dashed around, charging up and down the stairs, in a last-minute splash of excitement before the announcement of bedtime. Serena, meanwhile, moved smoothly from kitchen to dining room, chin raised, dishes of food balanced in each hand, wearing a tiny skirt and diamanté hair clips, every inch a budding ice cool hostess.

It was easy for Granville to see why the girls would want to imitate their mother. Edwina was glamorous, capable and sophisticated all at the same time. Her authority in the kitchen was watertight, her clarity of purpose beyond contradiction. He could not help standing back and watching her: the attention to detail and orderly control of procedure, all accomplished with such calm grace. She hurriedly stirred the sauces, drained colanders, breathed in the steam from simmering pans, and squatted low to check the meat in the oven, yet her clothing and make-up remained immaculate. With age she had mastered the craft of how to get the best out of her looks and at times like this he found her compellingly sexy. Her eyeliner was unusually pronounced this evening, a deliberate retro touch, like an actress from an old Fellini film, which he wasn't used to but thoroughly approved. He went up to her at one point and put an arm around her waist. Her concentration was momentarily broken and she smiled at him, going on tiptoe to kiss him quickly on the lips, a soft kiss with a hint of warm breath behind it, the sort that promised greater expression later. He was relieved that they seemed to have stumbled into a truce. It would make for a more relaxed evening.

Piet Steyn arrived on the dot of eight o'clock, the time that Granville had given rather vaguely when he'd issued the dinner invitation a few days before. He was wearing a dark blue double-breasted jacket dating from the eighties, wide shouldered and narrow at the hips; the trousers were from the same era, voluminous and turned up at the bottom. His hair was neatly brushed and parted, something Granville had never seen on him before, and he carried a small gift wrapped in festive paper.

'Come in, come in,' said Granville, ushering Piet through to the sitting room, where he introduced him to his daughters. Edwina then came in, all smiles, hand extended. They had met once or twice, she confirmed, adroitly ironing out any awkwardness, but never properly until now.

'The pleasure is all mine, I assure you,' replied Piet, shaking hands with a slight bow of the head.

Granville had so far not told Edwina about the peculiar contents of the room next to Piet's kitchen. He hadn't wanted to darken his wife's opinion about the South African further than necessary in the run-up to the dinner. The days when he and Edwina had shared every snip of intrigue, come what might, now seemed distant because he knew what she could be like, how she could receive fragments of news with apparent uninterest only to archive them for later strategic use, most often to fortify her stance on some issue. Right now he did not want her to start compiling a secret file against Steyn before giving him the chance to prove what a decent fellow he was.

Edwina excused herself from the sitting room and disappeared back to the kitchen. Granville offered a drink and Piet asked for fruit juice, which Serena went off to fix. Amelia was by now crouching behind the sofa, teasingly popping up her head over the back at regular intervals. Piet engaged her.

'Hello, little lady,' he said. She ducked down out of view again. 'You want to be careful,' he went on, though he couldn't see her. 'If you come up for too long a sniper might take a potshot.' She darted up again, all smiles, and Piet mimed the raising of a rifle, but she was down again, with a giggle. When she next came up, Piet had stepped quietly to one side and got a clear shot without her expecting. 'Bang!' he said, and she fell back once more. She kept on jumping up but by now Piet had turned his attention to Serena, who was handing him a tumbler of orange juice. 'My, what a beauty. You're a lucky man, Father,' he said to Granville, 'to have such a lovely family.'

'I am indeed.'

Still unsmiling, Serena held out a plate of minute and exquisitely prepared canapés, but her cool poise was broken when Amelia, jumping up from behind the sofa, caught her eye and made her grin at some shared secret. The platter she was holding wobbled in her hand but she quickly recovered.

'Is Janet not yet here, then?' asked Piet.

'Sadly, she can't make it,' replied Granville. 'Something's come up.'

'What a pity.'

'Another time.'

'Yes, yes.'

'I don't think we need to worry about her. She seems to be doing all right, thank God.'

'Yes. Thank God, indeed.'

A commotion in the kitchen announced the arrival of their other guests, Martin and Oonagh Benson, at the wrong door. Martin Benson, who cared nothing for what people thought of him, nor for the trail of consternation his provocative manners left in their wake, made a point of ignoring the front door, preferring to come straight into the kitchen from the garden. It was the privilege of a good friend, he announced, and a sign of intimacy; but it was also obvious he relished the opportunity of catching his hosts with their guard down. His wife, Oonagh, whose quiet intelligence counterbalanced the weight of her husband's bombastic ways, gave Edwina a hug and a long-suffering smile.

'So this is it!' Martin bellowed from the kitchen doorstep, holding out an arm towards the blackness of the garden. 'The great work of art! Am I supposed to be impressed?'

'Wait there! Don't move,' called Granville who had now come into the kitchen. He planted a kiss on Oonagh's cheek and introduced Steyn to them both. 'Back out into the garden, all of you. Come on, Piet. You too.' He flicked a switch on the kitchen wall and the garden was suddenly illuminated by floodlights.

'Well, well,' said Martin, sinking his hands deep into the pockets of his corduroy jacket. 'Building blocks for trolls, how very interesting. Any chance of a drink?' He pulled out and lit a rolled-up cigarette.

'Serena will be out with one in a minute. Come on. Seriously, though, what do you think?' Edwina remained in the kitchen while the four of them stood in a semicircle around Granville's statue. It was Martin who spoke first.

'What is it?'

'It's a polished granite cube with a polished granite sphere on top of it. Both the same width, both the same height, but otherwise opposites in almost every way imaginable. Perfection opposed.'

There was another silence, during which Serena glided across the grass with a tray of champagne in her hands. 'It's extraordinary,' said Oonagh, staring up at the colossal object. 'Each part of it must have weighed a ton.'

'About three ton apiece, actually.'

'How did you manage to get it up?' she asked, and her husband grunted a laugh.

189

'Don't ask.'

Oonagh went on, 'It's so precise. Where the two surfaces meet. It doesn't look like more than a square inch, how's that possible? All that weight on such a small spot. Won't it just . . . roll off?' Her accent still had a trace of Irish in it, even though she'd left her County Wicklow home many years before. She'd been barely eighteen back in the mid-seventies when she'd joined her maverick boyfriend, Martin Benson, on his global travels, a move thoroughly disapproved by her Catholic artisan father.

'That's the whole point,' said Granville. 'Theoretically, of course, the two parts shouldn't meet, like Zeno's famous paradox. But then, paradox is at the heart of the whole thing.'

'But what is it?' asked Martin again, drinking deep of his first glassful. His stomach protruded over the belt of his blue denim jeans and he wore his almost grey hair quite long, combed back, Tarzan style, over his collar.

'It's whatever you want it to be,' replied Granville.

'Oh, come on,' said Martin, with disgust, 'OK, what do *you* want it to be?'

'A monument to the divine aspirations of humanity.'

'A what?' said Martin.

'The meeting point of reason with the immeasurable. Look – ' he said, gesturing from the lower to the upper section: 'matter, trapped in thought and time, encounters a dynamic energy that's in perpetual variation. It's what Christ was all about.' At this, Steyn raised his chin and took a sip of juice.

'How can Jesus have anything to do with this?' asked Oonagh.

Granville looked at her with an expression of innocent

joy. 'It illustrates the meeting of mortal flesh with the divine. Immanuel. God with us.'

'Oh Lord,' muttered Martin and drained his glass.

'That's just beautiful,' said Oonagh.

'I'm glad you think so. Edwina doesn't get it at all.'

'I'm off to join her, then,' said Martin, stubbing out the remains of his cigarette underfoot and heading to the kitchen door.

'What do you think, Piet?' asked Granville.

Steyn's face hardened in thought. 'As a symbol of faith, I prefer the cross,' he said.

'Of course,' replied Granville. 'This is no substitute for—'

'No, no, you don't need to apologize. I just see the cross as the unparalleled illustration of the union you speak of. The upward shaft of the cross is man's eternal aspiration to the divine, while the horizontal piece shows the descent of God to mankind. Where they meet, at the heart of the cross, we have a symbol of Christ Jesus, God made flesh.'

'I like that, too,' said Oonagh.

'I think if I had a giant crucifix in the garden,' Granville said, ushering them back to the house, 'the neighbours really would be up in arms.' Oonagh laughed at the remark and pulled her ample shawl around her shoulders with her free hand. Piet followed them into the kitchen.

'You know, Father,' he said to Granville from behind, 'if you like, I'd be happy to do a bit of gardening for you. Help you tidy the place up a bit.'

'You noticed, then?' said Granville, amused again by Steyn's tactlessness.

'I don't mean to be rude.'

'Of course not, and thank you. I suppose it is a bit messy, but I kind of like it, in a funny way.'

'You like the disorder?'

'I wouldn't describe it as disorder, exactly. More as . . . a miniature wilderness.'

'Same thing. I'd be happy to help. For no charge, of course.'

As they entered the kitchen, Martin was standing beside Edwina at the cooker with his hand resting on her rump. He let it drop as he turned to greet them. 'Aha. Back from the philosopher's stones.'

'Time to eat,' Edwina cut in and moved briskly away from him to check the oven.

When they were seated, the girls came in to say goodnight. Amelia was drawn to Piet because of their earlier sofa game, but was too shy to manage anything more than the barest squeak as she said goodnight. 'Do I deserve a kiss, little lady?' he asked but got no reply, and so took her hand and raised it to his lips in the manner of a Prussian *Graf*. Amelia retreated into smiles and pulled her hand away. Serena formally kissed each guest on both cheeks and disappeared to the sitting room to watch television.

Granville made a point of saying grace before the meal, something which the others had never known him do in the past, but realizing it was being performed for Steyn's benefit they made no comment.

As the food was being dished onto Martin Benson's plate, he regarded Steyn properly for the first time and addressed him.

'I must say, you look very smart, my friend. '

'I'm sorry if I'm overdressed,' replied Piet. 'I thought that's how things were done in England.'

'Don't apologize. You just put us all to shame.'

Piet eyed him. 'Are you local to these parts?'

'God, I hope not,' came back Martin.

'Don't listen to him,' said Granville to Piet. 'He's lived in Shaftesbury for more than fifteen years. He just doesn't like the idea of being branded a settled English gentleman. Prefers to think of himself as a citizen of the world. A bit of a Lord Byron.'

'In his dreams,' said Oonagh.

'You don't like Dorset, then?' Piet asked Martin, who was chewing ferociously while stacking his fork as if the food might escape if he didn't pin it down quickly.

'Awful bloody place. Filthy people.'

Granville interrupted on his friend's behalf again. 'You wouldn't believe, Piet, looking at this rotund specimen of declining manhood,' he held out his hand elegantly towards Martin, 'you wouldn't believe that this was once a dynamic investigator of some of the world's more remote corners. And not bad looking, rumour has it. Our very own Indiana Jones once upon a time.'

'Rumour has it my arse,' spluttered Martin.

'Some kind of explorer?' asked Piet.

Martin shrugged. 'Anthropologist, some people like to call it.'

Edwina explained, 'Martin and Granville first met by accident when they were travelling in Nepal about a century ago.'

Granville nodded towards Martin. 'He was slouching around pretending to write a paper about – what was it? – Sherpa marriage customs, or something. Never finished that one either, did you, Mart?'

Martin Benson pointed his knife across the table. 'And *he* was walking shoeless across a holy mountain observing a year's vow of silence. Fat lot of use to man or beast.'

'It was only three months, not a year.'

'Same idea. You were pretty hardcore then. When people met you, they thought you were some kind of prophet. Big beard, all the right answers, wisdom, permanent smile on your face, and too bloody handsome to boot. No wonder everyone fell for you.'

'You included,' said Oonagh.

'Don't start that again. I'm just saying: for a young man, Granville St Clair made big waves wherever his shadow passed, so don't tell me off for going to seed. Look at you now! Mister Compromise in his safe little parish, dishing out tea to old ladies.' The two women were used to this kind of banter between their husbands and seemed to enjoy it.

'Do be quiet, Martin,' said Edwina. 'You're sounding just like Granville's father.'

'That's why I like him,' said Granville. 'Let him be.'

'And it's exactly why I can't stand him,' Edwina said, and they laughed.

Steyn turned to Granville. 'Is your father a pastor as well?' The others now suppressed their chortles.

'No,' Granville replied. 'I don't think my father's set foot in a church since his parents dragged him kicking and screaming to the font as a baby. Not quite true. He did deign to put in an appearance at my ordination.'

'I'm sorry,' said Steyn. 'In my country you often find sons following their fathers into the Church. Like a sort of family business.'

'Quite right too,' said Martin. 'It used to be a bit like that over here, but nowadays priestcraft is not considered a normal occupation. You've got to be *called*, or some such rubbish. This lamb's bloody good, Eds.' He winked at her before looking back at the fast-diminishing portion on his plate.

'I haven't eaten as well as this in years,' said Steyn, and nodded appreciatively at Edwina. 'You are a wonderful cook and hostess.'

'But you've had such a small helping,' replied Edwina. 'Wouldn't you like some more?'

'No, thanks. My appetite seems to have shrunk in the past year or so. Probably age.'

'Wish that would happen to me,' said Martin.

Steyn turned to Granville. 'I bet when you were trudging without shoes across the Himalayas, Father, you never dreamt you'd end up in a comfortable home like this, with a glamorous wife and two such beautiful daughters.'

'I did have shoes. Don't listen to Martin. He exaggerates everything.'

'Did you keep to your vow of silence?' said Steyn.

Granville nodded, finishing his mouthful. 'Not a word until I got to Lhasa three months later. Then I ordered tea from a wrinkly old man at a *chai* stall and a wonderful chapter in my life suddenly vanished as if it had never happened.'

'And which God – if you don't mind me asking,' said Piet, 'did you observe your vow of silence for?'

'Good question,' said Martin Benson, chomping. 'Which of your spiritual supermarket trolleys were you pushing around at that particular time?' He mimed a shopper in front of a store's shelves. 'I'll have a bit of this, a bit of that, please, and, oh, what's this? Transubstantiation? Sounds tasty. Bit of that, too.'

Granville took the jibe in good spirit but his smile was slightly forced. 'I've only ever had one God, Piet,' he replied. 'Same as you. Please don't think otherwise.'

'I don't mean any offence,' said Steyn.

'None taken, needless to say.'

'Tell me about you, though?' Oonagh asked Piet, leaning in towards him as she spoke. She had hoped to divide away from the general chat, but in the event the others all listened in. 'Granville says you're a man of strong faith. How do you practise your religion?'

'Are you really interested?' Steyn asked.

'For sure.'

'That's very kind of you.'

'Well?'

Piet thought for a moment. 'I observe a disciplined and orderly life. I constrain my personal desires and subject my choices to continual scrutiny.'

'That sounds a bit punishing,' Oonagh said gently.

'You are right,' he replied. 'But I rejoice in that kind of punishment. It casts light upon my path.'

'Monkish, I'd say,' said Martin.

Granville was intrigued and leant forward, elbows on the table.

'Is it all about denial, about suppression?' he asked.

'The self, with its desires and wickedness, has to be suppressed, yes.'

'But is there no place for freedom in your philosophy? Or for laughter and rejoicing?'

'I understand that you might think me a little bit old-fashioned, Father. I apologize for my clumsy way of expressing myself.'

'Don't be silly. If that's your way, you're more than entitled to it. What's fascinating, though,' he continued, enlivened by a line of thought and pausing mid-sentence to take a sip of wine, 'is that you and I are sitting here, opposite one another, both devout Christians but with completely contradictory views about how to express our faith.'

'Well that's that sorted, then,' said Martin. 'Anyone else for seconds?'

Granville ignored him and went on, 'You believe in constraint and regulation, while I think the core of a spiritual life is liberation, a release from constraints, dissolving and letting go of divisive things like opinions. Only that way can people be free of their selfish nature.'

'There speaks the old Buddhist again,' muttered Martin to Edwina beside him, before speaking out more generally and waving his wine glass in the air before him. 'What is all this bunk about suppressing the self, anyway?'

'Martin, do be quiet,' scolded Oonagh.

'Take no notice,' Edwina said to Steyn. 'He loves to be the devil's advocate.'

'It's by negating the self, the individual,' explained Granville, 'that we free ourselves from the temporal and ascend to the divine.'

'I agree with that,' said Steyn.

'How can you both talk such crap?' scowled Martin. 'The self is magnificent. The human condition is all about the marvel of individuality. Isn't it supposed to be God's great miracle that each of us is made unique? Isn't that why he gave everyone a different fingerprint, for heaven's sake?' Bolstered by his own logic, he began to sound almost angry. 'And doesn't history, culture, everything about us glorify self-determination? We lionize individuality! Look at you!' he gestured towards Piet. 'You've chosen an independent, self-determined life.'

'That's different.'

'Why is it? You guys with your high and mighty theories about negating the self! Open your eyes to the world around you, for God's sake.'

'High and mighty theories are what I'm continually fighting *against*,' said Granville.

'In which case you're a hypocrite,' concluded Martin and drank half a large glass of red wine in one shot.

'Are you an atheist?' Steyn asked Martin.

'I tell you,' interrupted Edwina, looking at Oonagh but pointing at Martin, 'I think he's deliberately trying to be Granville's father now. As if we need another!'

'Nonsense,' said Granville. 'My father never talks theology with me the way this airhead does. Dad is frightened that I know his evangelical atheism is just a rabbit's blink away from religious zeal. Turn the lens a notch and my father would be up at the Communion rail faster than a cardinal's choirboy.'

'Do you really believe that?' asked Edwina, standing up to collect the dishes.

'Of course. He's as churned up about the question of God and what happens next as the best of us.'

'Or maybe he just swings whichever way his polar magnet decides to take him next,' said Edwina.

'I didn't know your father was bipolar,' Oonagh said to Granville.

'He's not,' replied Granville.

Edwina flashed back, 'Yes, well, you're not exactly on the ball when it comes to recognizing strange things going on inside people's heads, are you?' She filled her own wine glass to the brim, Granville looked down again and Oonagh thought better than to pursue the subject further.

Martin Benson was the next to speak. He turned to Piet. 'Tell us about the new South Africa, though,' he said, stacking somebody else's empty plate onto his own – a token gesture because his wife and Edwina were already on their feet, doing the clearing proper. 'Do you approve of the coloured man's rise to supremacy?' Oonagh exchanged a look with Edwina and rolled her eyes.

Piet replied pensively, 'Let's just say that we can all see

now that the whites got a lot of things wrong in the past.'

'Good for you,' said Granville. 'Now what about pudding for anyone?'

'But are you happy with the new state of affairs?' insisted Benson. 'Can you sit beside your black fellow countrymen in church, sing hymns with them, embrace them as your political, biological and spiritual brethren?'

'OK, Mart,' said Granville, 'rein it in a bit.'

'I'm interested,' said Martin.

'That's all right, Father,' said Steyn, patting the air with his hand. 'I can answer Mr Benson.' Oonagh and Edwina slipped away to the kitchen carrying the stacked plates and dishes, and Granville followed them out. He closed the kitchen door quietly behind him. 'I hope he can cope with Martin all on his own,' said Edwina and lowered her stack of china into the sink.

'I think he's charming,' said Oonagh. 'Such good manners. And quite sexy in a funny sort of way.'

'He walks like a tramp,' said Edwina.

'Oh, come on,' said Oonagh. 'You can't fault him. Not on the way he's been this evening.'

'I suppose not,' said Edwina.

'So you take back all the negative stuff you've been saying?' said Granville, placing the dirty plates in the dishwasher.

'What stuff?' asked Oonagh. 'He's a sweetie. What could you possibly have against him?'

'He's just a bit of a misfit with the locals,' answered Granville, 'and there've been the most stupid rumours spread around. It's like ducking the witch in the village pond! I sometimes feel we're back in the Dark Ages.'

'Someone crucified a badger to his door,' said Edwina.

'Serious?' said Oonagh. 'What sort of person would do that?'

'Things have settled down a bit since then,' said Granville.

Edwina looked over her shoulder as she rinsed a serving dish at the sink and smiled at Oonagh. 'Granville's decided to be his saviour.'

'Hardly,' said Granville. 'Just trying to integrate him a bit, introduce him to a few people, so they'll stop thinking he's some kind of bogeyman. It's working. He told me so.'

'That's not really a good enough reason to have him to dinner,' said Edwina.

'Why not? The good Samaritan didn't look the other way. We've got a parable unfolding before our eyes.'

Edwina looked at Oonagh again. 'See what I mean? The saviour speaks.'

'I agree with Granville,' Oonagh said. 'Give the man a chance.'

'I still think there's something a bit creepy about him.'

'He's a solid guy,' said Granville. 'I'll stand by him.'

Edwina looked tired. 'You always make out you see the best in people,' she sighed.

'Isn't that a good thing?' asked Oonagh.

'It's naive.'

'Give me naivety any day,' Oonagh said resignedly, picking up the clean pudding plates. 'It's better than cynicism twenty-four seven. Your new friend's just fine. The strong, reliable sort. Admit you find him a little bit attractive.'

Edwina smiled and took the pudding from the fridge. 'I can see what you mean. In a rugged sort of way.' Granville gave her a puzzled look and they all three went back to the dining room, with the pudding on a large platter.

Piet was getting to his feet. 'Can I excuse myself?' he asked as they came in. 'I need to visit the boys' room.'

'Of course,' said Granville and directed him to the lavatory on the other side of the hall. They could hear him struggling for a while with the key in the lock until Granville called out that none of the locks in their house worked properly. This seemed to amuse Martin.

'So,' he said, 'we've had it all out and put the world to rights.'

'Sshh,' replied Granville, 'keep your voice down. You'd better not have offended him.'

Edwina gave Martin a conspiratorial smile. 'I told you he was sensitive about his new best friend.'

'Of course I didn't offend him. We agreed about pretty much everything, as it happens. Splendid fellow. He told me how his folk consider the blacks to be the descendants of Ham, youngest son of Noah. The story has it that good old Captain Noah got drunk one day, fell over and slept off his hangover starkers. The unfortunate Ham stumbled on his old man asleep in the buff and for no better reason than that, had his descendants given the black mark and cursed into slavery for all eternity. Hence we have black people.'

'Are you being serious?' asked Oonagh.

'Absolutely; and not a bad theory, I think.'

'Finished yet?' said Granville.

'No. The other notion is that blacks may be descended from Cain, therefore marked and cursed by God for slaying brother Abel. Unfortunate bunch of ancestors, all in all, I'd say.'

'Will you stop taking the mick, just for one second?' whispered Granville.

'People in the modern world can't think things like that,' said Oonagh.

'I'm just telling you what he said,' said Martin, all innocence.

'I'm sure he doesn't believe such tosh. Did he say he did?'

'Not quite,' replied Martin.

'There you are, then.'

'But he explained it in a way that left me thinking he was not – how shall I say? – entirely unconvinced by the hypothesis.'

'You were egging him on, willing him to put his foot in it,' said Oonagh in a half-voice, 'the way you always do.'

'Listening to the way you all talk about me,' said Martin, 'anyone would think I had a wicked streak.'

'Wicked's not the word,' commented Oonagh. 'You're positively deviant.'

'In my book,' said Martin, 'deviant means some sort of pervert.'

'That too,' said Oonagh. 'You and your peculiar penchants.'

Granville looked from Oonagh to Martin, and then glanced towards Edwina but she did not look up. At that moment they heard the lavatory flush in the distance and Edwina stood up to serve out the tiramisu. Steyn came back to the table.

Granville quickly filled the silence. 'I was telling Martin and Oonagh that your mother came from Dorset,' he said to Piet.

'Did she emigrate to South Africa?' asked Oonagh.

'She met my father when she was a nurse in the war.'

'Very romantic,' said Oonagh, and raised a hand to Edwina to refuse a pudding.

'Talking about the war, I hope you're going to come to the lecture in the village hall next month,' Granville said to Steyn. 'Part of the Battle of Britain commemorations. A historian from Bristol University is coming down. Did you know, Britain was only a week away from folding in 1940? But then Hitler ordered the Luftwaffe to stop bombing the airfields and concentrate on the cities instead. The runways that weren't full of craters were able to carry on sending up Spitfires to fight back, and we clawed back from then on. Our airfield in this village was one of the survivors, although apparently Goering had it in his sights to obliterate it just before the German change of plan. Quite a little piece of history, here on our doorstep. I hope you'll come to the talk.'

'For sure,' said Steyn.

'There'll be quite a few people from the church there.'

'I'll look forward to it. Maybe drag Janet along.' Edwina darted a look at Granville.

'Actually, she's helping to organize it. The whole thing was Bertie's brainchild. He was quite an RAF enthusiast. Hasn't she mentioned it to you?'

'No.'

The telephone began to ring. Edwina had just finished doling out the pudding and was still on her feet, so she went next door to answer it. She was back quickly.

'It's for you,' she said to Granville.

'Who is it?' he asked, making for the door.

'How should I know?' She was used to the daily quota of total strangers phoning the rectory. 'Female.' Granville went straight out and closed the door behind him.

They started to eat their pudding in his absence. 'So,' began Oonagh, looking at Piet, 'what made you decide to come to England?'

'You can call it a bit of a folly,' he said, and Oonagh smiled at him. 'Something I'd always wanted to do at some point in my life. A new chapter. I dare say there'll be others.'

'You're obviously a free spirit,' replied Oonagh.

'Or can afford to be,' chipped in Martin.

'I've been careful with money all my life,' said Piet without embarrassment. 'My savings have done pretty nicely. I've no complaints.'

'There you go!' Oonagh turned to her husband. 'Here's a prudent man for you. A man who plans for the future and eventually reaps what he's sown.'

'I never understood much about farming,' muttered Martin, trying to tease a sympathetic smile from Edwina.

Next door, Granville's head was bowed low. He was gripping the telephone tightly to his ear and his eyes travelled across the carpet at his feet as he listened. It was difficult to understand everything she was saying.

'Just try to stop crying for one second. All right? I can't make head or tail of this. Stop crying and tell me, calmly.'

The sobbing slowed.

'OK. Now, what is it?'

'I – just have to see you.'

'Why? What's happened?'

'I – I – need to see you again.'

'The last time we met you were so happy, so positive. What's gone wrong?'

'I – love – you.' She began crying again.

'You didn't say that, OK? Don't say it again, don't even think it. What's gone wrong? Did you get the job in Bristol?' There was silence at the other end. He tried again. 'I said what about Bristol, the job interview?'

'There – wasn't an – interview.'

'What d'you mean?'

'I – made it – up.'

'Why would you do that?'

'I wanted – you – to be happy – with me.'

Granville shook his head. 'What about the car, the money?'

'It's my – mum's car. I took it.'

'And the money Bertie left you?'

'I – made – that up, too.'

'So there's no money? It was just a story?'

Silence.

'When – can I see you – again?' she said.

'That's not a good idea.'

'You kissed me.'

'I did not—' Granville looked wildly around and walked to a corner of the room. He bent over and bowed his head, as if lowering the conversation might help keep the secret in its box. 'You know that's not true. You sprang a kiss on me out of the blue, and—' There was a groan at the other end of the line, and Granville changed his tack. 'Are you moving back to your mother's flat?'

There was no answer.

'Is she giving you a hard time, or something?'

Still silence.

'Let me organize professional help for you,' he said.

She began to break down again. 'I – I – have to – see you.' She was sobbing convulsively between each word.

'Hetty, you must understand that's not the answer.'

'If – I don't – see you – I'm going to – kill myself.' The last words were almost shrieked.

'So do you think there's a chance you'll settle down and stay here for ever?' asked Oonagh.

'Who can say what's around the corner?' answered Piet. He savoured a spoonful of the pudding and nodded slowly. 'I have to say,' he announced, 'this is the very best dessert I have had in my whole life. Or, right at this moment it seems that way. I'm sorry that it's beaten me. I suppose I'm used to eating a bit less.' He patted his

stomach. Just then the door opened and Granville came
back in.

'My God, man, you look white as a sheet,' said Martin,
swallowing a mouthful. 'What's happened?'

'Nothing,' replied Granville quietly. 'Everything all
right here?'

'Who was it?' asked Edwina.

'A parishioner.'

'Bad news?'

'No, no. Just the usual. Grist to the mill.' He stole a
glance at Piet and returned to his seat. 'Everybody else
finished?'

'I'll put the coffee on,' said Edwina.

Steyn was the first to leave. He shook hands with everyone and expressed his thanks to Edwina laboriously.
Martin Benson then sat down again, ready to settle in
for a while longer until Oonagh coerced him back onto
his feet and towards the door. In the interests of self-
preservation she always opted to do the driving. Martin
tumbled noisily out of the house and at last, guided by
his wife, got into the car.

By the time Granville and Edwina reached their
bedroom, half an hour later, they were tired. The erotic
voltage that had flashed between them earlier in the
evening had withered away and Granville seemed
distracted.

'I had to work bloody hard to pull that off,' Edwina
yawned and pulled her blouse over her head. She flung
it towards the heap of clothes on a chair, but missed and
it fell on the floor next to a discarded pair of tights. 'I
hope you appreciate it.' She unhitched her bra and let
her breasts fall free. The shoulder straps had left pink
indentations in the skin of her shoulders.

'Of course I do. It went well, I thought.'

'There are so many people we should have had for dinner. People we owe. And you go and insist we have that weirdo and—'

'Please don't call him that.'

'And the combination of him with Martin! Honestly. They're hardly likely to see eye to eye.'

'It was OK. Stimulating, in a way.'

'For you, maybe. While Serena and I slaved in the kitchen getting it all together you were out in the garden lecturing them about that idiotic piece of stone.'

'Is that what Martin said? He seemed much cosier in your company.'

'What's that supposed to mean?'

'He had his hands all over you when we came in from the garden.'

'*What?*'

'Don't pretend you don't know what I mean. I suppose we all know what he's like.'

'But what are you saying *I'm* like?'

'I'm not saying you're "like" anything.'

'What then?'

'I would just feel more comfortable knowing that if he crosses a line you'll stop him in his tracks. That's all.'

'You think I wouldn't stop him?'

'I don't know what to think, if I'm honest.'

'You are unbelievable.'

'And you're tired, you should just go to sleep now.'

'You can't just drop in a comment like that and expect to get away with it.'

'Well, I'm not getting away with it, am I?'

'God!' she aspirated, threw her clothes aside and pulled her nightie down over her breasts in angry silence.

'Please don't let's go to sleep on a bad note,' he said,

but she did not answer. He sighed deeply and went to undress by his chair.

Edwina lay down on her side and put out the bedside light. Then she remembered her earrings and sat up again to take them out. 'Have you even noticed I'd changed the sheets?' she said.

'Of course.'

'If my father had any idea how much housework I have to do he'd pass out on the spot. It's not what he had in mind for me.'

'Well, your father is a great peer of the realm.'

She looked away. 'You had to say something else nasty, didn't you?'

'It wasn't nasty. He is a peer. And I'm a humble vicar. Fact.'

'Who was that girl on the phone?'

'The who?'

'You know who I mean. The girl who phoned and left you looking like you'd seen a ghost.'

'Just someone I'm giving wedding instruction to.'

'Why d'you say "just"?'

The veiled perceptiveness of the question stalled him.

'To minimize the relevance of it, or her, to our home life. Isn't that what you want me to do with my job?'

'What's wrong with her?'

'Boyfriend trouble.'

Edwina rearranged her pillows and found another of her nighties scrunched up under them. She tossed it onto the floor and reached up to pull off her hair tie. 'Was it the same girl who looked so upset after Bertie's funeral?'

'No.' He didn't understand why he'd said it but felt as though every word he spoke took him step by step further into a dismal no-man's-land.

'Don't wake me up in the morning,' she said, rolling over away from him, arms cradled in front of her. 'I want a lie-in.' That was the last she said, and he finished undressing at the end of the bed in silence.

Chapter 18

The night before the Easter Grill, Granville could not settle comfortably in bed. He knew there was something he was going to have to do first thing in the morning and the anticipation of it disrupted his sleep as effectively as a broken spring in the mattress. It was dark and cold in the bedroom when he decided to get up and go downstairs. The sooner this was done the better. There wouldn't be time later, once the day's festivities were under way.

Because of the chill, he went straight to light a fire in his study, taking a generous pile of kindling from a basket and assembling a miniature pyre in the grate. The coal embers from the previous evening's fire were still warm and he blew softly into them, sending an apocalyptic ash cloud across the diminutive landscape of the hearth. Suddenly, an orange glow gave birth to a young flame without him even having to strike a match, which was gratifying to watch. A man has a personal relationship with the fire that he builds, Granville mused, and he gets better at it as the years go by. It was a selfish, private joy, one that could not be shared, and the thrill of it was as great now as when he'd first tried it, wide-eyed, with a match between his fingers, as a boy of about ten.

It was then that he noticed Amelia standing there in the open doorway, as if magically summoned by her father's childhood recollections. He had not heard her coming down the stairs, nor had he often known her get up so early. Her eyes were empty, her posture upright. It might have been eerie to see her so composed and yet detached, framed by the darkness of the hall beyond, had it not been for the complete absence of a supernatural property in the girl. She was half dreaming, barely registering him, but sufficiently cosy by instinct to walk over and curl up in his lap where he sat. He stroked her hair and she physically reduced herself, in the way of a cat that settles and shrinks into an empty shoebox for warmth.

Granville realized he would not be getting up to go to his desk just now, after all. Instead, he sat cross legged in front of the healthy fire, hand resting on his daughter's temple. Beneath his index finger wound the river-like course of a delicate vein, pale blue and precious, barely protected by an ivory film of skin. Who, or what, decreed the precise path that vein should take, he wondered? Who patterned its capillaries, the cooperation of its cells, or the edifice of the girl's greater being? If there was not a divine plan behind it, had it emerged from the ghostly imprint of his own structure? Or Edwina's?

The sharpness of the irritation between him and Edwina from the night of the dinner had by now sunk into a state of dreary antipathy in the light of which he felt annoyed with himself that he wasn't able to ignore her incessant erotic appeal. It was something she carried about with her everywhere she went, almost complacently, it seemed, as if quietly to remind him of the great distance that would need to be bridged if his mounting hunger for her were ever to be eased. It did not look as if there were any possibility of that in the short term. Their relationship's topography had become like a mountain landscape seen from a passenger jet – endless craggy peaks and glacial valleys, one after the other, an indistinguishable sequence across a vast, misty wilderness. Certainly not a kind place for children. Looking down at Amelia's fragile head, he did not want to find a trace of Edwina's imprint there. In fact, he did not like to think that this unblemished girl could be predetermined in any fashion, and certainly not burdened with the resonance of his or his wife's doubts and troubles. Yet, if the pattern of an individual's being derived in part from those who came before, how much of himself came likewise from the design of his own forebears?

The momentum of his thoughts was streaming, as it so often did, full flood towards an inevitable destination: the person of Mounty St Clair. His father still loomed large in his thinking, elbowing his way past all contenders to occupy centre stage, just as he had done throughout Granville's childhood. Mounty's impermeable self-assurance – some might call it conceit – had dazzled and embarrassed Granville by turn as he was growing up. In a certain light he might have been considered quite trendy. It was cool to have a sort of anarchist for a dad in the era of Johnny Rotten and The Clash. But it wasn't genuine, of course. Mounty Sinclair was anything but an anarchist. He basked in his own family's undemocratically achieved wealth and distinction. Though he had no time for the trappings of social rank, he was fascinated by his ancestry and revelled in the inherited chronicles and treasures piled up at his baronial home. He would take Granville aside as a boy and relate stories, examine portraits, trace the lineages, from baronet to baronet, back to the Fourth Earl, from whose second son's loins their branch of the family descended.

It had grown light outside, morning had arrived, and he knew he had better get this job over with. He would have to do it in the kitchen. He lowered Amelia's head onto a cushion and wriggled free of her. He went through, put on the light, retrieved his mobile from where it was charging and dialled the number.

'Hello?' She sounded croaky.

'Hetty? I'm sorry to ring so early.'

'That's OK.'

He paused for a second. 'Look, I'm not going to beat about the bush. I can't treat you like a child. You've got to understand that it's . . .' He stalled.

'It's what?'

'That I'm not going to have a relationship with you.' The words were reluctantly formed. 'The very idea of it is just ridiculous. Outrageous, even. What I'm saying is: I think it's better if I don't come and see you after all.'

'OK.'

'Do you understand?'

'Yeah, yeah, I do.'

'I'm sorry if you were counting on me coming. I was in a tight spot the other night. But it's just madness. We have to stop this, and stop it now. You've got to be strong for me, Hetty.'

'OK.'

'Are you all right?'

'Yeah, I'm fine. OK, then. Bye, then.'

'Hetty?' Silence. 'Hetty?'

'Yep?'

'It's going to be better this way. Believe me.'

'OK.'

'It would've ended in disaster. You do understand that, don't you?'

'Yeah.'

213

'All right then. We'll leave it a few weeks and then I'll give you a call to check you're OK.'

'OK.'

'You look after yourself now.'

'I will.'

'OK. Goodbye, then.'

'Bye.'

The phone went dead. It was over. It had taken about a minute.

Chapter 19

By the time Granville arrived at the abbey grounds, at eleven o'clock, the ladies had already got the bunting up, the car park signs had been staked and one or two gazebos were half constructed on the grass. A local marquee company had reluctantly agreed to donate a stack of trestle tables and some wooden folding chairs, but, as a protest at having had their arm twisted for yet another charity event, dumped the furniture just by the gate to the grounds, which meant that volunteers had to be found to put them up and distribute them around the stalls. It was a fine day with a good strong breeze, which George Atkins – a local farmer who'd brought his clay pigeon trap – said would make the shooting competition a devil of a challenge.

Piet Steyn's spit lamb roast was already well under way. He had arrived at six o'clock, along with the barbecue that he had built and two sackfuls of charcoal. It gave the meat that extra special something, he explained, to roast it slowly and let it drip for hours into the hot coals.

'It's magnificent,' said Granville, walking around the barbecue and inspecting it from top to bottom. 'You've worked very hard. All the welding and everything. I don't know how to thank you.'

'Well, it'll last a long time, for sure,' said Piet. 'Probably see me out.'

'We'll make sure it's stored carefully,' said Granville. 'You are a clever so-and-so. I wouldn't know where to begin to make something like this.'

'Don't mention it.'

'By the way, Piet. I keep forgetting to tell you: I've been asking around about the name Newland.'

'Why should you do that?'

'Just interested.'

'And?'

'I may have a lead. We'll see. I'll let you know if something exciting comes to light.'

'You know, Father,' Piet said, frowning, 'I'd rather let sleeping dogs lie, if you don't mind.'

'You're not curious about your background?'

'Not particularly. I'm sorry if that sounds ungrateful.'

'Not at all. Of course. I'll do as you say.'

Piet began once more to turn the lamb on the spit. Hot oil secretions streaked its torso as it rotated, glistening like abundant tears, until they grew too heavy and plopped, hissing, into the coals. The skin was turning brown, with pockets of fat fizzing and popping just beneath the surface. There were at least a couple of hours of cooking left before the meat would be ready but everyone who passed commented on the delicious smell and said it made them feel famished.

The site for the Easter Grill, as ever, was the unconsecrated patch of pasture beyond the old cemetery, fifty yards or so from the ruined east end of the abbey. To reach it, visitors had to follow a chalky path through the graveyard, weaving between ancient trapezoidal tombs that had been destabilized over centuries by the slow churning of the turf. A man in a panama sat at a fragile camping table next to the path's gate and politely offered people an entrance ticket in exchange for one pound fifty. He explained to them one by one that the tariff also entitled them to a photocopied A4 sheet carrying details of the afternoon's activities. A raffle ticket was available here as well, if they wanted it, he said, for a further fifty pence, an offer that was impossible to refuse.

Granville tested the PA system, 'Hello, hello,' his voice boomed across the little valley, and he nodded at the technician; it was all working fine. Closer to lunchtime, village residents arrived in greater numbers, children yelped and charged around the gravestones, dogs strained at leads to sniff one anothers' backsides, and a talented pair of young brothers from the parish began to play duet arrangements on brass instruments. Most people, when they arrived, headed straight for the stalls selling surplus domestic junk. Clusters of parishioners craned like vultures over them, searching for bargains. A handful of more affluent looking villagers browsed a second-hand book stall, while a group of elderly ladies was already forming a queue in front of the tea counter. Few people as yet seemed interested in placing bets on the sheep race to be held later in the day, despite the farmer's raucous attempts to pull them in, but quite a number of children were buzzing around Mrs Perkins' new Mini Cooper, trying to guess how many balloons had been stuffed into it, at fifty pence a guess.

Janet Gosling arrived with her sons, and wherever she went people came up to talk to her, tilting their heads with sympathetic smiles, so that her progress to the heart of the event was hampered. Piet spotted her and began to slice some meat from the better-cooked parts of the lamb. He assembled generous portions in three cut white rolls and put them on individual paper plates. 'I will pay for these,' he said to Granville, who was standing beside him, holding the microphone, ready to open the afternoon's proceedings. Piet took out his wallet and dropped the money into an empty Tupperware basin next to the grill. He then abandoned his post for a moment and hurried over to where the Goslings were standing. Janet was smiling and listening to an ebullient lady with a large straw hat who talked incessantly at her. Piet stood on the sidelines, waiting for a break in the woman's conversation, while balancing the three plates in his hands. Janet stole him a quick glance, which caused the woman who was talking to pause, and this allowed Piet forward.

'Allow me to offer you these,' he said formally, handing a paper plate to each of the boys and one to Janet. Her plate had been creased by his grip, which meant that the roll was tilted and juice spilt out of it over her fingers. She had to step back quickly to stop it dripping onto her dress, holding the plate at arm's length in front of her.

'Oh. Thank you,' she said. 'I might . . . Could you . . .' She handed her roll to one of her sons and the creased plate to the other, while she retrieved a handkerchief from her handbag. Piet apologized and tried to help. 'No, no, that's quite all right,' she said, 'no harm done.' Having quickly wiped her fingers she took back the roll, holding it at a distance, between her thumb and index finger. 'What do you say, boys?'

'Thank you,' each of them grunted in turn.

'You don't need to pay for these,' said Piet, 'and if you want any more just come and see me.' He pointed to the spit. 'I'm in charge over there, so I'll look after you.' Janet thanked him again and wandered away with her sons, who had already begun to devour their rolls. They quickly finished and she handed them her own, which they broke in two and consumed half each.

'Good afternoon, everyone,' began Granville into the microphone and paused. He looked at the man fiddling with the PA's amplifier knob. 'I'm waiting for the obligatory whine of feedback,' he said, and a few people laughed. 'Welcome everybody to our sixth – would you believe it? – our *sixth* Cheselbury Abbas Easter Grill!' There were cheers. 'It's a beautiful day, there's plenty of food, wonderful raffle prizes, all sorts of stalls, and a treasure hunt for the kids starting at three o'clock.' He went on to recite the litany of thanks to all who had contributed so generously to make the event possible, concluding with a special tribute to Piet Steyn. There was a lone, exaggerated cheer from somewhere at the back of the crowd and one or two heads turned. Granville went on, 'Not only has Piet cooked the lamb with an authentic touch – lighting his coals here at the crack of dawn this morning, I might add – but he actually built the barbecue apparatus himself and has generously donated it to the church.' The patter of polite applause was superseded by the voice from the rear which called out, 'Where've I seen that drum before?' The comment was gone before anyone particularly registered it and Granville finished with a short prayer. Then he raised his hands and told people to get on and spend as much as they could, because it was all in a good cause. The microphone was switched off and everyone dispersed.

For most of the afternoon, trade at the spit roast was fast and furious. Piet toiled like a man possessed over the coals. His sleeves were rolled, the muscles of his forearms bulged and he sweated heavily. A succession of volunteers came up to help cut rolls and take money, which left Piet free to concentrate on carving, basting and stoking the charcoal. Every so often he would pause, knife in hand, and look up over the top of the carcass.

He would scan the scene from left to right until he got a sighting of Janet, and then, satisfied, returned to his work. At one point, when he was particularly hot and busy, he noticed a child worm his way to the front of the queue rather than waiting his turn. It was a boy of about twelve. 'What do you think you're doing, man? Hmm?' Piet snapped, pointing his carving knife and staring at the child with angry eyes. 'You think you're more important than anyone else here, do you?' The boy was speechless with fear. Piet leant towards him. 'You get to the back of the queue right now or you don't get any food. Understood?' The boy nodded and fled, his chin puckering.

The abbey's remains, a towering and seemingly random conglomeration of flint and sandstone, began to cast shadows over the festivities as the afternoon wore on. The medieval masonry was swallowed in parts by ivy, but stood monumental and permanent in the turf, as much part of the landscape as the interlocking hills that surrounded it. Outcrops of towering beech and oak trees flanked the abbey grounds on the west, their fresh spring leaves swaying in unison with the breeze. These old plantations were the legacy of another era's yeomanry, the work of farmers with the vision to tame the wilderness around the abbey and grace the hills about their homesteads with clumps of forest. Leading steeply away from the same tall trees were the indented remnants of an ancient track, unused for decades. Its ruts were clearly discernible in the grass despite their disuse, and were all that remained to show where men and beasts had toiled daily up its gradient for centuries. Higher up, away to the left, all sign of the track disappeared where the grassy meadow ended at a tangled woodland glade. A few villagers, who had eaten their fill and seen enough of the Easter Grill, now started to wander up that way, with a collection of Labradors and spaniels bounding at their heels.

Granville and Janet Gosling sat together on wooden chairs in the shade of a huge old apple tree, and both had cups of tea on their laps. She was doing most of the talking and he was pleased by what he heard. As he listened, he spared a glance for his own family. Serena was sitting cross legged in the grass with a couple of well-groomed friends from school. They were chatting, laughing and picking petals of wild flowers that grew by their ankles. Amelia, meanwhile, was labouring to master a pair of stilts in the circus skills area. Edwina hovered at her side, helping to balance her and calling out instructions.

Janet explained to Granville how she'd been making up an album of photographs from Bertie's life, hundreds of them, and was having them digitally reproduced for a printed volume. She would probably have twenty or thirty of the books printed and distribute them to family and friends. The whole enterprise was bringing her close to the boys, she said, and they, in turn, were getting on with each other better than ever in the past. They were working hard at school and doing everything they could to make their father proud of them. 'In a most bizarre way,' she concluded, 'I think Bertie's death has had one positive effect on them. It's made them stop in their tracks and think: "Hang on, mate. Maybe it's time to grow up a bit."'

Granville silently thanked God he'd never wavered. He had been right to keep the secret. All would be well, after all. 'And you?' he asked. 'Are you coping all right?'

She sipped her tea, narrowed her eyes and looked into the distance. The breeze loosened a lock of her hair and there were distant shrieks of children laughing. 'I feel he's with me still,' she said, 'guiding me, watching over me. I know it sounds like a woman in denial. I know all the clichés.'

'It's early days.'

'I know. I'm no fool. I'm perfectly aware that he's gone, and gone for good, and that's what he wanted, for whatever reason. But I get this feeling he's at rest now. Content. Like the man I stood beside on my wedding day. It's that man who's watching over me. Yes, to answer your question, I'm coping just fine.' She smiled at him.

There was a cough behind them. Piet was standing there. Janet looked down into her teacup. 'Janet. Father. Sorry to interrupt. Am I intruding?'

'Not at all,' said Granville, and then, noticing that Janet had not raised her head, he quickly looked at his watch and added, 'The clay pigeon contest's under way by now. I insist that you take part, Piet. I bet you're a crack shot. Come on, let's make our way over.'

'No, I . . . I'll have to get back to the cooking.'

'Nonsense. I'll take over the lamb for a bit. You go on. Be my guest. I'll even pay for you to enter.'

There was no refusing him, so Piet walked slowly, hands in pockets, over to the area that had been cordoned off for the competition. A man wearing earmuffs and holding an over-and-under barrelled shotgun, stood at the ready, facing the crest of the hill. On the command, 'Pull,' George Atkins – the compere and adjudicator – pushed a button on his remote control and a black saucer spun up into the air, launched from an invisible spot higher on the hill. The man fired and missed, but shattered the disc with his second barrel, which elicited a solitary whoop of approval from his wife, standing close behind. The gun was opened, two spent, smoking cartridges ejected themselves, and George Atkins stepped forward to replace them with fresh ones. He had hold of the PA system's microphone and was providing a running commentary in a broad Dorset accent. The sound of his speech was echoed and distorted by the acoustics of the surrounding landscape.

'*Mister Mullins has scored only five in his second round and therefore is sadly eliminated from qualifying. We now have . . . who do we have? . . . oh yes, we have a lady contender, ladies and gentlemen, to show the boys how it's done, we have the lovely Mrs June Watson. Let's have a round of applause, then please, for Mrs June Watson . . .*'

Granville had taken up position behind the depleted remains of the lamb and had started to slice. Few were coming now to buy filled rolls and he wondered if he should start giving portions away rather than having to slice up remnants of greasy cold meat later on in the evening. As he was contemplating this, the young Gosling brothers came up to the spit.

'Can we have two lamb rolls, please?' asked Robert, the elder, his father's namesake. He held out a handful of coins.

'That's all right,' said Granville. 'You can have these for nothing.' Their shy faces broke into smiles and they both thanked him.

'*And June kills the first clay dead with her first barrel. There you are, gents. Watch and learn from a master at work.*'

'Like it?' asked Granville as they scoffed their buns. They nodded their answer appreciatively, mouths too full to speak. 'Steady on, there's plenty here. You look as though you haven't eaten for days. You should've come earlier. Piet would've given you VIP treatment.'

Robert began to say something but had to wait until he'd swallowed. 'He's always doing stuff like that.'

'Cos he wants to move in on Mum,' said Owen, the younger boy.

Granville smiled at them. 'It's not that,' he said. 'Piet just wants to help cheer you guys up a bit. He's a really kind man.'

They both made a noise of distaste, as if they'd caught something rotten on the breeze. 'He's always turning up at the house or phoning or something. He said he'd back off a bit but nothing's changed. Mum hates it. Why can't he leave us alone?'

Granville began to cut slices to make up a couple more rolls. 'You say your mother doesn't like him calling?'

Robert checked over his shoulder and turned back to Granville. 'No. She's scared of him.'

'He shouts at us,' said Owen.

'She thinks he might get violent,' continued Robert. 'What does he want with us, anyway?'

Granville frowned. 'What has he done to make her think that?'

'A wonderful score of twelve kills for Mrs June Watson. Now, before we start the semi-final, we . . . we have a last-minute late entry, a Mister . . . what's your name sir? . . . Mister Pete Stain, let's have it for Mr Pete Stain, everybody.'

Someone jeered. 'Whassat? Piss stain?!'

Robert Gosling went on, 'He gets angry. He tells Mum what she should do and stuff, what's right and what's wrong for a woman when she's lost her husband. It gives her the creeps.'

'Really?' said Granville. 'Well, I know for a fact he thinks the world of your mother. And you two, as well,' he added quickly. A pair of sharp cracks echoed around the valley, two shots fired.

'None of us want that, though,' said Robert. 'I wish he'd just go away. We all do.'

'Yeah,' agreed Owen.

'We'll just pause for a moment, ladies and gentlemen. Er . . . there seems to be a bit of a . . . everything all right, sir?' A muffled bumping sound came through the speakers as George Atkins put a hand over the microphone to have a quick word. Granville strained his eyes over the heads of the onlookers and saw that Piet was leaning forward, holding one arm across his abdomen. But the problem, whatever it was, seemed to pass quickly and he eased himself back upright, nodding to George that he was fine. After a few seconds he was ready to continue his round.

Granville walked with the Gosling boys over to the site of the shooting contest, where the remaining crowd had assembled to watch. Janet was there as well.

Piet had failed to touch his first three clays but was now alert and held the shotgun tucked under his arm at the ready. Granville noted the way his hands gripped the weapon, his finger resting alongside the trigger guard and the wooden butt touching lightly against his hip. It was the stance of an experienced shot, as he imagined the Wild West cowboys might have looked, rugged, self-reliant men on the frontier, for whom a gun was a natural extension of their hands and fingers. A clay flew high into the sky. Piet whipped up the barrels and fired, shattering the clay into a cloud of miniature splinters. 'That's more like it,' he muttered, and nodded that he was ready for the next one. The remaining eleven clays were similarly dispatched and the announcer confirmed Piet's place with four others in the semi-final.

The contest had caught the imagination of the small crowd and there were raucous noises of support when a local farmer stepped up to take his turn. He had quite a paunch for such a young man, and a grin that never completely left his face. The clays now came higher, at a faster rate and two at a time; competitors were supposed to try to hit them both, one with each barrel. The young farmer achieved the feat once, but otherwise shot one out of each pair, and once missed altogether. He was patted on the back, nonetheless, as he stepped down, giving way to the next contestant. When it was Steyn's turn, there was silence from the crowd until after his first two shots, both of which shattered their clays. Then there was general applause; but in the quiet that followed, a voice was heard to say, 'Oh yeah?' Granville looked across and noticed Colin Futcher standing close by, grinning. His son Rufus was beside him, and three other men in the group, each carrying a pint of beer in a plastic glass.

Steyn finished the heat having destroyed fourteen out of sixteen clays, and was through to the final. His rival for the trophy was a pale-faced telecom salesman who lived in the village, called Gordon Daniels, who was known to be against blood sports but a keen member of a local clay pigeon club. He stepped up to the marker spot carrying his own high-calibre Beretta twelve bore. He was wearing a quilted green waistcoat with a suede patch on the shoulder and a baseball cap advertising Eley cartridges. He donned a pair of transparent eye-protection glasses.

'Oi, George,' Colin Futcher called out to the announcer, 'you never told us this was a ladies-only final.' The men around Colin laughed.

The clays now flew out of the wooded ridge on the hill at a devilishly high trajectory, two at a time, and in random directions. Gordon, a veteran of many clay shoot competitions, who had only come to the Easter Grill in order to take part in this contest, knew the form.

He pirouetted from left to right, in neat sportsman's sneakers, confidently anticipating the flight of each disc as soon as he spotted it in the air. At the end of his turn he had shattered all but one of the clays. Steyn then walked up to the spot.

He was asked if he would like to borrow some ear-muffs, but politely declined.

'*Now Mr Pete Stain takes his stand*,' said the announcer. Alongside the clapping there were a couple of muted boos and a snigger.

'*Quiet, please.*'

Piet held his gun tensely and stared out at the sky.

'Here comes your ladies' man,' Colin Futcher called out. 'Shouldn't that be lady-man?' his neighbour added, just at that moment two clays flew up in different directions. Piet clipped the first, sending it wildly off course, which counted as a hit, but when he turned to fire at the second, nothing happened. He lowered his gun, staring at it in his hands. 'I'm sorry,' he said to the announcer. 'I think the safety catch may be faulty, or something.'

Futcher and his friends laughed. 'Oh, I see. The gun's not good enough, now, is it?'

'I'm sorry,' Piet repeated to George Atkins, ignoring the comment.

Granville now edged towards the group of drinking men. 'Come on, chaps,' he said quietly to them, lowering his head in the crowd. He didn't want to make a scene. 'Can't we just simmer down a bit?'

Colin turned to the man next to him. 'Did you hear that, *chaps*?' he said, mocking Granville's accent. 'We've got to simmer down a bit.'

Piet had asked the other competitor if he might borrow the Beretta, a request that caused Gordon

227

Daniels to hesitate, though with everyone watching he felt compelled to acquiesce.

'*We're all good sportsmen here,*' announced George Atkins, '*so we'll start Mr Stain's round all over again.*'

Piet held the Beretta at the ready.

'He don't look too comfortable, do he?' said one of Colin's friends. Others in the crowd, annoyed by the heckling, now tutted and called for quiet.

'Maybe those ladies' undies are a bit ticklish,' said Colin, and the group of men burst out laughing. Several people groaned disapprovingly and shook their heads. Someone said, 'Just shut up and watch, can't you?' Janet Gosling called her sons away. She waved briefly at Granville to indicate that she was leaving, and walked off with the boys towards the cemetery path. Piet noticed her departure and his expression darkened. He turned back to face his challenge. There was a clacking sound as the spring of the trap released the first clays into the sky. One after the other they vanished in two explosive black mists. Direct hits. Granville led the applause, and then turned to Futcher and his friends and whispered sharply, 'If you can't keep your mouths shut, then get out of here! There are children around.'

'Like being back at school,' one of them muttered in response and drank deeply from his glass, 'Sorry, teacher.' All the while, Rufus Futcher kept his head low, not wanting to dissociate himself from his father's group but embarrassed by them at the same time.

Steyn now held his gun ready for the second pair to be released. Colin Futcher, grinning, was watching George Atkins' hand as he held the remote control, and in the silence just before his thumb pressed the rubberized button, Colin called out quietly to Piet, 'Careful, now.' The distant trap released its charge but

Piet lowered his gun and the two clays flew untouched over the crowd's heads in an arc, falling and smashing in the field behind. There was complete stillness as Piet unlocked the Beretta, handed it back to Gordon and thanked him very much for lending it. He then turned to the announcer and apologized for withdrawing from the contest, saying that the trophy should rightly go to the other competitor. George Atkins was stumped for a response. Piet then approached him and asked politely, 'Would you mind, sir, if I were to trouble you for a couple of those cartridges?' He pointed to one of several open boxes.

George turned off the microphone. He looked confused. 'Help yourself.'

'Thank you, sir,' said Piet and took two cartridges from the box. He turned back to the crowd and began to walk towards Colin Futcher and his friends. There were four of them, all big men, excluding Rufus, who shrank away. Futcher stood his ground, stomach protruding, and took a swig of beer from his plastic pint. 'What's she going to do now?' he said in a public aside to the friend next to him, 'ask me to dance?'

'You think you're very funny, don't you?' said Steyn.

'Come on, Piet,' said Granville, stepping forward and laying a hand on his shoulder. 'Let's walk away from all this, shall we?'

'I asked you if you think you're funny,' Steyn repeated.

'What? Funny ha ha, or funny queer? I'm not half as queer as you, that's for sure.' His friends laughed again and Steyn walked straight up to him. He had the cartridges in his hand. 'What you going to do, then . . . ?' began Futcher, but the rest of his sentence was lost. There was a tussle, a sharp shove and a muffled cry. It was difficult with all the people in the way to see what was going on.

Steyn was holding Futcher's head tightly in the crook of his arm. He had the cartridges in his hand. The people next to him seemed too shocked or confused to intervene as he pushed one of the cartridges roughly, up to the hilt, into Colin's nostril. A couple of the men now yelled and grabbed at Steyn. One of them thumped him in the ribs, but he moved quickly, too quickly for any of them. Before they could get a proper grip on him, he had forced the second cartridge into the other nostril, causing the skin to split on both sides of the nose. He then smacked his fist upwards against the pair of them, punching them in deeper, so that Colin's head jerked back savagely and he let out a cry of pain. There was blood pouring over his lips, teeth and chin. The two-inch red plastic cylinders of the cartridges had disappeared completely into his nose, distorting the shape of his face, with only the shiny brass tops of each protruding. Colin's friends now grabbed hold of Steyn, pulling at his clothing and began to haul him back. There was a sound of clothes ripping, a hand slapped at his head and another grazed past his ear. Granville pushed forward and managed to position himself between them. 'Get him out of here,' he said to a bystander and shoved Steyn backwards, 'and call an ambulance.' He then turned to face the group of angry men. Futcher had sunk to the floor and a couple of people squatted down to help him.

'If you've got something to say,' Granville said, 'say it to me.' Steyn was right behind him.

'Get out the way,' one of the men shouted, 'or you'll go down with him.'

Granville held out his hand in front of him. It was shaking and he was panting but he stood his ground. 'All right, then. Take me down, if that's what you want to do.'

The man did not hesitate. He raised his hand and

punched hard into Granville's mouth. There was a sound as of fresh meat slapped against a butcher's block, and Granville fell backwards. 'Stuck-up prick asked for it,' said the man, shaking his grazed knuckles as his friends pulled him back. Steyn stared at Granville for a moment, then allowed himself to be ushered back from the fray, whereupon he shook off the arms that restrained him, turned around and walked away on his own. No-one tried to stop him. Attention had shifted to the two injured men on the ground. Granville's lip was split and he held a handkerchief to his mouth. He was indicating with his other hand that he was all right and should be left alone.

Steyn did not look back, but went over to the abandoned spit roast and collected his jacket from the chair. He then walked straight down the cemetery path and disappeared from sight behind the ruined walls of the old abbey.

Chapter 20

Later on in the evening after the Easter Grill, as they were going to bed, Granville at last told Edwina about what he had seen in the room adjacent to the kitchen in Steyn's house.

He had had his lip stitched at the local surgery and it was misshapen with the swelling. He felt shocked by the violence, and was also disturbed by what the Gosling boys had confessed. This was enough to make him confide in his wife that he had begun to have slight misgivings with regard to Piet Steyn. He put the bedside light off and lay on his back, staring into the blackness. Edwina moved over and curled in close to him, sensing his vulnerability.

'Why didn't you tell me before?' she asked, with no hint of accusation in her tone.

'I'm sorry. It was a mixture of things. I didn't think it was my business. I also felt guilty for stealing into that room behind his back and wanted to pretend it hadn't happened. I don't go in for tittle-tattle. And I didn't want to make you think worse of him.'

'Do you think he knows you went in?'

'He hasn't said anything. And he's just as friendly and polite as ever.'

'Too polite.'

'He's certainly up to something.'

'Spooky,' she murmured.

'Maybe he just deals in antiques or something on the side. Odd that he's never mentioned it. But it's very easy to think the worst when you're dealing with an offbeat character like Piet.'

'So you admit he's weird.'

'I didn't use that word.'

She smiled. 'I like the way you still want to think the best of him. You're a much better person than me.' It was as if a fault line had opened, revealing a glimpse of the wife, the girlfriend she had once been. In their early days together she had been dazzled by Granville's generosity of spirit and had tried to improve herself by his example. But his goodness was natural and she had never fathomed its origin. For years she had observed it and tried to manufacture something similar in herself; then she had grown envious and begun to pick holes in it; nowadays, more often, she resented it, but not tonight. Right now she felt, for the first time in years, as she had done at the start, full of quiet admiration for all that was best in him. She edged further in and he kissed her on the top of the head. She turned her face up to him and presented her lips, which he gently brushed with his own, flinching slightly at the soreness, and moving the hand that was resting on her hips down to her crotch. Her legs parted easily and he felt the intense heat of her, a warmth like no other on earth, close and humid. They began to make love.

When they got up the following morning there was a pleasant equilibrium between them. They gave each other a hug before going downstairs. 'I do love you, you know,' Edwina said, smiling up at him. It was the warmest moment they had shared for months, perhaps years.

'I know you do.'

'And now I've got your attention,' she said, still holding on to him, 'will you phone the doctor and make that MRI scan appointment?'

'No,' he replied, but he was smiling. She put on a fake grimace and pinched the skin on either side of his waist.

'Fatty,' she said.

'All right, all right,' he said, wriggling free and laughing.

'Promise me.'

'I promise.'

Granville was out for most of the morning. As well as Cheselbury Abbas, he was responsible for the affairs of three smaller satellite parishes, their church buildings, service schedules, groups and committees. This morning he was visiting the village of Trenthow, and dealing with a tricky situation. A retired female vicar had recently moved there and was keen to lessen Granville's burden by offering to take regular services at the village church on a voluntary basis. It seemed a great idea until the churchwarden notified Granville that he would resign if a woman was permitted to celebrate Holy Communion in their church. This warden also happened to own most of the surrounding land, had been born in the village manor house where he still lived, and had four prosperous sons, all of whom were settled with their own families in the immediate vicinity. Granville did not want to go upsetting so influential a local clan.

He tried to be as tactful as possible and explained that this was not something he was entitled to permit or not permit. The issue of women priests had been debated and accepted by the Church of England, for better or for worse, depending on your opinion, years ago. Without causing terrible offence and getting himself into trouble with the bishop he felt powerless to do anything about it. Not that he would necessarily want to do anything about it on a personal level, he added, nailing his own colours to the mast as gently as he could in the circumstances.

'Then I shall write to the Archbishop of Canterbury personally,' said the rebellious churchwarden almost nonchalantly, and the morning meeting was concluded in an awkward impasse. Granville chewed over the problem on the journey back and was still thinking about it when he arrived home, fifteen minutes later.

Edwina had said she was going out for the whole morning and that the girls were visiting friends, so he expected the house to be empty. He was therefore surprised to find, when he put his key in the door, that it had not been double-locked. Edwina must have forgotten to do it when she left, he assumed. The dog, caught off his guard, came charging into the hall, barking fiercely, until he recognized his master and then crept down low, wagging madly. Granville bent down to stroke him but at the same moment heard a noise from somewhere in front, and looked up at the open living room door. He felt a sudden pulse of alarm when he saw Edwina there, in profile, sitting upright in an armchair. She had not gone out after all. She did not look up at him, even though she must have heard him come in and greet Luther.

'Darling,' called Granville, but she still did not look around. So he came into the sitting room, opening the door fully, and then he saw. Sitting in another armchair, facing Edwina, on the far side of the fireplace, was Hetty. His stomach fell away inside him.

'Hello, Granville,' said Edwina. 'You're back early.' Hetty was looking up at him. She was dressed smartly

235

and modestly and looked older than usual. Her eyes were red. Granville went over to Edwina. Her face was pale and she would not make eye contact with him.

'What has she been saying to you?' he asked.

'Just about everything I need to know, I'd say,' replied Edwina flatly.

'Like what?' he turned to Hetty. 'What have you said?'

'I think I'd better go,' said Hetty quietly.

'Oh no you don't. You tell me what lies you've been telling.'

'Let her go, Granville,' sighed Edwina and her forehead sank into her hand. Hetty got up and walked over towards the door, coming right up in front of him. She looked him square in the eye.

'I'll never forgive what you've done to me, Granville,' she said calmly, her voice starting to crack, 'but I still love you.'

'What . . .' began Granville, but she walked straight past him and let herself out. 'You can't just . . .' he called after her. He followed her out to the driveway. 'Come back! What have you done?' It was too late. She slipped out into the road and walked quickly away. Granville wheeled around and ran back into the house to Edwina. 'You don't believe her, do you? I mean . . . that's the first time she's ever used my Christian name, for heaven's sake, I swear it.'

'Using a Christian name is not going to break a marriage. Fucking a teenaged girl when you're a married man of the cloth, might, though.' She turned and looked at him for the first time and her face creased up. 'How could you?'

'I didn't. I haven't. Is that what she told you?'

'And you made love to me last night. All the time knowing. I feel like filth. Like filth!'

236

'It's lies. Can't you see she's unstable?'

'Why didn't you tell me you'd been seeing her, then? If she's one of your fucking good shepherd projects, why did it have to wait till I found out about her myself? Seeing her outside the church that day. Then the phone call during dinner. You can't explain this one away as parish business. It just doesn't add up. And since when was your parish in Bournemouth coffee shops and romantic trysts up at the Hardy Monument?'

'It wasn't a . . . I can't even use the word, for God's sake!'

'You've thrown everything away. The girls . . .'

Granville stalled. 'Didn't she explain? I mean . . . how much did she tell you?'

'How *much*?' said Edwina and almost laughed. 'She told me quite enough. Do you mean there's more?'

Granville could not bring himself to mention Bertie Gosling. Not yet. Not while it could still destroy Janet and the boys. Later, perhaps, when Edwina had calmed down. 'You have to believe me,' he said, and he squatted down in front of her, but she stared ahead, sightlessly. 'Think what we've been through together. You used to trust me. Where's your trust gone?'

'So now you're the wounded party, is that it? Isn't that what men always do when they're caught red handed?'

'I haven't . . . look, Edwina, please,' but it sounded lame and she put up a palm to silence him.

'Just have the decency to give me some space,' she said, her voice breaking. 'Get out of the house and don't come back for a few hours. Then we'll see. OK? Then we'll talk. Just leave me alone for a bit.'

'OK, OK. I'll go. But just remember she's made it all up. I have met her a few times, it's true. And yes, she's developed a sort of crazy infatuation, but—'

'*Shut up!*' screamed Edwina at him and buried her face in her hands.

He said no more but went out of the house, got into the car and reversed out onto the road.

When he returned, three hours later, it was dusk and he could see immediately that there were no lights on in the house. Unless she was sitting in the dark, he knew this meant she had left. The brief note propped up against a vase full of wilting flowers in the hall confirmed his suspicions. She had gone, and taken the girls with her. They were flying to Aberdeen and would be staying at her parents' house until further notice. She told him not to call until she called him.

Chapter 21

'It must be spring outside.'

'Yes, it is,' Steyn answered. He was standing in front of the bookshelf, examining the row of book spines through his spectacles. He had paused the recording because he said he didn't feel up to that sort of work today, and she had suggested having some tea. She was now back from the kitchen and carrying a tray. There was a plate with a small cake that she had baked and a plastic knife beside it. None of the cutlery in the bunker was made of metal. Steyn had been careful to make sure there were no potentially dangerous implements down there and Rose had to select her choice of menus according to what she could manage with the tools available.

'Spring arrived proper about a week ago,' he added. He started changing around the books on the shelf, pulling some out and replacing them with others from a box on the floor. Every month or so he would bring a batch of carefully selected new titles for her to read, and take the old ones away. 'The sun has been shining pleasantly these past few days. Quite warm, as a matter of fact.'

She poured the tea into two mugs and sat down in her armchair. 'The sun shines every day in here,' she said, vacantly. 'The weather never changes. It never gets any warmer or colder, the leaves never fall from the trees and darkness comes at the same time every evening.'

'Have you read this one yet?' Piet asked, holding up one of the books from the shelf.

'No.'

'I'll leave it here, then. It's a good book.' She cut a slice of cake and handed it to him. 'Are you tired of the view from your window?' he asked, without looking up. 'Is that what you're implying?'

'I didn't say that.'

'Would you like me to change it in time for next winter, perhaps?' His back was turned and he did not see her eyes slowly seal shut. 'I could find a snowy landscape, I imagine. I've seen such things. Pine trees, mountains, a church spire. We've a few months to decide.' He turned to look at her over the rims of his glasses, and added, 'Is there anything else here you'd particularly like to change?'

'The sound of the fan drives me crazy.'

'That's a strong statement, Rose.'

'You say I should be honest.'

'Watch your tone.'

'I don't mind the clock so much because the tick helps pass the time until you come back. Like a kind of time tape measure. But that fan—'

'Keeps you alive.'

Tears sprang spontaneously to her eyes. 'I can't live the rest of my life with that noise.'

'We'll see.'

'And the lights.'

'What's wrong with them?'

'Can't I have a bit of control about when they come on or go off? Nine o'clock every single night is such a cold, horrible deadline. For about half an hour I dread the clock's hand reaching the twelve. Then there's a great click and everything goes black. I can't explain. It's like a kind of execution every night.'

'You're being hysterical.'

'Like a countdown to the hangman opening the hatch under my feet. Can't I control my own light? It's a small freedom. It wouldn't hurt anyone. Please.'

He turned to face her. 'Freedom is not always the cure. There is a greater fulfilment through self-denial. Through discipline.'

'I do understand that,' she said, encouraged by his unusually conciliatory tone, 'but this is not about me trying to break free from you or your plans. It's about me having . . .' she held out her palms and looked around the room, searching for the right words, 'it's about me managing my household, my castle. About trying to be a better wife for you.'

'You're wrapping this plea in a way that will make me think better of it.'

'I wrap *myself* to make you think better of me. Isn't that exactly what you want me to do?'

Steyn looked at her carefully and removed his spectacles. He smiled, almost nostalgically. 'Do you remember when we met?'

A flicker of alarm danced across her eyes at the change of subject. 'I remember.'

'All those early meetings,' he continued. 'How warmly you welcomed me in on those frosty winter mornings when I would call at your caravan for an early cup of tea? You got used to my visits and would have the kettle ready and boiling. You would be there, waiting, with a great big happy welcoming smile, just like my mother in her youth, and we would sit at your table and chat about a better world, a place where people could trust each other. You were a good listener, always eager to learn from my old stories.' Rose said nothing. 'It was the small, insignificant things that persuaded me, you know. Like your lovely old teacups with flowers on them, and their matching saucers. I used to like to help you get them down from the cupboard because it was a stretch for you. It was those cups as much as anything that convinced me you were the one. Did you know that? And your sweetly impressionable nature. There was nothing modern about you. I would walk away from that funny little caravan up on the hill, thinking: this woman could be the one.' He sighed and the sentimental smile fell from his face. 'And now you think I'm some kind of monster. After all we've been through.'

'I don't think that.' Her voice was tightly wired.

'You're afraid of me, though. Don't deny it.' He put out his hand and held hers, as if to offer reassurance.

'I am afraid.' She looked down. 'But I need you as well. You are my only hope.'

'Do you want to be free of me? Tell me truly.'

She seemed momentarily stumped by the question. 'I think that deep in your heart you are a good man,' she said, and then added quietly, 'But everyone makes mistakes.' He let drop her hand, leant forward over his thighs, and hung his head. He was gazing at the floor. 'What's wrong?' she asked.

'What makes you think that something's wrong?'

'I've never known you be like this before.'

'You can't expect things to be the same any more. Not after what happened between us the other day.'

'I thought we'd got over that.'

Steyn shook his head. 'I don't think so.' He brought his hands up, buried his face in his palms for a moment and sighed again.

'Husband?'

'It's all right, it's all right,' he said.

'You're upset.'

'Nah.' He raised his head.

'Yes you are.' Nervously, she extended an arm and put it around his shoulders. 'It's fine to cry, you know. It's fine to admit that sometimes we can be wrong about things.' Steyn did not answer, neither did he cry, he remained leaning forwards, staring into space, with her arm around him and her cheek resting against his shoulder. 'You know,' she murmured, 'for all the hours, weeks, months together, for all the learning and the questions, endless questions, I don't think we've ever been closer to one another than right now.'

'Is that what you think?'

'I think I can be a good wife for you.'

'You could have been.'

She did not move. 'What's that supposed to mean?'

'Ach, quiet. No point in any more upset just now.'

She jerked back fractionally. 'Are you giving up on me?' He did not answer. 'Husband!' There was contained panic in her voice. 'Let's build on this new closeness. It will be better, you'll see. Nothing until this point has meant anything.'

'Is that so?'

'Nothing compared with this. All that endless questioning about my past. It hasn't helped you to get to know me properly.'

He almost laughed. 'I have a very large archive, you know. Tapes, notes. Books of them. I think I know just about everything there is to know about you.'

She slipped down onto her knees in front of him and took his hands. Her voluminous pale blue silk skirt spread out over the carpet. She shook her head. 'But you don't. You really don't know me at all. I'd like you to get to know me, though.'

'What about all our work?'

'None of that was really me,' she said. 'I'm always just trying to please you. This is the real me. Isn't it better?'

He looked at her and frowned. 'You've made things up, you mean?'

'Some things.'

'Like what?'

'Like all the sex business. Especially recently.'

'The men?'

'No, the men were all real, but the rest of it . . .'

'Like?'

'All those questions about my preferences, my . . . so-called cravings. You know. I had to make half of it up.'

'Why?'

She was looking pleadingly into his eyes. 'Because I try to say what you want to hear.'

'You think that is what I want to hear?'

'I get the feeling you do, in some secret way.'

He did not speak but shut his eyes and his face tightened.

'It's all right,' she said and put an arm around his hunched shoulder. 'I think I understand what's going on. You've been struggling with this for too long. I can help you. We can work through this whole horrible business together. It's wonderful that we can be honest with each other at last. Husband!'

'Honest at last, eh?'

'Yes. You are my only hope, the only other human being in my life. You're my saviour. We can make this work now. If we're friends, anything is possible. I can forgive you everything.'

He nodded slowly and the tight strain on his face eased into a smile. She smiled back. 'Let me make you something to eat.' She massaged her fingers into the cavities around his collarbone. 'You're getting too thin. I'm going to feed you up a bit.' Quite spontaneously, her tears began to well up again, which must have blurred her vision, so that she did not see what was coming until she felt it full and hard against the side of her head. It almost lifted her off her knees and left her lying in a heap about a yard to his left. He stood up and walked over to her.

'Too thin, eh? That's because I have worked myself to the bone for all this,' he said. He raised his right fist again and the tendons in his wrist flared, but he changed his mind because she was too low, and so he kicked her, instead, in the ribcage. She groaned. 'And I'm not going to let you throw it all away. Not when I've come so far. I don't have all the time in the world, you know. No-one lives for ever. You should be aware of that.' He bent down and rolled her onto her back. She seemed only half conscious and her mouth hung open. Bunching her hair in his fist he dragged her up into a sitting position and was about to smack her around the face when she fell forwards, eyes rolling, so he hauled her up again and lowered himself to speak to her, this time in a quieter voice. 'You have disappointed me very, very much.' She did not respond. He let go of her hair so that she slumped to the floor at his feet. He remained staring angrily at her motionless form, and kneaded his fingers deep into the muscles either side of his upper vertebrae, feeling them click.

Rose had still not moved from the floor when the time came for him to leave the bunker, an hour later. He took no notice of her; instead he drained a coffee he had earlier made for himself, banged the empty cup down on the kitchen table, and locked the doors one by one behind him.

Chapter 22

It came to him in the night again, waking him up with a jerk, as if to remind him of something he needed to get up for. Was it developing a sense of humour, he wondered, or was it just playful like a puppy, impatient for him to be up and at it? It was certainly insistent, and very regular, nowadays, which did make him wonder what would happen if it arrived in full force when he was out, or up in front of the congregation in church. It had a way of leaving him speechless, in a stupor of wonder, unable to move or communicate in any way, which might prove embarrassing in public. People would think he had lost his marbles altogether.

It did not remain long with him this morning and was succeeded by a headache that left him in a dull daze for most of the day. He had work to do and ground on through it conscientiously, but as the afternoon waned he began to count the minutes until he could reasonably justify going back to bed.

By seven o'clock in the evening he was sitting alone in the living room, still not tired enough to go up, and flicking through TV channels. He could not put up with any of them longer than it took to register what was showing, and checked the TV guide for programmes coming up later. He was privately wounded that all the razzmatazz was carrying on as if nothing had happened. Not that he really expected the cataclysm in his own life to have rippled across the nation and diminished people's appetite for dog-bowl entertainment. He glanced down the schedule of programmes from the top again. Did it take a personal crisis to be able to stand back and see all this for the drivel that it was? The crud that passed for comedy: freeze-dried laughter on cue, smug quiz show panellists, incessant jibes at other people's expense. The so-called human interest features: documentaries that turned deformities, diseases and catastrophes into showbiz. Or the cunning commercial breaks: high-sheen car ads, dancing mushrooms, superhero indigestion tablets, complacent gits in banks promising wealth and security. Even the news: reportage from all corners of the world, nicely sanitized but bleak and scary, spelling out the inevitability of global hatred, as if it were a cliché of contemporary culture – insuperable dangers, unending threats and calamities. Granville turned the television off and went upstairs.

A family photo montage on the bathroom wall stabbed at him when he switched on the light. Happy faces and blue skies; damp baby skin in towels with beach sand stuck to buttocks; Christmas lunches, party hats, silly faces; the tousled hair, adults and infants wrapped in each other's arms, displays of affection and hilarity. He'd chosen the pictures deliberately for their off-guardedness. Now, it was the very indignity of the faces and poses that pushed the knife more deeply into his wound. There were far better family photographs downstairs – handsome black and white studio portraits in frames – but they did not have half the poignancy of these idiotic ones.

He brushed his teeth, peed into the toilet bowl,

neglected to flush it, and went out to check he'd left the landing light on. Then he realized the girls weren't home and that he needn't bother, and so switched it off.

Earlier he had brought a pile of books to the bedroom, thinking he might prefer to come up and read in bed: a couple of specially chosen sacred texts, a bit of Ramana Maharshi and some old notebooks from the days when he'd had the luxury to jot down his musings. He'd hoped to discover something here to cling to but found himself staring at the page, reading the same sentence over and over again without getting anywhere, and eventually gave up trying. He switched off the bedside lamp. A bit of daylight was still finding its way around the edge of the curtains and he wasn't remotely tired. He lay there for a while with the prospect of sleepless hours ahead, and at last got up to try Hetty again.

He arrived downstairs in his slippers and dressing gown and went to the kitchen to put the kettle on. His mother always said that tea put the world to rights. It made him wonder whether he should invite her to stay for a while, but he shied from such an infantile impulse. Run to Mummy and bury his frightened face in her skirts? What was he thinking? Besides, it would mean having Mounty to stay as well, and he did not feel up to having a rollercoaster in the house just now. Anyway, they were just about to leave for a hiking trip in Nepal.

He took his tea into the study and sat down at his desk. There were books and papers collated into piles, chaotic to anyone else's eyes but he knew exactly where everything was. The desk, the room, the whole house, was a mess, as full of stuff as it ever had been. The difference now was that the unfolding drama of four dynamic lives had been paused, and every room of the house felt like a frozen snapshot. Until this moment, their loosely reined lives had woven around each other like spinning pods on a fairground waltzer, exciting, edgy, but more or less under control. Now the buzz was still and the domestic jumble of lives and minds in motion was just so much beached detritus from yesterday. For all the quantity of stuff here, the photos, letters, treasures and personal knick-knacks, the house had the feel of an abandoned warehouse. He was the night porter, come to check the empty shelves, turn out the lights and shut the place down.

He stared at the telephone. There had been no word from Edwina or the girls in the three days that had passed. He would respect her wishes for a couple more days and then do something about it. In the meantime, he had tried continually to contact Hetty but there had been no answer. She held the key to the situation but she was unpredictable and could just as easily make everything worse if she chose to bare her full story or twist it at whim. Every time he phoned her, when the ringtones elapsed and the answer service cut in, he felt secretly relieved.

He was about to try her once again when the loud old Bakelite phone on the desk began to ring, and his heart jumped. He picked it up straight away. It was his father; the first time he had phoned back since the crisis began. Granville had left a message for him but now explained properly what had occurred. The bare facts of the news almost stuck in his throat, but at last the thing was out, the awful words spoken.

Mounty did not – could not – respond to this kind of incident in a normal way, and it was obvious to both of them that it would be better if he did not even try. Instead – and this, more than anything, indicated the magnitude of the effect the news had on him – his conversation skittered tangentially around the issue. He talked of a grander cosmic pattern and the inherent architecture of destiny, but he talked nervously, without pause and at a raised pitch, making sure that awkwardness would not be allowed to get a foothold, even if it meant failing to engage Granville properly in a dialogue.

'Is Mum there?' Granville eventually asked.

'She's somewhere else in the house, I think, no idea where.'

'Well, could you go and get her? Or take the phone . . . ?'

'Why don't I get her to call you back when she's sitting down and got a calm five minutes?'

'What's she doing now?'

'I don't know. Rushing about. Are you going to listen to Radio Four tonight? There's a very interesting programme about seals.'

'Look, you know, right now I'm not really interested in anything on the radio.'

'No, I don't imagine you are. I'll see if I can record it for you. You can hear it when we get back from Nepal.'

'Just ask Mum to give me a call when she gets a minute. I'd hate not to speak to her before you go.'

'Will do.'

'Bye, then.'

Granville put down the phone. Not for the first time he wondered how Mounty would react if the news arrived that his only son had unexpectedly died. It could go either way. He might theorize about it and drone on to anyone tactful enough to listen. Or he might fall apart completely. In a warped kind of way, Granville almost wished he could be there to see. How gratifying it might be if some state of post-necrotic consciousness, some out of body experience, allowed him, when the time came, to watch his father crumble in an outpouring of

251

conventional affection he had been unable to articulate during life.

As Granville sat at his desk the ghosts of the past began to descend, landing with gentle feet and smiling their way into his thoughts; deep impressions from his earliest days, the happenings and atmospheres that had shaped him. They were more than mere memories, they were the sealed and treasured ingredients of his very nature. Slowly ripened to goodness over the course of his life, they were jarred like a vintage preserve and safely shelved in a dark locker within. Right now, however, they served not to comfort but to plague him, and he could not block them out. He decided that a change of scene might help and wandered out in his dressing gown onto the back lawn.

The polished square base of his monument gleamed in the moonlight and he leant against it. The grass was freshly mown all around and the perfume of the cuttings was pungent in the spring evening air. It brought to mind a tableau of him and Edwina lying at night on a school's cricket pitch years before. The temperature had been wonderfully mild and the two of them were cushioned by a perfectly cropped stretch of turf. A half-moon was riding high and a bird of prey shrieked in the woods beyond. How royal the blue-black of that night sky! The scent of tickling grass blades on their cheeks as they lay looking sideways at each other, holding hands. Granville had only just been ordained and taken his first job as chaplain of a boys' public school in Buckinghamshire. She had loved it there. She played violin in the school orchestra, taught the cookery club, and the boys all fancied her rotten. Did she really have no idea of their stares or was she quietly teasing out their interest when she crossed her legs during orchestra rehearsals?

Her skirts were always just short enough to hold their attention, but if ever she caught them glancing up her tights they would look away, blushing. She would come home afterwards and laugh about it with Granville and he could tell that she quite enjoyed it.

During that first summer at the school, the two of them would steal out from the chaplain's cottage at night to enjoy the freedom and openness of the playing fields by the light of the moon. Once, they made love on the cricket square, and she'd had to stifle her cries as she came, all the while giggling at their recklessness. There would have been a scandal if they'd been discovered and he would have probably been sacked on the spot. As it turned out, he did not stay long at the school anyway but resigned after only a couple of terms in protest at the unfair expulsion of a promising pupil. So ended a short but happy chapter for the two of them. He now wept quietly about it; about the sunlight that had flooded their little kitchen on summer mornings, about the sofa they would curl up on together to watch television, about the narrow cottage staircase he would playfully chase her up, putting his hand up her skirt to feel around the cotton of her knickers on their way to bed.

Tiredness now began to overwhelm him and he went back indoors from the garden to bed. At last he fell asleep with his head turned towards the empty pillow beside him.

When he woke up the next morning, too early, it took a moment as always before he recalled his new circumstances, which meant having to rediscover the weight of her loss all over again. Anguish like this was new to him, his hunger for all three of them boundless. He kicked off his covers, got out of bed and thought about driving straight to the airport: drop everything and fight like a lion to salvage his family. But after he'd washed and dressed, the passion subsided. He retrieved his shoes from under the bedroom chair, put them on and slid back into the groove of a more or less normal morning. A sense of diligence and duty returned, and with it the bare bones of a more reasoned schedule of action. It was at this point, having forced himself to eat something for breakfast, that he decided it was time to see Piet Steyn.

He waited until eight o'clock and Piet picked up the phone almost immediately. Granville did not go into detail but asked if they could meet today, in person. 'There's been a development. About the girl,' he said, cryptically, 'and we need to decide on the best way forward. It's only fair that we agree, because we're both in this together.'

Piet said it was not a very convenient time for him. He was busy for most of the day but could meet in the evening, if necessary, at about nine o'clock, by the bench in the abbey grounds.

'I don't mind coming over to your house,' said Granville.

'Impossible,' Piet replied.

'Or would you like to come to me? I can make us something to eat.'

'I don't eat on Fridays.'

'Yes, I think you did tell me that once. Sorry, I'd forgotten.'

'Let's stick with the abbey.' The evening appointment was set.

Before beginning his day's work, Granville tried Hetty once more and left another message asking her to call him. He had just settled back at his desk when the front door bell rang and he went to answer it. The huge figure of the old farmer, Alan Burnside, was standing there, leaning on a stick, a cap gripped in his free hand. He nodded at the rector.

'Morning,' he said. 'Sorry for all your trouble, an' that.'

'News travels fast.'

'Well,' Alan looked down, 'you know what it's like once the women's tongues start wagging.'

'Thanks for your concern. Is there something . . . ?'

'Yes,' said Alan, and heaved his weight over to the other leg to ease the pain in his joints. Granville stepped back and allowed him into the hall. The waistband of Alan's trousers was exceedingly wide and held up by braces, the clips of which were visible on the under-curve of his paunch, where his jumper could not stretch. Granville offered him a seat but he declined, saying that he wouldn't be staying for long.

Getting straight to the point of his visit, he began, 'You remember you asked me about that farm down Petershot way, the one bought by old Neville Eggers?' Granville frowned, trying to recall what this was all about. 'That farm called Newland,' Alan prompted. 'You asked me about the place called Newland, and who'd lived there, an' such.'

'Yes, of course.' Granville remembered the conversation outside the church hall. 'Have you found something out?'

'In a manner of speaking. I saw Jim Eggers the other day, and mentioned it to him, seeing as it was his grandfather's brother that bought the place sixty, seventy-odd years ago.'

'And?'

'The Eggers family sold it on in the eighties.'

When it seemed that Alan had nothing more to add,

Granville said, 'Ah. OK, then. Thanks for letting me know.'

'Jim did say something about the people who sold it to old Neville.' Another pause followed by another awkward smile from Alan.

'Oh yes?'

'Finlay.'

'What?'

'That's what their name was. Finlay. Bit of a sad story there, it seems.'

Alan stood there, still smiling, either reluctant to spill the beans or just enjoying making the rector wait. Granville's mobile phone began to ring in his pocket. He took it out and glanced at the screen. It was Edwina. Looking up at Alan, he said, 'One moment, if you wouldn't mind, this is really urgent,' and hurried back through the hall into the kitchen to answer it. 'Hello?'

'It's me.'

'I know. How are you? How are the girls?'

'We're all OK. You?'

'Pretty bloody awful.'

There was a brief pause and they started talking simultaneously. She stopped first. 'Can I call you straight back?' Granville asked. 'Someone's here. Let me get rid of him and I'll get straight back to you.' He thought he heard something like a laugh at the other end. 'Darling? Edwina?'

'Please tell me I didn't hear you say that.'

'What d'you mean?'

'Nothing changes, does it? Even at a time like this.'

'Come on. That's not fair. He's standing in the hall. I can't just—' The phone had gone dead. He closed his eyes for a second, pocketed the phone and went back through to the hall.

'Look, Alan,' he said, 'I've got a real bowlful at the moment, could we talk another—'

'Their daughter ran off with a soldier, they say. Came to a bad end.'

'Who's that?'

'The daughter of the Finlay family. Took up with some African farmer after the war. Not a black. I mean one of them white South Africans.'

'What sort of bad end?'

'No-one can remember the details. Just that it didn't work out and she died young.'

'Were there any children?'

'There was a son. His mother's brother tried to get the boy back to England but that didn't work out either.'

'Why not?'

'Don't know. Jim seems to think the whole thing ended badly. Either the kid died or something. South Africa. Hell of a long way away. Long time ago.'

'What happened to the family in Dorset?'

'After the place sold, they went up north somewhere. One of them married into a Yorkshire family, or something, and went to farm their place up there. No more Finlays round these parts after that.' He seemed to have finished the story.

'Is that it?'

'You interested for some particular reason?'

'No, no,' replied Granville. 'I was looking for a family called Newland, you'll remember. Just something I read about. Nothing special.'

'Oh, I see.'

'I don't think the two things are connected.' He knew he probably did not sound very convincing.

'Ah. Oh, well, then.' Alan looked down, a little disappointed. He sucked his breath in and grimaced heavily, gripped by a new pain in his hips. 'I'll be on my way, then.'

As soon as he was gone, Granville dialled Edwina's number. For a while it seemed she wasn't going to answer.

'Hello, Granville,' her voice eventually came through. Using his name like that sounded too formal, detached.

'I'm more sorry than I can say,' he began. 'About everything you're going through. If you can find it within yourself to believe me or trust me, I promise, I absolutely promise that there's an innocent explanation to this whole stupid business.'

She sighed through her reply. 'It's not just the girl, though, is it?'

'What do you mean?' She did not answer. 'Edwina? Tell me what you mean.'

'This business with the girl has just brought it to a head. It's given me the chance to stop and think. Things haven't been right for quite a while, have they? It's only now that I'm away from it all that I'm beginning to feel sane again.'

Her words pierced like a needle's point.

'I know it's been a bit of a strain, but nothing that we can't work out, surely. For the girls' sake, if not for—'

'You don't need to worry about the girls. They're as happy as larks up here.' Another stab. Insensitive, he thought, but said nothing. 'I've got to tell you,' Edwina went on, 'I've started looking at schools.'

'For the girls? Take them away from me completely, you mean? Take them away from home, their friends? Just like that?'

'A clean break. Now that we've finally done it.'

'*We* haven't done it. It's *you.*'

'Father says—'

'I don't want to know what he says.'

258

'It's better this way.'

'No it's not. You can't do this to me. You can't.'

'Couldn't you see this coming? You could have done something about it. Instead, you pick a time like this to go off and have an affair with a . . . with a *child*?'

'Edwina, you cannot believe I would do such a thing.'

'I've got nothing more to say right now. It's best if we don't speak for a while.'

'Let me talk to Serena.'

'Best not.'

'You have to let me talk to my children.'

'They don't want to.'

'What have you told them?'

'Look, maybe in a few days' time.'

'Edwina!'

'Don't call on the landline. Father and Mummy will put the phone down on you.'

'Please—'

'I'll ring in a few days.' And the line went dead. He stared at the phone for a moment before letting it drop to the floor.

Chapter 23

It was dark by the time Granville arrived at the abbey grounds, but he could see well enough because the moon was up and nearly full. He reached the bench where he had agreed to meet Steyn, and it was empty, so he sat down and pulled his coat close in around him. There was a nip in the air. To his left towered a free-standing wall, intersected at a right angle with remnants of another segment of the fallen abbey. By day, this stonework was the colour of beach sand but in this light it had turned milky grey. The seemingly random punctuations of flint stones in the walls looked like small black pockmarks in the dullness, the scars of an ancient architectural plague. There were occasional blind arches in the structure, and one or two redundant mullioned entrances that had been filled in with brick or stone to suit the purposes of forgotten generations. The muddle of decay, ancient alteration and destruction made it impossible to ascertain how the storeys or partitions of the place might once have been divided, where new chambers had succeeded old cells, where cloister had been linked to chapter house or nave to chancel. Illegible remnants of inscriptions on lintels still pronounced partial Latin sentences, while here and there, pale outcrops of stone were all that remained of gargoyle faces that had once spat fear into the hearts of passers-by. Granville looked around and thought that if ever there were an illustration of how far the Christian ideal had strayed from the simple warmth and kindliness of the man Jesus, it was here in this bleak and mournful place.

All at once he was aware that Steyn was present, standing in the shadow of the ruins. 'Is that you, Piet?' he called quietly, but it was not until he had called a second time that Steyn stepped wordlessly out into the moonlight. He stood with his hands in his pockets, leaning back slightly, eyeing Granville, as was his way. He seemed thinner and his face had a skeletal quality, reminiscent of the villains in old-fashioned horror movies. Granville had seen the same look in a row of sculpted busts along a colonnade in Italy: portraits of pious ecclesiastical grandees, glowering down from rococo niches with faces like vampires. He called out, 'Don't worry. We're quite alone,' and Steyn came slowly forward to join him by the bench. 'Were you hiding?'

'Just taking in the atmosphere.'

Apart from the short telephone conversation the previous night, Granville had not spoken to Steyn since the incident at the Easter Grill five days earlier, and had assumed there would be a comradeship between them, since they had stood shoulder to shoulder in front of a common aggressor. But any goodwill there might have been seemed to have been blighted by the incident and was noticeable only because of its absence.

'How long were you standing in the shadows over there?' Granville asked.

'I saw you arrive.'

'Why didn't you come out?'

'I wasn't ready. I come to this place quite a lot, to think.'

Granville looked around. It was suitably Wordsworthian

here, with an atmosphere that might encourage contemplation of the intercourse between man and nature, but he did not suppose Piet came to ponder along these lines. 'What do you particularly like about the place?'

'The thought of the men who lived here in times past. Men governed by the rules of their order and who were purified by it.'

'I shouldn't romanticize their lives too much. It was a harsh world. Desperately confined. Cruel, at times.'

'But close to God.'

'With the threat of hellfire hanging over them. The obedience of those medieval monks was held together by blind fear, believe me.'

'You don't know everything, Father.'

'Of course not, but I do think we've got beyond the age of horned devils with tails and forks.'

'You don't believe in Satan?'

'Roasting people on barbecues? About as stupid as the idea of angels fluttering around with feathered wings.'

Granville was sitting on the bench, leaning forward, elbows on knees. He let his head sink. 'Edwina has left me,' he said, 'and taken the children.' His breath lightly clouded the cool air in front of him as he spoke. 'That girl, Hetty, has been making out I've had an affair with her.'

'Hetty?'

'Bertie Gosling's girlfriend.'

'I didn't know that was what she was called.'

'She made up the other name. Turns out she's a pretty convincing liar.'

'So you have been seeing her.'

'Not in the way she's implying. I've seen her once or

twice, trying to sort out her problems, smooth over the whole mess about Bertie, that's all.'

'You didn't tell me.'

'I know.'

'Did she regard your meetings in the same light?'

'Clearly not.'

'So are you completely without blame?'

Granville raised his head and looked towards a distant meadow. There were cows lying in the grass out there, bulbous black ink splurges against a marginally paler backcloth. It took him a moment to answer. 'I suppose not.'

'You allowed her to . . . ?'

'I didn't think so at the time.'

Steyn came over to the bench and looked down at Granville before sitting next to him. 'Your lip is still swollen. You shouldn't have stepped into that fight.'

'Thought you'd never mention it.'

'I didn't ask you for your help.'

'All in the past.'

'If you're expecting me to be grateful—'

'Least of my problems.'

Steyn sighed and leant back. 'What has this business of your wife got to do with me?'

'The girl is out of control. I think she might spill the beans.'

'Tell people what really happened, you mean? Who would she go to?'

'I don't know. The police. The papers.'

'What would she gain from that?'

Granville thought for a moment. 'Revenge.'

'For what?'

He sat up. 'For me refusing her. She's desperate and sick in the head.'

263

'She must be stopped, then.'

'There is another way,' said Granville. 'We could pre-empt her. Come clean ourselves.'

Steyn stopped short of laughing but his contempt for the suggestion was clear. 'Are you crazy? We'd have to admit we've been lying from the start. Think how it would affect Janet.'

'Yes, but if we enter into a battle of denials and counter-claims the girl will start inventing a load of hogwash and we'll end up digging ourselves into a deeper hole. At least if we go to the police now we'll have a chance to stop her in her tracks.'

'The police? That might be all right for you, Father, as a pastor, but the officers of the law might not be so charitable to me. I'm sorry, but I don't want the police breathing down my neck. What would Janet think of me then?'

Granville sighed and shook his head. 'Piet, what exactly do you want from Janet?'

'With respect, that is my business.'

'I feel a duty to protect her.'

'As do I. You obviously have decided she needs protection from me.'

'Does she really welcome your . . . interest?'

'Has she said anything to you?'

'Not directly, no.'

'Then keep your nose out of my affairs.'

'Harshly put.'

'You've brought up a sensitive subject.'

'You know she's put her house on the market, don't you?'

Piet neither replied nor moved a muscle.

'She wants to be nearer her sister,' Granville continued. 'She'll be leaving Dorset for ever.'

They sat in silence while a gust of wind sent a heavy whisper through the heights of the surrounding beech trees, like a theatre audience stirred by a surprise and unwelcome announcement. The noise settled and quietness returned to the shadowed masonry and neighbouring grassland.

'What about the girl?' Piet said.

'If you don't want to go to the police, have you got any better suggestions?' asked Granville.

'Give me her address. I'll talk to her.'

'What would you say?'

'Reason with her. I'm an old hand. It would be better coming from me. Her feelings for you sound a bit complicated.'

'I don't know if it would get you anywhere. She needs psychiatric help.'

'Let me try. If it doesn't work out, we'll think about doing as you suggest.'

Granville thought about it. 'How long would you give yourself?'

'Have you got the address?'

'It's on my phone.' He took out his BlackBerry.

'Give me two days. If she's still making a nuisance of herself after that, you and I will go to the police together.'

It seemed a reasonable enough suggestion to Granville. He was too tired to argue, and used to settling for compromise solutions on a daily basis in the course of his work. 'All right,' he said, and handed over the phone. Steyn took the device, inspected it with hostile caution, and then retrieved a pencil and notepad from his jacket pocket. Granville watched him carefully take down the girl's details. His handwriting was slow, laboured and angular, almost Gothic, and reminded him of his grandmother's style, a relic from the Victorian era.

Piet finished writing, read through what he had noted, and folded away the pad. 'I'll deal with this,' he murmured and stood up to leave. Granville walked behind him along the narrow path that led away from the ruins. At the exit, they passed a glass-fronted display case, put there by a heritage organization for the benefit of tourists. It showed an artist's reconstruction of life in and around the abbey in the days of yore, with sack-clad bearded serfs touching the forelock to gentlewomen in conical hats, but the illustrations were little more than vague shapes in the near-darkness.

'You've learnt one thing, at any rate,' Steyn said out of the blue as they left the abbey grounds and came out onto Church Street. 'You now understand that there are people around here who have decided, through no fault of mine, to make an enemy of me. They've got it into their heads that I am some kind of monster.'

'I'd say that's a bit of an exaggeration. But you don't do yourself many favours. You could have handled that situation differently the other day.'

'I was provoked.'

'No amount of provocation justifies sending a man to hospital. I mean, what made you think of . . . ?'

'I don't like being treated unjustly.'

'That may be so, but you'll probably find Colin Futcher will press charges. He may have the last laugh.'

'He can do what he wants.' Steyn seemed almost to rejoice in the threat. 'I've seen a lot worse in my time. Let him show me what he's made of.'

'Our Lord recommends a different approach.'

Steyn stopped in his tracks and looked straight at Granville. 'You presume to teach me the Gospel?'

Granville smiled, though for the first time he felt unnerved by Steyn. A splinter of the anger he had

266

witnessed at the Easter Grill was there now and turned towards him. 'It is my job,' he said, 'and you are part of my congregation.'

'Don't make me laugh! You said that joining your church would help me to be accepted here. It hasn't made the blindest bit of difference, as you can see. People here still look down on me. Maybe my association with you has made it even worse than it was before.'

'The likes of Colin Futcher don't take any notice of what goes on in church,' replied Granville. They had reached the point where their ways divided. The pavement that headed out of the village towards Steyn's house disappeared into utter blackness, whereas Granville's led off right towards the housing estate enclave, the entire way illuminated by orange street lights. 'You must understand that it's nothing personal. Rightly or wrongly some of these people just see you as an outsider.'

The comment brought a sharp look from Steyn. 'I was not born here, it's true, but my people came from these parts. Generations of them. By blood I'm as local as the best of them.'

'That may well be so, but the sort of people I'm talking about have no grasp of history. To them you are a foreigner. You just need to be patient, show a little bit of tact, and give them time. To broaden their outlook and be educated.'

Steyn laughed out loud and turned away from Granville. He began to walk off.

'Piet!' called Granville, to no effect. He repeated the call, louder, and Steyn turned around. 'Does the name Finlay mean anything to you?'

Steyn's head tilted stiffly backwards and that same look of dark suspicion came into his eyes.

'What are you trying to do?'

'Nothing. What do you mean? I was just wondering.'

'Why do you ask, then?'

'Because there was a family called Finlay that lived at Newland Farm. Near Petershot.'

Steyn looked to the ground and brought a fist to his nose as if to relieve an itch. 'I had a brother whose name was Finlay. He died as an infant.'

For a moment Granville's face lit up. 'That's it, then. He must have been named after your mother's family. And they farmed land not ten miles from here. Isn't that a discovery?'

It took a while for Steyn to respond. When he did look up his face was hard as stone, and Granville felt a fizz of shock.

'You have been snooping into my background, again, then,' he said.

'I meant no harm. I've just asked some locals a couple of questions. I'm interested in family history. I thought you'd be pleased. You always seem so proud of your Dorset roots.'

Piet took a step back towards him. His fists were buried deep in his bomber jacket pockets and a cold anger came into his eyes. It dawned on Granville with a jolt that their friendship was not only irretrievably lost but had probably never existed in the first place. It had been a sham all along.

'You should perhaps spend more time sorting out your own family,' Piet began, 'than picking around in other people's. Tidy up your own house first.' Granville did not offer a response. 'It's no wonder your life is in ruins. Look how far you've let your women sink. You have a headstrong wife who defies you publicly and a daughter who dresses like a harlot. D'you know? I pity you. I pity your drink-fuelled opinions, I pity your blasphemous friends spewing godless filth without restraint. I pity you for having every advantage life can offer and throwing it to the dogs, but above all I pity you for your spinelessness.'

He stared at Granville, ready and waiting to tear down any attempt at a retort, perhaps pitching for an all-out fight, but Granville did not give him the satisfaction. Instead, and without a word, he turned and walked off towards the orange glow of the street lamps, leaving Piet standing alone in the shadows.

Chapter 24

Rufus Futcher got straight on his scooter and rode out to the high fields behind Charlton Blackmore, where the annual point-to-point meet was already under way. He had not intended to come to the races today but his discovery was too important not to share with his father right away. By the time he found Colin he was out of breath, having run from the car park to the bar tent and then on to the paddock.

Colin Futcher was wearing a short-brimmed grey trilby, and had a plastic splint on his nose, held down by surgical tape. In one hand he held a racecard, folded back on itself, and with the other he had just put a pencil behind his ear. He was with a couple of friends, leaning against the paddock rail and watching the horses for the next race parade past, when Rufus came puffing up to him.

'Dad,' he said, but Colin took little notice. He was busy assessing the rump muscle of the Gizzard horse everyone had been talking about.

'Looks like 'e'll do the distance anyhow,' said one of his friends.

'Ain't done much yet, though, has he?' said the other. 'Look at that form.' He pointed to his racecard. 'Third, pulled up, nothing, nothing, second. And 'e's carrying too much weight.'

'He'll come in with the first three, mark my words,' Colin said sagely, watching the horse pad slowly around the ring.

'Dad!'

'How d'you know that, then?' said the friend, grinning at his mate. 'Got a nose for it, have you?' They both sniggered.

'You wait and see,' said Colin.

'Dad. Can I talk to you?'

'What the fuck d'you want?' Colin did not take his eyes off the horses. The announcer's voice boomed around the site from a variety of lofty speaker cones, issuing race stats, entry details and pieces of local hunt news. The meet was taking place on a high plateau between Sherborne and Sturminster, the views of surrounding countryside were wide ranging and the amplified sound travelled far, echoing across the rolling grassland on all sides. The sun was out and a colourful patchwork of car roofs sparkled, like a quilted bedspread, in the adjacent field where the vehicles were parked.

'I have to talk to you alone,' Rufus said, lowering his voice and his head.

'After this race.'

'No. Now. It's important.'

One of Colin's friends smirked out loud. 'Run along then. Don't upset the boy.'

Colin tutted. 'Better make it quick,' he muttered, and reluctantly turned away from the paddock. When they were out of the hearing of his friends, he said, 'Come on, then. Out with it.'

Rufus was still breathing deeply, as he thought about

how best and quickest to get his information across. 'He's got a secret place.'

'A what? Who?'

'Steyn. At the end of his garden. Right thick in the brambles. Some kind of hole in the ground. I seen him go in there. Goes in and stays in. For hours.'

'A hole? What, like a fox hole?'

'No, not like that. Like something out of James Bond. Underground. It's got one of them metal lids like when you get into a submarine.'

'In his garden?'

'At the bottom. He's got, like, a bit of woodland and brambles, all overgrown, like, and there's a secret way through. I saw him go in there an' I see him open this lid and go inside and close the lid again behind him.'

'What's 'e do down there?'

'I dunno.'

'So that's where he goes when he's not in the house.'

'That's it.'

'That's where you're going to have to do it, then.'

Rufus' panting stopped. The animation froze on his face. 'Do what?'

'You know. Like we said.'

'I dunno.'

'You can't go backing out now. You know what we got to do.'

'Yeah, but . . .' He stalled and slowly shook his head. 'I don't think I could do that, Dad. Not come to thinking about it.'

'You too scared? Well, we'll have to talk it through down at the pub, then. See if we can find someone with enough balls.'

'No!' Rufus stared fiercely into space. 'I can do it. Don't go telling people I won't.'

Colin smiled and patted his son on the shoulder. 'Right then,' he said. 'That's that. I'll be going up to the finishing post to watch this race, then.'

Chapter 25

Granville was sitting in silence at his desk with no light in the room other than that generated by the computer screen. His face was floodlit by the glare and his eyeballs were animated, darting quickly from one side of the screen to the other as the content flitted and refreshed itself; but otherwise he was completely still, captivated, transported to another world. The usual, almost erotic intensity of gratification he felt when chasing a scent as strong as this was darkened this evening by a deepening sense of alarm.

He possessed a genuine talent for this sort of research, as he had discovered when gathering material for the two books he'd written. The feel and clatter of the keys beneath his fingertips, the luminous moments of revelation, the stumbling into unexpected chasms which turned out to offer solutions more grand and far-reaching than he could possibly have hoped for – these were the silent joys of the perspicacious internet researcher. The process itself focused Granville's thought into a prism from which it was difficult to be distracted, so that his own present plight, even Edwina and the girls, were for the moment sidelined.

Within a couple of hours he had sifted through essays about the Dutch Reformed Church, Afrikaner Calvinism and Boer farming communities, and had come to a reasonable understanding of the sort of world in which Piet Steyn had been nurtured. He read about the Boer people's northern European roots, about their proud struggle to survive in the face of hostile conditions and invading colonizers. He learnt how they had clung to their old faith like besieged soldiers who hold high the flag to strengthen their resolve; and about how they carved a kind of civilization out of the wilderness, under the perpetual threat of an engulfing chaos. He began to perceive a culture of pugnacious defensiveness, frugality and self-determination, traits which in time evolved into sanctimonious complacency and prejudice. But above all, he came to see how those remote farming communities regarded themselves as lonely Christian outposts where life was precarious, where the menfolk armed and entrenched themselves against the heathen, and where it was the women's job to rear hardy, determined heirs to keep the flame alive. They were white-skinned, European stock, and nowadays spoke English as well as Afrikaans, but were otherwise foreign in almost every respect, as different from Granville as almost any people on earth.

He then turned his attention to immigration records, Second World War regimental lists, Ministry of Defence registers of nursing staff and colonial troops. It was not a straightforward path through the tangle of websites, but he found a thread which gathered strength and direction as it progressed. Rose Finlay, the twenty-one-year-old daughter of Henry and Rebecca Finlay, he discovered, travelled to Egypt from Southampton in 1943 as a member of Queen Alexandra's Imperial Military Nursing Service, where she worked in one of the British Army's tented hospitals. After the war, Rose Finlay married Johannes Greef, a soldier in the 6th

South African Armoured Division. The only window of opportunity for them to have met would have been in Sicily, where the South African regiment had been sent for training prior to moving further north into Italy. Rose's hospital had also moved to Sicily after the German surrender in North Africa, but how they found one another and the circumstances of their romance remained a mystery.

A little bit of digging into the surname Greef brought up some references to a Transvaal family of farmers who had made local headline news in the early 1960s. For four generations the Greefs had occupied a huge corn and grazing ranch in a treeless area of the middle veld, having trekked there years before to escape British colonizers in the Cape. But it was their involvement in a notorious local incident that lent the name Greef more prominence than others of their ilk in that area at the time. It was a news file reference that first gave mention of the occurrence, and, though it sprang off the screen like a bolt, Granville felt its arrival as a moment of grace. It was late, dark and deathly silent in the room, but his mind was ablaze.

The remains of missing girl Louise Wiedemann found, the article began. Granville read the content of the piece slowly, and then read it again. The fate of the young man Louise had fled with – Jan, son of the late Johannes and Rose Greef of Olifantsfontein, and nephew of respected farmer Hendrik Greef – was still unknown. Police were continuing to search the surrounding area for his body, and hoped to have more news in due course. That was it. There were no further links or references. The trail had come to a dead end. But it was enough.

*   *   *

He could not let the matter rest. It was too late to go and see Janet that same evening but he decided to call her and make a time to visit the following day. When she picked up the phone he could tell by the hushed surprise in her voice that she was alarmed to be called so late at night, but he quickly put her mind at ease and arranged to come over and see her; just for a chat, he said. She could only manage the evening, she replied.

He arrived at her front door punctually at seven o'clock and she embraced him warmly. She had heard the news about Edwina and wanted to let him know she sympathized. She asked if he was all right and he said he was managing. They went into the house and sat down at the kitchen table. She asked if he wanted to talk about it and he explained what had happened as best he could, omitting the detail and avoiding any hint of self-pity.

'You're a good man,' Janet said, when he'd finished. 'No bitterness, no blame, and you only say lovely things about Edwina, though goodness knows how you must be feeling.' Granville absorbed her soothing words gratefully. It was good to be here. A wholesome, tidy kitchen, everything put away, tea towels folded, a pot plant in bloom on the table, Labrador asleep in front of the Aga. It felt like a fortress of kindness in the midst of a turbulent, volatile world. She listened to him intently and seemed to understand without having to ask for elaboration, without the need to gratify her curiosity. For the first time since Edwina's departure – though he had not come here with the intention of opening his heart – he felt like breaking down. He could feel the physical effects of it coming on, involuntarily, as if some demon within had punctured a hidden spice pod under the bridge of his nose. Janet clasped his hand on the table as his tears began to spill over.

What she didn't realize was that Granville was not crying for Edwina, nor for the girls, nor with the pain of abandonment. He was weeping because unexpectedly he had caught sight of a better place, and, in glimpsing it, knew he would never look back. It was just a faint and vague sighting but its appearance marked the turning of a page, the passing of his former life. Perhaps it had always been there, waiting for him, but he had never noticed it before because of the smokescreen of his busy life and the storm of his marriage. It felt like a quieter kingdom, and promised a future of gentle smiles, tolerance, acceptance. Janet had unintentionally lifted a film from his eyes, had allowed him a moment to reflect on his own needs for once, and he realized that he deserved a kinder partnership, a better life. His tears were tears of farewell.

She said nothing, but kept hold of his hand as he let his feelings subside. After a couple of minutes he took control of himself, sat up and coughed away the last traces of emotion. He apologized and Janet said not to be silly; would he like some tea? It was as he took out his handkerchief and turned aside to blow his nose that he noticed the slip of paper sitting on the low table nearby, beside the phone. A name was written in blue ink, along with a telephone number, and at the sight of it Granville froze. Janet noticed and followed the direction of his eyes.

'What's the matter?' she asked.

'Who's that?' He nodded towards the slip.

Janet looked at it. 'I don't know. Someone who phoned this morning when I was out and wants me to call back. My cleaner wrote down her number.'

'Do you know what she wants?'

Janet frowned. 'Not a clue. Why?'

Granville suddenly stretched out his hand and took the piece of paper, scrunching it into his fist. 'You mustn't call her.'

'What?' Janet looked mystified.

'You just have to forget this person, all right? Trust me.'

'Do you know her?'

'Yes. She's a troublemaker.'

'What does she want with me?'

'I don't know.'

'You're frightening me.'

He looked up at her and forced himself to smile. 'You don't need to worry. Hetty Swanley is just a young girl with a lot of problems and she's started spreading vicious rumours.'

'Is she the one who . . . ?'

'Exactly. She's made up all sorts of nonsense about me, and not content with poisoning Edwina's mind, she's obviously now made it her mission to spread muck to my friends and parishioners as well.'

'Is that why she's trying to get hold of me? How horrible. What's her connection to you?'

'There isn't one, really. Just one of those problems that springs up out of nothing in the course of a rector's work. You're better off ignoring her. If she calls again just put the phone down.'

'OK.'

The piece of paper was a tight ball in the palm of his hand. He let it drop into his jacket pocket.

From upstairs came the sound of a deep thumping bass. They smiled at each other. 'Which one's that?' he asked.

'Probably Owen. He loves something called dubstep. He wants to have a soundproof room when we move. I think we'll need it!'

'Have you had any interest in the house, then?'

'Oh yes. Didn't I tell you? We've had an offer.'

'So soon?'

'And we've found somewhere we want in Hertford-shire. It's all with the solicitors.'

Granville raised his eyebrows. 'That is news.'

'We're really excited about it, actually.'

'I bet. You'll be sorely missed here, of course.'

At this, a darker thought seemed to cross Janet's mind. She stood up without saying anything, and went over to fill the kettle.

'Janet? Is everything all right?'

Her back was turned; she stopped what she was doing and leant with both palms against the work surface. 'Not exactly.' She said no more and Granville had to coax her. Eventually, she turned and said, 'It's about Piet.' Granville waited for more. 'He's partly the reason we want to move so quickly. The sooner the better, really.'

She had stumbled into the subject Granville had come to discuss without his even having to prompt her. 'You can tell me,' he said.

'Can I? I've been so worried about it. You seem such good friends. And he's a great support in the church, a good Christian and everything. I felt embarrassed to say anything negative about him. But . . . you should know.' She stalled again.

'Know what?'

'He scares me.'

'Why?'

Janet stared wide-eyed into space, flicking her thumb-nails against one another as she considered what to say next. The kettle clicked off, she made the tea and then came back to the table.

When she began, her tone was confessional. 'He was

so proper, so considerate, a great support in those first days. Nothing was too much trouble.' She hesitated, as though she had lost her nerve again, and Granville encouraged her on.

'Everyone needs help in times of distress.'

'I allowed him to get close to me. I relied on him. Something about the way he took control of situations. It was – stupid of me, I know – he was just very gallant. Old fashioned. And fatherly. You see, it started off quite innocently, but . . .'

'Don't blame yourself.'

'He began to buy me presents. First of all flowers, then things for the boys, classic novels and stuff they didn't really want, but very thoughtful. And then it got more personal. Just when I was starting to get uneasy about the amount of time we were spending together.'

'Did you tell him you were feeling uneasy?'

'Yes, and he seemed to agree. At least he said he did, but it was as if keeping him at a distance made him even more determined to push himself on me. After that he wouldn't let up. There'd be something every day – a present, a note in the letterbox, another visit.'

'Why didn't you say something to me?'

'It was difficult to explain to anyone, because he probably meant well. I didn't want to seem ungrateful. And I wasn't completely blameless, I suppose. I'd let him spend more time with me than was appropriate, probably. I felt ashamed to say anything. I still do.'

It was Granville's turn now to act the comforter. He got up, pulled his chair over beside hers and put an arm around her shoulder. He told her not to be hard on herself, that bereavement was an unpredictable process that had left countless of his parishioners high and dry over the years, if not half crazed.

'But I should have drawn the line and I didn't,' Janet went on. 'He started buying things like dresses for me, shoes and furs and jewellery, stuff I really didn't need.'

'Old-fashioned things?'

'That's right.'

'Wartime, or 1950s style?'

'How did you know?'

Granville nodded, remembering. 'It just fits.'

'And then he would start telling me how to behave, as if he had a hold over me, as if I was answerable to him in some way. And he would question me endlessly, about what I'd done, what I was thinking, even about what I'd dreamt about the previous night, and nothing I said seemed to satisfy him. Then his questioning became really horrid.'

'What do you mean?'

She sighed and looked up at Granville, resolved to go on regardless of embarrassment. 'He wanted to know about my sexual history. Not that there's been much. Even down to the boys I'd snogged at school. Their names, how tall they were, whether they were hand-some, clever, sporty – I mean, this was weird stuff.'

'Did you go along with him?'

'I felt helpless. Then he began to get very bossy when he came around, dictating this and that about the house, about what I ate, when I went out, who I should spend time with. And he would get angry with the boys – supposedly in defence of me, but I didn't ask for it. Of course, they got frightened and in the end hid away in their rooms if he came to the house. And so I started to make excuses every time he tried to see me. And we'd lock the door and pretend not to be in if we saw him coming up the drive. It was awful.'

Granville shook his head. 'I feel ashamed that I wasn't there for you.'

She hung her head. 'It's not your fault. I was weak and stupid. I let myself fall into it.'

When she had calmed down Granville said that it would probably be wise if she kept clear of Piet from now on.

'Do you think he's dangerous?'

'No, no, of course not. It's just that it would be sensible to keep a distance. You don't have to come out fighting, but just let him know that you'd rather be left alone. It is your prerogative, after all. And, as the good gentleman he purports to be, he should respect your wishes.'

'Do you think he'll do as I say? He's very insistent.'

Granville looked straight at her. 'If you're worried, come to me. How long until you complete on the new house?'

'A month or so.'

'And then it'll all be over. So don't worry.'

He left her feeling much happier for having un-burdened herself, and kept up his smile, waving back to her all the way down the gravel driveway, right up until the moment she closed her front door. Then he turned to face the darkness ahead and the cheer fell from his face. He contemplated walking straight to the end of the village in hot blood to call at Steyn's house, and was still debating with himself whether to go or wait until the morning when he turned the corner at the end of the churchyard wall and entered his own road, Tennyson Terrace.

Then he saw something that made him stop in his tracks. The flashing brightness of the blue lights on top of one of the parked cars looked almost festive against the night sky. Three men were waiting outside his house, facing the entrance. Even from this distance he could hear Luther barking furiously from the other side of the door. Granville was instantly anaesthetized by the sight and could think of nothing for the moment other than how best and quickest to shut the bloody dog up. The neighbours were suspicious enough of the bull terrier as it was. Luther was doing himself and the St Clair family no favours by making such a racket at this time of night.

Chapter 26

When the men saw him coming up to the house they strolled down the path to meet him and it dawned on him that a crisis was about to break. He prepared himself to absorb its impact and began to speculate wildly about what might have happened. He tried to measure just how bad it was from their eyes as they edged around the camper van towards him. On the other side of the door Luther had sensed their retreat and his barking began to slow.

It was a cold evening and the men were wearing quilted fluorescent jackets. All three had fleshy cheeks and the nearby orange street light lent their faces a kind of Yuletide glow. Had it not been for the young leaves on the trees and the utter solemnity of their expressions, they might have been a deputation of carol singers sent to bring good cheer and sample the neighbourhood's mince pies.

'Is it my wife?' Granville asked. His voice was hushed and strained. 'My girls? Has something happened to my daughters?'

'Mr *Saint* Clair?' The man in front bore a serious expression and took off his peaked hat. He was older, corpulent and balding.

'Yes.'

'Is your wife at home? Or due home, sir?'

'No. Is she all right, then?'

'Your wife?'

'Yes.' The confusion was maddening.

'This isn't about your wife, sir. I just thought I ought to check if she was at home. It's business of a sensitive nature. You might want to break the news to her at the right time and place.'

'What are you talking about?'

The policeman frowned and raised his chin. 'I'm afraid I've got some bad news. Can we come inside?'

'Tell me first,' said Granville.

The policeman glanced over his shoulder at his colleagues, whose faces remained impenetrable, before returning his attention to Granville. 'Very well,' he said, and flicked open a notebook in his hand. 'I take it you know a Miss Henrietta Swanley?'

'Henri— You mean Hetty?'

'Henrietta Swanley.'

The possibilities of what the man might say next made Granville light-headed. 'What's she gone and done now?'

'What's she gone and done now?' repeated the policeman, none too impressed with Granville's attitude. He exchanged another look with a colleague, who swallowed and cast his eyes down. 'She's just gone and been found dead, sir.'

'Oh God.'

'Can we come inside now, sir?'

Granville unlocked the front door and leant down with a shaking hand to calm the dog, who pushed past him, bristling, to sniff the first policeman's trouser bottoms. 'Hello, boy,' said the second, cheerily, leaning down and holding out his hand for the dog to inspect, 'aren't you a big fat fella?' The policemen filed through the hall and into the sitting room. They filled the room, almost too bulky for the space available, and looked jarringly out of context there. Policemen at close quarters always seemed like an alien species to Granville. Although they looked and behaved like reasonable human beings, their presence had a way of rendering all normal social devices invalid. One was stripped bare by their suspicious *politesse*, made vulnerable; even a glance over the shoulder was an implication of guilt, a possible sign of intent to escape.

The senior man stood comfortably, legs apart, in the middle of the sitting room and relayed the raw facts of the situation to Granville. It came out like an inadequately prepared speech, recited straight from notes and without any feeling. Granville glazed over as he listened and his eyes fixed on the polished accessories of the policeman's uniform, the padded waistcoat with its stuffed compartments, the walkie-talkie and handcuffs. The man's choice of words was foreign to the culture of everyday communication, which added peculiarity to the already shocking news: the listing of the deceased's full Christian names, the circumstances of the body's discovery, the references to points in time in terms of hundreds of hours, and then, ultimately, the cause of death, rattled out in one bland, unpunctuated sentence.

'Subject to the final ruling of the coroner it would appear that the deceased died by her own hand and that death was caused by a fracture to the neck the result of self-inflicted hanging with no evidence as yet to support a theory of suspicious or third party involvement.' It was only when he closed the notebook that he seemed to relax and spoke to Granville in a more compassionate tone. 'I'm sorry to be the one to bring you this news, sir.'

'I can't believe she'd be up to it. Not just the courage to

do such a thing, but the planning. The . . . you know, the mechanics. It's so awful.'

The policeman's eyes darted momentarily to one side and back again. 'I won't distress you with the details, but the young lady seemed to know what she was doing.'

'How could she? Don't most people bodge it? Do you think she had help?'

'There are a lot of nasty websites out there. If someone wants to do something like that properly, they can get all the help they need just by going online.'

'Did she use a ladder?'

'No. She jumped from an attic hatch. Rope was attached to the ridge of the building in the loft. Very strong piece of timber.'

'How did she think of that? She wouldn't have thought of that.' Granville sounded faintly outraged. 'She must have been helped, or something. She wasn't the type to be so . . .'

'So?'

'So methodical.'

'When people are desperate . . .' The policeman's tone was polite but brusque. He didn't need to be educated by a layman on such matters. He wanted to wrap up this part of the discussion and move on.

'You're sure she wasn't with anyone else? A visitor? Did the neighbours . . . ?'

The officer was too irritated to smile at this, but his expression suggested that Granville's comment might earn a laugh or two when it was repeated back at the station. 'It goes without saying that we asked the neighbours all the relevant questions.'

'Of course,' said Granville quietly. 'Do you think she . . . do you think it happened quickly?'

'Death would appear to have been almost instantaneous.'

'Was there a note? Is that why you're here?'

This seemed more relevant territory for the officer. 'Not a note as such. But the young lady does appear to have been writing bits and pieces over the past few days. Her table was covered in little jottings, bits of paper with doodles, drawings, that kind of thing. Seems she was very preoccupied with you.'

'I know.'

'We wondered if you might be able to shed any light on the situation.'

Granville hesitated. 'Well, I knew she was very depressed. Problems at home and things. I'd been trying to help her but she grew too dependent on me. It got complicated.'

'We know all about her family, especially that father of hers.'

'I think there may have been a history of abuse,' said Granville.

The policeman pursed his lips and raised his eyebrows but did not comment. 'The neighbour says she was about to be evicted from her flat,' he said, 'because she couldn't pay the rent. Were you aware of this, sir?'

'She told me two different stories.'

The policeman went on. 'You say things got complicated between you?'

'Yes. She was making things up. Poor girl was completely deluded. She visited my wife behind my back, stirring up all sorts of nonsense. It upset my wife terribly. I'd tried to put her in touch with someone who could help, a priest in Bournemouth, especially when it was clear that her seeing me was doing more harm than good.'

'I can well imagine. It's obvious from her notes she had a crush on you. Seems she was heartbroken because you told her it had to end.'

Granville shook his head. 'It never began.'

The policeman raised his eyebrows and looked around the room, clocking the details. 'I dare say it didn't, sir. Must be an occupational hazard for a man in your position. A vicar. Happily married man, an' all.' His eyes met Granville's and he waited for a response.

'Perhaps I should get in touch with her parents.'

'I don't think that would be a good idea right now. In fact, we may have to think about putting a restraining order on the father. He's got a history of violent offences.'

'You mean he might come after me?'

'He was very upset.'

'Understandably.'

'Well,' said the policeman, conclusively, and put his notebook in his pocket, 'I think we've taken up enough of your time. That's all we need to know for the moment. If, for any reason, we need to contact you again . . .'

'Is there anything more I would be able to add? I mean, I'd be happy to help in any situation, but . . .'

'The young lady was over the age of consent, so there's no issue of sexual offences.'

'What do you mean? There was never any . . . any contact of that sort between us.'

At that moment the walkie-talkie carried by the policeman behind came raucously to life. The man turned away and held it to his mouth, answering with words that swam unintelligibly past Granville. The officer in front of him conferred with his colleague for a moment, checked his watch and then turned back to Granville.

'So, we'll be on our way, sir. As I say, if for any reason we need to make any further inquiries, we'll be in touch.'

'Look, this business of sexual offences . . .' Granville began to protest.

'As I say,' the officer did not attempt to conceal his impatience, 'we are not pursuing that line of inquiry.'

'But you know what the press are like. One whiff of scandal involving a clergyman and an under-aged girl.'

'She was seventeen.'

'Only seventeen?'

'Yes, sir.' He nodded and gave Granville a last, summary look. 'Quite a shock, isn't it?'

'I never touched her.'

'It's not for me to get involved in that side of things.' The policeman turned away, the ones behind nodded their thanks, and all three now shuffled in single file towards the front door.

Right up until the moment when they said their final goodbye and headed for the cars, Granville expected one of them to turn around and place some strategically timed question about Bertie Gosling. Partly because of that and partly because his conscience was writhing, he wondered during each of those last seconds if he should pre-empt them by volunteering his information. But no question came and his knowledge therefore remained sealed. Perhaps they had no idea, anyway. Perhaps in the whirlwind rapture of her new passion Hetty had obliterated all trace of the former one, and had taken the secret with her.

After they had gone, he came back into the sitting room and looked around. Everything in place; the same quiet; the clock ticking. He did not stop to ponder but functioned automatically, moving to the kitchen to make himself some tea, and from there to his study. It was Sunday tomorrow, Palm Sunday. There was a sermon to write for the ten-thirty. But he had barely started work when his chain of action stopped. He pushed back his chair from the desk and bent over double, cradling his head, like a cartoon character on an airline safety card, adopting the brace position before the final impact. He remained like this, his abdomen heaving with the effort of each breath because his lungs were compressed, and then, with a sudden flash of fury, sat upright and swiped backhanded at the teacup, sending it flying across the room. Boiling fawn liquid sprayed the wall and the cup smashed in pieces. Luther, who had earlier padded after his master into the study, hurried guiltily from the room to find a place to hide. Granville, meanwhile, picked up the phone and punched in a number.

A man's voice answered.

'Hello, Digby. It's Granville.' In the short silence that followed, he could picture his father-in-law's impatient sigh. 'Is she in the room with you?'

'No she's not,' came the response. 'To be honest, I don't know why you keep calling. Why don't you just leave her until she feels ready to speak to you?' His voice was gravelly, military, and his accent finely sculpted.

'Actually, Digby, I don't want to talk to her. In fact, I was rather hoping you'd pick up the phone.' This took the old man by surprise and he refrained from saying anything until Granville went on. 'You see, I've decided Edwina's probably right. Maybe this trial separation isn't such a bad idea after all.'

'She's going to want answers to a lot of questions, but right now she needs time to think, and you've just got to accept that.' The words were drawled even more than usual. Digby was going deaf, and although he sounded as much of a bully as ever, his mind was clearly not as agile as it had been. Granville knew he would have to spell his point out more plainly.

'What I'm trying to say, is—' He froze on the instant as a rush of feeling overwhelmed him. Suddenly he felt his daughters there on either side of him, dressed in sleeveless nighties; he felt the hairs on their bare upper arms tickling against his own skin and caught the warm minty scent of their toothbrushed breath. Was this it? He squeezed his nose as his face creased into a spasm, and then, recovering, tried to carry on. 'What I'm saying is that she's right.'

'What?'

'Look, just tell her I won't be calling back. She's right. Things have been bad for a while. It's time to make some changes. Lots of changes. Maybe we should try some time apart. Do you see what I'm saying?'

'Really! Don't you think you should be trying to make things better? I mean, what did you expect? She's been a damned good wife for you and it's hardly a girl's dream to end up living in a council house. Especially a girl with Edwina's background.'

'You're right. It's not a council house, actually, but you're right, of course. It just isn't right for her. Never was.'

'What's that you say?'

Granville spoke up. 'I said you're absolutely right, and so is Edwina.'

'Glad you think so,' came the defiant reply.

There being nothing else to add, Granville allowed a pause to see if his father-in-law wanted to say anything. When no further word came down the line, he said, 'Goodbye, then, Digby,' and put down the phone. He held tight on to the receiver for a full ten minutes before finally letting go and leaving the room.

Chapter 27

Granville did not go to work on his sermon, nor did he sleep that night, but lay on his bed staring into the darkness of the unlit room. Part of him hungered like a junkie for the miraculous to descend, for benediction to swallow him up, take him out of this maelstrom and put everything majestically in its right place. But it was idiocy to ask. He could no more believe in emergency pain relief from a dial-up God-entity than he could expect divinity to descend at the rub of a genie's lamp. He heard the old family grandfather clock in the downstairs hall strike two, and though he had not planned to get up, he knew in a profound way that his time had come.

That clock chime was familiar to him, part of the domestic soundtrack of his childhood. It brought to mind the memory of creaking floorboards on early Saturday mornings in winter, when his father would get up in the dark to have breakfast before going shooting. Reassured by the sound of the same chime, he roused himself out of bed and switched the light on. He had no idea what he had got up to do but thought that he had better get dressed anyway. The room was a mess, it was always a mess. Edwina's things were still all over the place: solitary earrings missing their pair, empty glass tumblers that never found their way back to the kitchen, freshly pressed clothes waiting endlessly to be put in drawers, dirty clothes bunched up on the floor because the laundry basket was too full, and other clothes more carefully laid on a chair because they could squeeze in one more use before going to the wash.

He left the bedroom and went quietly downstairs in his socks. Luther looked up from his basket, confused to see his master breaking the nocturnal routine like this. Granville knelt down to stroke him, and then bent over to kiss his massive forehead where the white fur was short enough to show an underlay of pink skin. Luther snorted happily at the attention and tried to roll over, tail quivering. Granville whispered a few words close to the dog's head, and felt the velvety texture of its ear between his fingers, then got to his feet and went through to his study. He switched the computer on, found the email address he needed, and began to type.

A quarter of an hour later he was out of the house and had locked the door behind him. It was cold and dark, still not even three o'clock.

He let himself into the church at the west end and made his way down the aisle to the vestry door without turning any lights on. There was an electric fire in the vestry which normally he would have switched on when it was as cold as this, but tonight he did not, because he had no interest in anything outside the single purpose that had brought him here. Despite the dark, he moved comfortably around the room because it was his place of work and he had it well mapped, yet right now he was curiously disengaged from both the vestry and its contents. His limbs moved as normal but his thoughts were denied choice and cross-reference. It was as if his freedom had been suspended, netted like an animal in a hunter's trap, and he had not the will to struggle against it. Instead, he submitted to what he had come to the church to do with deliberate and unquestioning obedience, like the monks of olden times who had lived, studied and worshipped just a stone's throw away from here. His every movement, thus detached from the urges of personal choice, seemed almost part of a ritual.

He took off his jumper, shirt and trousers, let them fall to the floor, and bent forward to scoop the socks from his heels. Then he put his thumbs inside the elastic of his underpants and pulled them down to the ground as well. He proceeded naked from the vestry up the aisle, passing beneath the arch of a Tudor rood screen, and stepped up into the chancel. The flagstones in this part of the church were broad, polished and ancient, quilted here and there with massive grave tablets belonging to forgotten Dorsetshire squires. Granville's bare feet walked across their worn commemorative inscriptions and he felt the slender grooves of the lettering like insect legs beneath the skin of his soles.

He unlatched the twin gates of the altar rail as he had done a thousand times before, swung them open and walked towards the niche of a lancet window. Here, he retrieved a box of matches and lit the candles on a pair of tall brass candlesticks either side of the altar. Stepping back and facing the altar, he lowered himself to the ground, kneeling, hands clasped in front. He then lay down flat and stretched out, face down, nose and forehead pressed against the cold flagstone, with his arms spread out either side of his naked body.

He remained like this for a long time, breathing condensation against the black stone beneath his face and murmuring an ancient prayer over and over again: three short lines of Greek that could trace their origin to the practices of the ascetic Desert Fathers of fifth-century Egypt.

Kýrie Iesú Christé, Yié tou Theóu, eleisón me ton amartolón.

Faint, blotchy Plantagenet frescoes on the chancel walls looked down on him where he lay – partial images of Jesus and the Apostles, clad in robes like togas, with severe faces and hands raised in the act of blessing. Their colourful clothing and stylized curling beards had faded to a pale terracotta from the centuries of damp, and their haloes were flaking.

Lord Jesus Christ, Son of God, have mercy on me, a sinner.

It must have been well after five o'clock when the treeline of a horizon outside began to gain slight definition against the night sky. Granville looked up, straining his neck, and saw its silhouette in the fields beyond one of the plain glass windows. The palest of lights now crept from the same source across the interior fabric of the church and bestowed presence upon formerly invisible contents: a heavy oak pulpit, an Evangelist's fierce-eyed eagle at the lectern, the Ten Commandments painted in great Jacobean letters on lofty timber panels between the nave's arches. Dimly, an oak board which listed the church's incumbents – from Robert de Planke in 1290 to Granville St Clair most recently – arose out of the dark, together with elmwood pews, wrought-iron flower stands, and a hymn board showing sets of stark numerals. Prostrate nuptial effigies of praying Elizabethan ladies and gentlemen emerged atop tombs through the gloom, and colour at last began to grace the generous span of stained glass behind the altar.

Granville rose stiffly to his feet, stood for a moment facing east with his head bowed, and began to walk back towards the vestry.

The cold was biting through his skin and flesh, sending a morbid resonance all the way to the bone, and an oppressive ache weighed on the sutures of his cranium. The contents of his brow seemed bruised, and throbbed at each heartbeat. Limb joints and ligaments resisted movement, and his genitals shrank away in shame. Exhausted, stripped down and half mortified, he at last gave in to the pain of his body and went to find his clothes.

Over the top of his shirt, jumper and trousers he donned a black cassock and above it all a clean cotton surplice. Thus robed for Sunday and rubbing his hands for warmth, he put on the vestry's electric heater and made himself a cup of tea; he took it, steaming, with him into the church proper and sat down at the edge of the Lady Chapel, located off one of the transepts. The sky outside was clear, though still dull, and he could tell that in an hour or so the sun would be streaming in through the windows.

He sat thus quietly on a side bench in his fine old church, dressed like an ordinary village clergyman, a cup of tea hot between his hands. The austerity of his earlier devotional posture had passed, giving way, with the darkness, to a more moderate and modern sort of meditation.

He wondered distractedly about the nature of divinity and his perception of it. Was there some Almighty pattern at work which he had yet to fathom, or was it all just pressure on the temporal lobe, as the doctor had suggested? Was his understanding and celebration of the mystery of creation, the ground and unity of all being, just a clinical response to a piece of diseased tissue in his head? Perhaps it had always been thus, ever since the blinding pastoral wonder that had started it all, so long ago out there on the water meadows between Cambridge and Granchester.

He gazed across the chapel at an early nineteenth-century marble plaque on the far wall. It was one of several he had looked at many times over the years but he was particularly moved by it. It had been placed by a young widow to commemorate the untimely death of her husband after a riding accident in the parish, and its top was bedecked with an elegant neoclassical relief of a grieving woman, bare-armed, head bowed, draped in Romanesque folds. The bereft wife had ordained an eloquent inscription and its text was as poignant this morning as it must have been on the day the masons had first mortared it into the church wall two hundred years before. She tells of an unending devotion that will last to the sunset of her years, and her 'unutterable love' for the deceased. Strong words, and perhaps generated in part by the romantic culture of the times, but deeply touching nonetheless. Granville wondered how long it had been since Edwina could have described her love for him as unutterable. Years, probably, a tired decade or more. Her love had somewhere along the way mislaid its unutterability and had learnt instead to speak in plain and simple words. It spoke a language of selfish entrenchment, accusations and injury. Perhaps even something worse. He envied the young squire commemorated on the plaque, and could almost picture him in his tight riding breeches and heavily pleated shirtsleeves that fluttered in the breeze, standing beside his unruly stallion, holding it by the reins. He could imagine his smiling rosy face, tousled hair and dark curling sideburns. He could picture his lady, too, waving farewell for the last time as he galloped away; and then gracefully leaning over her dead husband's casket before it was sealed, weeping warm tears onto the pale, handsome face. And still he envied him. Granville would take an early death any day in exchange for the unutterable love of a good wife like that.

Chapter 28

When Brigadier Finch, the churchwarden, entered the building by the west door at eight-thirty, he was convinced that the organist must have come in to practise the night before and forgotten to lock the church up. Then he spied the rector, already robed, kneeling at the altar rail of the Lady Chapel. The Brigadier didn't like the look of it. It was out of the ordinary and a touch too ostentatious for his taste. He knew that something was afoot but thought it best to get on with his own tasks, keep a beady eye on things, and try to fathom out what might be happening as and when the rector felt inclined to talk to him. On the other hand, he did not want it to seem as though he was spying from the shadows, so he made his arrival plain by walking a short way down the aisle and coughing lightly.

'Good morning, Peter,' said Granville, distantly.

'Good morning,' replied the Brigadier, and glanced towards the east window. 'Looks to be a fine day, at any rate.'

'Yes,' replied Granville. 'So it does.'

'Let's hope it holds till next Sunday. Better for the children's Easter egg hunt.'

'Quite.'

'Busy week ahead for you, I should imagine. Holy Week and all that.'

'Rather.'

Granville then bowed his head and appeared to resume his prayers. Brigadier Finch muttered an excuse, turned away and began getting everything ready for the service. He put on his glasses, checked some details on a piece of paper and opened the lectern's Bible at the appropriate page; he then moved on to the hymn board, followed by the linen cupboard and the vestry safe for the silverware. One by one he completed all his duties, avoiding Granville, who he now conjectured must be involved in some esoteric piece of priestly devotion to mark the approach of Easter. The rector was full of surprises, quite a few of which were not to the liking of those in the congregation who hankered after a more conventional approach.

Brigadier Finch left the church at nine-fifteen, as he always did, giving himself enough time to pop home, have breakfast and pick up his wife for the service. When he returned, just after ten, he half expected to find Granville still kneeling in the Lady Chapel, but to his relief the rector had withdrawn. However, there was another person in the church: a young man in a leather jacket, sitting alone in the back row. He had a notepad on his knee and a large camera resting on the pew beside him.

'Good morning,' said the Brigadier.

'Morning,' the young man chimed back enthusiastically. He was not a regular member of the congregation, looked uncomfortable in his surroundings and was too early. Brigadier Finch smelt a rat.

'Have you come for the ten-thirty?' he asked.

'Is that when it gets going?'

'That's when the service starts.'

'Oh, right. That's when Mr *Saint* Clair will be coming, is it?'

'It's pronounced Sinclair. He should be here already.'

The young man put out a hand to pick up his camera. 'Really? Great! Is there any chance I could have a quickie with the vicar, then, before the, um, service thingy gets going.'

The Brigadier looked disgusted. 'I'm afraid you'll have to wait until after the service if you want to talk to the rector. You can stand in the queue with everyone else.'

'Oh, come on, just a quickie. Then I can go.'

'Certainly not.' The Brigadier looked at the camera the man was holding. 'And it's not permitted to take photographs in the church during a service.' He saw the disappointment on the man's face but did not soften. 'What do you want with the rector, may I ask?'

The man smiled and began to explain why he had set off from Bournemouth at such an early hour. His informal friendliness was tailored to charm, but the more Brigadier Finch heard, the harder his face set.

Far more people than usual came to church that morning. Granville looked tired and gaunt as he glanced down at them from the chancel step at the start of the service. A light bristle peppered his chin, and his hair seemed thinner and unclean. He guessed from the faces of the congregation why most of them were there. The regulars had come, as ever, but some of them were not in their usual pews, having arrived to find them already occupied by strangers. On any other occasion this might have been a heartening sight, but the atmosphere this morning was unsettled.

The newcomers' eyes followed Granville closely, but

303

their diligence owed nothing to the sacramental content of the service. They did not kneel for the opening prayer and they did not look down to consult their service books. Not once did they participate in congregational responses, nor open their mouths during the hymn, but watched and waited, their eyes glued to the master of ceremonies, ready for a sign. Piet Steyn was also there, sitting in his customary place because he had got there early, as usual. He was dressed in jacket and tie, his posture upright and his hands resting on his lap. His weather-worn face gave nothing away.

Granville had not progressed far into the service when he paused mid-sentence, let out a long breath and looked up into the expectant eyes of the assembled. There was a rustle as people readjusted themselves in their pews, an indication of their acknowledgement that something was about to happen. The few faces that were not already trained on him now looked up with a jolt. They silently urged him onwards.

Granville closed the service booklet, gently clasped his hands together and raised his chin to the congregation. A lone child's voice yelled into the silence from the rear of the church and the sound of it rang cavernously around the building. Granville smiled and there was a gear shift down in the level of tension. He might almost have been about to announce the results of a charity whist drive or the new president of the Ladies' Group.

'So nice to see so many of you here on Palm Sunday, and what a beautiful morning it is,' he began conventionally enough. The pleasantries concluded, he lowered his head, paused for a moment, and began again in a different tone. This time the winning smile was absent.

'The regulars among you will have noticed that I've interrupted the usual order of service to preach my sermon a bit early. I didn't think there was much point in carrying on with the other. I genuinely apologize to those good people who've come to worship their God in the normal way. You deserve better than me, truly. But most of you here this morning are not particularly interested in the service, and, to be honest, neither am I. So shall we move on to the bit you've all been waiting for? To hear what I've got to say for myself? It won't take long.' A few looked down with shame, but most froze in anticipation, while one or two folded their arms.

'Most of you will have heard that my family has left me because my wife thinks I've been involved with a girl less than half my age. Some of you might also have heard that the police were at my house last night and that there's more to this scandal than you might first have thought.' There were a few gasps, whispers and shakings of heads. The old pew timbers creaked at their joints. 'It's no secret. You'll find out all the details soon enough. It'll be in the local papers, perhaps even the nationals, and it won't matter much what I say in answer to the accusations.' The young man in the leather jacket at the rear of the nave was writing furiously into his notepad, and a small plastic device that sat on top of his hymn book flashed red.

'But I'm not going to talk about me, except to let you know that this is the end for me. The end of my time as your rector, in fact the end of my life as a clergyman.' The silence was complete down the length of the nave, tangible up to the highest points of the arches. Higher still, the coffered roof timbers, with peeling medieval paint and death-watch beetle scars, looked down on the events unfolding far below. Immaculate and untouched for centuries, the heights of the church were exactly as they appeared in a framed Victorian photograph by the north entrance. The fabric of the place had survived through the centuries without blemish. Only the people had changed, their ideas, their joys and tragedies, breezing through this basilica like spectres, passing out beyond, and fading from memory. The people had come and the people had gone, generation after generation, with the landmarks of their passage logged thrice per head in dusty church ledgers stored in the vestry: baptism, marriage and funeral.

Steyn sat still as stone and watched Granville, as did everyone else. One well-groomed family – parents and three school-aged children – abruptly rose from their pew, collected their coats and left quietly by the west door. An elderly lady, with perfectly set hair beneath a pudding basin hat, took a minute handkerchief from her handbag and began to dab gently at her eyes. The air was brittle but Granville himself was serene. Having dropped his bombshell he now stepped down from the chancel into their midst, informal again, and held open his surpliced arms. 'You might think I should express remorse for leaving the parish in the lurch in the run-up to Easter, for letting everyone down, for preaching all this moral and worthy stuff to you over the years, only to fall flat on my face in a sea of scandal and rumour. But what I'm really sorry about is that I've allowed myself to go on for so long. In fact, now is the first time I'm going to speak to you about God from my heart. The truth, no nonsense.'

A few more people now rose from their seats in different parts of the nave, and for a moment it seemed as if a genteel stampede for the exit might commence, but in the event everyone else remained rooted to the pews, enthralled by the drama.

'I'm going to talk for just a moment about gardens.'

There were some frowns and looks exchanged. 'We all have them. Some of us take more pride in them than others, some of us have whole acreages, others have little more than a window box. Have you ever thought why we have them? I'll tell you: a garden is an expression of man's wanting not just to exist in harmony with the natural world, but to exert benign dominion over it. And what's the alternative to dominion? What happens when we ignore the ingress of nature and decide we don't want to tame it into pretty little portions? What happens if we don't cultivate, prune and weed? If we decide not to mow, plant, and mulch around the places where we live? The answer is pretty obvious: the wilderness of nature begins to reclaim the land, like it or not. Who, then, would have dominion, we or the natural world? To our way of thinking, that notion represents a kind of chaos which might threaten to overwhelm us, our homes, our jobs, our children, our civilization.

'People began to carve gardens out of nature at about the same time that they began to invent laws and morals out of lawlessness and amorality, and no bad thing it was either. No sensible person would question that we need a consensus for what should be considered right and wrong in society. But don't let's muddle these cultural building blocks with divinity. The divine truth has nothing to do with culture and therefore nothing to do with religion. When we proclaim a regulatory system in the name of God, the thing we create – called religion – is just another brick in culture's wall. And culture has rules, structures, an elite brigade of officials – ' he lifted his surplice with the thumb and forefinger of each hand and then let it drop – 'we have the operational manuals – ' he raised the Book of Common Prayer; 'we have monuments, temples of excellence – ' he opened wide his arms; 'and very picturesque the whole thing becomes. We also fight wars, slaughter innocents and build walls to defend our ways. We judge, belittle and detest those who do not join us. All this is culture, it is established nationhood, and historically it is also religion, but it is not the Godhead. It is a perfect, workable, man-made, house-proud front garden, a demonstration of our dominion over potential chaos. But it blocks our view of our true nature, what we've come from and what we will inevitably return to; and as far as divinity is concerned, it seeks to cage and monumentalize that which by its nature cannot be stilled or contained.

'Take a look at a newborn baby. Does it possess any notion of morality, right and wrong? Does it tread the treacherous path between heaven and hell? Of course not. And if it were not taught, preached at and legislated against from an early age, it would continue to grow in a moral vacuum. Socially prescribed behaviour is hammered into a growing person's head from the start, and each strike flattens further that person's ability to choose or act in freedom. By adulthood most people have forgotten what freedom means. They have conformed, through repetition, habit and discipline. They have dropped anchor according to a prescribed set of rules and they feel a whole lot safer for it. That's what it's all designed for, isn't it? To make people feel more secure, in this life and in the great unknown hereafter. That's why, for centuries and centuries, people have relinquished their freedom in supine surrender to the so-called Will of a so-called God. But here's the tragedy: our code of morality – necessary though it is for the working of society – is the product of nothing more than a set of Graeco-Judaean philosophical theories, laws and political statecraft. It is not prescribed by a god or gods, and any man who sets himself up, who stands up and tells people what they should and should not do *in the name of God*, is a fraudster, pure and simple.' The shuffling grew to an agitated murmur, and there was a sudden flash of light from the rear of the church. Heads turned. The young man in the leather jacket was on his feet, camera in hand. Brigadier Finch got up at once and strode over to confront him. The young man held up his hands in surrender and sat down.

'I'll just finish with this,' Granville said, riding the disquiet, and the noise settled down. 'God cannot be taught in lessons, cannot be reached by repeating the same words over and again, or by obeying threatening commandments. All these just build up a theory of God, draw up a man-made, speculative map of how to curry a hypothetical God's favour and earn a place in a hypothetical next world. But I tell you this: none of these things lead to the Kingdom. Anyone – myself included – who preaches ways to practise religion, is preaching ignorance, is preaching divisiveness, is spreading un-truth, is a force for darkness in our world. I will go so far as to say that our established religion of Christianity,' he held out wide his arms again, as if encompassing the whole church edifice, its shining organ pipes, ancient furnishings, marble memorials, stained glass, brass, silver and gold, 'Christianity, its beliefs and its tenets, are a monumental deceit. Priestcraft is an obstacle to an understanding of the true nature of God. Coming to church, my friends, I'm afraid, is utter folly.' Several old ladies were now weeping quite openly. Brigadier Finch had not returned to his seat, but glowered at Granville from the back of the church, as yet undecided if it was his prerogative to intervene.

'We need culture,' concluded Granville, 'we need

language, we need law, horticulture, we need the thought process that formulates all these necessary tools for living. But we must not confuse them with the immeasurable Godhead. The truly responsible life – I might almost say the truly holy life – is spent on the boundary of garden and wilderness: quietly acknowledging and celebrating the wonderful ways man has invented to tame and enshrine his raw nature – the literature, art, music, and the rest; but also breathing deep the freedom and clear horizons on the other side of the great divide. In this territory, matter meets the divine. In this kingdom man embodies God. This is the Christ principle.'

In the silence that followed, most of the people looked down with embarrassment. Some of the regulars still kept their eyes on Granville, either in sympathy, because they knew at heart he was a good, compassionate priest, or even in hope that he would pass on from his maverick speech and resume the service as usual. One man, a teacher from the village school, began to clap and actually rose to his feet, but no-one joined in his show of support, and other than causing a few people to turn around to see who it was, most pretended to ignore him.

Granville bowed his head and automatically walked towards the chancel, but then stopped himself, as if suddenly remembering what had happened, and turned back to the congregation. He smiled. 'I suppose in the circumstances no-one will particularly feel like singing the next hymn.' He looked over to where the organist sat at the keyboard but she had gone. Still the congregation seemed to wait for his lead. 'I suppose you'd better all go home, then,' he said, and opened his arms in a final, almost benedictory, farewell. People began to get to their feet in silence, and Granville walked down towards Piet Steyn. 'A word, if I may,' he whispered: 'in the vestry.'

310

A few minutes later, after Granville had hung up his cassock and surplice, there was a knock on the vestry door and Piet let himself in. He closed the door behind him but did not come further into the room. There was a distance between them like a field of battle, and Piet eyed Granville warily.

'Tell me what happened when you went to visit her,' said Granville.

'The most important thing is that our secret is still safe,' said Steyn.

'The most important thing is that a young girl is dead.'

'I know that, but—'

'So you already knew she was dead?'

'The reporter in the church told me when I arrived this morning. The girl has gone now, for better or worse, but it means she can't tell anyone anything. That's good for Janet and it's good for you.'

'I don't give a damn about me, isn't that clear by now? And, compared to the death of a human being, I don't particularly care about Janet's discomfiture, either.'

'Well, like it or not, the fact of the matter is that Janet can be spared any further unhappiness.' He tilted his head sideways, half enquiringly. 'Unless you decide to blab, that is. I thought you were about to just now.'

'We've got no business keeping this secret any more.'

Piet tensed and leant back fractionally. 'What do you mean?'

'We should go to the police. Finish this thing once and for all.' Granville looked at Steyn and shook his head in disbelief. 'You've got some explaining to do, Piet. Or should I call you Jan? Jan Greef?'

Steyn was looking away from Granville when the comment was made and remained like that, frozen.

'I've found out a few things, and now I want to know

what happened to Hetty. You'd better have some bloody good answers.'

Steyn raised his eyes and looked at Granville full on. He spoke quietly. 'We need to talk this through properly. Why don't you come over to my house? I'll tell you about what happened.'

'I'll come right now.'

'Give me half an hour.' He looked at his watch. 'Or a little bit longer. Come around at one. I'll make some lunch for us.'

'I don't want your bloody lunch.'

'Either way. I'll see you at one o'clock. Just hold off from telling anyone anything until you've heard my side of the story. I ask only that.'

They held each other's gaze before Granville sighed and nodded his agreement. Piet left the vestry without another word.

By the time Granville got home, Luther had defecated in the hall, having been locked in since the previous night. Granville smelt the mess before seeing it and tutted at his own thoughtlessness. The dog hung his head with guilt as he walked over to greet his master by the door. Granville squatted down to mutter apologies and reassure him with a few strokes before letting him out into the garden. He then picked up the faeces with toilet paper, flushed them away and began to scrub the hall carpet. It was already getting on for one o'clock and he realized the dog needed to stretch his legs, so he decided to put Luther on his lead and walk him down to Steyn's house, rather than drive.

There wasn't time to do anything else before leaving the house. He neither checked his messages nor moved anything on his desk. Books remained open where he had left them, his bed upstairs was dishevelled, and the contents of the fridge untouched. He simply left by the front door, locked it behind him and walked away from the house, with the dog on its lead and nothing else in his hands, as he had done hundreds of times in the past.

Chapter 29

'Ah, there you are, Father.' Steyn welcomed him into the house with a smile and straight away offered him something to drink. Granville quietly declined. They walked through the hall and Piet held out a hand to usher him into the sitting room. 'I'd better put your dog in the boot room while we chat,' he added. 'He's a little muddy. I can put a towel down for him to lie on.'

Granville had never been in the sitting room before. It was tidy and predominantly pale brown; the wallpaper, thick pile carpet and paintwork all displaying variations of the same flat umber. A few chipped and characterless pieces of furniture, the sort that would go for a handful of coins at a jumble sale, sat symmetrically around the fireplace. There were no pictures, though some hooks and bleached squares on the wallpaper showed where frames had once hung. Before Steyn bought the house, a shy old couple had lived here for fifty-two childless years. They were both dead now, having spent the last days of their lives in a concrete care home on the outskirts of Yeovil. Their Cheselbury Abbas house had been empty for four years before Piet Steyn came on the scene, but other than rescuing the building from dereliction and tidying up inside, he had done little to it and lived mainly in just two of the rooms. The lounge into which Granville was led smelt stale, a residue of its previous inhabitants which had never quite lifted.

There were two armchairs and a sofa upholstered in a tan tartan fabric, but Piet conducted Granville to an upright wooden chair at the table. He sat himself opposite on a matching chair.

'That was quite a sermon this morning, Father,' he said, pursing his lips into a smile. 'It sounded like it was personally directed against me, if you don't mind me saying. As if you'd set out to highlight the very issues which set you and me apart. Phew!' He nodded and half chuckled. 'But interesting, I have to say. All that business about nature and chaos. You've definitely pinpointed something there.' Granville was sitting straight, one arm resting on the table, and looking at Piet without expression. 'It struck a chord with me,' continued Piet. 'Every day of my life I have been aware of that slipway to chaos just there in front of me. All of us face it, each time we make a decision, even a small choice. It takes discipline not to slip. The alternative – ' he raised his elbow and slanted his arm rigidly downwards, ' – the inferno.'

'What did you do to her?'

'Ah,' Piet said. 'Hetty, you mean?'

'We can talk about Louise Wiedemann later.'

'Who?'

'The girl whose body was found a few weeks after you went missing together in 1961.'

Piet half smiled and shook his head. 'I don't know what you're talking about.'

'What about Hetty?'

Piet now sighed and leant forward, elbows on the table. 'You want to blame me, I can see that. Well, perhaps I should accept some of the blame for what happened.' He was nodding, and pushed his thumbnail

315

thoughtfully into a groove in the wooden tabletop. 'She was determined to do away with herself, that much is certain. But I was probably the wrong person at the wrong time. If someone else had been there in my place, she might have been persuaded to change her mind. You, for instance.' He looked up. 'I can confess that with an open heart, Father.'

'What happened?'

'She was in a distraught state when I got there. Wouldn't listen to a word I said.'

'What did you say to her?'

'That it would do no good to anyone to keep making up lies. That you were a married man, married in the eyes of the Lord, and that it would be a terrible sin to try to harm your marriage.'

'You talked to her about sin at a time like that?'

'I was doing my best but it was probably the wrong approach, you're right.'

Granville let out a long breath, and tautness seemed to flush out of his body like a departing ghost. His shoulders dropped and his head fell forwards. After the night he had been through and the burdens the new day had brought, the exhaustion felt suddenly crushing.

'Did she say she wanted to kill herself?' he asked.

'She said she had no desire to live, yes.'

'She couldn't have done it without help.'

Steyn laid his palm flat on the table and looked directly across at Granville. He had an expression of solid, man-to-man sincerity. 'Father, speak plainly. Are you suggesting I may have had a hand in this girl's death?'

Granville looked away and closed his eyes. 'I don't want to leap to that conclusion,' he said. His voice was rough and deeper than usual, like a smoker's.

'But you can't help suspecting. I understand,' said

Steyn, frowning with forced empathy. The old guarded-ness was absent. 'There are things I've got to tell you. A lot of things. You deserve some answers.'

'Your past—'

'Yes, yes. I can explain everything and I will. Trust me.'

'And this business with Janet.'

'We'll talk it all through. Maybe you're right about it being time to come clean,' he said.

'About Bertie?'

Piet nodded. 'Absolutely. We should talk that through, too. It might be best for all.' They sat for a moment without saying anything until Piet pushed back his chair a little to give himself space and placed his hands wearily on his thighs. He smiled across the table at Granville. 'I think I need a cup of tea before we begin. Sure I can't tempt you?'

Granville eased up. 'OK.'

'You'll feel better for it.' He got up, patted Granville on the shoulder and went around behind his chair towards the door. There was a spring in his step and he half ran, rather than walked, to fix the tea.

While he was gone, Granville sat and stared into space. There were noises from the kitchen where Piet was putting on the kettle but Granville's mind grew still. He breathed in the lifeless vacuity of the room, was infected by its stagnancy and began to feel sleepy.

When he heard the sound of Steyn's footsteps returning from the kitchen his eyelids stirred to life but he did not look around. He wondered, drowsily, if he could even be bothered with a cup of tea now. A noise from the door informed him that Piet was back and there was a slight rustle directly behind his chair but nothing to alert him, which meant that he was caught off his guard when it happened. Not a word was said, and it was over before he could move a muscle.

Granville found himself unable to make a sound or even breathe. There was a wire around his neck which was being tightened with two wooden handles crossed behind, just above the dog collar. Steyn gave them a twist, which pinched Granville's skin at the back and split the capillaries in a horizontal line around his throat. Domed scarlet beads arose glossy, like spotless ladybirds, in a row along the line of the wire, either side of which his neck ligaments bulged. He tore hopelessly at it, scratching the skin of his neck, but it had sunk too deep into the flesh. Steyn maintained the tension. 'Put your arms down flat on the arms of the chair,' he said quietly, close to Granville's ear, 'or I'll take your head clean off your shoulders, I swear I will.' Granville began to judder. 'Put them down, put them down now.' Keeping a grip of both handles with one hand, Steyn guided Granville's wrist down onto the polished veneer arm of the chair. Then, expertly twisting a roll of brown parcel tape round and round, he bound it to the wooden arm and began the same procedure with the other wrist. After that, he applied tape over Granville's mouth and around his ankles. Only then did he loosen the cheese wire from behind, and Granville's head drooped forwards, blood dripping from the thin pink line.

Steyn came around to face him, pulled up a stool directly in front, and flopped down on it with a sigh. He put down his cup of tea, opened a drawer in the table, and removed a large hypodermic syringe. Its plunger was fully extended and the barrel filled with a clear liquid. A plastic cap covered the needle, which he removed, and then rested the syringe on top of the table, next to his mug.

'Phew,' he said, 'that was quite a to-do. Well, it's all over now.' He slurped up a tiny sip of tea because it was too hot to take a proper mouthful. 'Ah, that's good. I've worked up a thirst. Sorry you can't join me.' Granville was trembling from shock and wheezing. 'You see, I gave her a fair hearing but guilt was written all over her, and she knew it before the end. Guilty on two counts, if you think about it, with the addition of intent to spread yet more mischief. That female would never have been able to lead a good and upright life. I've known her kind before. You see,' he turned to glance out of the window, choosing his words carefully, 'she was one of those women that live in perpetual debt to the demands of their sexual organs.' He nodded, satisfied with the way he had worded it. 'Look at the way she dressed. Sweaters stretched over the swelling of her breasts. Trousers cut tight against the slope of her genitals.' He raised a schoolmasterly finger. 'Do you know what the word *pudendum* means, Father? It is the gerundive of the Latin *pudere*, and means "that of which to be ashamed". Interesting, don't you think?' Granville began to raise his head slowly and looked into Steyn's eyes. 'It is a gender affliction,' he enunciated the words percussively, 'the assumed irresistibility of that part which brings shame to her sex.' He shook his head with distaste. 'Pah! It is always the same thing that brings them down, they never change! Anyway,' he slurped some more tea, 'I believe she understood before the end. I'm happy to say she even repented. So perhaps the Lord will have mercy on her soul.' Granville kept his eyes fixed on him. 'She understood that it could only end one way. She did it of her own free will, I promise you. I just pointed her in the right direction, you might say.'

A single high-pitched bark cut the air. Steyn blinked and looked over Granville's shoulder, then relaxed back onto his elbows and took a longer draught of tea. He was about to start talking again when another bark came, and this time he pursed his lips. 'I'd better go and deal with that.' He got to his feet and drained his mug. 'Why did you bring the dog?' he asked. 'Stupid thing to do,' and he pulled out something that was stuffed tightly in his trouser pocket. It was a black satin cloth bag, which he opened up and slipped over Granville's head. Granville convulsed and began to grunt. 'Careful,' said Steyn, but Granville heaved from side to side, rocking the chair so that it tipped over and crashed onto the carpet. The side of his head smacked against the ground but his hands and feet remained tightly bound. 'Now look what you've gone and done,' said Steyn, and tutted. 'You'll have to stay there while I pop out for a minute, but I won't be long.'

Granville could hear noises from the kitchen – a drawer opened and the clatter of hard objects being rifled through. Then, distantly, he heard a door open and a low growl commence, as Steyn went in with the dog. The door closed again but the growling continued, more distantly. Then there was a brief pause before an isolated sound, like a nail being struck cleanly into a soft wooden board. A single penetrating knock, after which there was silence.

Chapter 30

Leo Flowers had been a loyal member of Cheselbury Abbas church ever since the days of the old rector, who had taken him in after his disfiguring accident and given him employment; but he had never cared much for Granville St Clair. He couldn't pinpoint exactly why he didn't like the current rector but over the past few years had found fault in everything that took place at St Peter's – the functions, the announced notices, every word of every sermon. The recent embarrassing incident had provided a justification of sorts for Leo's years of grumbling. He could not remember exactly why he had always thought it would end badly for Granville St Clair, but he didn't see the need to look for a reason. He knew that his opinions were cooked over a slow fire, and that although his memory was too shaky to recall chapter and verse of everything that might or might not have happened, it did not render his overall perspective any the less valid. There was just something about this rector that didn't add up, pure and simple, and Leo had seen quite a few of them come and go over the years. Mr Wright – the incumbent who had baptized Leo in the same church eighty-odd years before – had himself been born in 1858. Leo looked the year up in his encyclopaedia and found out that the Prime Minister then had been

Lord Palmerston. Leo had a keen sense of history and it excited him to think that he had been held at the font by someone who'd been governed by a man from the same generation as the tyrant Bonaparte. That so few markers in time linked him to such great epochs made Leo feel his life had greater relevance.

Puffed with confidence that his age and significance in the village lent him special reasons to be outraged by the latest turn of events, and secretly pleased – for reasons he could not particularize – to have the opportunity to strike a blow at Granville, Leo was gratified, one evening, to find his memory jarred into recalling the morning when Bertie Gosling had been found dead. That was it! he thought to himself, and lightly thumped the arm of his chair. That was what had been niggling him. He decided to go across the yard and knock on the Old Rectory's kitchen door to share his information with Mrs Gosling straight away.

Janet received the news expressionlessly. 'You're quite sure?'

'Sure as day is day.'

'Might you not have made a mistake? Your sight's been playing tricks on you.'

'I can see well enough to see what I needed to see that morning.' Leo remained where he stood, his one eye staring out defiantly, awaiting grateful plaudits that never came. Somewhat deflated, he eventually looked down, shuffled on the spot and added, 'Of course, it's none of my business, but I thought you ought to know.'

'Yes. Thank you, Leo.' She managed to raise a smile. 'You can leave me to deal with it. I'd be grateful if you could keep it under your hat. Don't mention it to anyone at all, please.' Leo nodded his agreement because it was not in his interests to get on the wrong side of Mrs Gosling.

Within the hour Janet had left her house to walk over and visit Granville personally. Shaken, but fully in control of herself, she refused to leap to conclusions. Leo Flowers was a decent and loyal old sort at heart, but also a bigot with a little sack of poison always at the ready; like so many of the locals of a certain age around here, she reflected, particularly the farmers. Give them the slightest provocation and they liked nothing better than to spout off cantankerously about everyone and everything; in the light of which, Granville's goodwill and nobility of character could not be glibly dismissed. There must surely be a reasonable explanation to all this.

Janet had not been present in church that Sunday, but had heard all about it and had seen what was being written in the newspapers. She tried again and again to call Granville to offer her support but he had never picked up the phone and no-one seemed to know where he had gone. She had been too busy sorting out the sale of her house to do much else about it, but now decided to go and see if he was at home.

When she arrived in Tennyson Terrace she saw three men standing on the pavement wearing what looked like ski jackets and fleece hoodies. They had cameras slung over their shoulders, and were waiting by the garden gate. Two of them were smoking and laughing and the third was yawning hugely on a collapsible stool. As she approached they turned towards her, chucking away their cigarettes and taking hold of their cameras. Instinctively angered by their presence, Janet took them to task but quickly discovered that they were friendly and harmless. They told her that as far as they knew Granville had not been home since the incident in the church the previous Sunday morning, but that their newspapers had instructed them to keep the site covered, just in case. Janet therefore returned to the Old Rectory and thought about how she could get in touch with Edwina.

After calling one or two locals, she was pointed in the direction of Brigadier Finch, who, as churchwarden, had all the relevant contact numbers for Granville in case of emergencies. The Brigadier picked up the phone after a single ring. He said that normally he would not feel at liberty to pass on telephone numbers, but in the circumstances, and given Janet's recent misfortunes, he supposed it would be all right this once. 'You know he's handed in his resignation?' the Brigadier drawled as he flicked through his address book to find the right page.

'I didn't know.'

'He must have sent an email to the Bishop's Office on Saturday night after the police had been to see him. The Diocese has forwarded it on to me. They say they've got a couple of retired priests who'll fill in until they find a permanent replacement. Might help if Granville showed up. He'll have to clear out of the house, for a start.'

'What did he say?'

'Ah! Here it is.' He read out the contact number he had for Edwina's family home in Scotland, which the Brigadier knew was a frequent holiday destination for the St Clairs. 'Would seem a bit odd if he's run off there, though, considering everything.'

'What did he say in the email?'

'Just apologized for the inconvenience. Said he'd be writing more formally and explaining himself in due course, but until then thinks he'd better lie low for a while.'

'Lie low?'

'That's what he says. Because he wants to protect the Church from any more scandal.'

'What else?'

'Not a word. Just two lines, that's all we deserve, it seems.'

Janet finished the conversation quickly and moments later had Edwina on the line. She relayed the news, but Edwina did not seem particularly surprised.

'He didn't actually tell me he was going to resign,' she said, 'but it seems like a logical step. I haven't spoken to him for a week.'

'Did you know what had happened? About the girl's suicide?'

'Word has got through.'

Edwina and Janet's relationship in the past had been cordial but shallow rooted. They neither called each other regularly nor lunched together, and seemed content to let matters roll on that way, which, for two neighbouring housewives of a similar age, with small children and an equivalent social status, was tantamount to an admission of mutual dislike. Right now, Edwina was not even attempting to cushion her words or hide her eagerness to get off the phone.

'You haven't heard from Granville either?' Janet asked.

'Not a squeak, but that doesn't surprise me. We've agreed to keep our distance. He's probably holed himself up somewhere with a pile of books and an iPod full of meditation chants. Run away from it all.' The weariness in her tone was theatrical rather than heartfelt. 'My guess would be he's left the country. Hidden away in some *Gasthaus* in the Black Forest, or maybe done the full whack and got on a plane to India. He might try and *find* himself all over again. It's been brewing a while.'

'Do you think we should report it to the police?'

'God, no. It's a free country, isn't it? Why would the police be interested?'

'I don't know. People are whispering. Wanting answers.'

'Well, they should mind their own business.'

'It's for you to decide, I suppose. But there is something else. Something closer to home. I'm afraid it's rather disturbing.' She went on, haltingly, to relate what she'd been told earlier by Leo Flowers. When she had finished she waited for a response, but none came, and Janet wondered if they'd been cut off. 'Edwina? Are you still there?' Then came the click and flat tone of disconnection. She rang back straight away and a man's voice answered. Edwina was upset, the man said, and just wanted to be left alone with her children.

The following morning was clear and sunny, a premature hint of full summer, and Janet took the opportunity to go out early and deliver leaflets about the forthcoming Battle of Britain lecture in the village hall. An eminent historian from Bristol University was coming to give the talk, a friend of Bertie's, and Janet had taken it upon herself to make sure the event was a success.

She had not gone far before she saw Piet Steyn coming from the opposite direction. His determined stride was unmistakable, fists buried deep in his jacket pockets, glaring at the path ahead. It would be impossible to avoid him.

He greeted her formally, keeping a respectable distance, and said he had been on his way to visit her. Her face flushed and she stumbled to make her excuses, but he put a hand on her arm and interrupted. 'I understand why you might not want me to come into your home,' he said. 'I realize I have been too forward. I've come to

326

apologize and to ask you to remember me in a better light.'

She pulled away her arm. 'Why?' she asked. 'Are you leaving?'

'No, but I hear you may be. I would like to part as friends. Can I make a time to come over? Just to say goodbye properly.'

'What's wrong with here and now?' she answered. 'Actually, I've got something to ask you, and I'd like an answer, too.'

If Piet flinched inwardly at the unexpected belligerence in her tone, he concealed it, and regarded her in silence before lowering his eyes. 'Of course. Where shall we go? Over there?' He held out a hand in the direction of the bench beneath the church field's solitary standing stone, close by. It was not an unreasonable suggestion, and the bench was bathed in morning sunshine, but Janet wanted to demonstrate her control of proceedings. There was a place down by the stream, beside the remains of the old mill, she said, where people would be less likely to notice them. The implication that she did not wish to be seen in his company did not escape Piet. 'I understand,' he said, and they began to stroll down towards the leafy shade of the old millpond.

The mill itself had been redundant for half a century or more and was now a ruin. A few collapsed roof timbers remained, angled down into the damp turf and covered with moss, but otherwise the walls of the miller's cottage, which had stood on this site in some form since troops had mustered to fight at Agincourt, were now open to the slow ingress of nature from beneath and the dissolution of rainwater from above. All around, the trees, ground and hedges were a mass of unkempt ivy, fallen boughs ridden with fungus and impenetrable brambles. Birds flitted merrily in and out of the crisscross jumble of leaves and thorns, relishing the privacy and abandonment of the place. The air was thick with the scent of last year's mouldering leaves, which lay dark and spongy in the wet earth underfoot.

Silently they entered the cottage precincts and found a place to sit on smooth old pieces of stone beside the waterfall that fed the millpond.

'I'd just like to say this, and I won't say any more on the matter,' began Piet, but faltered, and looked out towards the river. It was quite broad at the point where it passed the cottage and fell smoothly over a shallow drop, creating a gentle roar. He had to raise his voice to be heard. 'Let's just say that I've come to recognize that I am capable of mistakes.'

'What mistakes?'

'As far as you're concerned, my mistake was to think you were the sort of person who needed a strong man to take control. You did not ask for my help. I pushed myself on you and I want to apologize for that. I think I have reached a sort of crossroads in my life.'

Janet watched as he appeared to struggle with his feelings. 'What's brought this on?' she asked.

'A mixture of things, I think. I've found the house where my poor mother was born, for a start. Where my whole story begins, you might say, not far from here. I've been to visit my ancestors' graves and walked the fields they tilled. It means a lot to a man like me, a lonely man, you might say, who's had to fight every inch of the way just to find a place to call home. Suddenly I feel I might have found where I belong, where my mother was before she married my father, what she might have been if she hadn't . . . and I no longer need to . . .' He lost his thread, and Janet stole a glance at him, afraid that he might break down.

'It all sounds very positive,' she said matter-of-factly.

'Forgive me,' he said, and smiled at his own folly. 'I shouldn't be burdening you with my feelings, especially after all you've been through.'

'You're right. You shouldn't. In fact, you haven't been quite straight with me from the start, have you?'

'What do you mean?'

'Do you really need me to spell it out? What about the woman who was there the morning my husband died?'

For a moment there was no sound other than the water falling, then Piet looked up at her and his eyes were full of remorse. 'Thank heavens you've asked. I've been struggling with this for weeks. Now at last I can shed the burden.'

'Oh really?' It was a statement rather than a question.

'Again, you have deserved better. I can't carry on protecting that man for ever. Especially after the way he behaved in church. He's heading for a mental collapse, I believe.'

'You mean Granville? What's the woman got to do with him?'

'I'm not sure how much you know. Something, clearly. But in case you don't know, it's my unfortunate duty to be the one to tell you that your late husband was having a relationship with that young woman.' Janet made no immediate response, but her eyes began to sting and there was nothing she could do to stop tears pricking up of their own accord. 'Perhaps it was guilt that made him end his own life, I don't know,' continued Piet. 'I'm afraid you have been given a misleading account of the events. I will never forgive myself, except to say that

329

Father Granville was trying to protect everyone at the time: you, your children and the girl in question.'

'Go on,' Janet managed, and stretched a hand into her bag to find a handkerchief.

'Father Granville arrived on the scene some time before me. He found Mr Gosling on his own. And then the girl came downstairs. She was in a terrible state and he, well, I suppose, in a manner, he took her confession. At least, he regarded it in that light. By the time I arrived—'

'Why did you go into my house?' Janet's voice sounded almost shrill. 'What possible reason or motive did you, as a complete stranger, have for entering my house so early in the morning?'

Piet raised his hands in front of him. 'Father Granville saw me through the window, walking along the path at the bottom of the lawn and he called out for help.' Janet received the justification silently and brought the hankie to her nose. 'By the time I arrived, the girl had sworn Granville to secrecy. He felt he had to honour that. You know the sort of person he was. Generous, but perhaps a little weak.'

'I don't think he's weak in the slightest.' Her voice trembled.

'Anyway, he'd made up his mind to protect everyone. He'd heard the girl's confession, and his lips were sealed. His next job was to make me agree to do likewise.'

'And you did.'

'I had no choice, without betraying a priest's confidence. The problem came later.'

'What do you mean?'

'Father Granville grew close to the girl. Too close. In fact, he used his position as her confessor to take advantage of her. With fatal results.'

'For goodness' sake!'

'You don't believe me? He told me all about it. About his sexual obsession with the young girl. And look what happened. The evidence would suggest things were pretty far advanced.' Janet said nothing but remembered Granville snatching Hetty's telephone number, viciously, almost, and scrunching it into a tight ball. 'And as he grew more obsessed with the girl,' Piet went on, 'he became more paranoid about me, about what I might tell people, especially you. He realized too late the mistake he'd made and went crazy trying to cover his tracks. It took over his life, and then everything exploded after the girl went to visit Edwina. Now the girl's killed herself, he's abandoned his life and done a runner.' He shook his head. 'I imagine he may have tried to poison you against me, too, to make me seem like some madman, in case I told you the truth.' Again, Janet did not answer, but blinked down into her lap. 'I thought as much. I mean, I'm no angel, for sure – you know that as well as anyone, but I'm certainly no monster.'

'He never said you were a monster,' she said quietly. 'He never has a bad word to say about anybody.'

'Well, now you know the truth. You know about my involvement, which I hope you can understand, and you know a little more about our lamented pastor.'

'You talk as if he's dead and buried.'

'He may as well be.'

She put her hankie away, closed her handbag and stood up. 'I think I understand,' she said.

'And you won't hold it against me?'

She brushed some moss from her skirt and looked around to find the path that led through the tangled ground cover. 'It doesn't matter any more what I think about you.'

'It matters very much to me. It brings me no pleasure

to tell you about your husband's infidelity, I assure you.'

'Don't concern yourself too much,' Janet replied blandly. 'In fact everything seems to fall into place now. All sorts of things, going back months, if not years.'

'Are you all right?'

'Of course. I'll be on my way now.'

Piet stood up abruptly and blocked her path. 'I hope you won't feel the need to go to the police about this.'

They were in a lonely spot, probably not even within calling distance of the nearest person, especially with the roar of the waterfall close by.

'Why should I want to do that? Do you think I could put my boys through another trauma, just after they've begun to get over the first?'

'So you won't? For all our sakes?'

'Even if it did become common knowledge, you could just tell the police the same story you told me. They could hardly blame you for upholding a clergyman's confidentiality.'

'I know what the police can be like.'

'You needn't worry,' she said. 'This is between you, me and Granville, and as far as I'm concerned, it's over.'

He held her gaze for a moment longer, still blocking her path. 'Can I see you one more time? When things have calmed down, in a day or two?'

She stared at him, too afraid to give any answer other than the one he wanted to hear. 'Perhaps.'

Apparently satisfied, he stood aside. She stepped past him and across the rough ground as quickly as she could manage, catching her foot on the brambles. He remained where he stood, watching her, hands in pockets, until she disappeared from sight.

*   *   *

Some time later, Steyn arrived back at his house. His head was bowed and he seemed preoccupied as he opened the gate that led into the garden, which is why he did not notice the young man lying hidden in the undergrowth, watching him from the other side of the road.

The observer was dressed in camouflage, complete with balaclava and khaki gloves, so that not a single piece of flesh was exposed – an outfit he usually put on to decoy and shoot pigeons in the flat land beyond his parents' home. Even his eyes were concealed behind a narrow mesh band, against which he now pressed a pair of green rubberized binoculars. He was watching Steyn's approach closely, as he had watched several times before, at dawn, dusk and in the dead of night, hidden by foliage at a variety of different locations in a semicircle around the foreigner's property. One night he had crept right into the hedge behind the brambles, and, using the night vision scope from his rifle, had got a clear and close view of Steyn lowering a box on what seemed to be a pulley through the hole on top of the raised mound. He decided to keep a simple record of the movements to see if there was a pattern to his comings and goings. That was the only way to be sure of not making any mistakes. He was paralysed with fear as it was, and knew that he would only be able to do what needed to be done if he could be confident that Steyn would be there when the time came, and that no-one else would be around.

He was pretty sure about everything now, and he'd go back and tell all to his father. Once he'd done the job, and done it properly, they'd all be pleased with him. And that would be an end of it. Rufus' neck was stiff from watching, so he laid down the binoculars and rested his head in the grass. A ladybird was scaling precipitously the narrow cusp of a dried old leaf, just a few inches in front of his face. It fell off and vanished into the long grass. Rufus closed his eyes. He longed more than anything else for this nightmare to be behind him.

Chapter 31

As the sedative receded, his eyes and ears came to life and he woke to the tick of the mantelpiece clock. He did not recognize the sound for what it was at first, but it fascinated him, the speed, texture and resonance of it, every beat slow, multi-layered and complex. It seemed to possess harmonic character, shades of happiness and sadness, like a musical statement encased within a gentle rhythmic structure. After what seemed an interminable progression, the sound evolved into something new: a regular sequence of muffled tones, deep, hollow and ominous, like the thumping of a muted gong. As his senses arose this, too, began to mutate and accelerate, finally surfacing from its journey of self-discovery into the cold light of consciousness where it became harsh, uncomfortably close and insistent.

His neck ached from having been too long slumped, and he saw that he was bound to a wheelchair by four tubular bicycle locks. They were brand new ones, made of blue unscratched steel and they looked incongruous hooped over the ivory cuffs of his brushed cotton shirt. The shirt was not his own, neither were the other loose-fitting clothes he was wearing: heavy, pleated trousers turned up at their bottoms, a sleeveless cable weave jumper with moth holes, and brown lace-up brogues.

Still nauseous and shivering from the effects of the drug, he raised his eyes to take in the surroundings. There were layers of tape over his mouth which nipped the skin of his cheeks when he tried to turn his head and the sharp pain of this brought him to his senses. He was conscious of a continuous humming, which reminded him of waking up in the cabin of a cross-Channel ferry as a child. His first thought, for no other reason than this, was that he might be at sea. But then Steyn appeared and the chain of recollection began.

Steyn did not say anything to begin with but came up to the wheelchair, hands on hips, and searched Granville's face. When he did speak, his manner was courteous but weary, like the manager of a hotel who still makes the effort to account for his establishment even though he's been in the job too long and no longer particularly cares about the welfare of his guests.

He outlined what he described as the rules of the house, though the words breezed over Granville's head, barely registering, which did not matter, as there was no call for dialogue. Steyn talked of an exercise programme to be undertaken twice a day, strictly supervised, with all necessary restraints, and said something about sleeping quarters for Granville in the study, though they would leave this until later on. He gestured here and there, describing the layout of the place and Granville's eyes followed the direction of his arms, not really understanding where or what he was referring to. There was mention of a bathroom procedure, mealtimes, and other parameters of a daily routine that Granville was expected to live within, 'at least until a decision can be reached about what to do in the longer term'. Then Steyn leant down close.

'We are in a sealed bunker thirty feet beneath the

ground, partitioned and secured with toughened steel-plate doors, to which I alone hold the keys. Not a splinter of sound or light can pass from here to the surface. We're cocooned, you might say, in a fortress of rectitude. You'll be comfortable,' he said and pulled up a chair, 'but you'll do as you're told and there'll be no second chances.' His arm travelled in a wide arc around the room. 'What you see is the culmination of more than forty years' planning. The fruit of my life's labour, saved cent by cent in gold krugerrand. Men will speak of it in time to come.' He let his words sink in and then got to his feet.

He walked across to a door on the far side of the room, opened it and said quietly to Rose that she could now come in. He held out an arm as if ushering her into a stage spotlight and she presented herself before Granville, chin raised, front knee kinked, smiling. She did not look directly at him but fixed her eyes on a spot behind his head.

Piet introduced her and explained that she would be looking after Granville's emergency needs during the times when he himself was absent from the household. He stood back to look her up and down. She was dressed as if about to go for a spring walk in the park, in a yellow and green floral dress, with a broad white belt, flesh-coloured stockings and large, white circular sunglasses resting above her hairline. 'Rose will take care of you adequately,' said Steyn. 'She might even sing for you,' and taken with the idea, added, 'yes, come on, Rose, let's have a little song now.' She blinked and appealed with her eyes to Steyn for a reprieve, but he insisted with a shake of the head. 'Come on, now,' he said, 'do as you are told.'

Granville stared at her as she stood there in front of him, stock still, a picture postcard housewife from a bygone era. She looked down and swallowed, preparing herself for the ordeal, and opened her mouth. Her face strained with the effort, and a birdlike voice emerged, quite frosty and only approximately in tune, singing, 'My bonny lies over the ocean'. Steyn smiled and began to sway slightly at the repeated chorus lines, 'Bring back, bring back'. At the end of the first verse she looked up at him fearfully and Steyn clapped. 'A pretty sound,' he said, 'better every time.' Granville kept looking at her, and for an instant her eyes shifted and made contact with his, a hairline fracture in her presentation, but a blink later she had turned away and walked off to attend to something next door.

Granville remained staring at the space that she had occupied while Steyn talked on. Rose, he explained, would not be permitted to release him from the wheelchair under any circumstances, nor did she have the means to unlock his restraints. 'Which might result in complications,' he added, and because of this offered Granville the use of an adult's incontinence diaper, 'just in case you feel you are unable to control yourself while I am away from home. Nothing to be ashamed of.' Granville did not seem to hear the suggestion and was still gazing ahead, so that Steyn had to make the offer again. This time Granville declined with a barely perceptible shake of the head.

Steyn now removed the gag, peeling off the tape strip by strip, which ripped the stubble from Granville's chin and upper lip. When he had finished he left the room, though the rumbling sound of his voice talking to Rose continued next door for a minute or so, before a succession of metallic thuds, each more distant than the one before, indicated his passing through the bunker's three access chamber doors.

The recirculated air smelt warm and tainted, like the atmosphere of a basement factory canteen. Opposite Granville was a small brick-surround fireplace with a pair of comfortable looking armchairs either side and a low table between them. All four walls of the sitting room were decorated in a heavily patterned paper. A pair of thick, lined curtains beneath a pelmet were drawn to, as if it were dark outside, and the clock on the mantelpiece showed ten to eight. Daytime or evening? The only light came from a pendant fixture in the centre of the ceiling, a type of inverted glass bowl, frosted and engraved. It gave a yellowish glow, not quite bright enough, and occasionally flickered, which, together with the dull tick of the mantelpiece clock and the canned air, added to the room's dreariness. Granville could see from the glint at the edges of the door that the room next door was much brighter.

For some while he listened to the sounds between the silences that came from the next room. The clatter of plates being stacked. The rhythmic swish of a cloth. A tap turned on, then off. Disjointed footsteps. Several times he was about to call out but stopped himself. He could not reach to spin the wheels of the chair and move himself, and so had to make do. A clock in another room chimed and then chimed again a quarter of an hour later; and again and again, quarterly, distant notches in the emptiness, neatly slicing up the passage of time into recognizably right-angled portions.

When it seemed that Rose had no intention of coming back uninvited, he spoke out for the first time, but his voice cracked and he had to repeat himself a little louder. 'Can I come in there, please?' The sounds from the next room came to a stop and after a moment she appeared at the door. 'Can I join you?' he asked. 'If you don't mind.'

She walked over and came around behind the chair. There was a rustle of underskirts and a smell of scented soap as she passed. She pushed the chair forwards, negotiated it through the door and into the kitchen. The light in here was dazzling. Different sorts of bulbs had been used, all concealed, to provide a daytime brilliance that was clean, white and invigorating. The hum of circulating air persisted, but not so oppressively in here. She parked him in front of the large glazed window, with its open curtains and pastoral prospect, then went back to her work at the kitchen surface. He was facing away from her and could not see what she was doing.

'That's some poster,' he said, looking at the pane of glass and the illusory view beyond. It showed meadows, a forested ridge and a perfect village nestled distantly between interlocking hills. 'Where's it supposed to be? France? Seems Alpine, at any rate. Amazing.' She did not answer. After a pause, he tried again. 'How long have you been here?' No reply. He looked around and spotted a newspaper on the kitchen table. 'Did he bring that one today?' He nodded towards it. 'I know where he keeps them.' He strained his neck to try and face her. 'Don't you remember me?' he asked. 'I'm the rector. I got to know Bob quite well – you know, your friend, the traveller who came and stayed with you in the caravan. Seems ages ago now. Lily. That's your real name, isn't it?' Still no reply. 'Well, I remember you, Lily, even if you don't remember me.' He lurched to the right to try and swing the chair around. It moved fractionally and he tried again. He could now just about see her. She was trying to cut some vegetables with a plastic knife, rounded at its tip, and was finding it hard work. Her back was turned.

'How long has he been keeping you here?' Granville

asked again. Still she did not answer, nor even indicate that she had heard him. When eventually she did turn around, he could see that her eyes were red from chopping onions, and she discarded the outer layers into a compost bin. She blew her nose. 'Would you rather I didn't speak?' he said. 'The only way we're going to make anything better here is by doing something together. The only hope we'll ever have of getting out—'

'Don't say such a thing!' She hissed the words, and doubled over, violently. 'Don't even think it!'

'I'm sorry, I didn't mean—'

'He knows everything.' Her face was taut. 'He'll know what you've been saying.'

'You mean he's recording us?'

'He just knows.'

'All right. I'm sorry.' He allowed her to calm down. She hesitated and then turned back to carry on with the cooking. 'I don't think he meant us not to talk,' Granville continued. 'He would have said so.' She did not respond, and for the moment he gave up trying.

For the next hour or so Granville had nothing to do except watch her at work in the kitchen. When she had finished, she glanced up at the clock on the wall and said, 'Would you like me to leave you in here or shall I push you back into the drawing room?'

'Where are you going?'

'To my room.'

'Can we talk?'

'I have things to do.'

He did not want to let the thread of contact drop. 'Really? Too busy to talk for five minutes.'

'It's eleven o'clock.'

'So?'

'I do my Bible study at eleven o'clock.'

'Perhaps I can help.'

'No.'

'I'll wait in here, then. It's a bit more cheerful.' She accepted his decision and walked away, but before she left, he called, 'What time do you expect Piet?'

She stopped in her tracks and said hesitantly, 'I don't understand you.'

For an instant Granville considered the possibility that she might be mentally deficient, that the years down here had left her partially brain dead, but then he understood. 'You don't know his name, do you? He's never told you his name. He's called Piet. Piet Steyn. Didn't you know?'

'No.' That admission and the dull pain that came into her eyes when she spoke it told Granville that he had gained a foothold.

'I'm sorry,' he said. 'Don't let me keep you. We'll talk later.' She lowered her eyes and turned to go. Granville felt a sudden urge to say something else, if only to keep her in the room, but thought better of it.

Chapter 32

Steyn returned to the bunker for a light lunch. He said he could only stay for a short while but promised, like a diligent family breadwinner, to be back with them in time for an early supper.

While he was there, he escorted Granville to the toilet, making sure first to lock Rose in a separate room. He chained shackles to Granville's ankles, removed the bicycle locks from his wrists, and then parked the wheelchair right in front of the lavatory door, which meant that Granville had just to stand up and shuffle forward a couple of steps before he was inside. Steyn warned him that he was holding an electronic device at the ready, in case of what he described as 'any mishap during the procedure', but Granville could not see what it was.

After a brief moment of privacy and freedom in the lavatory, Granville indicated that he was ready to leave by rapping on the door. He was then required to reverse out slowly, wrists held together behind his back, and cuffs were put around them before he lowered himself back into the wheelchair.

Later in the day, the three of them were back around the kitchen table again for supper. Granville was still bound by the ankles but his arms were now secured just above the elbow, which meant that he could move his forearms and freely use the cutlery to eat. The menu was shepherd's pie, with a generous crust of mashed potato and a pile of carrots on the side. Piet seemed to be in a good mood and talked most of the time. He was particularly appreciative of the cooking, though he ate little, and what he did take, he churned up into a small brown heap on his plate – mince, gravy and vegetables together – before shovelling it by the forkful into his mouth.

He spoke continuously, sharing with them his various observations of the day, a blend of news and commentary with much moral substance woven in. His style was different from that of the man Granville had come to know. The old guardedness was gone and he seemed relaxed, almost affable, his manner tailored to suit the role of a respected domestic overseer whose spiritual authority over his brood was absolute. He would leave pauses after pronouncements so that the two of them could reflect on his words, and Rose accepted everything he said with a thoughtful nod. In any other context than this Piet might have seemed a kindly family patriarch, a man of faith and far-reaching thought; but there was no other context, Granville reminded himself, and more than once he glanced across the table at Rose and caught a tiredness in her eyes. Like the reused air they breathed, the flickering light and imperfect silence of the place, her vitality had been tarnished.

After dinner, while Rose stacked the plates and began to wash up, the direction of Piet's conversation changed, though his tone remained disconcertingly pleasant. He was addressing Rose.

'So, tell me, what does it feel like to a see a man again after so long?'

'What do you mean?' she asked, without turning away from the sink.

'You know exactly what I mean,' he replied without pause, and gazed at her directly, waiting for an answer.

'It's . . .' she stumbled, 'it's strange for me, of course. It's been just you and me here for so long.'

Piet turned to Granville with a smile. 'Rose and I have no secrets,' he said. 'One of the rules of the house is absolute, unconditional honesty, though Rose struggles with this.' He spoke out again to her. 'Tell me honestly now: has the presence of a new man in the house – quite a young man, at that, and good looking, some would say – has it made you think about sex? Even for an instant?' She was silenced by the question and tried to carry on with the washing up. 'Come on, Rose. Absolute honesty now. Has the smallest thought of this nature passed through your mind today? The tiniest, passing fragment of a thought about physical intimacy with this man?'

'I . . .'

'Speak up!'

'I can't even remember every thought I've had,' she ventured.

'Don't pretend you don't know what I mean.'

'Hundreds of thoughts go through a person's head every minute. We don't choose them. Particularly when something unexpected like this happens.'

'I await your answer.'

'Piet,' cut in Granville, 'please don't.'

'Silence, please. Allow me to judge the success or otherwise of my teaching these past years. Rose: my question.'

'You shouldn't—'

'*I shouldn't?*'

'I would never normally think of things like that. It's only because you—'

'The truth and nothing else, please.'

She lowered her head and stopped what she was doing. Her hands, which were covered by a pair of pink rubber gloves up to the elbows, sat still in the soapsudded water. She seemed paralysed, unable to move, speak, find a way out or retract what she had already said.

'Piet,' Granville spoke out again, 'can we please talk in private?'

Steyn looked from Granville to Rose and back again. 'Ach,' he replied, 'I see. The knight in shining armour comes to the rescue of the maiden in the monster's castle. A fairytale ending. Is that it?' Steyn pondered the implications of what he had said for a moment, staring into space with his arms crossed and the corners of his mouth drawn down. Then, clapping his hands, he snapped out of his reverie and stood up. 'Rose, I have business to discuss next door with the good pastor. We will be stepping down from the table.'

'Yes, husband,' she said uncertainly. Steyn went over to Granville, took hold of the wheelchair by its handles and pushed it through to the study. Granville looked back and caught a glimpse of Rose. She was still leaning forward over the sink, motionless, head hanging, her studied grace poleaxed.

The room he and Steyn now entered was small and dull, with one chair, a desk, and a little steel-framed bed neatly arranged in the corner. Granville assumed it was intended for his use.

'Okey dokey,' sighed Steyn. He reapplied the wrist restraints and explained that at night Granville's limbs would have to be securely attached to the bed frame. 'It may not be all that comfortable,' he said, 'but you'll

have plenty of time to catch up on sleep during the day.'
He parked the wheelchair opposite him and sat down
heavily in an armchair. His head rested against the spread
fingertips of one hand and his eyes were closed. For some
while he remained like that, in silence, then breathed
heavily and looked up. His conviviality had gone and
heavy creases had returned to his brow. In a matter of
seconds he had become thin and hunched again, like
the Piet Steyn that Granville had always known, though
suddenly older and more troubled.

'What an unfortunate situation,' Steyn muttered.

'How long has she been here?'

Steyn chewed on the corner of a thumbnail. 'Does it
matter?'

'Ever since she went missing from her caravan? Three
years?'

'Her disappearance hardly caused a ripple. A good
candidate for my purposes. No ties, no dependants, no
accountability.'

'Just a human life.'

'Don't be so melodramatic, Father. It hasn't been so
bad. At the start, yes, it's always hard. They shout and
scream, beat the walls, tear their hair.'

'They? How many have there been?'

'But they get over it. The secret is to get them to
understand the purpose. As soon as Rose understood
what I was doing here – that it had nothing to do with
punishment or persecution – she started eating again.
She realized I was offering her a decent life. Our first
Christmas was a watershed. Very special. The tree, the
decorations, little gifts, carols on the tape machine. She
was beginning to learn.'

'Learn what?'

'How to be a good wife.'

Granville stared at him. 'Where did you get these ideas from?'

'Feminine purity and trustworthiness are the salvation of family life and one of the cornerstones of civilization. Qualities more precious than gold. By the same token men have to be strong, hard-working and morally courageous. There's no mystery about what you call my ideas. It's the way everyone knows in their hearts that things should be.'

'But you say that every woman lets you down.'

'Their failure is no reason for me to abandon my mission. I must carry on or die in the attempt. What kind of a Christian soldier would I be if I just gave up?'

'What kind of Christian soldier would incarcerate a fellow human being for years in an underground bunker?'

'So you prefer a world populated by adulterous whores?'

'Is that the only alternative?'

'It's black and white. Why does no-one have the courage any more to stand up and say "this is the right way of doing things and this is the wrong"? You tell me, Father, based on your own experience of marriage. How would you have your woman behave, given the choice?'

'We do not have the prerogative to choose on behalf of other people, only for ourselves.'

'Wrong. It's just that sort of spineless attitude that's got us into such a mess.' He pinched forefinger and thumb together professorially. 'Our present culture – obsessed above all with freedom – encourages selfish, unregulated indulgence, and it is irresistible to the weak. Schools with no discipline, children who think it's embarrassing to do well, who prefer to get fat and sit in front of screens. Young men with no ambition, bunking off work or

348

getting drunk. Wastrels who can't be bothered to find a job, but queue up for free money from the state. Married couples divorcing at the drop of a hat, leaving their children high and dry. You know what I mean, even if you pretend not to. But we can undermine the disease, slowly, surely. I will have success and one day others will follow my lead.'

'What do you intend to do with her?'

'You mean Rose?' Steyn chewed on his finger again for a moment, spat out a fragment of hard skin he had bitten off, and leant forward on his elbows. 'To be honest, as far as Rose is concerned, we've come to the point when it's a matter of choosing the appropriate time and circumstances for closure.'

'What do you mean?'

Steyn thought before answering. 'I mean that one cannot just do these things on impulse. The chicken farmers back home used to say that as soon as you wring their necks the clock is ticking. Better by far to truck them around while they're still breathing because it keeps them fresh and doesn't fill up your refrigerator.'

Granville absorbed the implication of the words. 'Why?' he asked.

Steyn looked up with surprise. 'Because it takes time and planning to dispose of human remains in such a way as not to be traceable, of course.'

Granville closed his eyes. 'I mean, why do you have to get rid of her?'

'She has failed. I need to make room for a new candidate.'

As they sat in silence, the background hum of the ventilation system rose up a semitone in pitch. It would always happen when a high-consumption appliance, like the vacuum cleaner or fridge, came on in the bunker. It altered the slant of tension in the sound landscape of the room.

'What's the point in humiliating her, then?' asked Granville.

Steyn looked up. 'What?'

'If you've decided you're finished with her, why do you taunt her like that? Making her sing in front of me, and all that other stuff. What's the point?'

'I suppose it's because I am disappointed, and I want her to know it.'

'You make a mockery of Christian values.' Steyn shrugged but did not answer. 'So you're going to do away with her and look for someone else to imprison down here. Is that the long and short of it?'

'I don't have to look, I've already found the right person. In fact, I'm going to have to act more quickly than I'd thought. Time is running out.'

Something in the almost humorous way Steyn now regarded Granville answered his next question before he had articulated it. 'It's Janet, isn't it? You're planning to kidnap Janet Gosling.'

Steyn acknowledged the assumption with a wink and a cock of his head. 'She's a fine candidate, Father.'

'Have you gone completely mad?'

Steyn shook his head and waved a finger in the air. 'Don't presume to know the situation,' he said. 'Janet and I are closer than you imagine. I had a long talk with her just yesterday and she's keen to see me again. We've been through a shaky patch but that's all over now. It won't be easy to start with, it never is. I know she'll find it hard to adjust, but I'm patient.'

'You're insane.'

Steyn just smiled and shook his head. 'It'll turn out fine.'

'Don't you understand? She's terrified of you. She wants to get as far away as possible. And have you thought about her boys?'

'It's unfortunate for them, but I have to think of the bigger picture. Anyway, they have uncles and aunts to turn to, and more money than is good for them. They'll be provided for.'

'Janet's not like some rootless traveller with no family, living in a caravan. There'll be trails everywhere. The police are not idiots. They'll be all over you in a matter of hours.'

'If it comes to that, I've got a story in place. You have a starring role in it, as it happens. She's been asking a lot about you. Some might think she was ever so slightly in love.'

'What are you trying to say?'

'If the police come asking me about Janet Gosling, I have information and pieces of evidence that will nudge them down a different trail. She's run off to join her lover. The two of you, fugitives, running away from your lives and responsibilities.'

'No-one will believe that.'

'Don't you worry.' Steyn patted the air in front of him, 'Janet's the one. I'll make it happen. She's just perfect. Such untrammelled material, such maturity and innocence.'

Granville quietly asked the inevitable question. 'And where does all this leave me?'

Steyn puffed his cheeks and opened wide his eyes before exhaling but gave no answer. Granville looked away.

'Oh. I found this on your person,' Piet suddenly said, animated by the recollection, and produced Granville's BlackBerry. 'I'd no idea how to work the thing, of course, and had to go to a telephone shop in Dorchester to get hold of an instruction book. Anyway, I took the liberty of looking through your messages. Quite a few people have been wondering where you are.' He waved the device in the air. 'Plenty of stuff from Janet, as you might expect. But on the whole most people respect your desire to get away from it all for a while. As for your wife . . .' He whistled and looked down at the phone screen, flicking his thumb over the roller ball. He found what he was looking for, and pulled down the corners of his mouth, discouragingly.

Granville's voice was calm. 'What does she say?'

'Not very pleased with you. I think that's a fair summary. Let's see . . .' He took his glasses from a pocket and put them on. 'She calls you a coward for running away. Yes, she's pretty angry. She says . . . yes, here we are: she says she's in touch with the Church Commissioners—' He looked up. 'I suppose you know that organization?'

Granville nodded.

'She's in touch with the Church Commissioners and she's going to begin clearing the house out next week. That was . . .' he checked the date, 'three days ago.' He turned the phone off. 'A decisive lady.'

'Does she say . . . ?' The question stuck in his throat. 'Yes?'

'Does she say anything about my daughters?'

'Not a word,' Steyn replied, and dropped the phone back in the breast pocket of his shirt. He regarded Granville studiously before speaking again. 'She's a bad egg, that woman of yours. You could have handled her better. All this time, you've been clinging on, like a sloth under the branch, instead of getting on top like a real man and straightening things out.' Granville did not reply. 'Oh well,' said Steyn, 'she's history now, as far as

352

you're concerned. And not too soon.' He got to his feet, stiffly, and looked down at Granville in the wheelchair. 'All things considered, it would have been better if we'd never met that morning,' he said. 'I did not particularly wish to extend our acquaintanceship, if you remember. But you were most insistent.'

'I know.'

'You had your own reasons.'

'I suppose I did.'

'I would not have chosen to bring you into this situation. Everything got complicated, and then there was the girl.'

'Did you kill her?'

Steyn scowled. 'We've already talked about this. My role was purely mechanical. I told her that if she chose to put an end to it I could show her the way to do it right.'

'Is that what you do with people who don't measure up? Help them dispose of themselves?'

'I only try to enact the Will of the Lord.'

'What warped sense of divine mission informs your conscience to carry out cold-blooded murder in the name of God?'

Piet smiled again. 'You've read a lot of books, Father, but perhaps you should have concentrated more on the only one that counts.' He stretched over to his desk and picked up a Bible. 'It's all in here, you know. Everything I have ever done and every justification required to do it is written in the Law.'

'Can you imagine Jesus tightening the noose around Hetty's neck?'

'Who are we to judge? I don't read between the lines when it comes to the Holy Scriptures. I act upon what I read.'

Granville began again. 'Look, Piet, I know how hard

353

your life has been. I understand a bit about you. I know your religion has been your great fortress. The only way your ancestors could survive in the wilds was by—'

But Steyn interrupted him with a raised hand and an almost kindly smile. 'Forgive me, Father, but we're not going to start all that now.'

'You can't be blamed for growing up in—'

'Enough.' He said it with quiet finality and stretched, arching his back, which made his spine click. The background hum of the ventilation fan sank down again to its normal running tone. 'Time for bed, I think.'

'You don't have to do this,' Granville persisted, 'any of this. It's not too late.'

'Spare me the clichés.'

'We can talk it through. Tell me the story from the start. I'm good at listening.'

Steyn just smiled and ambled over to a chest of drawers. 'I don't do bedtime stories,' he said, opening the top drawer, and rifling around. 'Actually, I was always a little scared of them as a child.' He found what he was looking for and closed the drawer. 'And I don't think my tales would be the kind to give you sweet dreams.' He turned back to Granville and held up the bunch of plastic cable ties that he had retrieved. 'Let's see how we're going to do this, shall we?'

Chapter 33

When she was convinced that her husband had no intention of showing up in the short term, Edwina St Clair returned to her former home in Tennyson Terrace to begin the process of clearing the place of her possessions. Until now, other residents of the estate had tended to look the other way when they walked past the closed windows of number 3 – either out of a sense of neighbourly camaraderie or bourgeois disgust – but today, with the removals truck parked on the driveway, the front door open, and Mrs St Clair coming in and out of the house, there were few who could resist the temptation to stare, some of them pausing for a minute or more to feed their curiosity.

Edwina took no notice but went about her task with a sense of purpose, telling herself repeatedly that she had no affection for this bloody house anyway, nor the village, nor many of the memories associated with it. She was still bristling with righteous anger about her husband's behaviour but she also knew that her tub-thumping had begun to ring hollow. The truth was that her fury lay just a hair's breadth away from a depth of despair she had no desire to fathom. She therefore did what she had to do quickly, moving from room to room without stopping, and refusing to dwell on the provenance of all the old possessions she was boxing, bagging or binning. She disembowelled the contents of wardrobes whole and churned out drawerfuls, ignoring detail for the sake of the general goal; but all the while her cheeks were wet with streaming tears which would not let up, no matter how hard she tried, and this infuriated her still further.

All around the house lay black and white bin liners some filled and tightly tied, others partially full, the black ones for keeping, the white for the charity shop. A waste disposal skip had been parked outside and was filling with alarming speed. She had hired the help of two hefty Lithuanian boys who normally worked at the local car valeting centre, and they came into the house in their boots every now and then to ask if she wanted to throw something out or put it in the pile for the removal lorry. Every time she condemned an item to the skip, they would turn it over, examine it from every possible angle, mutter unintelligibly to each other for a while and eventually make a judgement as to whether or not it was worth taking on for themselves. Their own pile was now also growing and they promised to come with a van for it the following day.

She stopped for a coffee with her two helpers mid-morning, and they asked her in broken English if she was OK, to which she replied, yes, fine, smiling through red eyes, but they looked unconvinced and embarrassed. She drained her mug and went to rinse it in the kitchen sink, steeling herself for the next round. The family photographs had been a challenge and she had put them straight into cases marked 'very fragile', face down, layering them with blanket linings so that the glass would not break. She refused to be drawn by the children's milk-toothy grins in the studio portraits, nor would she indulge herself with a glance at the happy holiday shots on the sideboard. The wedding album was transferred to a packing box with a minimum of finger contact, like a contaminated laboratory article. A few pieces of the girls' infant clothing, which she'd kept back for sentimental reasons, were folded quickly into a trunk, as were the special birthday cards and drawings they'd laboured over in early childhood. All in all, Edwina thought, she was managing to get through memory lane with the rose-tinted spectacles firmly folded and locked away.

She moved on to Granville's study, which she had been dreading, but found was easier to clear than she'd feared, because the shambles of his desk and the clogged shelves of theological books filled her with renewed annoyance. All this academic theory and pedantic gibberish had got in the way from the start. It had driven them into separate worlds and silted up the channels of communication. With something like revenge, she now slung hardbacks and journals by the armful into boxes which she marked with a large 'G St C', part of a load that would be delivered to her father-in-law's house, for want of anywhere else to put it. The old St Clair family treasures could go the same way, for all she cared, and good riddance to the lot of them. She did toy with the idea of holding back the magnificent ancestral portrait of her husband's namesake in their bedroom, partly for the girls' sake and also to punish Granville, but decided in the end to include it with the rest of the stuff bound for Mounty's house. She couldn't bear to live with that name emblazoned on the gilded title panel.

She finished Granville's desk surface, emptied the left-hand drawers and got as far as the second drawer on the right, when something at last caused her to stall, and the pause proved fatal to her resilience. There was not much in the drawer other than a few pieces of redundant office tat: a hole puncher, dried-up ink bottle, loose clips and an unused rubber date stamper. But beside them, just lying there and rocking to a standstill as she stood and stared down into the drawer, was a large pale grey pebble. She picked it up and held it in her palm. It was smooth, cool, and filled her hand so that she could not quite bring her fingertips together around it; just as she remembered. Had it been here all these years? She could see Granville, so young and excited, with backpack and boots, dipping his hand blindly into the Snowdonia river and bringing the stone out of the water to illustrate a point he was trying to make. He'd had to speak up because the broad stream burbled so loudly. The pebble was utterly perfect, he had said; it had waited thousands of years for him to lay his equally perfect hand upon it, something which might never have happened, but which, after the event, was incontrovertible and a milestone in its way, be it ever so small. Thus was occurrence carved from the random abyss of potentiality, he pronounced, eyes full of joyous wonder; thus was made explicit what would otherwise remain implicit in all creation for all eternity. Thus was the potentially world-changing chain of cause and effect kept in motion. He had shaken his head at the vastness of the concept, baffling himself, as he always did. What role did the hand of God play in all this? he'd asked in a half-voice, staring at the stone and turning it over in his fingers, even as she now turned it over in her own.

She could admit now that she had felt a needle-prick of spite even then, by that river in Snowdonia. A trace of poison had been there so early in their lives together, the precursor of something uglier that grew as the years progressed. Why? she asked herself. Why had she allowed herself to belittle him? Granville's innocence and inspiration were the very things that set him apart from others, everybody said so. If she could not personally grasp the wondrousness he thought he beheld with his own eyes, was that a reason to despise it? All the time that she had been sneering at the supposed flaws in his character she had been blind to the disease in her own. She had invented a whole lot of nonsense over the years, and fed it with plain envy. Her tears spilled over and splashed onto the pebble, darkening its pale smoothness, and she knew that she would never again meet a man of the calibre of the one she had married.

The door to the study opened and she turned, startled. One of the Lithuanian boys was standing there, like an awkward bull, trying to explain that they needed some things – tools, staples and tape. She pursed her lips and smiled. She needed some bits and pieces herself, she said, and thought it might be a good time to pause from her work. She could go to the local agricultural superstore, part of a West Country chain known as FAIR – Farm and Industry Retail – which was not far from Cheselbury Abbas and would have everything they needed. She told the boy she'd be back in half an hour or so, and he nodded, shuffling out of the room.

It was as she was locking her car at FAIR that she noticed the man pushing a low flatbed trolley on the other side of the car park. He was heading for the front entrance of the store, and even as she watched, frozen with a peculiar interest, the double glass doors opened automatically and he disappeared inside. She had neither seen nor thought much about him since the incident at the Easter Grill, but somehow the sight of Piet Steyn aroused her interest. Perhaps the telephone conversation with Janet had struck a chord and it was only now that she thought

359

about it. Steyn had been there with Granville on the morning of Bertie Gosling's death. He had known about the girl from the start.

Curiosity made Edwina follow Piet from a distance inside the store. It was not difficult to stay unseen because he seemed detached from everything and everyone outside his purpose, though twice he went up to sales assistants who pointed him in the right direction. He picked up some sponges, scourers, a carton of industrial cleaning fluid and a packet of latex gloves. Edwina, tailing him, wondered if he had an interest in ceramics, because he was examining some tile saws and eventually put one in his cart. He then noticed a leaflet about kilns in the same section of the shop, put on his glasses and began reading it. He remained at the same place in the aisle for some while, before heading off, leaflet in hand, this time towards the customer services desk. Edwina followed and hid behind a rack of gun dog accessories close by, so that, by the time Piet reached the front of the queue, she could hear parts of his conversation with the assistant.

He was asking how to purchase a poultry incinerator. Nothing too big, he specified, and preferably front loading. She stole a glance and saw the assistant checking various models on his computer. 'What sort of usage do you anticipate?' Piet leant over to look at the computer screen and gave an answer Edwina could not hear. The assistant's voice was clearer. 'They're all ministry approved,' he was saying, 'subject to the usual inspections and ash disposal regulations.'

'It's all right,' said Piet, 'I'll put an application in the post. What about fuel?'

'LPG, natural gas, biogas.'

'And delivery?' His slow speech and style of

questioning began to frustrate one or two people in the queue behind him, who exchanged glances. When at last he was satisfied that he had all the information he needed, he jotted down some notes on a piece of paper provided by the assistant, took off his spectacles and turned away sharply to his left. Edwina had moved out slightly to get a better view and now had to look down quickly to avoid eye contact. But, on lowering her eyes, she saw something which made her stop in her tracks. It was clear as day, but before she could think again, it was too late to get away. She looked up and he was there in front of her, staring straight into her face.

'So, you're back,' he said.

'Yes. I've come to clear out the house.'

'Ah. Any word from Father Granville?'

Edwina's hands were trembling. She averted her eyes and struggled to appear at ease. 'No.'

'I'm sorry for the trouble you're going through. It must be a terrible time for you.'

'Thank you.'

'Your daughters are well?'

'Yes. Very well, thank you.'

'Have they come with you?'

'No,' she replied. 'They're in Scotland with my parents.'

'Ah. Scotland's very beautiful, I hear.'

'Yes, parts of it are quite stunning.'

'Good walking?'

'Very good.'

'Perhaps I'll make my way up there some day.'

'You should.'

He nodded. 'Well, I'd best be getting along. If you need any help with the house . . .'

'Thank you, but I've got a couple of strong boys helping.'

Piet nodded again and smiled at her. 'Goodbye, then. And best wishes for your future.'

'Thank you. Goodbye.'

Steyn turned away and pushed his cart towards the exit, which opened and closed behind him. Edwina stayed exactly where she was for some minutes after, staring into space until a shop assistant came up to ask if she 'needed any help at all'. The distraction brought her to her senses and she quickly went around the store, picking up what she had come to buy, before moving to the checkout. Minutes later she was back in the car and hurrying home.

As soon as she was back indoors, she handed over the tools to the two boys and closed herself in the sitting room. She went straight over to the telephone, checked a number in the local parish magazine and began to dial. It took a little while and several redirections before she was put through to the right department.

'Mrs St Clair? This is Detective Sergeant Walker.'

'Was it you who spoke to my husband after that girl's suicide?'

'That girl?'

'I'm sorry.' Her face was flushed and sweat was welding the receiver to her cheekbone. 'I'm not thinking straight. Her name was Hetty. Hetty Swanley.'

'Yes, you're speaking to the right person.'

'There's somebody else involved, I think. A man in the village. I think he might have something to do with my husband's disappearance.'

There was a pause at the other end of the line, and when the policeman spoke, he did so slowly and carefully. 'Take your time, Mrs St Clair. Now, tell me why you think this other man is involved.'

'Because I've just seen him. He was wearing a pair of my husband's shoes.'

Another pause. 'How do you know they were your husband's?'

'I just know. They're ones I hate. A particular design. Made by Clarks. He thought they were comfortable and didn't care about the way he looked.'

'Quite a lot of people wear Clarks shoes, you know.'

'Not like this. They have a little green tab on each heel. The first day my husband got them, the dog chewed the tab off the left one. It was the same with this man's shoes today. The left tab was missing.'

Chapter 34

Rufus Futcher could not run away from his anxiety. It was like an ache that he carried around with him everywhere. It was there when he woke up and still there as he drifted off to sleep at night, and nothing during the course of the working day could distract him from it for long. He bitterly regretted putting himself up for this job but had to tell himself it was no good moaning about it now. There was no way out.

Everyone had been so pleased with him when he said he'd do it. They'd slapped him on the back, cheered fiercely and punched the air. Pint had followed celebratory pint and then, later, swaying, they'd asked him quietly: was he sure he could manage it? Yeah, sure, easy peasy, he'd answered scoffing, and they'd gripped him around the shoulders again. It had made him feel great, like a real man, top of the tree. Since then, he had been planning, watching, and making notes back home in his slow, laborious way. As every day passed and the date drew nearer, he'd felt his bowels constrict. Now, he had no appetite for food whatsoever.

He'd done a lot of groundwork, he knew Steyn's routine and had practised the whole plan again and again. Surely nothing could go wrong. But, confident as he was, he could not stop wondering about ways to get himself off the hook. They boiled down to three options: owning up to everyone that he was just too scared to go through with it; running away from home altogether; or doing himself an injury that would make it physically impossible. All three filled him with almost as much dread as the job itself, and this made him loathe himself all the more.

Twice now, when he had seen Steyn climbing out of the bunker in the late evening dark, Rufus had hooted an owl call. On both occasions Steyn had stopped in his tracks to look up into the surrounding trees. Rufus knew it was insanely reckless and told himself he was doing it because the damned foreigner deserved to be spooked. But part of him secretly wanted to alert Steyn. If his owl calls were not quite right or just a little too insistent he might put the wind up the old bastard and that might just scupper the whole plan. What a relief that would be.

But nothing had happened to justify him aborting or backing out, and so now he had to pack everything up in preparation. He had a khaki game bag, one he used to bring rabbits and pigeons back home when he'd been out rough shooting. It was just about big enough to fit in all the kit. He looked around his room before leaving. He didn't want to see or talk to anyone just now. He just wanted to go, do the bloody thing and get back home. It wouldn't be long before he was back here again, surrounded by all his old stuff, with the dog curled up at his feet, and the whole horrible business would be over and done.

*

Time was running out, but Granville knew that he would have to go carefully with Rose. He observed her quietly, without interfering, allowing her to move freely around the space, command the silence and keep to the daily routine she was used to. He spoke only occasionally, dropping pleasantries and practical requests that were easy for her to accommodate, with the result that by the third day it was as if he had brushed away a layer of protective dust from her and had begun to catch glimpses of the delicate personality beneath. He spied subtle fractures in her expressions, remnants of spontaneity behind the perfect mask of make-up and mannerisms. From time to time she would even smile at him; nothing dramatic, no moment of awakening or sudden realization, but a quiet hint that his presence and kindness were appreciated; enough, he felt, to encourage him gently onwards.

One morning, after breakfast, he asked her to pass him a pencil and a couple of sheets of blank paper. He then asked her to push him up to the table, and he proceeded to tear the paper into small squares, inscribing a letter on each and a numeral on the reverse side. She glanced at him from time to time without saying anything, but interested in what he was doing. Once he looked back at her and smiled, which made her turn away. He then took the spare sheet of paper and carefully drew lines across it, turning it into a large grid, each square of which was about the same size as the pieces he had earlier torn and inscribed. 'That's it,' he murmured to himself when it was complete. She was working on the other side of the kitchen, folding clean linen into a basket, and she looked across at what he had done.

'What is it?' she asked.

'A word game. Just a home-made thing, a poor man's Scrabble, but quite fun, actually. I play it with my daughters on camping holidays. Do you want to have a go?' She looked away sharply and did not answer. 'It won't hurt you,' he said. When he noticed her look back again, hesitantly, he added, 'And I'm pretty 'armless, as you can see.' He was attached to the chair by the elbows, and waved his forearms around like a seal's fins. She could not suppress a smile at this and came over slowly, taking a seat next to him at the table.

'How do you play?' she asked.

He explained the simple rules, demonstrated how to put together an easy word, how to score it, and how it opened up opportunities for the next turn. She had a go and he applauded her effort as best he could, flapping the tips of his fingers together, which amused her again. As the game progressed, he watched her concentrating quietly on her turns and her face seemed transfigured. For those brief interludes when her guard was down, her eyes had the vulnerability of a homesick child. There was no call for rescue, nor anything demanded of him, but her frailty was unmasked and he wished he had the power to protect her.

When he thought the moment was right, he spoke up. 'Rose.' He had interrupted her concentration and she looked up, startled. 'We have to talk.'

'Please don't.'

He kept his voice low so that it barely imposed on the quietness. 'If you help me, I can help you. It's our only chance.'

'Sshh.'

'Why?'

'He hears everything.'

'You mean he's listening in to what we're saying? I doubt it. It was never in his plans to have two people down here. He won't be bugging the place.'

'He'll still know.'

'OK, let's speak really quietly, if you're worried. The fans will blot out the sound.'

'But the Lord sees everything,' she whispered, her eyes pleading. 'I can't break his Law.'

He held her eyes, calmly. 'Rose.' He was also whispering. 'Rose. You must believe me now. There is no Law. There is no Law. The Lord has given us our nature. It's through our true nature that we can get close to him. And our nature is beautiful. You are beautiful just as you are. It's that simple.'

Her face was alive with turmoil. She could barely speak. 'How do you know?'

Granville smiled straight at her. 'Because I've seen the face of God.'

She frowned and shook her head in disbelief. 'What?' she whispered.

Granville's eyes were shining. 'It's true. I don't know how to explain it, but it's true. I have been face to face with the Lord. I have felt the breath of God pass through me.'

Rose drew breath sharply and put a hand to her mouth. 'Husband says you are the instrument of Satan.'

She was close to him, because they were speaking so quietly, close enough for him to be able to rest his fingers on hers and smell the warmth of her breath. He felt her jolt at his touch but she did not take her hand away. 'There is no Satan, Rose. The devil is a vicious rumour made up by people who want to enslave us. There is nothing but God. I am part of God, and so are you. You don't need to be afraid any more.' He kept her attention suspended by the assurance and vigour of his own smile, but it was no more than a slender thread that held her, and he could see it starting to fray even as he watched.

'Do you remember your life before you came here?'

He wrestled to bring her back. 'Your beautiful life, your free life. I knew you a little. Do you remember?' She shrank away from him, her hand falling from under his, and she let out a deep, animal cry. Granville could not tell if it was a collapse into hopelessness or a release of pent-up tension, but either way he had lost her. She got to her feet, barely keeping her balance, and staggered across the room towards a sofa. He called but she was deaf to him. She fell, face forwards, onto the sofa and buried her head in a cushion. Another long, guttural cry, and then silence. There was nothing he could do. Words and reasoning were irrelevant, so he let her rest in her oblivion and waited for it to subside.

There was more than an hour of absolute stillness and he thought she had fallen to sleep, when she stirred, rolled over and got up. Her hair was a mess and her eye make-up smudged. She said nothing and did not look at him, but walked straight through to the next room. He heard a more distant door close and he was alone again.

The faintest residue of her scent remained, enough to keep the image of her alive, tired as he was after a succession of sleepless nights. In his boredom he pictured her like a spectre, moving around the room, doing all her usual jobs. He tried to reconstruct in his mind's eye her dignity, modesty and deportment. She reminded him of a kind of womanhood he had once depended on for everything, so long ago, but which he had all but forgotten. It brought to mind the nursery rhyme and children's story records he'd had as an infant – Beatrix Potter and the like – read by actresses of the day with cut-glass accents and matronly kindness in their tone. Caring, assured and prim, those storytellers had transported him to castles in the clouds and far-off desert islands, through realms of giants, lands of magic beans and princesses; and, despite the dangers, the sky would never fall on his head, nor would the dragon's mountain swallow him up, nor rats, nor witches devour him. The women of his boyhood would put all things right before the light went out, before they leant down elegantly, ample skirts rustling, and kissed him, hush, to sleep. They had all been like that to a greater or lesser degree: the nanny at home, the school nurse, the matrons, his mother's sophisticated friends, even the presenters of 1960s daytime television. Their words were milk and honey, their medicines the cure to all ills, their easy, unconditional goodwill a panacea of oceanic depth. It made him wonder at what point he had reformed his view of femininity. As he sat there, bound to the wheelchair, contemplating the absence of Rose, he tried to recall the moment when womanhood no longer represented to him a detached and unassailable seat of maternal goodness, but became, instead, a thing very much to be assailed. At what point did he cross the boundary and find that he had scaled the previously insurmountable, had arrived at the summit of the holy mountain, face to face, on equal terms with the mother goddess in all her sepulchral finery, and realize his needs had changed, that, when all was said and done, he wanted nothing more than to unharness her breasts for his private delight, to prey upon her, mount her, pin her down beneath him? He wondered if the dichotomy had ever really been resolved, for him or for any man alive, or whether it was just one of those cultural paradoxes that afflict every generation, that are slammed into the back room of post-pubescent consciousness, never satisfactorily confronted and forever branded taboo.

Chapter 35

Piet Steyn had made up his mind. It was just a matter of when precisely to act. He had known for some while that the moment was getting close, but hadn't thought it would have to be quite so soon. In the past, he had always taken his time in situations like this. His usual method was to watch and ponder from a distance, and he would find that, magically, as if from nowhere, the bare bones of a strategy would take shape of their own accord. The project seemed to have a soul of its own, or perhaps the whispering of the archangel was secretly directing events. This time, however, it was going to have to be different. Matters had come to a head prematurely and his hand was being forced. It wasn't a disaster. He had always been good at snap decisions and had never yet slipped up. For as long as he had breath in his body his courage and determination would see him through.

He had watched her coming this way often enough on a Wednesday morning and knew that it would be the best place to act when the moment came. He knew exactly what time she would walk past and had even worked out where to park his van. There were a couple of perfectly good spots to choose from, each with its own minor advantages, and different only in detail. A slight snag was the possibility of another car passing at the wrong moment, and he calculated from his observations that the chances of this were quite high – about thirty-five per cent. But he would park the van slightly off road, where a passer-by would really have to be looking to notice it. Approaching cars could be heard from some way off, so that if one were to come he could either move things along a little faster or, at worst, engage her in a bit of conversation for as long as it took for the vehicle to pass. The procedure itself would be pretty straightforward; what to do afterwards was more of a problem. One thing at a time, though. Nothing was insurmountable.

He double-checked that everything was in his bag before carrying it to the van at ten-thirty. Absolutely no point in going any earlier. The less time he was out and about the better. He drove down to the village, straight past the church and past the stone pillar gateposts of the Old Rectory without seeing a single soul, which suited his purposes just fine. Passing the entrance to Tennyson Terrace, he turned left, skirting the perimeter of the church field, with its paved path and single standing stone. The van's seats were high and he could see over the hedge that there was no-one just now taking the short cut across the field to the village centre. A bend to the left brought him up to the little patch of woodland at the side of the road where a dirt track led off to the right, and this he took, stopping his van just yards from the tarmac but sufficiently hidden by an outcrop of blackthorn. He got out of the driving seat and waited beside the van, screened from the road, for a minute longer. There was a distant pish of tyres on tarmac and seconds later a more violent ripping sound as a car came round the corner and sped on past, then silence again, and he checked his watch. Any minute now.

Every morning, at ten o'clock, she took the longer

pavement route around the field to the village shop to pick up a few bits and pieces, including her daily newspaper. She could have had it delivered, but preferred to have the exercise of the walk. She had told Piet that it was part of a familiar daily routine that kept her going, and that she also felt a duty to support the village shop and be seen to drop by there regularly in person. Come rain or shine, she could be relied on to arrive at that shop at twenty-five past ten, almost exactly, and would return, about fifteen minutes later, by the shorter route across the field's flagstone path, Labrador at her heels. Today was fine and warm, he had seen her car parked in the Old Rectory driveway, and it was impossible that she would not show up on time.

He was still hidden from view when he caught sight of her coming around the hedge at the corner. The dog was on its lead and her other hand carried an empty shopping basket. She was moving fast, as usual, to maximize the good effects of the walk. Piet took a deep breath to prepare himself for what he had to do, but just as he was about to exhale he felt the first twang of a pain beneath his ribs. It was not bad enough to paralyse him this time, but it was worse than an ache and had become irritatingly familiar. It seemed that there was something alive in there, feeding on his organs from the inside, and he wished he could just take a knife and cut the damned thing out once and for all. He put a hand to his abdomen and felt the muscle of his diaphragm contract involuntarily. Janet was no more than twenty yards distant and he tried to stand up straight. He would have to come out of hiding now or miss his moment. The pain clutched at him harder and he curled over, pummelling angrily at his midriff to put a stop to it. In that state he stumbled out of the bushes to accost Janet. She saw him and stopped in her tracks. The animation drained from her face and her mouth fell open. Piet stood up straight and tried to smile.

'What do you want?' she asked.

'Janet! What a surprise,' he said, sticking to the prepared script. 'Thank God it's you.'

She frowned and did not move. 'What do you mean?'

'I've had a . . . had a—' This time it took his breath away completely and he put out a hand to steady himself. His fingers accidentally caught hold of a healthy young bramble cane sticking out of the hedge, and the thorns tore his flesh. He cursed.

'Are you all right?' she said, and took a step towards him.

'Yes, yes. I've just . . .' A far off rushing sound gave warning of a car approaching, and Piet looked up at her. 'I've hit an animal in the road. I think it's injured. Come and look. Quickly.'

'Where?'

'I've put it in my van.'

'I didn't know you had a van.'

'I rented one to move some stuff. Will you come and have a look, quick? It's bad.'

'What kind of animal?'

'A . . . a dog.'

'Shall I just call the vet?' she said, and reached into her bag for her mobile.

'No!' he said. 'Come and look first. I think maybe I should put it out of its misery.' The car was just out of view around the corner and he beckoned her towards him with his hand, but was interrupted by another sharp stab to his abdomen. He clutched both arms around his middle.

'You're not well. Let's sit you down.'

'No, I'm fine,' he said, fighting the pain, but lost strength for a moment and went down onto one knee. She was beside him now and leaning down. The car had appeared around the corner and the driver was slowing down to see what was going on. Hazard lights went on and the car pulled over.

'I don't need help,' said Piet, and got back to his feet.

'Come and sit down,' said Janet, and tried to lead him towards the van that she could now see parked behind the bushes.

'Everything all right?' A youngish man in a striped shirt and tie had stepped out of the car. 'Do you guys need some help?'

'He's not well,' said Janet.' Can you help me get him to his van?'

'I don't need help,' said Piet impatiently.

'Over there,' Janet said to the newcomer. They took an arm each and began to haul him towards the van but Piet shook them off angrily and turned on the man. 'Can't you just mind your own business?' The man jerked back, as if stung.

'No need for that,' he said.

'Come on, Piet,' said Janet, reaching the open door of the van, 'just sit down and take a deep breath.'

'Do you know him, then?' asked the man.

'Yes. I'm sorry, he doesn't mean to be rude. Shall we call an ambulance?'

'No you won't!' snapped Steyn, and sat down heavily in the driver's seat of the van. He looked quickly over to the passenger side, where some things were visible through the open top of his canvas tool bag, including a bunch of cable ties, some bandages and an emergency first aid kit, and he pushed the whole lot into the foot-well, out of sight. 'Just leave me be.' He looked up at the young man. 'I'm sure the lady can manage on her own, thank you very much.'

'No, don't go!' said Janet quickly. 'Where's the dog?'

'The what?' said the other man.

'He said he'd run over a dog.'

'Go away! Both of you, get out!' shouted Piet and fumbled with the ignition key.

'You mean there isn't a dog?' Janet put a hand to her mouth and took a step back. 'Were you making it up?' Piet gave her a furious look but said nothing and slammed his door closed. He started up the van.

'Watch out!' called the man as Piet reversed speedily over the bumps out of the rough. He only just missed colliding with the parked car on the verge behind, before slamming into forward gear and driving back the way he had come.

Chapter 36

Granville looked up when he heard the metallic clang and watched the door directly in front of him open. Piet Steyn stood in the doorway and looked around the kitchen. 'Where is Rose?' he asked.

'She went to her room.'

Piet saw the basket of linen half filled, with a pile of laundry beside it. 'Why didn't she finish her work?'

'I don't know.'

'What's this?' asked Piet, coming up to the table and pointing at the improvised word game.

'Just something to pass the time.' Piet looked at it for a moment, then turned and walked in the direction of the next chamber. Granville called out to stop him. 'Would you mind taking me to the lavatory?'

'In good time.'

'I would appreciate it if you could do it now. It's a little desperate.' Piet came back and began to wheel Granville over to the bathroom.

'I've managed to have a few words with Rose today.'

'Have you indeed?' Piet replied flatly.

'She's very shy, of course. But I think you've got it wrong about her.'

'I see.'

'It's just my opinion. I think she has the sweetest, purest mind of any woman I've met.'

'You've only known her a few days,' said Piet.

'I just don't think you should feel let down by her. She's doing her level best to be everything you want. Just give her a little more time.'

'Time, eh?'

'Yes.'

'As if you would know what to do.'

'I'm only trying to help.'

'Trying to get her off the hook, you mean.'

Granville lowered his voice to a whisper, afraid that Rose might be able to hear. 'Of course I don't want you to harm her, but I—'

'Maybe you're getting a little fond of her yourself. Very touching.'

They had arrived at the bathroom door and Piet began the procedure of releasing Granville so that he could step into the room.

'You're being paranoid,' said Granville.

'I'm being realistic. I know I've created a good woman there. Any man would see that. Any man would want that. It's a measure of my success.'

'Why condemn her, then?'

'So you don't deny you're attracted to her?'

'Come on, Piet.'

'You can go through now.'

Granville hesitated. 'Why do you feel so let down by her?'

'For the same reason they've all let me down. I thought I'd told you. She's a whore through and through, and always will be. Even I cannot change such deep-rooted corruption.'

'You're wrong.'

378

'Go through or I'll put you back in the chair.'

Granville, with his ankles chained, shuffled over the bathroom threshold. 'You'll never find another like her.'

'I must carry on trying or die in the attempt,' said Steyn, shoving Granville forward and closing the door behind him.

'Perhaps the problem is with you, not the women,' Granville shouted from the other side, but Piet had walked away from the door.

Piet spent a long time alone with Rose, and Granville could hear nothing to hint at what might be going on. It was not until the old farmhouse clock in the kitchen said twelve-thirty that the door adjoining the next chamber clanked open, and both Steyn and Rose came through. She had changed her clothes, reapplied make-up and seemed composed.

'We're running a little late,' said Steyn as she walked over to the fridge. 'You'd better make a sandwich or something quick. I don't need much but you should make something for our guest.'

'Don't put yourself to any trouble on my account,' said Granville, but neither of them took any notice of him.

The snack lunch was prepared and they sat around the table in silence, after which Piet thanked Rose, escorted Granville once more to the lavatory, and left the bunker without another word.

*

Steyn reached the exit shaft, turned on the lights and glanced up to check the ropes were untangled. He sat himself on the seat of the block-and-pulley lift, released the scarlet weight-bearing rope from its cleat and began to haul himself upwards. The mechanism was well balanced and easy to pull. He sometimes liked to climb the old steel rungs instead, for the exercise, but had recently begun to find it tiring and preferred to get to the surface with breath to spare.

At the top, he secured the rope in double cleats and tied the slack off tightly to the uppermost rung before releasing his grip on it. The rope's fibre sank back into the cleats and the mechanism creaked as it took the strain of his weight. He then stretched up to turn the hatch release wheel above his head and found it hard work, which irritated him. Maybe it just needed a bit of oil, he told himself, and made a mental note to bring a lubricant spray back in the evening. Extending his foot out to one of the wall rungs, he slid off the seat, grasped a higher rung with one hand, and with the other heaved open the hatch above him. Daylight, air and garden sounds flooded in; the sun was shining as brightly as it had been when he'd come down a few hours earlier.

His head was barely out of the ground when he saw the shoes and trouser bottoms of someone standing there, close to the opening. He looked up sharply to see who it was but the sun was directly behind the man's head and Steyn was half blinded by the glare. He raised a hand to block out the rays but struggled to get a clear view. 'What the hell d'you think you're playing at?' Steyn said.

The stranger held his ground, right next to the open hatch, but said nothing.

Steyn scrambled up the remaining rungs, slammed the hatch closed behind him, then turned on the intruder. 'I said, what do you think you're doing here? This is private property, you know.'

The man took a step backwards. He was about the same age as Steyn but well-groomed, in jacket and tie, slightly corpulent and bald. He had a book and a notepad tucked under one arm, and carried a digital camera in the other.

'My name is Philip Porter,' he said, eyes wide with shock. 'I'm sorry, I hadn't expected to see anybody. I thought everyone was out.'

Steyn walked up to him, aggressively. 'What do you mean "everyone"?'

'I've called at the house several times. There's never been anyone at home, so I took the liberty—'

'Took the liberty!'

'I only want a photograph of the bunker. I'm doing the lecture in the village hall. About the Battle of Britain.'

Steyn winced with disgust. '*What?*' he rasped.

The man now looked a little indignant. 'I'm doing the lecture. It's for charity, you know.'

'Why should I care?'

'The Cheselbury Abbas fighter base was quite import-ant in the Second World War. And this,' he pointed to the ground, 'was the central operations bunker.'

'So what?'

'Well, I've asked around a bit, and as far as I can tell no-one's been near this bunker for fifty years or more.'

'Who've you been talking to?'

'Anyone. Locals, villagers. Hardly anyone even knew it was here. I've got copies of all the old RAF maps, of course, and I—'

'Look, mister, you are trespassing. I haven't got time for this.' Steyn jabbed an index finger directly at the man's chest. 'Now you clear off my land.'

Mr Porter looked deeply shocked and began to blush. 'There's no need to be so rude. This happens to be a site of historical significance. I don't want to, but there are protocols I could pursue. The Imperial War Museum and Ministry of Defence are doing this sort of thing all the time. Applications for easement of access for historical research and so forth.'

'Are they, indeed?' Steyn eyed him carefully, his face trapped between anger and contempt.

'They are. I'm very sorry for intruding and all that, but I meant no harm. I'm just trying to get some pictures for the lecture.'

Steyn paused, staring at the ground, and nodded to himself. He then looked up, as if miraculously transfigured, and smiled at the stranger. 'It's me who should apologize,' he said, and held out his hand. Mr Porter hesitated but took it. 'I just got a shock to see you standing there. Of course. Please.' He gestured with his arm towards the hump of the bunker. 'Feel free to photograph away.'

'Thank you,' said Porter, still uncertain, and began to walk around, clambering carefully through the brambles, taking pictures. The occasional thorn snared his trouser bottoms and socks, and he bent down to disengage them. 'What's it like down there?' he asked, standing on top of the hump and nodding towards the hatch. 'Anything of interest?'

'Not much.'

'All right if I take a look? I don't mind a bit of mess.'

Again, Steyn stalled, and bit his upper lip. 'Mr Porter, I see I'm going to have to let you in on my secret. But I'm going to ask you to promise to keep it to yourself.'

The man smiled gleefully. 'Of course,' he said. 'Something exciting?'

Steyn manufactured a laugh. 'Yes, as a matter of fact it is. It's also another reason why I was a little sharp with you earlier.' He stopped to contemplate for a moment, raising his eyes to the blue sky with its peppering of cumulus clouds. A breeze was teasing the fresh shoots and delicate new leaves at the tips of tree branches. 'Funny to think of them buzzing around like angry wasps up there, isn't it? This very sky on a day much like this. Dogfights. Machine guns strafing the air, blood, petrol fumes and burnt flesh, all up there, and then coming back safely to base. Right here.'

'Not all of them came back. Fewer than half of this lot, actually.'

'It was a wonderful time. Clear purposes. Pure hearts. Right and wrong. We could learn a lot from those folk.'

'Wartime spirit. They say the adversity brought out the best in people.'

Steyn turned to face him. 'Maybe I'm a bit sentimental. Anyway, I want to recapture some of the spirit of that time. You see, I'm something of a handyman, DIY and the like, and I've been doing a bit of restoration work down there in the bunker.'

'Really? What sort of thing?'

'Promise me you won't tell anyone just yet. In fact, I'd be grateful if you don't mention this bunker in your lecture at all.' Steyn held up his finger again. 'I'm going to let the world in when it's all done and dusted, but I just need a few more weeks. Agreed?'

'Well, it would be difficult not to mention—'

'Talk about the air force base, the runway and what have you, but please, not the bunker itself, I ask you as a special favour.'

'You're restoring it all by yourself? To look like a proper 1940s operations HQ?'

'Something like that. I hope I haven't got too much wrong. It's a bit of a hobby of mine.'

'Fascinating.'

'I'm glad you approve,' said Steyn. 'Now if you leave me your card and swear on your mother's life not to tell a soul, I'll make sure to contact you personally as soon as I'm ready with it so that you can have a sneak preview. Maybe put me right on the details before I open it up to the wider public.'

Porter came over to stand in front of Piet. 'Mr Steyn, is it?'

'That's right.'

He took out an address card from his wallet and handed it over. 'I think you are doing an excellent thing. I can't wait to see it. I wish more people in this country had such a lively sense of history.'

Piet smiled modestly. 'Just a little something to keep me busy in retirement.' He ushered Porter down the garden and they walked side by side towards the gate in the hedge.

'What line of work were you involved in before you retired?' Porter asked.

'I was a mortgage broker, back home in Durban.'

'Ah,' said Porter, nodding, and asked no more.

Chapter 37

Janet Gosling stood perfectly still in the hall of her home with five matching suitcases lined up neatly beside her on the floor. Her hair was immaculately styled and brushed, she was wearing a pale blue cashmere twinset, and a double string of natural pearls around her neck. Her hands were cradled lightly at her navel and her chin was raised. The front door was open behind her and she was looking back into the body of the house. She had made her decision and there was no going back. All the essentials were packed and ready to go, and the boys – surprised at the suddenness of the upheaval, but not objecting to it – were already on their way in a separate car. The removal men were due in a few days' time to start boxing everything up into tea chests. She glanced for the last time at the paintings on the walls and the bronze on top of the tallboy. It would be some while before she would see any of these things again.

On a whim she meandered deeper into the hall and opened the drawing room door on her right. She stood for a moment, contemplating the space where her husband had last drawn breath, taking in the surroundings, the large sash window casements and elegant plaster friezes. She also glanced briefly up at the heavy ceiling beam, and the mark, beneath wood-filler, that showed where the noose's screw had been fixed, before she turned and walked out of the room.

The light from the open front door was partially blocked. There was a man standing under the door frame, and she regarded him, half in a dream.

'Just these last suitcases, madam?'

She smiled. 'Thank you. Yes.'

He picked up as many as he could manage and took them to a large car that was parked at the bottom of the front steps. Janet allowed herself a last look down the length of the hall. Her eyes fixed on the telephone, sitting in its charger on a side table, halfway down one wall. She ambled slowly towards it until she was standing right next to the table, and looked directly down at the phone. She put out a hand and was about to pick it up, but the man coughed somewhere behind her and she looked around.

'I'm ready whenever you are, Mrs Gosling.'

She smiled at him again. 'I'm coming right now. Thank you.' And with that she walked from her house.

*

Steyn did not return to the bunker after seeing Mr Porter off his property, but went back into the house and sat hunched in a chair, staring into space. At last, he got up stiffly, found a pencil and a piece of paper, sat down at a table and began to write out a long list. The first ten or fifteen items flowed quickly from his pencil, after which he went on more haltingly, stopping to think between entries. When he had finished, he read through what was written to make sure nothing had been omitted, added two more items to the bottom of the list and tossed the pencil angrily over his shoulder. He then walked across to his workshop in an outhouse on the other side of the lawn and locked the door behind him. The building had no windows, but a keyline of light around the door showed that he was still there several hours later, as did the incessant sound of activity from within – banging, sawing, the hum of electric appliances and the whine of cutting discs.

The following morning, early, he consulted his list once again and began work on the house proper. It was evening by the time he got as far as the item marked 'electricity box', three-quarters of the way down the page, and he erected a ladder in the hall, next to the mains power supply. He donned a pair of glasses, put a selection of screwdrivers in the breast pocket of his shirt and started working on the house fuse box, disconnecting, unscrewing, pulling out wires, breaker switches and RCD units. For a while he operated with a pocket torch held between his teeth because he had had to turn the power off altogether. Satisfied at last, he screwed all components back into place, put away the ladder and turned his attention to the room off the kitchen. He would need to fetch some things from the outbuilding for this next job, and it would be wet and messy, so he went first to find himself a drop sheet.

Without pausing for food, but occasionally drinking deep from a double-sized carton of orange juice, he worked right through the night. One by one the list of jobs he'd jotted down were ticked off, until, at five o'clock in the morning, he felt he had done enough and began to tidy up. He rolled out and straightened the carpet that he'd earlier cleared away from a hatch in the hall floor, shifted back the furniture and put everything in its right place. Then, like an athlete pacing on, out of breath, after crossing the finishing line, he began to slow, eventually making himself a cup of tea and collapsing into an armchair. For some minutes he just sat there, until his head sank back, his jaw fell open and he drifted off into sleep, the tea untouched beside him. He was still asleep in the chair at eight-thirty when the doorbell rang.

It rang twice before he realized what was happening. He got up and walked into the hall.

'Who's there?' he called.

'It's Detective Sergeant Walker, sir. Police. Come to have a word. It won't take long.'

'What's it about?'

'I'd prefer to come in and talk, if you don't mind.'

Steyn unlocked the door with two sets of keys, slid aside the top and bottom bolts, and opened the door a few inches on its security chain. Satisfied that the uniformed officer on his doorstep was genuine, he eased the door forwards, released the chain from its slot, and opened it fully.

'Mr Piet Steyn, is it?'

'That's right.'

'Very security conscious,' said the sergeant, looking up and down the locks in the profile of the door.

'No bad thing.'

'Had an unfortunate experience, then?'

'Just a little aggravation from a few local drunks. Is that what you're here about?'

'No, it's not. Mind if I come in?' He already had his pad and pen in hand. Steyn let the policeman into the hall and ushered him through to the sitting room.

'Would you like some tea or something?'

'No, thank you.'

'Do you mind if I make one for myself? I've only just woken up.'

'Not at all. I'll wait in here.'

Left alone, Sergeant Walker began to scan the contours

of the room, circling slowly on the spot, looking from top to bottom, eyes occasionally resting on something and logging it, before moving on to something else.

Piet returned with a cup of tea in one hand and a file of papers in the other. 'I've got everything here,' he said, opening up the file on a low coffee table. 'Please,' he held out his hand towards an armchair, 'take a seat.' Sergeant Walker sat down, and craned his neck to see what Steyn was trying to show him. 'This is a police certificate from Natal province,' Steyn said, handing across a thin sheet of old A4 duplication paper, tanned at the edges. Its type was blurred and purple. The text on it began, 'To whom it may concern' and was dated September 1976. 'And this one,' he laid out a new sheet neatly next to the first, 'is from the same police department, enabling me to possess a firearm. You see?' He pointed to his own name in heavy print. 'I don't actually possess a gun, but I keep the certificate as a kind of character testimonial.' He then turned to a sheaf of papers containing old employment references, some of them folded up like precious archives, and reached for yet another file with documents relating to his immigration status, but Sergeant Walker held up a palm to interrupt.

'Mr Steyn, I'm not here to inquire into your past history or your residency rights. I've come about something different, something quite specific.'

'Oh yes?' Steyn looked up over the top of his glasses.

'That's right.' The policeman held his gaze in a territory between politeness and challenge. 'Let me start by asking: do you have any knowledge of the whereabouts of the Reverend Granville St Clair?'

Steyn raised his eyebrows and let droop the corners of his mouth. 'None whatsoever.'

The sergeant was reading the questions written on his

pad and noted down the answers. 'Since the morning of Mr St Clair's disappearance have you either seen or been in contact with him in any form?'

'No. Why should I have?'

'He was seen talking to you in church on the morning that he disappeared. Did he say anything to you that might give us a clue about where he has gone?'

Steyn shrugged his shoulders. 'I've already answered that. I would guess he'd go as far away from this place as possible. His life was in a bit of a mess.'

'Never mind about what you would guess. What do you know?'

Any hint of a smile that remained on Steyn's face now fell away. 'As I said, nothing.'

'I think you may know a little bit more about what you call the mess in Mr St Clair's life than you've been letting on.'

'I've never let anything on, as you describe it. No-one's asked me anything until now.'

'Well, that's not quite the case, is it, sir? You were interviewed on the morning of . . .' he checked some notes in the back of his pad, 'of 19 February, at 8.10 a.m., the morning you and Mr St Clair discovered the body of Mr Robert Gosling.'

Steyn sighed. 'That's correct.'

'And your account of what happened that morning, written up by the interviewing officer, Police Constable Ewing, appears to differ substantially from what we've since learnt to have been the case.'

'Substantially, you say?'

'Mr Steyn, I'm going to caution you,' Walker began in a quiet voice. 'You do not have to say anything. But it may harm your defence if you do not mention when questioned something which you later rely on in court.

390

Anything you do say may be given in evidence. Do you understand?'

'Yes.'

'Perhaps you'd like to tell me now in your own words the bit you chose to leave out before. The bit about Henrietta Swanley.'

Steyn lowered his face, pinched the bridge of his nose and swept a hand up over his forehead. 'You realize that in telling you this I am breaking the confidence of a man of the cloth? That girl swore him to silence and he in turn extracted a similar oath from me. And for a God-fearing person like myself that constitutes—'

'Mr Steyn,' interrupted Sergeant Walker, leaning forward and fixing Piet with his eyes, 'I'm not here to play games. Just tell me what happened and we'll see what's to be done about it.'

Steyn stared blankly at the policeman then seemed to come to a decision, nodded, and began to recite his account, the same version he had told Janet. Walker took notes throughout. When he had finished, the policeman asked, 'And have you seen or heard anything of or from Miss Henrietta Swanley since the morning of 23 January?'

'Just once. She came to Mr Gosling's funeral.'

Walker raised his eyebrows and noted it in his pad. 'Anything else?'

'Only what I heard from Father Granville. She was telephoning him and they met up from time to time. That's all I know.'

'And you never saw her again?'

Steyn assessed the question before answering. 'No. Though I am aware, of course, what befell the poor girl. Everybody knows that, I imagine.'

There was a long pause now while Sergeant Walker

jotted more material on his notepad, after which he snapped it shut, smiled at Piet and said, 'Thank you very much.' He got to his feet.

'Will that be all?'

The policeman was standing a few metres distant and looked Steyn over. He lowered his eyes to glance at Piet's feet, craning his neck slightly as if to see something on the floor behind. Steyn turned and looked down at the carpet, wondering what the policeman had spotted, but saw nothing out of the ordinary.

Walker asked, 'As I'm here, do you mind if I take a look around?'

'Am I suspected of something?'

'We're just checking under every stone,' said Walker. 'It's pretty routine when there's been an irregularity of some kind, evidence withheld, that sort of thing.'

'There were good reasons for what I did. And I'm prepared to stand by them.'

'A man of principle. I'm sure it'll all be taken into account. But we have our procedures. Do you mind?'

'Help yourself,' said Steyn, and followed him out of the room. They first went upstairs, where Steyn opened the doors to the three bedrooms in turn. Sergeant Walker glanced around each of them for a few seconds, stepping in no further than just beyond the door and saying nothing at all, except 'thank you very much', identically, three times, before moving on to the bathroom. They then returned to the ground floor and went into every room, finishing with the kitchen. This had more contents than any of the other rooms and was clearly the one most used by Steyn. The policeman examined it with a little more care, opening cupboard doors and drawers, before ending up in front of what looked like the door to a connecting pantry.

'What's in there?' he asked.

'I sometimes use it as a bit of a storeroom,' replied Steyn.

'Mind if I take a look?'

Steyn nodded, Sergeant Walker turned the handle and went in. The shutters were closed and it was dark, so he put out a hand to switch on the light. It came on and lit up a completely bare room with textured wallpaper. Walker pouted, went in, sniffed the air and circled around, looking up to the ceiling and down to the floor, before turning back to the door to leave. Something caught his eye at the bottom of the wall just beside the entrance, and he walked over to look at it.

'Wet plaster,' he said, putting a finger to the edge of the smooth terracotta square. 'Thought I smelt it when I came in.' He leant down, looked closely and pressed his fingertips against the fresh work. 'Very wet.' Steyn did not say anything. 'Neat piece of work. May I ask what you've been plastering over?'

'There used to be an electrical box there but I got rid of it last night.'

'What kind of electrical box?'

'Fuses, trip switches and the like, for my workshop. I've got three-phase power over there. Some heavy duty appliances. But it's more convenient for me to bypass this and handle everything from the mains box.'

Walker raised his eyebrows. 'It's all Greek to me. You know a bit about electrics, do you?'

Steyn smiled. 'Where I come from, sergeant, you have to handle everything practical yourself, because if something goes wrong there's no-one for hundreds of miles around to help.'

Walker nodded and stood up tall again. 'Could I have a look at your workshop? Won't take a minute.'

Steyn hesitated but then led him across the garden to the outbuilding, which he unlocked, using a key from a large bunch that he had in his pocket.

'You carry around a lot of keys,' said the policeman.

'As you noticed, I'm very security conscious.'

They went into the timber-framed building and were hit by the alluring smell of a petroleum-based solvent, blended with the softer, more comforting scent of pine sawdust. A workstation along the entire length of one side contained a variety of vice grips bolted to its surface, and beyond them a lathe and a range of other machines, including a bench grinder, pillar drill and welder. Various hydraulic instruments and an air compressor stood to one side, together with a free-standing industrial cabinet on castors, full of every type of manual tool. All of it was clean, everything in its place, surfaces swept, bottles of fluids and nail jars arranged neatly on shelves according to size. Against one wall rested sheets of ply and lengths of timber, all sorts and varieties, while another wall supported racks of tubular pipes, plastic and copper, and a third held coils of electrical cabling. Sergeant Walker let out a whistle. 'Some workshop.'

'DIY's a bit of a hobby, you might say,' said Steyn.

'There's enough kit here to build a brand new holiday home in the garden!'

'Well, it keeps me out of mischief.'

The policeman turned to look at him. 'Done a lot of work to your house, then, have you?'

Steyn blinked. 'It may not look like it, I know. You'd be surprised, though.'

Sergeant Walker switched on an instant smile. 'Always that way, isn't it? Homes eat up your time and money. My wife's on at me all the time about it: "Why can't you just

leave the house be and spend the money on a holiday?"
That's wives for you, I suppose.'

Steyn smiled back. 'If you say so.'

The sergeant wandered in and looked at one or two of the machines, bending down to cast an expert eye at some detail close up. There was an old-fashioned moped parked in the far corner of the room, and he went up to it, glancing at the tax disc. 'Bit of a classic nowadays,' he said. 'Use it a lot?'

'No, I prefer to walk whenever possible, but sometimes I have to go further afield. It's for emergencies only.'

'Nice condition.'

'I restored it myself. I can show you the insurance documentation, if you like.'

'No need for that,' replied Walker. 'How about the van?'

'Van?'

'The white Ford Transit, parked on your drive.'

'Oh, I've rented that for a couple of days.'

'I know.'

'You what?'

'I checked it out.' Walker smiled again. 'One of the benefits of the computer age. Tap in the details and you get an instant result.'

'Aha.'

'Mind me asking why you're renting it.'

'I'm getting in a load of plants for the garden. Spring planting, you know.'

'Plants?'

'And sacks of compost. A whole lot of stuff. I don't have a car.'

Walker looked down the length of the garden. 'Good for you. You've done a great job.'

'Thank you.'

They walked away from the outbuilding and towards the house in silence. 'Would you like to come back indoors?' asked Piet.

'No thank you, sir. I think I've seen everything I need to see. If we've got any more questions we'll give you a call. Thank you for being so accommodating.'

'It's my pleasure.'

Steyn walked him down to the garden gate. 'Just one thing,' he asked, as the policeman was about to go to his parked car.

'Yes?'

'I know it was probably wrong in a sense to hold back the business about Mr Gosling and that girl. I shall have to answer for that.'

'That's not for me to say, sir. I'm just collecting information.'

'But could you tell me how you found out the truth about what happened that morning? I was under the impression nobody knew about it other than myself and Father Granville.'

'I'm afraid I'm not at liberty to discuss that.'

'I suppose it might have been Mrs Gosling. Janet.' At this, Sergeant Walker looked up. His face betrayed a look of slight surprise, which he suppressed. 'It wasn't her, then?' asked Steyn.

His guard momentarily down, Walker replied, 'Off the record, I don't think it matters if I tell you I've never met or spoken to Mrs Gosling. I had intended to but it seems she's left the area. Packed up and gone down to her sister's just yesterday. Very sudden. I shall have a colleague in the Hertfordshire Police interview her when the time is right. No particular hurry, but she may have something to add, I suppose.'

Steyn's mouth opened fractionally but otherwise his expression gave nothing away.

Sergeant Walker did not delay further but said a last goodbye and got into his car. Steyn was still at the garden gate, staring down the path as the police car drove off and out of sight. He then checked his watch and walked quickly back to the house.

Rolling the hall carpet neatly away again, he leant down to grab hold of the recessed handle of the hatch in the middle of the parquet floor. He pulled the lid open on its hinges and lowered himself into a shallow cellar that stretched beneath the house's ground floor. There was not enough head height down there to stand upright and so he worked at a stoop, which strained his neck. One by one he brought out the stuffed black bin liners and boxes that he had earlier filled, and dumped them on the hall floor beside the open hatch. There would be enough stuff here to fill the van comprehensively, he thought. Perhaps even twice over.

Chapter 38

Rose had recovered from the upset of the morning, so that by the time she and Granville were alone together again after the hurried snack lunch she seemed to be able to go about her work in the kitchen as normal and barely spoke a word.

Granville was now alert to any signal that she might be getting distressed and took care not to interfere with her normal pattern of activity. He never waylaid her but spoke only if she happened to be doing something in the same room, and then only in a one-sided way. He would talk quietly about his own life, his pretty daughters and their friends at school, their games, hobbies and all the holidays they had had as a family. The girls were his whole life, he said, and at times he felt his love for them was a merciless dictator, irrationally sucking him dry and laying waste his interest in almost anything else. Old hobbies, indulgences, moments of self-pity, the endless possibilities of life – they had been pushed aside and forgotten, he said. Rose smiled at this and said that she had also had to leave a lot of things behind, but for different reasons. It was a short and quiet admission, but Granville saw it as a possible breakthrough.

By late afternoon, after she had returned and made him a cup of tea, she came and sat down on a chair next to him to listen to a bit more of his narrative. There were ten minutes or so until the time set aside for her afternoon prayers and he asked if she would like to play the word game again, but she shook her head, and so he continued to talk, now adding little questions. Did she like this or that kind of apple? Did she prefer retrievers to terriers? Had she ever noticed a particular star in the summer night sky? He chose his subjects and imagery carefully, trying to bring to mind the beauty of the world beyond the bunker and slowly awaken her memory of it, but lightly, and always with a trace of humour. Above all, he took care not to ask her directly about her past life, because it was clear she had survived down here only by curtaining a part of herself off.

As the afternoon turned to evening, and the automated master control began to dim the lighting of the landscape behind the windowpane, Rose returned to the kitchen and Granville noticed she was restless. She sat down at the table opposite him but kept glancing at the kitchen clock, then got up and looked around for something to do. For want of anything better, she went over to the fridge, opened the door and started logging its contents from top to bottom. Granville watched but said nothing.

She eventually came back to sit at the table, checked the wall clock again and scratched at her wrists. Granville said, 'He's later than usual. Is that it?'

'Something's wrong.' She got up and began to pace around the table, arms crossed tightly beneath her bosom.

'Rose,' Granville said gently. 'Just think about this sensibly. If something has gone wrong for Piet, it might just be good for us.'

'How?'

'The police might be on to him.'

'That's impossible.'

'Why do you think that?'

'He's too clever. He thinks of everything.'

'He's only human, Rose. And I've got a feeling he's out of control and doesn't realize. He's making mistakes.'

'He never makes mistakes. What if he's just gone? What if he's had an accident and been killed? No-one will ever know we're here. We'll just die here, trapped for ever.'

'Don't think like that. We've got food, we've got water. We could survive for ages if push came to shove, but it won't. Someone would find us.'

She turned on him. 'How can you be so sure?'

'Because anyone who does a thorough search of his house up there is going to find some sort of connection to this place. He's got rooms full of stuff, provisions, the clobber he brings over and takes back every day. Then there's the controls for the lights, the air, the temperature. And they'll have sniffer dogs and all sorts. You know what the police are like. Piet's clever, for sure, but he's not very good at covering his tracks. It's as if he belongs to a bygone era. The detectives, pathologists and whatnot will be on to it in no time. Just – please, Rose – sit down. Let's sit together.' She stared at him, teetering on the edge of oblivion. 'Or better still,' he said, 'let's have something to eat. Can you make me something, Rose? I'd love that.'

'What would you like?' she asked.

'What were you going to do anyway? Everything you make is so good.' She turned away and went back to the fridge. 'But I'm afraid I'm going to need your help with something,' Granville added, 'and it's a little bit embarrassing.'

Rose looked up and knew what he meant. 'I can't get you into the bathroom. You'll have to do it in something.'

'A bowl will do. Or a pan? I'm sorry.'

She brought him a porcelain salad bowl and went through to the next room, closing the door behind her. A few minutes later he called out and she came through, picked up the bowl from the floor beside him, and emptied the urine into the lavatory. She pulled the flush and returned to the kitchen sink to wash the bowl. Granville was surprised at her lack of coyness. She went about the job in the straightforward, no-nonsense way of a ward nurse, something he found comforting.

Steyn did not return that evening and as the time passed, Rose's eyes came to life. After she had cleared up their supper, she sat hunched and tense at the kitchen table, hands gripped together.

Shortly after seven o'clock there was a loud click and they were suddenly in pitch blackness. Rose drew breath sharply and Granville asked her to move her hand towards him. Her fingers floundered across the arm of the wheelchair, over his lap, eventually finding him and grasping his hand like a lifeguard's rope. Not just the lights, but the buzz of the ventilation fans and the interminable hum of appliances had also stopped. Even the kitchen clock stood still. For the first time in more than three years, Rose was experiencing utter silence. 'It's like a tomb,' she murmured. 'He's cut us off. He's done it on purpose to punish us.'

'Is there a torch somewhere?'

'No.'

'Matches?'

'One box and it's half finished. Next to the stove.'

'OK. When you're ready, you're going to find your way over to the stove and get those matches. All right?' They said nothing more for a moment but sat motionless together, hand in hand, until she said she was ready to go.

He listened to her shuffle slowly across the floor. She knocked into a chair but managed to get to the stove and find the matches. 'Now light one and come back to me,' said Granville, but before she had the chance, there was a brief buzzing sound, a loud click, and the electricity came back on. Rose's eyes darted up at Granville. 'What's going on?' she asked.

'Probably nothing more sinister than a power cut. Have you ever had one before?'

'No.'

'Well, we've got light again. Come and sit down and bring the matches with you, just in case.'

She pushed his wheelchair over to the three-piece suite on one side of the room and sat down on the sofa next to him, dropping her shoes and curling up tightly on the cushions. There was a blanket draped across the back of the sofa, which she pulled over herself, and then stretched out to take hold of Granville's hand again. They looked like a pair of war-torn refugees sheltering from an air raid.

'Think rationally,' said Granville. 'If he had the worst in mind, he'd just come down and do it. The fact that he hasn't means that he's probably jumping ship, abandoning the whole project and doing a runner.'

'He'll never abandon it completely.'

'Why do you say that?'

'I know him.'

'He might—'

'If he fails this time, he'll just go somewhere else and start all over again.'

'How do you know?'

'It's happened before.'

'Has he talked to you about his past?'

'A little.'

'About his family?' Rose said nothing. 'Has he ever spoken to you about his childhood?'

'Quite a bit.'

'Really?' encouraged Granville. 'Was it a happy one?'

'No. It went badly wrong. His baby brother was killed. It had something to do with his father. An accident of some kind, when he'd been drinking.'

'A man killed his own child?'

'Not purposely. The father and his little son were on their way back from another farm. The boy fell out of an open-backed truck. They'd been driving for miles along a dirt track and he must have crawled out of his seat. He was not much more than a year old and his father didn't even notice until he got back home.'

'And that was it? They never found the boy?'

'The father was drunk and set off back along the road with a couple of farmhands. But it was getting dark and they didn't know where to begin looking. It could have happened anywhere. It took a few days before they found parts of the body.'

'Parts?'

'Wild dogs.'

Granville said nothing.

'It drove the parents apart,' Rose continued. 'His mother refused to go near her husband again. She started drinking and would spend whole days in bed. The household fell to pieces. She seemed to forget about her other son altogether. And then the father went off the rails. He started messing around with a young girl on the farm, the daughter of one of his cattle men, no more than a child.'

'Piet shared all this with you?'

'He said that within a few weeks he lost both his parents.'

'Which is why he feels betrayed.'

'And then his mother disappeared.'

'Where to?'

'With another man, a neighbouring farmer. But it wasn't long before news came through that she'd been found dead in a hotel bedroom in Durban.'

'What happened to Piet?'

'His father wasn't interested. The place went to ruin, farm workers left, animals died. In the end his father killed himself.'

'It must have been difficult for him to tell you all this.'

'He told me the story several times. I think he wanted comfort. Once he even curled up and cried like a baby.' She was gazing into space. 'He said his parents had everything and threw it all away. He said it was his duty to make right the great wickedness of their lives.'

'Take revenge of some sort?'

'Not that. Just put right the balance, put things back to where they were before their transgressions.'

'But why should he have to carry the burden of his parents' sins for the rest of his life?'

'The archangel told him it was his duty.'

'The what?'

'St Michael. The archangel.' She said the words simply.

'He claims he saw an angel?'

'That's what he said.'

'What else did he say about it?'

'He was miles out in the country. Alone in a huge wilderness. Then the clouds opened and a great figure came down from heaven.'

'Wings, sword and the like?'

'He was very sure of what he saw.'

404

Granville thought he might snigger but stopped himself. There was something here he recognized. A young man alone in a landscape, graced by what he feels sure is a message from God, something which remains with him for the rest of his life, a refuge and an inspiration, informing his ways, shaping his actions. If he himself had been raised in the wilds of the Transvaal, with all the cultural inheritance that went with such an upbringing, might he have interpreted his own moments of benediction as something just like that, the voice of an archangel?

'But what I can't understand,' he said, 'is the connection between this so-called divine visitation and the compulsion to go out into the world, find women, and—' Again, he zipped his mouth and looked away. 'I suspect the truth is that Piet was desperately scarred by what happened to him as a child and he's spent the rest of his life inventing a way to justify trying to claw back the paradise he imagines was there before his mother fell apart. That's what a shrink would say, anyway. He's chronically sick.'

'I just wish he was dead.'

Her words came out of the blue, savagely, and shocked Granville to silence. Her performance as the good wife had remained intact since he had arrived, until now. He looked at her. Her eyes were huge and still, like those of a reptile that holds its prey in sharp focus for minutes on end before striking out with lightning speed. And then she began to shake, as if suddenly cold, though it must have been an inner chill because it was as warm as ever in the bunker. She was lost in an enemy wasteland, insufficiently clad and blind with terror; but her mind was free of him.

Chapter 39

Steyn drove quite a distance, across the county border into south Somerset, in order to empty the contents of his van at a local authority waste and recycling centre. He found the place attended by a weather-beaten man wearing a fluorescent waistcoat and rigger boots, who looked as though he had spent much of his life living rough, and in this regard resembled Piet himself. They might almost have been related, and the affinity extended to the way they spoke to each other, as if they shared a common wavelength. There were a few obligatory questions the man had to ask about the contents of the bags, but he did so in a spirit of one kindred soul bemoaning the trials of life with another, and then turned his back, went into his Portakabin, and let Steyn get on with his business without interfering further.

The job was done in just a few minutes, the whole lot slung into a huge skip labelled 'General Household Waste', after which Steyn drove his van to the nearest town, which happened to be Yeovil. He turned into a car park near the town centre, stuck a parking ticket with two hours' allowance onto his windscreen, and strode off in the direction of the High Street.

He disappeared into a bank for nearly an hour before emerging and making his way downhill along the same street. He had not got far when his attention was drawn to a display of handwritten special offers in the window of a travel agency, and he stopped to examine them carefully, moving slowly from one end of the double shopfront to the other. The pavement in this part of the street was narrow, which meant that other pedestrians – mostly overweight mothers with pushchairs, and teenagers in hooded tracksuits – had to navigate their way around him or step down into the road to get past, but he did not seem to notice.

Eventually, he went into the travel agency, and after staring, bemused, around the interior for a moment, was invited by a uniformed assistant to make his way over to her desk with his enquiry. It was not long before she was tapping away at her computer to see what she could find for him.

'Just a single, you say?'

'Yes, just one ticket.'

'I meant just one way? You won't be wanting to come back?' She spoke with the kindly condescension of a young person who assumes everyone over a certain age needs a nursery school explanation.

'That's right,' said Piet. 'And I'm not so concerned with cost. Just with last-minute availability.'

'Does it matter which airport you travel from?'

'Not at all.'

'Just bear with me, then, and I'll see what I can find for you.'

*

By the time Steyn walked across his lawn towards the bunker it had been dark for some while. He carried with him his canvas bag, now heavy with tools, which he had to lower carefully on the shaft pulley because its zip was broken and he didn't want the contents to fall out.

Rose and Granville distantly heard the unmistak-able sound of the first outer chamber door being un-locked, unbolted, slammed and locked again. The noise increased by stages after each door, and all the while the two of them looked at each other but said nothing. Rose had been preparing supper and was standing by the stove, waiting for the kettle to boil so that she could transfer the water to the pasta pan.

The keys turned in the inner door's locks. There was terror in Rose's face and Granville said something to calm her before the door swung open and Piet was suddenly there. He stood in the doorway, as he always did, regarding them, one at a time, and looking around to assess the place; but from then on his manner was recognizably different from usual. The self-consciously patriarchal benevolence had gone. He wasted no time on pleasantries, but locked the door behind him, returned the keys to his pockets and heaved the heavy tool bag onto the kitchen table. A hacksaw blade together with the stumpy wooden handle of another implement poked through the broken zip.

'What happened to the electricity?' asked Granville.

'Never you mind.' He pulled the top of the bag over to hide its contents.

'We thought you had abandoned us. Rose was fright-ened.'

'Was she, indeed?' muttered Steyn, distracted.

'Shall I make enough supper for you too?' asked Rose in a shaky voice from where she stood by the stove. Steyn smiled grimly but neither looked up nor answered.

'Could you please take me to the lavatory?' asked Granville.

Steyn looked at him, then nodded, and wheeled the

chair over to the bathroom door. He took the keys from his pocket and Granville watched him select the right ones for the bicycle locks that were binding his elbows. 'You must be pretty desperate,' he said to Granville. 'I apologize for that.' Granville did not reply but shuffled into the lavatory.

All the time he was locked in there, Steyn and Rose did not exchange a word. She took a bag of pasta from the cupboard with trembling hands, while he leant back against the lavatory door, arms crossed, watching her every move.

There came the sound of the toilet flushing and shortly afterwards a light knock on the door to indicate that Granville was ready. Steyn saw him back into his chair, replaced the locks and returned his attention to the tool bag on the table. Now he opened it fully, pushed aside some of the contents and took out a brand new tarpaulin, still folded in its shop packaging. He began to tear open the plastic.

Rose was uneasy. 'I don't know whether to put pasta in for you or not.'

'No. I shan't be needing any, thank you,' replied Steyn quietly. He unfolded the tarpaulin on the ground. It was bright blue and surprisingly large. 'In fact, there's no need to cook this evening at all. You'd best take off the water.'

Rose whipped around and Granville looked up simultaneously. 'Why not?' she asked.

Steyn frowned at her as he rolled up his sleeves a few yards away. 'Rose,' he eventually said in a quiet voice, 'would you mind going through to your room for a moment, please?'

'Why should I?' She backed against the stove, grasping its rail with both hands for support. 'This is the time I make supper every night. We've never done any different.'

'Since when did you start questioning my instructions, may I ask?'

'I'm not—'

'In which case please do as you're told.' A tremor stirred in his tone. 'I don't have a lot of time.'

'Why not?' She brought a hand to her mouth.

'Look, Piet,' said Granville.

'Silence from you!'

'Oh my God,' Rose whimpered from the stove, and Steyn turned back to her.

'Go to your room.'

But she could not move. She was staring at him, eyes wild with fear and both hands now clasped over her mouth. Steyn advanced on her. Granville called out again from the wheelchair but neither of them took any notice of him. They were entirely detached. Their long and intimate drama had come suddenly to a head, and they both recognized it. They were face to face, centre stage, on the brink of the climax, and the rest of the world had fallen away.

Steyn began to move and was just a couple of paces from the paralysed Rose when she acted. She wheeled around on the spot, grasped the pan of boiling pasta with both hands and, groaning heavily, slung it straight at Steyn.

Granville watched the saucepan leave her hands as if in a progression of stilled frames. It twisted in the air as it flew, emptying itself, so that its entire contents caught Steyn full in the face, followed by the pan itself, which struck his forehead with a clang.

Steyn cried out, bending over double and cradling his face in both hands. The stance unbalanced him and he

410

staggered forward, coming within a few inches of Rose. She arched away from him. He cried out again, louder, as the full force of the agony overtook the initial shock, and yelled, 'My eyes!' He was disoriented and in a reflex movement put out a leg sideways to stop himself falling, but over-compensated and toppled, like a dizzy child stepping off a roundabout. Out of control, he fell forwards. Rose might have cushioned his fall had she stayed put, but, repulsed by his advance, she stepped aside and he crashed into the enamel stove, taking the force of the impact on the temple. He groaned and sank to the floor in a heap.

Rose stared down at his pink, scorched face. The fine skin of his eyelids seem to have melted away so that his eyes stared up at her, one of them strangely pale.

Granville spoke first. 'Rose! Get the keys from his pocket. Get the keys, Rose.' She remained glued to the spot. 'Rose, listen to me. He's unconscious. You have to get those keys. Just bend down and take them from his pocket. Quickly.'

'I can't.'

'This is our chance. Our only chance. Just free me and I'll do the rest. Rose!'

'Look what I've done.'

'You did the only thing possible.' He spoke more quietly. 'If you hadn't stopped him he would have killed us both. That's what he came back to do, don't you see?'

She did not respond.

'Get the keys from his pocket and release me. I know which ones you need to use.'

'I can't go near him.'

'You must.'

'He might come round.'

'All the more reason to hurry.'

Gradually Rose struggled to overcome her fear, encouraged every inch of the way by Granville. She lowered herself onto her haunches, all the while keeping her eyes on the comatose form of her captor, crumpled at her feet. Disgusted by the proximity, she edged her hand closer, as if towards a leper, and probed two fingers over the lip of his trouser pocket. Stretching further, she felt the warmth and intimacy of his pocket's insides, and turned her face away, closing her eyes. When she had hold of the bunch of keys, she snatched out her hand and inelegantly crawled backwards across the floor.

'Good, now come over here to me,' said Granville urgently, and she obeyed. He identified what he thought were the right keys, but after trying them both, found they did not turn in either of the locks. This brought on a renewed fit of panic in Rose, and he tried to calm her, suggesting another pair that looked similar, and these turned out to be the correct ones.

'Well done,' he said, stood up from the wheelchair and pulled her close in a hug. She hung limply in his embrace, arms dangling at her sides. He then went over to the prostrate figure of Piet Steyn. 'I'm going to lock his wrists to this radiator,' he said, 'and then I'll go for help.'

'You can't leave me alone with him,' she replied.

'Then you come with me. We'll go out together.' At this, a look of wild fear came into her eyes and she began to cringe back, shaking her head. 'All right, all right,' he said, remembering that she had not breathed fresh air or seen the outside world for three years. His own hands were shaking as he hauled Steyn by the forearms over towards the radiator. The body felt heavy; perhaps more than just unconscious, he thought, but did not know how to check, and there wasn't time. Patches of skin on

Steyn's face had started to blister and a trickle of blood streamed from a wound on his head.

'I'll secure him to the radiator and lock you in another room, so that even if he does wake up you won't have to face him. That way you'll be completely safe until I come back with help. OK?' She thought for a moment and then nodded.

Granville had to stretch Steyn's arms to make them reach, which had the effect of half lifting his bleeding head off the floor. His mouth fell open and he resembled a hanging carcass, the victim of a wartime atrocity, like photographs Granville had seen of the Holocaust.

Rose, looking on in horror, asked if he thought Piet was dead, and Granville answered that he didn't know, but that Rose should move through to the first exit chamber, which he would seal off until he came back. She had not entered this room since the day she had first come to the bunker and shrank from the idea of waiting in there alone. She asked if she could be locked in her own bedroom instead. This meant that Granville had to find the right keys and lock two connecting doors behind him before he could turn his attention to the business of getting out.

Returning to the kitchen after settling Rose, he glanced at Steyn's awkwardly stretched figure before hurrying over to the first of the bulkhead partition doors. He fumbled nervously to find the right keys for the twin locks, but forced himself to calm down and selected the correct ones through a process of elimination. He then put his shoulder to the heavy steel door, pushed it back on its hinges, and passed on to the next door, the key to which was easier to identify because the lock here was very old and matched one of the antique keys in the bunch.

When he had passed through the third door and reached the bottom of the shaft, he found the light switch and looked up at the swaying fall of ropes suspended from above. He saw a wooden swing seat attached to the end of a pair of them, and quickly worked out the mechanics of the pulley system. There was a wicker basket lying to one side, with a carbine hook attachment, which he saw could be clipped onto the rope's end as an alternative to the seat. He decided not to bother with the pulley, thinking that it would be quicker to climb the ladder, but the sheer vertical ascent proved an ordeal because the muscles in his legs were weakened after days spent in a chair, so that by the time he reached the hatch at the top he was out of breath and his thighs were contracting in spasm. Holding onto the topmost rung with one hand, he used the other to turn the hatch release wheel anticlockwise. When it would turn no further, he pushed upwards and felt the hatch swing open. He could see straight away the stars shimmering in a clear black sky and he climbed the last few rungs into the fresh air. Crawling up out of the ground, he stood tall and looked around to get his bearings.

He was not aware that a camouflaged figure had been watching from the rough as the hatch opened. The observer now crept noiselessly forward and Granville was looking in the other direction when the blow came. It caught him on the back of the head, hard and direct, and he fell face first into a nettle bed.

It was too dark for Rufus Futcher to realize straight away that he had knocked down the wrong man. The hair was the same colour. It was only after he had lit the wick of the petrol bomb in his hand that he had enough light to see exactly what he had done. 'Oh God. Fuck,' he repeated to himself, heart racing, and his eyes darted back and forth from the bleeding figure of Granville to the flaring bottle in his hand. It was too late to change the plan, and he didn't have a contingency for this situation, so he went over to the hatch and slung the home-made device into the shaft, anyway. It took two long seconds to reach the bottom, and Rufus wondered if it might have gone out, but then heard it smash and explode against the concrete floor far below.

The fire began to spread straight away, fed by the powerful underground ventilation system. A simultaneous counter-draw sucked air through the open doors of the interlinking chambers and up the shaft, as if towards an industrial chimney. Rufus went back to look at the unconscious body of Granville. He raised his voice as he leant over. 'I'm sorry,' he said, caught between shock and fury. 'I never meant to hurt you. It was that weirdo I was after. You shouldn't go interfering in other people's business, anyway.' The last words were shouted as he ran to the cover of the hawthorn hedge and vanished into the night.

Granville had not heard, and at least a minute went by before he stirred. He lifted his scratched and stung face from the ground and put a hand to the back of his head. The skin was split and felt wet to the touch. He looked around for clues to what might have happened but could see nothing other than a dim light coming from the mouth of the shaft over to his right. An ache, as if one side of his brain were being wrung dry, made him clench his fingers into the brambles on the ground without noticing the thorns, and sink his fingernails into the soil. He held his breath and shut his eyes as the pain peaked and at last began to subside, releasing him to look back at the open hatch. He could see a light coming from it that was neither pale nor steady but had begun to dance and was accompanied by a distant rumble.

He got to his feet and walked unsteadily towards the hatch. He paused to take hold of himself, then climbed through and began to negotiate the rungs.

As he trod downwards, a continuous breeze of warm air and smoke rushed eerily in the opposite direction, like a mass emigration of benign spirits, whispering warnings to him to flee the place. But he progressed on, focusing on the stolid rhythm of his descending foot-fall to fortify him, step by measured step, all the way to the bottom. It was only when he reached the hard floor and caught sight of the fire spreading through the access chambers of the bunker that he shook off the remnants of his delirium and remembered properly what he had come to do.

He ran through the entrance passage, holding a handkerchief to his mouth and nose, and came into the kitchen. One whole side of it was already being consumed, the side with the window. Flames lapped upwards through the pretty curtains like the tongues of ravenous dogs. Cushions and carpets submitted to a slower kind of incineration, while the wooden furniture, more resistant, had begun to scorch and blister. Occasional sparks spat pigmy fireworks across the room and smoke filled the expanse of the ceiling like a gathering of miniature storm clouds. A sudden smash marked the collapse of the windowpane, and the picture-perfect landscape behind it began to brown and boil.

The sound of smashing glass jolted Granville into remembering that he would need the keys, and he reached into his pocket in a sudden panic that they might have fallen out. But his hand found them, and he hurried towards the far door, searching for the right key as he went. He thought he detected movement in Steyn

416

as he ran past but could not be sure, and there was no time to check.

Rose was curled on her bed. The sealed doors in between had confined the fire to the kitchen, but now that they were open it greedily began to extend itself into the new territory.

'Come on!' Granville leant over her on the bed, and blood from the wound on the back of his head dripped onto her sheets. She roused herself almost sleepily and asked what was happening. 'Fire,' he said, 'we have to get you out of here now.' He picked up a cloth and told her to press it over her mouth.

When they reached the kitchen Rose looked at Piet. 'What about him?' she asked.

'I'll come back for him. We have to get you out first.'

'What happened? How did it start?'

'I don't know. We can only get out one at a time. Quickly – go through.' He pushed her towards the far door and the way out. He could feel her reluctance to leave the familiarity of the living space, despite the danger, and had to nudge her forward the whole way.

By the time they reached the access shaft, the fire had begun take hold of everything in its path. It seemed to leap and ignite spontaneously in different places, without connection to any source, catching items beyond its stretch. The wicker basket in the corner crackled festively, its dry willow weave quickly turning to carbon. Even the ropes were starting to blacken, scorched by a flame close by. Granville stamped out as much of the fire as he could, telling Rose to sit on the seat and hold on tight.

'As soon as you reach the top,' he said, 'climb onto the ladder and get yourself out through the open hatch. Once you're safe, call down to me. OK?' She nodded and held to the ropes either side of the seat.

When she was ready, he heaved on the ropes and she began to rise with ease. It was a well-engineered device, the several pairs of wheel pulleys counterpoised to absorb and lighten the strain. He thought of the skill of the hands that had fashioned it, the self-reliant recluse whose determination and pious grit invited enmity and doled out scorn in equal measure. When Rose reached the safety of the ground above, Granville would have to go back and find this man, bring him through fire and save him from peril. For what? What could the future possibly hold for Piet Steyn? Would he submit to the hierarchies of a psychiatric unit or prison community? Could he ever integrate? Did there even exist a society that could accept or mend the ways of the creature he had become? In the interval of time that it took for Rose to make her smooth ascent to freedom, while the pulley wheels turned and the flames began to reignite all around him, Granville wondered if he would not be doing a greater service to all by following straight after her.

A turbulence on the ropes told him that, high above, Rose was shifting her weight from the seat to the ladder. Moments later he heard her call. She had reached the outside world, a free woman; but there was no euphoria in her voice, nor even relief at breathing nature's good air again. Her call sounded more primal and desolate; like the howl of a farm animal watching impotently as its calf is pulled away and crated up on the market truck.

Another sound came straight after, this time from a different direction, and it was harsh, almost barked.

'Father!'

Granville stamped out the fire at the base of the shaft, ripped off his shirt, and used it to smother the flames that were licking up the pulley ropes. Holding the shirt in front of him, like the improvised sail of a desert island castaway, he ran back through the access chambers, now engulfed in fire, and blasted his way into the kitchen. The smoke was dense and fire raged victoriously all around.

'Father!' Piet called as loudly as before, because his blindness meant he hadn't seen Granville clamber through the chaos to arrive at his side. His head was hanging upside down and he was flailing around, every sinew strained in a hopeless attempt to free himself. The paint on the radiator to which he was bound had started to blister and one of his trouser legs was alight. Granville held the shirt to his mouth and with his other hand searched for the keys in his pocket. They were not there, and he thought he had probably left them in Rose's bedroom.

'I'm here, Piet!' he yelled.

'Father! There's a fire. I'm burning up!'

Granville used the shirt to smother the flames on Piet's clothing. 'I'll get you out,' he yelled. 'Just hold on a minute.' He did not wait for a response, but ran through the adjoining rooms, cloth to mouth, eyes watering, until he reached Rose's bedroom. The keys were there on top of her pretty chest of drawers, lying between a silver-handled hairbrush and a talcum powder jar.

As he fought his way back through the smoke to the kitchen, the contraction on the right side of his head took hold again. The savageness of the pain paralysed him and he could go no further for a moment until the grip began to ease, after which he stumbled on and arrived at Piet's side. He unfastened the bicycle locks that held him.

Piet was mumbling almost incomprehensibly, his voice transposed to a kind of fluty falsetto, through which Granville could pick out words calling for divine intervention. There was an intensity of feeling on Piet's face, but whether it was physical pain, despair, or an eruption of remorse, Granville could not tell.

Piet tried to stand up straight but cried out that he couldn't see, a realization that seemed to sap the strength from his body so that he stood there like a vulnerable fledgling, legs apart and knees caved, disoriented and shaking. Granville had no choice but to shoulder his arm and haul him from the room. The way ahead, a straight path through the fire and smoke, seemed impenetrable. Holding his breath and shutting his eyes, he heaved himself and his burden forward, step by step towards the furnace. The flames billowed and licked at them tauntingly as they passed, mocking their attempts to save themselves and closing in behind them with every step. There would be no going back from here on. They managed to reach the bottom of the escape well, scorched and half asphyxiated, and Granville straight away let Piet slump to the ground so that he could work quickly to put out the burning patches on their clothes.

The infant smatterings of fire which he had earlier smothered at the bottom of the ladder had matured and collaborated into a united force. He realized it would be hopeless to try and stifle them. His only hope was to get himself and Piet out of the place before it was utterly consumed. He lifted Piet onto the pulley seat. Flames danced up along the ropes, rejoicing at the ease of ascent. Plaited nylon fibres stretching thirty feet up began to blacken, and molten plastic drips fell from them, like hell's raindrops, onto Granville's arms as he tried to balance Steyn in the seat. He managed to snuff out the flames at the place where Piet could put his hands to grip the ropes and told him to hang on for all he was worth. Steyn's head was lolling from side to side.

'You should just leave me here to burn.' His words were slurred.

'Have you got hold of the ropes?'

'I'm dying anyway, didn't you realize? Some disease on the inside. I can feel it.'

'Then why bother yourself with killing Rose and me?'

'It would take more than the fear of death to stop me striving for good in the world. I have to persevere or die in the attempt.'

'So you keep saying. Just don't let go of the ropes. I'm going to start pulling.'

'I'm finished now. Better to leave me down below.'

'I'm pulling!'

'I've had a long life. If you had known what I've known, seen what I've seen, you wouldn't blame me.'

'We'll talk about it when you're out.' He began to haul Piet upwards.

'The seeds of a man's story are planted early. The rest of his life is just an elaboration of what is there at the start.'

'There isn't time to talk!'

'And my story began at the gates of hell. Hear me, Father: if you don't put them right they'll call me a monster. You must tell them. Just because something's not pretty doesn't make it bad. All I've tried to do is make the world a better place than the one I was born into.' He was swinging gently as he rose.

'Not far now!'

'You wouldn't have been any different. And with your advantages I might have been just like you.'

'You're beginning to sway. Reach out to the rungs and steady yourself.'

'You and I just travel a different path to the same truth.'

'No more talking. Concentrate.' He had no idea whether Rose was waiting at the top, but called out that

Piet was nearly there and that she would have to help. He did not hear a reply but neither did he expect to. The roar of the furnace had become deafening.

'Father, do you hear what I'm saying?'

'For God's sake!' yelled Granville from below as he pulled. He was stripped of his shirt, singed and blackened by smoke, and the fire lapped hungrily all about him. 'Just think about getting out.'

The knot in the rope reached the pulley block, which indicated that Piet had arrived at the top. Granville shouted for Rose again but there was no word from her. Piet remained up there, spinning slowly where he sat, held aloft by the device he himself had crafted, but now either unwilling or too weak to move. Still no sign of Rose. Granville was hoarse from yelling.

Holding tight to the end of the rope, Granville stretched it across to a rung of the ladder, tied it securely and began to climb. He would have to do this by himself. But he had gone no more than a few steps when he noticed the red weight-bearing rope, now covered in flames as far up as he could see, jar and twang slightly. Suddenly, a section of it quite close to him unravelled violently so that only a thin part of it was left to take the strain. He knew what was about to happen and scrambled back down the ladder to get out of the way. His feet touched the ground at the moment the rope snapped, and Piet began to fall. Granville could see him hurtling down the shaft towards him, like the wicked ogre in 'Jack and the Beanstalk', and managed to step out of the way just before he reached the concrete.

Piet hit the ground in a peculiarly well composed posture and remained upright where he sat, looking for all like a cross-legged Buddha, fattened and compressed by the force of the impact. Even his face seemed to have broadened, the eyes to have travelled slightly down towards the cheekbones, and his lips had worked themselves into a smile. He sat there, motionless for a moment before his body had a small convulsion, nothing more than a little burp, and a parcel of trapped air found its way out of his mouth. It was disturbance enough to cause the head to tilt slightly, and then slump, which unbalanced the body as a whole so that it fell over onto its side. Granville hurried over to see if there was any hope, and leant forward to lift the head off the floor, but it came up too easily in his hands. After so many years of stiffness, Steyn's neck was shattered, and his head lolled free at last, held to the shoulders by nothing but loose skin and ligament. Granville let go of it on a reflex and the skull bounced on the concrete before lolling to one side.

The fire in the access chambers now belched venomously, and a tubercular cloud of red and black burning gas billowed into the shaft. Granville could wait no longer and began his ascent up the ladder. As he neared the top, drained, scorched and exhausted, the vice inside his head began to squeeze again and stalled his progress. The last few rungs were an ordeal of biblical immensity. In his delirium the angel wrestled with him, interminably, timelessly, swallowing him whole, bent on his destruction. His grip on the steel rungs loosened. His hope was expiring, and a kind of happy carelessness seemed to be teasing him away from it all; but the pain drew back a notch, which felt almost disappointing, because he knew he would have to make the effort again, and with one last surge of strength he dragged the greater part of his body weight out of the top of the hole, slumped forward and crawled clear of the wreckage. He looked around the dark wilderness for Rose, and called her name, but there was no sign of her.

It was then that it happened. Preceded by a pain like a hammer blow to the crown of his head, it suddenly happened. And more powerfully than it had ever happened before.

The pain was no more. It no longer belonged to him but to a different man, in another place, another time. In its stead, nobility and kinship descended. And everything that had ever happened in the realms of space and time, every incident, thought and feeling, was peculiarly there, ranged before him to inspect, each constituent part a small, insignificant speck in the grander picture. Thus contained, fenced and scrutinized, the entire accomplishment of human endeavour through the millennia, from the first days of the species to the present moment, was reduced to nothing more than a quaint footnote. He could wink at it and let it go.

Ageless presence consumed everything – history, intelligence, life itself – elevating, concentrating, binding it all together in a sphere of complementary diversity. As always, tears sprang to Granville's eyes. And as always, he greeted it with the words, 'What are you?' He then lowered his face gently and sideways to the cold ground, with infinite thanks, and closed his eyes.

Chapter 40

Edwina had spent most of the time, since the bunker fire, by her husband's hospital bed. Now that he was back home, she wanted to make him as comfortable as possible. In the first instance, that meant insulating him from the horde of reporters, photographers and curious passers-by who kept vigil along the pavement outside their garden gate. Although she loathed the idea, she had been persuaded by her mother to hang net drapes across all the windows on the road side of the house; otherwise it would mean having their heavy blanket-lined curtains closed, which would leave them in pitch darkness all day long.

Granville slept a lot, which gave her the opportunity to start unpacking some of the boxes downstairs. Everything was labelled, so she knew where to find the necessaries, but she realized there was not much point in doing a full-scale unpack because the present arrangements were going to be temporary.

It was mid-afternoon on their first day back together at number 3, Tennyson Terrace and she was kneeling on the floor, encircled by boxes and open bin liners. Granville was resting in the bedroom upstairs. It was a warm day and Edwina wore jeans with a sleeveless, plunge-necked light cotton blouse that showed off her impressive cleavage. Her thick dark hair was up and fashionably tousled, strands of it falling either side of her face. She heard a car pull up in the driveway and leapt up with a smile. She had been expecting them, counting the minutes, in fact. Half-unravelled parcels of kitchen utensils lay on the carpet where she had been squatting, together with sheets of crumpled newspaper. She parted the net curtains to have a look and hurried through to the hall.

The doorbell rang before she could get there and a moment later she had the door open and both her daughters flung themselves into her arms. Amelia was shrieking and jumping on the spot, while Serena, more contained, clung to her mother as if quenching a long thirst. Behind them, beaming, stood Martin Benson. His corduroy jacket was heavily creased at the elbows and one shirt button had given way to the pressure of his corpulence. A pair of half-moon glasses rested on the end of his nose, and his thick long hair struck Edwina for the first time as definitely more grey than brown. They were all getting older, she supposed.

'Thanks for picking up the girls,' she said, and gave Martin a quick hug.

'Wouldn't miss it for the world,' he replied. 'Walking out of the airport with a stunning girl on either arm – I was the envy of the arrivals hall.'

'Good run down? Any traffic?'

Benson just winked to reassure her that she needn't bother with the pleasantries, and she went indoors with her daughters. 'Stay for a coffee,' she called out to Martin over her shoulder.

'Where's all my stuff?' was Amelia's first question as she stood in the middle of the sitting room, looking

426

around at the taped-up boxes and the peculiarity of the once familiar room.

'Well some of it's in boxes, and some of it's back in your room. I think I've found all the things you'll want straight away. But you know we're not going to be here for very long. There's no point in unpacking everything.'

'Why can't we stay?' asked Amelia. 'I like it here.'

'Because this house doesn't belong to us. It belongs to the Church of England, and Daddy's going to be getting a new job.'

'Whereabouts? Can we stay in the same road?'

'I don't know what he'll do next, but I doubt very much it'll be here. Don't forget he's just come out of hospital. We all need a bit of time to settle down.'

'So will we be going back to Grandpa and Granny in Scotland?' asked Serena.

'We'll certainly go back and visit.'

'But are we going to live there? Are we going to go to that new school?'

'We really haven't made any plans yet.'

Serena pursed her lips, not entirely satisfied with the noncommittal response. Amelia, meanwhile, was busy with a box. Things she had not found interesting in years were suddenly made thrilling by the process of having to unwrap them.

Edwina told Serena to wait a moment while she went upstairs to check if their father was awake. While she was gone, Martin squatted down to join Amelia in the joy of her discoveries, while Serena waited at the edge of the room, looking around wistfully. She did not have long to ruminate because Edwina was back within a couple of minutes, smiling. 'He's awake,' she said, 'and he can't wait to see you. You two go on up.'

'Aren't you going to come with us?' Serena asked her

mother, apparently shy at the prospect of the reunion.

Edwina did not let her smile drop. 'No. You have him to yourselves. That's what he asked for. I'll be along in a little bit. Now,' her voice fell to a whisper, 'have you got your cards and presents?' The girls nodded, took a couple of small, perfectly wrapped and ribboned packages from their overnight bag, and headed for the stairs. Edwina closed the hall door behind them. She turned to Martin, who had heaved himself up from his haunches.

'How is he?' he asked.

'OK, I think. In shock, of course. And very tired.'

'What's the consultant's latest?'

'Can't see anything wrong. A bad knock on the back of the head, and a few scratches and burns, but nothing serious. Slight concussion, that's all.'

'Well, that's good. Did you tell the doctors about the other stuff?'

She nodded. 'They can't pin it on anything medical. They gave him an MRI scan while he was in there but nothing came up. They say the only other thing that can explain the hallucinations is some kind of psychological disorder. Schizophrenia or something.'

'Christ.'

'They say we can look into getting a psychiatrist, but Granville won't hear of it.'

'Do you think he needs one?'

She crossed her arms and grimaced. 'I can't put my finger on anything really out of the ordinary. Nothing erratic, violent, or anything. Just . . .'

'Just?'

'He's just not quite there. Detached, somehow. But that could just be the shock and all the painkillers.'

'Can you persuade him to see a shrink? Overrule him, even?'

'Doesn't look like it. But it's early days. We'll see how it goes.'

'He's always had these hallucinations, you say?'

'He must have talked to you about them.'

'The religious thing, yes. The Holy Spirit and whatnot. What's the difference now?'

'Well, for a start he doesn't talk about the Holy Spirit. And there's the business at night, when he starts ranting.'

'Can you make sense of what he says?'

'It's mostly about these invisible "others" who are present somehow, in the room, torturing him, purifying him. He seems to be genuinely in pain, right the way through his body. Really spooky, actually.'

'And what does he say about it in the morning?'

She flicked her hair back from her face. 'Pretends it's nothing, writes it off. He seems so peaceful in the day-time. I don't want to spoil anything.'

'It'll pass.'

'God, I hope so.'

Martin walked over and stood right in front of her. He lowered his head to engage her line of sight because she seemed to be in a daze. He reached out and took the tips of her fingers in his hand. 'If you ever want a shoulder to cry on, you know, I'm always here. Always have been, always will be.'

Edwina smiled and shook her head. 'We're not going down that path again.'

'Was it so bad?'

'I try not to think about it. We were idiots.'

'I still think about it.'

'The fallout could have been awful. I've seen it with other people. Whole families, loads of lives ruined.'

'It never got out.'

'We got off lightly, you mean.'

'Which is why I'm thinking . . .'

'No.'

'Your shout.'

She looked up at him. 'I'm really going to make it work this time. For the girls' sake as much as anything. And because I do love him.'

'Did he ever suspect anything?'

She smiled. 'No. He trusts everyone. Including you. How about Oonagh?'

Martin shook his head and then put a hand to her waist.

'Don't,' she said, and raised a palm.

Martin dropped his hand. 'I think I'd better go,' he said quietly.

'You could stay. He'd love to see you.'

'Later. This is a special time for the family. I'll just slip out.'

She walked with him to the door and thanked him again for picking up the girls from the airport. He said it was the least he could do and leant forward to give her a quick peck on the lips. She opened the door and waved as he walked back down the drive to his car. Prompted by a pair of policemen, the paparazzi parted to let him through.

Amelia was lying next to Granville, her head in the crook of his arm. He had a bandage around his head and one on each hand. Serena sat at the end of the bed.

'And they're too strict,' Amelia was saying. 'We had to sit at supper for hours and hours after we'd finished eating, just to listen to boring grown-ups talking about boring stuff for hours and hours, and then we had to go straight to bed.'

'*You* had to,' corrected Serena. 'I stayed up longer and made conversation.'

'And we weren't allowed to watch television or anything.'

'Why are you only happy when you're in front of a screen?' scorned Serena, sounding like her mother. 'You're an addict with no other interests.'

'And *you* always think you're so clever, going off on your own, reading books and writing your stupid diary.'

'I'm writing a diary, too,' said Granville.

'Since when?' asked Serena.

'Since a couple of days ago.'

'Can I read it?'

'If I can read yours.' They smiled at each other.

'You'd think mine was stupid,' said Serena.

'And you'd think the same about mine.'

'But in fact you don't know anything at all,' Amelia kept on at her sister. All the while she was plumping a cushion on her navel. 'And you never practise the piano when you're supposed to, and the teacher's always saying you don't finish your homework on time.'

'No I – I *do*,' said Serena. 'It's you who—'

'I don't see why I have to like Scotland, anyway.' Amelia turned to face Granville. 'I don't like Granny and Grandpa and I don't like their creepy big house. It's got ghosts and it's cold all the time.'

'Did you see a ghost?' asked Granville. 'I'd love to see a ghost.'

'Why?'

'To see if all the stories are true.'

'They must be true. Billions of people have seen ghosts.'

'I think they all run away when they see me,' said Granville.

'Their house hasn't got ghosts, stupid,' said Serena.

'Ghosts can't run,' said Amelia, frowning at her father, 'and they can't see.'

'How do you know?' asked Serena. 'Since when did you become the world expert on ghosts?'

'If a ghost can disappear through a wall, why should it have to run? And what would it run on? Its feet would go through the floor.'

'How does a ghost move, then?' asked Serena.

'It just floats.'

Serena tutted and turned towards the window but Amelia took no notice. 'Lucky ghosts,' she continued, 'I'd love to float everywhere. I can't wait to be a ghost. Do you remember when we went to Greece and I was allowed just to float around on that big inflatable chair all day long with no work to do? That's what it must be like being a ghost.'

'I remember,' said Granville.

'Can we go back there this summer?'

Serena looked sharply up at her father, waiting for his answer, but he did not reply.

'Dad?' said Amelia, after a pause. She had by now flattened the cushion on her lap and twisted its corners to make them look like animals' ears.

'Yes?'

'Mummy says the nasty man killed Luther.'

'Yes.'

'Why would anyone want to kill Luther? Luther's nice.'

'The man thought he was in the way.'

'That's not a good enough reason to kill someone.'

'He thought it was good enough.'

'That's because bad men have different reasons from good men. What did he do with him after he'd killed him?'

'I don't know.'

'Do you think he gave him a Christian burial? I mean,

it wasn't Luther's fault that he got in the way, because he's only a dog, so the man could've buried him properly to say sorry for killing him.'

'Maybe he did. I don't know.'

'Why did you try and save the nasty man? He deserved to be killed.'

'Amelia!' scolded Serena.

'He did deserve it,' said Amelia. 'For killing Luther.'

'Well, he's gone now,' said Granville.

'How did he get killed? Did you see it happen?'

'Amelia,' said Serena, 'I can't believe you.'

'He fell down a hole,' said Granville.

'I miss Luther.'

'I'm sure Mummy will get you another dog.' Again, Serena glanced at him uncertainly, but said nothing.

There was the sound of footsteps coming up the stairs and a moment later Edwina appeared in the doorway. She was smiling and holding a steaming cup.

'Tea?' she asked Granville.

'Thank you.'

She sat on the bed next to Serena. There were two get-well cards on display which she picked up to look at. They were colourful and handmade. 'These are beautiful, girls,' she said. 'Don't you just love them, darling?'

'Love them,' said Granville.

'Look what Amelia's said. "To our brave Daddy. We are so – " Proud is spelled with a U, not a W, darling.' Serena raised her eyes to heaven at her sister's imbecility. Edwina looked at the fronts of the cards again, admiringly.

'And these!' said Edwina, reaching over to the window-sill where the girls had put their presents. Serena's was a glass photo cube showing pictures of all four of the family, and Amelia's was a box of mini chocolate Easter eggs, Granville's favourite. 'Have you had one, darling?' she asked her husband.

'Yes,' he answered. 'Delicious.'

'Now, girls,' went on Edwina, 'can you pop downstairs and put some pasta on for supper? We're going to eat early. I bought a ready-made sauce.' She turned to Granville. 'Would you like pasta, darling?'

'Thank you, but I'm not very hungry.'

'You must have something. No pasta?'

'No, thanks.'

'Please have some.'

'OK.'

'Go on, then, girls.' They both gave Granville a kiss on the cheek, left the room and Edwina closed the door behind them. She came up to him and sat down on a chair next to his bedside table. 'You've made the *Daily Mail*. They're calling you a hero. There's talk of the George Medal.'

Granville did not respond.

Edwina said, 'I thought you'd be amused.'

'It's a lot of hot air.'

'I don't think they'll leave you alone until they get their pound of flesh. You'll have to get used to being a bit of a celebrity.'

He heaved himself up into a sitting position. 'It'll be yesterday's news in no time,' he said.

'I shouldn't count on it. You know what the tabloids are like. The police are being great. Keeping them all at bay.'

'Any news from my parents?'

'Can't get hold of them. They're still in the Himalayas. Won't be in reach of a phone signal for another week at least.'

'Never mind.'

Edwina looked out of the window. In the distance, Rodyard's Ridge gleamed bright yellow-green against the spring sky, its beech tops swaying. 'Rufus Futcher is up for grievous bodily harm with intent to cause injury, and perhaps even manslaughter. They're questioning his father, too. Rufus has come clean completely. Says he never meant to kill anyone and was pressured into doing it. He had no idea what was going on in the bunker. Nobody did.'

'Of course he didn't mean to kill me.'

'He meant to hit Steyn.'

'He wouldn't have wanted to kill him either.'

'How can you be so sure?'

'He's just a boy. Probably terrified.'

'Very forgiving of you.'

'I won't press charges.'

'It's out of your hands, darling. A man was killed. That's a serious crime, no matter what any of us thought about him.' Edwina looked down into her lap and hesitated before placing her next question. 'When you were down there, locked into that chair, what did—'

'Is there any news of Rose?' interrupted Granville.

Edwina blinked. 'The woman? Lily Greenacre?'

'Where is she?'

'She's safe. The police handed her to social services after they'd checked her over at the hospital.'

'Where's she staying?'

'I don't know. Some council property, I imagine.'

'Where did they find her?'

Edwina's eyes travelled the walls, slightly confused. 'With you, of course. She went to get help after she found you on the ground. Don't you remember me telling you all this?'

'I'm sorry, it's all a bit of a muddle.'

'The press are pretty hot for her story, you can imagine. Like those tales from Austria about women being incarcerated for years on end. The police say they'll protect her for as long as she needs it. She's bound to get someone to ghost-write her story and make a fortune. They always do.'

'When can I see her?'

Edwina frowned. 'What's the hurry?'

'I'm just interested to know what happened.'

Edwina shrugged. 'I don't know. I suppose we'll hear from her sooner or later, when the time is right. For both of you.'

'OK.'

Now she leant forwards and took his hand. 'They say you rescued the woman and then tried to get Steyn out before escaping yourself. Is that how it was?'

'It's all over now.'

'Spoken like a true hero.' She smiled.

'Not intentionally, I assure you.'

Edwina looked at him, puzzled by the absence of humour. 'They're bound to want the full story at some point. They won't stop till they've heard every detail.'

'Details are a bit fuzzy, I'm afraid.' He said nothing else and Edwina stroked his hand in silence before starting on a new tack.

'How is it?' she asked softly.

'How is what?'

'This thing that's happened to you.'

'It's wonderful.'

'Is it still there?'

'All the time.'

'Like it used to be? You know, when you had those experiences every now and then?'

'Not really. That was just a whisper. This is grand opera.'

'Can you describe how it feels?'

He seemed to think about the question for a moment before smiling and shaking his head. 'Words don't do it.'

'Of all the evasive clichés!' She was trying to get a laugh out of him again.

'I'm sorry,' he replied.

'You used to talk about enlightenment, the unity of all creation, grandiose stuff, universal ennoblement, that kind of thing.'

'If you say so.'

'Well, is it like that?'

He thought again. 'I'm just in a place where everything's worked out.' This made him smile and she encouraged him on with a squeeze of the hand.

'You old swami, you. You think that's quite funny, don't you?'

'Only because the description is such a trivialization of the real thing.' He was altogether on a different plane.

'And what about the pains in the night?' She was serious now.

'They're nothing.'

'They're something when they're happening. You writhe around and cry. You drench the sheets with sweat and talk about people torturing you, purifying your brain. What's that about?' He drew down the corners of his mouth, shook his head but gave no answer. 'Do you remember anything about the nightmares?' she asked. He closed his eyes, saying nothing. 'Would you like to see someone about it?'

'No point. We've already discussed this.'

'Fine. I just want things back the way they were, that's all.'

'You don't really.'

'Yes I do.'

'Because it's the only way you know.'

'And what's wrong with that?'

'If you're frightened of change you'll never move forwards.'

'Well, let's talk about moving forwards, then. Can we chat about the future?'

'If you like.'

'The Church Commissioners are being very good about the house. In view of everything that's happened, they say we can stay on here as long as we need to, and they're going to hold back your offer of resignation indefinitely, to give you time to put this whole business behind you and think again.'

'That's thoughtful.'

'Do you think you might apply for another job? When you're feeling better?'

He sighed. 'To be honest, I don't know what I'll do.'

'There's no pressure.'

'But I'll never work for the Church again.'

Now she looked at him. 'But you said—'

'I could never do that,' he affirmed, quietly.

'In which case, at some stage we will have to start looking for a house of our own.' Her positive tone indicated that she was not entirely averse to this alternative.

Granville said, 'You'll be looking in Scotland, I imagine.' It came out of the blue and Edwina felt a peculiar sensation: legions of miniature, closely packed pinpricks passing through her abdomen and enveloping her like a greatcoat. Granville's comment hung in the air. She released his hand and clasped hers together on her lap.

'I was thinking we might look for a home together. As a family.'

438

'I don't think that would be a good idea,' he said, without a shade of hesitation or doubt. She took longer to respond.

'Is that the way you want it?'

'I think so, yes.'

'Could we not decide in a while? After everything that's happened, wouldn't it be best to let the dust settle a bit? Not make any final decisions until we're sure.'

'I am sure. I think in your heart you're sure too. You're just afraid.'

'What about the girls?'

'It will be better for them this way. They can see me whenever they want.'

Edwina turned away and kept her voice steady. 'You may not be in the right frame of mind to make drastic decisions like this. You're not yourself yet.'

A hint of a smile came to his lips. 'I am not myself yet? Take a minute to think about what a ridiculous statement that is.'

'Don't talk semantics with me, Granville. Not at a time like this.'

'I'm only telling the truth.'

Though softly spoken, his words carried such conviction, she knew it was hopeless to reason against them. After sitting quietly for some time longer, she sniffed deeply, searched for a tissue in her pocket, and asked, 'Why?'

'I thought we'd done this already.'

'And I thought things might have changed.'

'Then it's me who should be asking why.'

She dabbed the tissue under each eye in turn, found another one to blow her nose on, and stared into space for a moment before answering. 'I suppose the answer is that I understand a bit more about what you were going through. I know that girl was unstable, that you were only trying to protect her, and Janet. I'm prepared to listen and make the effort to start again. And I love you.' Her voice was breaking.

'I'll still be around. I'm not going to another planet.'

'I want things to be as they were.'

'They weren't great.'

'Doesn't everyone have ups and downs?'

'Ups and downs?'

'Yes.'

'Shall we lay our cards on the table, then?'

'Of course.'

'You'll be honest with me?'

She seemed confused by this. 'Yes. Why shouldn't I?'

'Have you ever been unfaithful?'

She looked up with a jolt. 'No.' She held his eyes and the silence throbbed, growing like a balloon until it could grow no more without popping; then she looked down. 'Yes.'

Neither moved for a while. Time now passed in a calmer silence as the news began to settle.

'I suppose you're going to want me to tell you the whole story,' she began.

'Not really. I think I'd better go. The sooner, the better, really.'

'Go where? You're not in a fit state to get out of bed.'

'I will be soon. Trust me. I'm feeling stronger by the hour.'

'Let me talk to you about it. It was nothing, a stupid, silly mistake that I'll regret for the rest of my life, but nothing.'

'Let's leave it at that, then.'

'Don't you think it's worth trying to work through this?'

'We can't keep lying to ourselves.'

Edwina felt the wave of pinpricks flood through her again as it dawned on her that this was really happening. 'What about practicalities?'

'I'll take the van. You can have whatever else you want. There's plenty of money to go around.'

'You always hated wasting money.'

'Money can't really be wasted. Just spent. What's money for if it's not to be spent?'

She took a deep breath and stood up. 'I'm not going to make a scene.'

'I know you're not.'

'We'll have to think about what to say to the girls.' This brought tears back to her eyes. 'They thought they were coming home.'

'Is that what you told them?'

'I suppose I never properly told them anything different.'

'Ah.'

She looked at the cup of tea on his bedside table. It was still full. 'That'll be cold,' she said. 'Shall I make you a fresh one?'

'No, thank you. I wasn't thirsty, to be honest.'

'Is there anything else I can get you?'

'No, thanks.'

'And you don't really want to have pasta with us, do you?'

'Not really.'

'I'll leave you to rest, then.'

'See you later.'

She left and closed the door quietly behind her. She spent a few moments composing herself on the landing before going down to the girls. She could already hear them cooking in the kitchen, and by the sound of their giggles they were getting on just fine together again. It was always that way, she mused. Give them a job and they'll forget all the niggling little annoyances that get between them when they've nothing better to do.

Chapter 41

A green Volkswagen Beetle was weaving along the narrow, hedge-lined lanes east of Lulworth, close to the Dorset coast. It was an old model, from the late 1960s, polished and in good working condition but not pristine, not quite a car clubber's pride and joy.

The countryside was undulating, and the rear-mounted engine of the Beetle throbbed noisily from its dual exhaust as the driver shifted down into third gear to negotiate a climb. Arriving at a junction on the hilltop, the car rumbled to a standstill in front of a white three-way signpost while its driver considered what to do next. It was a glorious sunny day and the blue horizon of the English Channel was visible in a dip between two oak-crested hillocks over to the right. This seemed to decide the driver's choice of direction, despite the logic of the signpost. But minutes later the Beetle was back at the same junction again, having performed a tight three-point turn down the road. This time it did not pause at the signpost but progressed along the lane in the opposite direction.

Shortly after, the car arrived at a farm gate attended by uniformed policemen and the driver rolled down his window to exchange a few words with them. One of them, a female officer, spoke briefly into her walkie-talkie, and then waved the driver through the gate. The Beetle bumped slowly across the field, passed through a gap in the hedge at the far end and drove over to where a camper van was sited on its own. A washing line, heavy with clothes drying in the sunshine, stretched from the van's wing mirror to a tree branch. Nearby, the remains of a fire smouldered beneath a tripod bearing a blackened saucepan, and muddy wellington boots stood upright next to the van's open sliding door. The views of the sea were expansive and a healthy breeze spun the blades of a wind turbine bolted to the back of the vehicle. On the other side of the field a family had set up camp, and a few adolescent boys were playing French cricket. A couple of dogs bounded around them, chasing the ball and following scents in the long grass, while sparrows danced in and out of the field's boundary hedgerow.

A thickset elderly man climbed out from behind the wheel of the Beetle and rapped his knuckles gently on the steel flank of the van. 'Anyone at home?' He wore a heavy old jacket with pens clipped to its breast pocket, and a pair of horn-rimmed glasses hung on a lanyard around his neck. His hair was grey, thinning, but just long enough to be tied in a knot at the back of his head. In one hand he carried three identical Moleskine note-books, and in the other a lighted cigarette.

Granville appeared at the sliding door. He was tanned, wearing a T-shirt and smiling. 'Hello, Dad.'

'God, you look ten years younger. What are you on?' The man's voice was deep, soft and gravelly, a veteran smoker's voice.

'Do you really want to hear the cliché?'

'Spare me.'

'Don't ask, then.'

444

Granville came down from the van and embraced his father. They remained locked tightly for a while and did not say a word. At last they broke apart and Mounty St Clair turned aside to dry his eyes on his jacket sleeve.

'Is this where you live, then?' he asked.

'Home sweet home.'

'You've been through the mill.'

'All over now.'

'We were on the other side of the world. We had no idea.'

'Haven't brought Mum with you, then?'

'No. She's been frightened off by what your wife's been saying. Thinks she'll be upset if she finds you've changed character. I've been sent to see if it's all true. Cup of tea?'

'Absolutely.' Granville turned back to the van. 'Rose?'

She appeared at the door and stepped down to the ground. She was wearing a light cotton dress and had sandals on her feet from which her toenails peeped out bright red. 'Rose, this is my father, Mounty. Dad, this is Rose. She's been looking after me.'

'Nice to meet you, my dear,' said Mounty, flicking the remains of his cigarette into the grass and kissing her on both cheeks. 'Well, this I was not expecting,' he added quietly.

'Sorry,' said Granville. Rose moved closer in and stood behind his shoulder.

'No need for apologies. We're all grown-ups. Christ, you sound as if I've caught you behind the bike shed. What about that tea?'

Granville turned to Rose and smiled at her. She went straight into the van to put the kettle on the gas hob. 'Just milk, no sugar,' Granville called after her. 'And one for me, too, if you wouldn't mind.' He turned back to his father. 'I thought if I warned you about her, you might not come.'

'Don't be ridiculous.'

'I didn't plan it this way. She came to visit, we talked and talked and it just felt right to be together. She didn't like where the Local Authority were housing her, she had nowhere else, so she asked if she could stay with me.'

Mounty nodded towards the van. 'Very cosy, I'll bet.'

'Our fairytale ending, you might say.'

'Good thing I didn't bring your mother, then.'

'I need someone to look after me. I'm still having rough nights. Rose handles it all very well.'

'Don't you think you should go back to the doctor?'

'No point. I know exactly what's happening. It's not a medical condition.'

'What, then?'

'They're purifying me.' He said it as easily and naturally as if he were acknowledging a passing cloud in the sky. His pleasant smile did not drop for an instant. Mounty looked at him uncertainly.

'They?'

'For want of a better term.'

'Who are they?'

'Not people. Not even entities.'

Mounty waited for a further explanation. When none was forthcoming, he asked, 'What, then?'

'The best way to describe them would be principles. But that's just a vague approximation.'

'A little more illumination, if you'd be so kind?'

Granville looked amused at so typical a remark from his father. 'I don't expect anyone to understand. Rose seems to know what I mean, though.'

446

'Are these "principles", or whatever, telling you how you should live your life?'

'Not exactly. I haven't progressed that far yet.'

'What's the purpose of this so-called purification, then?'

'I suppose it's sort of clearing out the old to make way for the new. I don't know quite what the new is yet, but I get the feeling that when I'm ready I'll have my work cut out.'

'Whatever that might be.'

'Exactly.'

Mounty sighed and searched in his jacket pocket for a cigarette packet. 'You're not making it any easier for yourself, you know.'

'How were the Himalayas?'

'Peaky.'

Granville smiled. 'One up on Belgium, then?'

'Don't knock the Netherlands.' Mounty raised a warning finger. 'Common-minded folk entertain a misconception that they might not be very interesting.'

'Next stop Brussels, then?'

'Actually, I was thinking about the Andaman Islands.'

'Different.'

'Depends on your perspective. But I'll probably end up going where I can find the cheapest flights.'

'You're rich enough to spend the rest of your life going first class anywhere you choose and still have bags to spare.'

'We all have our follies.'

'Your life is one long folly.'

They smiled contentedly, like old buddies who know each other better than words can express, before Mounty's face turned more serious. 'The bloke who kept you prisoner,' he said. 'His story's coming out

447

bit by bit. They think he might have been involved in cases of missing women going back to the seventies and beyond.'

'I can imagine.'

'One of the victims was only fifteen.'

'Nothing would surprise me.'

'Did you get any idea what made him tick?'

'He'd convinced himself he was some kind of saint.'

'Demon, more like.'

'Definitely not. He believed he was for the good guys. Maybe he did have what it takes to make a saint.'

'What's that supposed to mean?'

'Most of those early Christian saints were bloody-minded fanatics. Just the same, capable of anything.'

'Good riddance to the lot of them, then.'

'They'll never be forgotten, though, will they?' said Granville. 'People still venerate them. Those guys stuck to their guns and went down still flying the flag. And so people in churches go and kneel before their bones to this day.'

Mounty looked genuinely surprised. 'You talk as though part of you sympathizes with that creature.'

'The fascination of opposites, maybe. It's more complicated than it sounds. Let's talk about nicer things. Tell me what you're working on.'

'Never you mind.'

'Finished the new perspective on Euclid?'

Mounty puffed scornfully into the air. 'Yonks ago. I've done my translation of Alcaeus since then.'

'Alcaeus?'

'The Lesbian.'

'Never heard of her.'

'I don't mean a dyke, you dozy tart. Alcaeus was a man. He came from Mytilene on the island of Lesbos.'

Granville was trying to keep a straight face. Mounty stared at him. 'Are you taking the piss?'

'Sorry.'

Mounty tutted and shook his head. 'If you really want to know, I'm writing a novel.'

'I won't ask the intensely dreary question: what's it about?'

'Thank you.' Mounty held up the little pile of notebooks. 'I've brought these back.'

'You got through them fast.'

'You know what I'm like with light reading.' He lobbed them to Granville.

'You needn't have brought them back. They can go in the bin. I'm writing buckets of the stuff at the moment. Just thought you might like to see where I'm at.'

Mounty frowned. 'You don't want to throw them away. I've never chucked anything out.'

'That's why you need such a big house. What did you think?'

'What about?'

'My jottings.'

Mounty leant over with a sigh and picked up one of the notebooks. He put his glasses on, opened the book and began to read. '"The pain was still there until the first sign of dawn, when it started to withdraw into the shadows, like theatre cleaners who sweep down the stage and vanish into the night when the show is over and the actors have all left the building." Nice metaphor. "And with the pain's departure came the descent of joy. Such joy. Joy with no reason, no goal, no end in sight. Reasons, goals, ends in sight are all of the realm of thought, and thought is the physical response of memory, by its nature bound and inward looking, a tool for survival, nothing more."'

'You don't have to read it out.'

Mounty held up a palm to silence his son and went on. '"The search for joy, the pursuit of what tomorrow will bring – these things have a purpose, in that they strengthen our walls, feed our bellies, lay waste our enemies: tools for survival, as I say. But joy itself has no becoming, no destination, no point of arrival. Joy can be apprehended only through the death of becoming. And when we cease to become, cease to search, detach ourselves from the shackles of thought – what is there? Only stillness and emptiness. Outside the boundaries of thought and feeling is the ending of time and therefore the ending of fear and therefore the ending of sorrow."'

'Amen,' said Granville and laughed.

Mounty dropped the book on top of the others. 'I've read a dozen or more tinpot gurus with much the same sort of stuff to say.'

'I don't doubt it.'

'From Plato to Osho, with a few Christian mystics thrown in for good measure along the way.'

'Along the way.'

'Which isn't to say I'm belittling your adventure.'

'Thank you.'

Mounty lit himself a new cigarette and looked at the view. 'Is this it, then? Reinvent yourself as the wise old hermit of the Dorset Downs? The West Country avatar?'

'I'm not trying to do that.'

Rose stepped out of the van with the tea. The cups and saucers were decorated with a pretty floral pattern, and had delicate, gilded handles. She handed them to the men and brought up a couple of deckchairs for them to sit on. Granville asked her quietly if she'd remembered to put her sunblock on and she replied that she had.

He turned to his father. 'Rose has been out of the sun for so long, even a few minutes' exposure can burn her -skin.' Mounty nodded. Rose, meanwhile, had walked over to the washing line and taken hold of a pyjama top that was fluttering in the breeze to see if it was dry. Mounty watched her and waited until she had gone back into the van before turning back to his son. He leant forward in his chair and balanced his teacup on the ground between two tufts of grass.

'The clandestine element of my mission here,' he said, pausing to take a long drag on his cigarette, 'is to ascertain for the womenfolk's benefit if you've lost your marbles sufficiently to warrant medical intervention.'

'To what end?'

'I don't know,' Mounty shrugged. 'To bring you back to the fold?'

'Back together with Edwina, you mean?'

'Suppose so.'

'And they've chosen you as diplomat for their cause? They must be desperate.'

Mounty stretched for his tea. 'Well, if you think about it, there's no-one else who knows you as well.'

'If that's true, you'll see they're on a hiding to nothing.'

'Of course I can see that.'

Granville broke the silence. 'What are you going to tell them, then?'

Mounty thought about the question while he took a sip of tea. His smile had gone. 'Are you sure this is such a good idea?' he asked with a quick dart of his head towards the van.

Granville sighed. 'So you do want to rein me back in.'

'I just want to hear it from you. To set an old man's heart at rest, if you like.'

451

Granville got up from his deckchair and came over to sit cross-legged on the grass in front of Mounty. He took his hand. 'Dad, I understand completely what you must be feeling. I understand your fears, your doubts, I can hear the questions you want to ask but are afraid to, and I can sense your dread of losing me. I haven't lost all human feeling, you know.'

Mounty blinked and looked the other way. He was uncomfortable with this level of frank intimacy and it was uncharacteristic of Granville. He took back his hand. 'Lovely spot, I have to say.' He looked around at the landscape, anywhere but straight at Granville. 'Are the newspapers leaving you in peace?'

'So far so good.'

'They're still badgering Edwina. Cold callers, photographers. Difficult for the girls.'

'I'm going to get married to Rose. As soon as the divorce comes through.'

Now Mounty looked at his son. 'Are you serious?'

'We're great together. I really think we'll make a perfect marriage.'

Mounty rearranged himself in his seat. 'I'll say this once and once only, but it has to be said. What you went through in that bunker – you can tell me all about it another time – I understand it must have bonded the two of you together, it's only natural. But are you really ready to make decisions that will mean throwing everything away? Your life, your work, your marriage, your daughters?'

Granville opened his palms to the air and smiled. 'I am.'

'The girls miss you. They say you've changed. They say their dad has gone.'

'Maybe he has. No point in pretending otherwise.'

'I never thought I'd hear you say that. You were always such a devoted father.'

'Whoever they thought they had before is no longer here, pure and simple.'

'What was wrong with that person?'

'His whole life was founded on doubt and compromise. And he was trapped in a place of suspicion and resentment. It wasn't doing him or his family any good. But anyway, I don't have any choice in the matter. What's done is done.'

'Is that what you think?'

'From where I am now, it's clear as day. I can't live out my life in an unhappy lie.'

'Don't you love your daughters any more?'

'Do I love them?' He put the question to himself and looked up towards the sky. 'If, by love, you mean: do I want to own them? Do I want to clutch them to myself, carry around some culturally conditioned notion of responsibility and massage my own narcissistic urges? Then, no. You of all people should understand that.'

'I was always there for you. Maybe you thought I was busy with other stuff while you were growing up, but—'

'Dad. Please. There's no need.'

Mounty took refuge in more tea. 'So you sit here for the remainder of your life like a teenaged beach bum with nothing better to do than spout out so-called wisdom philosophy and be looked after by a woman who worships you as her saviour. Is that about the measure of it?'

'Not at all. I'm going to get a job. Got one already, as it happens. Part time, but it's a start.'

'Oh yes? Doing what?'

'Landscape gardener.' Mounty rolled his eyes to heaven. 'No, I'm serious.'

453

'But you've always hated gardening.'

'Not quite the same thing. I'm applying to do a degree.'

'A degree in landscape gardening?'

'Landscape design, it's called.'

'There's always one old hippie on every degree course. Whereabouts?'

'Bartle College. It's part of the University of Essex. A three-year BSc.'

'Essex man?'

'If I get on the course we're going to move up there and buy a cottage. Rose really wants to have her own house. And I want to give her – ' he opened wide his arms and looked around, searching for the right words, 'I want to give her everything she wants. A castle, if need be.'

'A castle. In Essex?'

Granville smiled. 'I don't mean it literally.'

'Do you know anyone in that part of the world? What sort of a life will you have?'

'We like to keep ourselves to ourselves. Rose will have her home at last – what she's always wanted – and we think we might try for a baby.'

'Is that what you really want? At this time of life?'

'Rose will make a good mother. She's still young enough. I'll have my work and my writing. And I want a large patch of land to develop. I've got a project in mind.'

Mounty was watching his son carefully as he outlined his ambitions. Granville's eyes were wide, wandering here and there, and hardly blinking. 'I've drawn up the plans already, a whole schedule of works and I can't wait. All I need is ten acres of redundant farmland, untouched is essential, wild, raw nature, uncultivated, unpolluted. I want to start from scratch and work it up into something truly wonderful, a model, something big, something that will enrich people, draw them in, elevate them.'

'That's going to be your new career?'

'Call it that, if you want.'

'What about God?'

'I don't use that word nowadays. It's too loaded.'

'What word do you use instead, then?'

'Depends on the context. But there's nothing more idiotic than the word God. We're not cavemen any more. It's like holding up the most sophisticated microsurgical instrument and calling it a lump hammer.'

'Then why not just sharpen your terminology?'

'Sorry. Words don't do it.'

Mounty nodded, looked aside and drew down the corners of his mouth. 'I see,' he said in his low, soft-grained voice. He sat back in the deckchair and finished his tea. It was almost cold. Putting the empty cup back on the ground, he looked around the site, taking in the coastal view. 'I think I could get used to this.'

'You're welcome any time,' said Granville. 'You and Mum. Bring a tent. Come and stay for a few nights, and bring the girls. They'd love it here.'

'They would,' said Mounty, heaving himself to his feet. 'And I will come back. I promise.' Stiff in the legs, he limped the first couple of paces over to the van, put his head through the sliding door and held out the teacup. Rose was in there, chopping vegetables. 'Goodbye, my dear. I'm very pleased to have met you.'

'Won't you stay for lunch?' she asked. 'We haven't had a chance to talk yet.'

'Another time,' he replied. 'Thank you for looking after him.'

Her return smile was radiant. 'I'm sorry if—'

'No, no, no,' murmured Mounty, waving her apology aside and leaning forward to kiss her. He turned back to Granville. 'Farewell, my boy.'

'Bye, Dad,' said Granville and hugged him. 'Mission accomplished?'

'I think so.'

They walked over to where the Beetle was parked.

Granville nodded towards the car. 'She's still going strong, then?'

'Just about. Gordon keeps her cleaned and tuned.'

'And how is Gordon?'

'Old.'

'And Betty?'

'Not as sexy as fifty years ago, to be sure.'

'Is that how long they've been with you?'

'Gordon started out as my father's footman after the war. Betty had the nicest pair of tits in the village. They were married in the late fifties some time. Pretty event. Sunny day. The whole village was there. Lovely, simple flowers everywhere. Bunting, lemonade. Everything seemed so straightforward then.'

'Those were the days, eh?'

'You might say.'

'Would you do it differently, if you could have your time again?'

'At the time we thought we had it all worked out, but I don't think we got it right, really. Chucked the baby out with the bathwater, as it were.'

'We?'

'My generation.'

They fell silent again and then Mounty looked up at Granville. 'I'll tell them the bits they'll be able to understand.'

'Who?'

Mounty nodded over his shoulder as if they were standing right behind him. 'The womenfolk.'

'OK, then,' whispered Granville, like a fellow conspirator.

Mounty remained where he stood, viewing Granville steadily, eyes creased up, as though by squinting he might see through some magic prism into the depths of his son's soul. 'Something's gone, hasn't it?'

'I think it probably has.'

'Do I need to worry about you?'

'I don't know the meaning of the word.'

Mounty snorted a laugh and then wagged an index finger at him. 'You are incorrigible,' he said, turning to the car and sinking heavily into the driver's seat. 'You've always been incorrigible. That bit hasn't changed.'

'Thanks for coming.'

Mounty turned the key and the old Volkswagen roared into life. 'Good luck with the university application,' he spoke up over the noise.

'Thank you.'

'Are there any courses there that I could do? I rather fancy the idea of student life again.'

'Why don't you come and do landscape design with me?'

He grimaced. 'Yuk. Too New-Agey.'

'Old fogey!'

Mounty raised his hand in a last wave and turned the car around.

Granville watched the Beetle bump its way over to the gap in the hedge and disappear from sight. He stayed there for some while before walking slowly back towards the van. Rose was standing there waiting for him, arms folded and head slightly atilt in expectation.

Granville stood in front of her. 'So. What next?'

'I'm going to finish getting lunch ready,' she said, 'and then go for a little walk. Would you like to come with me, dear?'

'I would, but I'd better not. I've got work to do.'

'Work, work, work. You shouldn't punish yourself so much. Take some time off to have fun.'

He smiled and stroked her cheek. 'No rest for the wicked.'

Epilogue

He was right. There was a lot to do today. He would write for about an hour, have lunch at one o'clock, as usual, rest for half an hour and then spend forty-five minutes in silent meditation with Rose. After that, he would unroll his large sheets of paper, work on his landscape design project for most of the afternoon, and then pause early evening to take a stroll down to the beach for exercise. There was some admin to do as well, forms, papers, lawyer stuff. He did not want to bore Rose with that and she didn't really understand much about it, anyway, so he would get it done while she was busy preparing supper. All in all, it would be a good, productive day with much achieved. As long as it was all clear by eight, then they could have their evening meal together and a good chat afterwards. Perhaps even a game. He was so proud of her, of the way she was managing, of the way she was progressing. He was proud of them both. It was a joint endeavour. She needed him to help her work through the trauma of everything that had happened, come to terms with it, expunge it. She was ready to begin again, a new life, with him as her guide. If she felt up to it this evening she might even tell him a bit more about her past. There were years' worth to catch up on, and he was finding it more and more intriguing. She was full of surprises and he was gradually forming a complete picture of her, in all her glory. He wanted to know every part, everything she'd done, everything she'd thought, leave no stone unturned. It occurred to him, just then, that it might be a good idea to start documenting their adventure, and he looked around to see if he could find a fresh notebook for the task.

A Dark Enchantment
Roland Vernon

Winner of the *Daily Mail* First Novel Award

GODWIN TUDOR, a young English photographer recently arrived in Athens, is intrigued by the mysterious and maverick British landowner Edgar Brooke, whose vast estate dominates the island of Pyroxenia.

Whilst visiting Brooke's remote home, Godwin is enchanted by the breathtaking landscape and captivated by his host's capricious young daughter. But all is not quite as idyllic as it seems.

Inadvertently drawn into a terrifying international incident, Godwin does his best to play the diplomat. But consequences prove more devastating than he can imagine.

'A rousing, red-blooded tale with colourful
characters in an exotic setting'
Joanne Harris

The Maestro's Voice
Roland Vernon

NEW YORK, 1926. Rocco Campobello, the great tenor and superstar of his day, has collapsed on stage. As he fights for his life, the world holds its breath. He emerges from this brush with death a changed man. Rejecting both celebrity and a glittering career, Campobello returns to his roots on the impoverished back streets of Naples in order to confront a dark truth from his past and lay its ghost to rest.

But Naples is in the throes of violent change. Fascism is on the rise, while the city's Mafia families feel their power slipping away. Caught between them, Rocco rediscovers a passion and an integrity he once feared lost and, in the face of blackmail, brutality and murder, hatches a plan to outmanoeuvre them all and reclaim his life . . .

Against the spectacular backdrop of Naples' crumbling palaces, decaying streets and ancient catacombs, a master storyteller weaves a rich, compelling tale of corrupted fame, personal crisis, violence and redemption.

'Intrigue on an operatic scale . . . an exciting and accomplished page-turner'
DAILY MAIL